Avenging Raymond

Jean Schick

Avenging Raymond

Jean Schick

Avenging Raymond

Paperback: (979-8-950072-24-6)
Hardcover: (979-8-950072-25-3)

This book is dedicated to the memory of James E. Thompson.

Dr. Thompson will be missed by many for several years to come. Jim will have a special place in my heart for the rest of my life. His farm in the hills gave me the idea for the setting in this book.

Thank you for giving me your opinion and encouragement Tammy Shepard.

I would also like to thank The Library of Congress for the use of Abraham Lincoln's picture.

Prologue

1988

The large kitchen in the ranch style suburban home near Chicago, with an open airy feel, was a cozy inviting place to be. It was a beautiful late spring morning, so all of the windows were open allowing the scent of flowers to drift through the house. The immaculate house was tastefully decorated, sitting in the middle of a perfectly manicured half acre lot.

An elegant, light-skinned black woman sat at the table reading. The woman's hair was pulled up into a bun, her makeup perfect, the small amount of tasteful jewelry she wore completed her outfit. When Opal stood to walk across the room the knee length silk tunic softly swirled around her slender form to accentuate her perfectly proportioned curves and above average height. Her movements were fluid and graceful enough to draw stares of admiration, while her fine aristocratic features stopped men in their tracks. The perfect modulation of her voice combined with her ability to articulate denoted her education. No one could have guessed this beautiful woman was old enough to be a grandmother.

It was Saturday morning. Opal leaned against the counter, worry lines creasing her forehead, as she looked out the window to check on her grandsons, ages eight and twelve. She smiled at the sight of her older grandson playing with his brother. It never ceased to amaze her at how patient Tony was with Raymond. It was obvious how much Tony loved him. The way so many of the other children teased Raymond, she was thankful he watched out for his shy bookworm of a younger brother. Satisfied that everything was as it should be with the children, she leaned her head back closing her eyes while she inhaled deeply. Lost in thought, she let the warm gentle breeze wash over her face enjoying the calming effect.

Her son and daughter-in-law hadn't come to pick the boys up last night. She had paced the floor most of the night because she had not heard a word from them since they left to have dinner with a business acquaintance. Opal was afraid something terrible must have happened. Normally they would call if they were going to be a few minutes late.

There was something about the man her son, Andrew was meeting that made Opal uneasy. For some reason that she couldn't quite figure out, he made her very uncomfortable, she didn't trust him. She had only met him twice. For all his good manners, fancy clothes, fluid speech, when he smiled it never came through his eyes. His smile was as fake as she was afraid that he was. That night after Opal put her frightened grandchildren to bed, she vowed she would contact the authorities the next morning.

Sunday morning Opal asked the next-door neighbor to come over to keep an eye on the boys while she went to the police station. When the woman arrived, they greeted each other warmly. Beth Ann had been a friend to Opal for several years. The women were dear enough to each other that they were almost like sisters. "Beth, I am so glad you were able to come so fast."

After hugging Opal in greeting, Beth looked closely at her worried expression. "You look awful. What's wrong?"

"Beth, I'm scared out of my wits. The kids didn't come home last night; they didn't even call. You know how funny they are about those boys. They normally call while they're out just to check on them. They are never late."

A worried look replaced her concerned expression as Beth attempted to ease her friend's fear. "They may have had car trouble and had to get a room. Don't get too upset until you know what's going on. You're about to worry yourself to death."

"I can't help it. I don't trust that man that was with them last night. There is something about him that doesn't sit right, and the way he looks at Beulah makes my skin crawl. He has been trying to push my boy to go into business with him. Andrew told him no more than once. The man is pushy and doesn't want to take no for an answer."

Beth had been lost in thought. She was worried about Andrew and Beulah as well. They were responsible young people that cared deeply and passionately about the welfare of their children. She had never known of them imposing on Opal in this manner.

"You go on. I will be more than happy to watch the boys; we'll have a good time while you're gone. Take as much time as you need." She tried to put on a pleasant face for her friend, so she couldn't see just how concerned she was herself.

When Opal arrived at the police station, she waited for what seemed like an eternity before speaking to someone. After telling the officer in charge everything she knew of her son's plans for Friday evening, including who she knew was to be dining with him and her suspicions about the man, she was asked for descriptions of both her son and daughter-in-law. The officer was gone for quite some time before he returned. He seemed a little too stern, almost like he was keeping information from her. She was told there wasn't any information on the disappearance of her son or daughter-in-law.

Several months after the disappearance, Opal's daughter-in-law showed up at her door. Her appearance had changed so much that Opal had a hard time recognizing her. The once vivacious, ebony skinned beauty, was now hollowed eyed with blotched skin, the once curvaceous figure was now skeletal in appearance. The woman she saw standing before her was dirty, unkempt, and acted like the hounds of hell were after her. Fresh scars were evident on her face and exposed limbs. Beulah's fidgeting gave her away as an addict. It was such a shock to her that Opal was thankful the boys were at school, so they didn't see what their mother looked like when she showed up.

Opal had a hard time convincing Beulah to go to the hospital to be examined. Even after agreeing, Beulah tearfully refused to talk about where she had been. On the way to the hospital, Opal tried to find out what happened to her son. If Beulah had ever known, she either wasn't telling or didn't know now. Every time Opal asked a pointed question, Beulah either stared blankly ahead or tears ran down her once beautiful face. Her large, dark brown, doe eyes that once were so expressive, now had a vacant look to them. Opal had a feeling that what little her daughter-in-law could remember was too painful to talk about.

After a three day stay in the hospital, Beulah went into a rehab center. Opal mortgaged her home to pay for it. While Beulah was hospitalized, she signed papers for Opal to try to find to out about her financial situation. With the help of an attorney, she found out that her son's home had been signed over to someone else and his savings and checking accounts had been closed out within a week of his disappearance. She went in search of the man she thought was responsible. Beulah admitted she had no recollection of being drugged. Existing in a drugged stupor, she was used as a prostitute until shortly before she arrived on Opal's doorstep. No matter how hard she tried, she couldn't remember what happened that night. She had no idea what happened to her husband.

Within a year the expenses added up to an astronomical amount, Opal was broke. She sold her beautiful home to pay expenses for the search of her son and her daughter-in-law's hospital bills. Living on a tight budget, she noticed money frequently disappearing from her purse, and expensive pieces of jewelry handed down from her grandmother vanished also. The family was soon forced to move into low rent housing. Beulah had started using drugs again and would disappear without a word for days at a time. One day an officer showed up at the door to tell Opal they had found Beulah's body. She had died of an overdose a few months after finding out she had the AIDS virus.

***

"Ms. Opal, Ms. Opal" Tony came rushing in the door dragging Ray behind him. He was waving his report card.

"Child settle down. I told you we don't put on airs. You call me grandmother or gram or Opal or something else; but I'm not going to have you call me Ms. Opal. I know your poor momma made you call me that, but we don't do it now. Let's see what's got you so excited." She grabbed both boys in a hug, careful not to knock Ray's glasses off, then kissed them each on top of the head. Holding out her hand and grinning at them she said "I bet you have good news. Is that your report cards?"

Both boys beamed up at their grandmother. Tony was almost as tall as she was already. Ray had been so sickly for so long she had worried but now he had started growing and filling out. Tony still watched out for him constantly.

"Grand we both got straight A's." Ray injected before Tony had a chance to speak. Tony grinned broadly at the sight of his younger brother dancing around while he told their grandmother the news.

Opal looked at both of them with warm loving admiration. "Your daddy would be so proud of both of you if he could see you now, I know I am. This calls for a treat. I am taking my two men to the movies and on the way home we will get ice cream."

Ray's eyes looked so big behind his glasses that Tony had to laugh out loud. "Really? Grand you're taking us to a movie?" Ray was amazed.

"Really, go clean up. We will grab a bite to eat and head to the theater." Opal pushed them toward the bathroom and began setting the table.

Tony knew how tight funds were. Even as young as he was he understood how hard it was for his grandmother to pay the bills and put food on the table. After his mother's death, a man claiming to be his father's old business acquaintance asked Tony if he wanted to earn some cash money on the side.

When his grandmother did something special like this, he was reminded of the offer.

With Beulah gone, Opal started receiving checks on the boys. She thought it prudent to teach Tony to manage money, so she added his name onto her checking account and had him to sit with her when she paid bills. Before long he helped make up their budget and learned to do taxes. When Beulah's funeral expenses were paid off, Opal opened savings accounts for both boys. Unknown to Opal, Tony had started running errands for Ronald Arnold.

A few days before Anthony Lewis Taylor, Tony, turned fifteen, he came home from school to find his grandmother in her bed. Opal was pale, sweating profusely, having trouble breathing, so weak she could barely speak, she knew she was dying. "Tony sit by me." She grasped his hand with the little strength she had. In a voice that was near a whisper she solicited a promise from her grandson. "I know how the system works. When they come to take me away you will hear the racket, go to the neighbor's. Don't come back in here and tell them I am raising you or they will take you boys and split you up."

"Grandmother, I am going to get help. You'll be alright." Tony was frightened. He tried to stand to go get help.

"No Tony, you have to listen. It's my time to go sweetie. You have to be the man and raise your brother. Finish school. Your name is on everything I have. You can sign my name. The funeral home won't notify anyone; I've already seen to that. They will be calling my old friend Beth. No one else needs to know. I have faith in you." Gasping for breath, tears of despair started slowly making their way down the face that Tony loved so very much. "I wanted to live long enough to see you both through college with families of your own. It just isn't going to happen that way. I love you." Her last words were spoken so softly it was hard for him to hear as she took her last breath.

When Raymond came home he found his older brother holding their grandmother in his arms. Tony sat on the side of the bed, rocking her lifeless body while he cried like he had never cried for anyone before.

"Tony what will we do now?" Raymond stood watching his brother. His coloring was light brown to start with, now he was pale to the point of passing for white. The trauma of what he witnessed was too much for him to bear. The room spun slightly for a moment before he passed out, sinking slowly to the floor.

Chapter 1

(Easter Sunday, March 31, 2013)

Brenda Lou, get your fat butt out here! Come on, you hear me? Get out here right now! — Where the devil are you? Damn it girl, I–" Chet was yelling as he stomped across the living room to throw open the bedroom door. His face flushed with more anger than he had felt in many years. Shock at what he saw stopped him in his tracks. "What in the Sam Hill is going on here?"

Brenda sat straight up in the bed drawing the sheet up to cover her bare chest. Seeing her dad standing in the doorway with his mouth hanging open, she went from half asleep to wide awake in .02 seconds flat. "What's wrong? Don't you ever knock? I was asleep." Before she could utter another word, she was startled when she felt a hand reach up pulling the sheet down far enough to expose a large amount of her oversized soft white breast. With her father looking on, the same dark-skinned hand groped for, then grabbed, the partially exposed breast.

"What in God's name have you done Brenda Lou? I know for darn sure that is not your husband in that bed with you. You have got a lot of explaining to do." Chet was shaking his finger at her while in the process of going from slow boil to popping a gasket in a heartbeat. He already had the whole morning for his anger to build.

A large black male stuck his head out from under the covers. Wiping at his eyes, he drew himself farther up into a sitting position.

He threw his arm over Brenda's shoulder, making it easier to reach the breast he had been attempting to fondle earlier, he turned his attention to Chet. "Who the hell are you old man?"

It took a moment for Brenda to process everything going on. At first, she didn't remember what happened the night before. It barely registered that her husband would not have exposed her, or attempted to fondle her breast, especially with her father in the house. When she heard the strange voice she went from shocked, to confused, to frightened, in the blink of an eye. "Oh no." She groaned when it dawned on her that the voice belonged to the man she met at a bar the night before.

"I see why you didn't hear me beating on the door, which by the way wasn't locked." Chet's color was fast going from bright red to pale as the sheet covering Brenda's bed. Chet's normally tanned skin appeared extremely pale. He looked like he had been whitewashed except for his dark brown hair. "Your husband is at the house, where you were supposed to be. I see why you forgot about leading choir this morning." All of a sudden Chet's eyes rolled back in his head, as he did a slow spin down onto the floor. He went into convulsions before he completely stopped moving.

The black man in Brenda Lou's bed peered down at the man lying in the floor. "He's still breathing. Hey Cotton Candy, wanna pick up where we left off last night?" He chuckled while he started fondling the large white breast once again. "I don't think the old fart will bother us again for a while." He laughed, bending to try to take the dusky rose-colored nipple into his mouth.

Brenda Lou turned toward the man she had spent the night with. Using both hands, she pushed him away from her as hard as she could before she swung her legs over the edge of the bed, launching all 189 pounds of her somewhat overweight body out of the bed. "Daddy, Daddy. Please don't be dead, Talk to me." She cried out in a panic as she threw herself down beside her unconscious father.

Bewildered, she looked at the man in her bed, "Tony, call 911 while I'm getting some clothes on, and then get out of here." She raised her pink tinted head full of matted blond hair away from her father's mouth. Once she figured out he was still breathing she started trying to figure a way out of the mess she had gotten herself into.

At just over six foot six, Tony was about as dark as any black man you would find anywhere. His handsome features were finely chiseled, with a body being that of an Adonis. Tony knew he looked good enough to play a Roman gladiator in any Hollywood movie. "That's your daddy for real? I'll be damned, I know who he is. I've seen him on TV." Tony laughed, shaking his head as he went in search of the phone. "Cotton Candy, I sure wouldn't wanna be in your shoes."

Trying to squeeze into a pair of tight blue jeans, she was pulling a roll of fat around so she could wiggle into them enough to get them to zip. While she worked with the zipper, Brenda stuck her feet into a worn pair of loafers. Finally getting her jeans snapped, she pulled on her bra and shirt. "Tony! Come on Anthony, please get a move on. You can't be here when they come to pick my daddy up!" She sounded hysterical. There were tears causing black streaks to run down her face from the smudged makeup left over from the night before. "What am I gonna do? I really messed things up this time! Larry Joe's going to hate me! I've never done anything like this before." She wailed.

Tony had disappeared for several minutes before he came swaggering into the room tucking his shirt into his pants. "So, Cotton Candy, when are we gonna do this again?" He grinned at her like he expected her to jump at the chance.

Her expression went blank, mortified by the shock of everything going on. "I am worried to death about Daddy right now. I don't even remember what happened last night. If there was time, I would be trying to find out how you ended up in my bed. I just need for you to be gone from here before anybody shows up, understand? I need to call my Momma. Go, now! Get out!"

Hearing the sirens getting closer, Brenda started to panic. "Hurry up! Get out of here, and, stop calling me Cotton Candy!" She was trying to talk between sobs. "Is my car here?"

"Yeah, it's here. How do think we got here since I didn't drive? You gonna take me back to my car?" While he finished lacing his shoes he looked over at Brenda Lou. "So, Girl, when we gonna do this again?" He repeated.

Brenda glared at Anthony Payne. When she spoke, it was between clinched teeth. "I told you to get out. I have no idea what happened last night. There is not going to be a next time. I want to know what happened, but not now. Go! I'm sure you can get a ride from someone else." On the verge of tears once again, she wasn't having much luck trying to push an apparently amused Anthony Payne toward the back door.

At the sound of the ambulance doors slamming shut in front of Brenda Lou's house, Anthony finally made his way out the back door. Brenda watched the fluid movements of all two hundred and twenty pounds of solid muscle disappearing from sight as the door closed behind him. What she didn't know was how badly he wanted to turn around to apologize for thinking the man that showed up was someone else she was seeing as well as for his words and actions in front of her father.

Never before had he slept with one of the women connected with a job. Something about this one drew him to her like no other ever had. Hearing her mention her husband's name had hurt him. Surely she had to have some idea of the kind of person she was married to. Anthony had crossed a self-imposed boundary when his desire for this woman took control of his actions. At the moment he did not like himself very much. He knew he had to come across as a complete jerk; but, he hadn't felt good about it.

The ambulance crew knocked on the front door ten minutes after they received the call. Cell phone in hand, Brenda Lou opened the door while dialing her mother's phone number. All she told her mother was that her dad had blacked out and she called the ambulance. Her mother said she would have Brenda Lou's husband drive her to the hospital in Dexter.

Before the paramedics could finish getting their patient's vital signs, Chet started to respond. When Brenda Lou saw that her daddy was waking up, she turned her back to him so she wouldn't have to witness the disapproval in his eyes. Since her daddy was laying in front of the bedroom door, she was able to help answer questions while she worked. As she started yanking the sheets off the bed, she told the medics she was trying to stay busy to keep from getting in their way.

"Mr. Perkins, can you tell us what happened?" The medic asked Chet while he was shining a penlight in first one eye then the other to check the pupillary responses.

Chet looked over at his daughter before he answered the question. "I can't say what happened." Brenda Lou caught her daddy's expression as he looked her in the eye before he looked back at the medic.

The medic had been doing this job long enough to know that there was something his patient wasn't going to tell him. "Well Mr. Perkins, we need to take you on to the hospital so the doctor can have a look at you." He was looking around to see if there was anything obviously out of the ordinary that may have caused Chet's problem. "They'll want to do some tests to see what caused you to pass out." The only thing the medic found in the assessment he did was a faster than normal heart rate, with an elevated blood pressure. The rate wasn't extremely fast nor was the blood pressure extremely high. His cardiac rhythm was only slightly faster than normal; no other abnormalities appeared on the monitor.

While the crew loaded her daddy onto the stretcher, Brenda Lou let them know they needed to take Chet to the Dexter Emergency Room, instead of Kennett. She told them her daddy lived in Bloomfield, so his doctors were all in Dexter. Normally they would have taken a patient picked up in Malden to Kennett or Poplar Bluff; but this didn't appear to be an imminently life-threatening emergency.

Housekeeping wasn't one of Brenda Lou's talents. After the ambulance pulled out of the driveway, she went to work like someone possessed. The sheets were thrown into the washer and the dishes into the dishwasher before the ambulance reached the end of the street. She set a personal record for running the vacuum cleaner before wiping down the kitchen counter. While Brenda checked her face and brushed her hair she checked the bathroom to be certain Anthony hadn't left anything there. While she put the clean sheets on the bed, she looked under the bed to make sure there weren't any traces of her having had another man in her bed. Satisfied that everything looked normal, she was as ready as she could be to go face her husband.

It was a twenty-five-minute drive from the Green's house to the hospital. Knowing that Larry Joe would ask questions, she tried to come up with answers she thought would satisfy him. Brenda Lou was confused about almost everything that happened the night before. On top of wondering about that, she didn't know what her daddy might tell her husband about what he saw. Brenda told herself there was no doubt about her being in love with Larry Joe. She was afraid if he found out about Tony, he would divorce her.

Easter Sunday was a beautiful day. The clear sky was a soft baby blue with a few fluffy white clouds floating across high up in the sky. Tulips had just started to push up through the ground. Crocus and Easter flowers bloomed brightly in the yards she passed as she sped along. There were children hunting Easter eggs among the clumps of grass and flowers at many of the homes. Lost in thought, Brenda Lou paid little attention to the scenery. Knowing how she had begged her dad to let her lead the choir for so long, she didn't blame him for being upset with her. She hadn't seen him angry enough to cuss since she was small. She knew she had hurt him to the quick. Seeing what he saw, on top of her not showing up—well, she didn't blame him. Her thoughts were racing all over the place. Try as she might, she couldn't remember how she ended up in bed with Anthony Payne.

By the time she reached the city limit sign of Bernie, she started to remember a few things. What she remembered upset her more than she already was.

Larry Joe had promised to take her out to celebrate because Chet finally agreed to let her lead the choir that Sunday. The Easter Services were to be televised live on all the local channels. While she was in the shower that Saturday evening, she heard the phone ring and Larry Joe answer it. He was only on the phone for a minute before he opened the bathroom door just enough to yell that he had to go out to meet her dad for a few minutes.

Finished with her shower, Brenda stepped out of the tub wrapping herself in a thick bath sheet. While taking special pains to apply her makeup and fix her hair, she surveyed the bathroom. Larry Joe had just finished remodeling it for her. She loved the new vanity. It was long with a marble top. There were double sinks, so both she and Larry could get ready for work at the same time. He even put up a full-length mirror for her. The new lighting could be dimmed or brightened, perfect for romantic evenings in the new whirlpool bath for two. The extra thick, soft mauve carpet was a shade darker than the walls. The wallpaper came halfway up the wall with a matching soft, silk, pastel striped print, while the flowered trim added the perfect touch to bring it all together.

She recently started worrying her husband was losing interest in her. He seemed distracted most of the time and he was gone long periods of time too often. Looking around she decided she was wrong; he had done all this for her.

Brenda checked herself in the mirror. She was wearing a mid-length black dress with a scoop neck which showed off her breasts. The dress hung the way it needed to, making her waist look smaller than it was. Appraising the overall effect after slipping on her three-inch black heels, she felt good about her appearance. Her dad objected to the pink streaks she put in her blond hair, but she thought they looked great. He told her with her bleached hair and thick makeup she looked like the wife of that evangelist that got in trouble.

Brenda didn't care what her daddy thought about her hair, not only did it help her business, her husband said he liked it.

It was taking Larry Joe a long time to get back home. Brenda had started to pace by the time her phone rang. Larry Joe finally called to say he had been held up longer than expected, asking her to meet him at the steak house in Dexter. She could hear a lot of background noise where he was. It sounded like he was calling from a bar; but, she told herself that couldn't be right. Not only was he with her dad, he swore he didn't go to bars.

Brenda circled the steakhouse twice without seeing Larry Joe's car. She thought while she waited she would run up the road to pick up a bottle of wine for later. Passing the bar, she spotted Larry Joe's car. She had forgotten her daddy was manning the suicide line that night. Wondering why his car would be in the lot, she parked her car and slipped in through the back door. There sat her husband at a table holding hands with a very attractive younger woman.

Chet came out of the bathroom in time to see his daughter, livid with anger, turn storming out the back door of the bar. Brenda Lou hadn't stuck around long enough to notice her daddy heading back to the table. Chet let her go, thinking it would teach her a lesson about jealousy. After their meeting, Larry Joe started to leave, that's when Chet told him he saw Brenda Lou. When Larry Joe got to the steakhouse, Brenda Lou wasn't there and wouldn't answer her phone when he tried to call her. He called her parents' house to see if she had gone to talk to her mother. Normally, when she got upset that's where she went. It was very late by the time Larry Joe arrived at the Perkin's home to wait on his wife.

Donna strolled into the hospital waiting room. She was a tiny little thing, looking much shorter than her five feet four inches. Brenda spotted her and steeled herself for what was to come. Donna pushed her glasses farther up on the bridge of her nose while looking down it at her seated sister. "What did you do to daddy?" She demanded, sounding as sarcastic as her smug expression implied. "He was fine when he left the house. I take that back, he wasn't fine.

He was upset– with you–again! You hurt his feelings really bad this time." She chewed on her bottom lip for a couple seconds before she went to sit between Brenda and their mother.

"Donna Mae, why do you automatically think the worst of me every time anything happens to anybody?" There was a pleading sound to her voice as she sat with her hands in her lap, fingers entwined, rolling her thumbs. "Other people do bad things too and on purpose. I don't do bad things on purpose, Donna Mae!" Tears were starting to well in her eyes. "Not everything is my fault." Feeling this was completely her fault, Brenda had a hard time holding back the tears.

When Donna started to speak, she was silenced by their mother. Lou held up her hand in front of Donna. "Girls, this isn't the time or place for bickering. I wish the two of you would behave. For goodness sake, you are both grown women." Lou stood up looking from one of her daughters to the other with a stern look of displeasure on her face. I'm going to go see how things are coming along. I'm surprised Larry Joe hasn't come back out here yet." Looking pointedly at Brenda Lou, she continued. "You have a fine man there. It's past time for you to get over your childishness. I don't know why he puts up with your jealous behavior, or your tantrums. You had him worried sick last night." Having said her piece, Lou turned and motioned for the receptionist to buzz her through the doors.

As soon as Lou was out of sight, Donna turned on her sister. "Okay Brenda Lou, spill it. I already heard rumors galore." She hissed through clenched teeth with a sly gleam in her eyes.

Sinking so low into her chair that if she went any lower she would go through the bottom into the floor, Brenda looked up at her sister. Donna was sitting ramrod straight on the edge of her seat, glaring down her nose at her. From the look on her face you would have sworn she smelled something that had gone bad. "I don't know what you're talking about. I don't gossip, remember? I'm worried about Daddy and all you want to do is gossip. Go figure." She kept her head down and rolled her eyes up.

"I don't know for sure what all happened. I hope it wasn't what I heard. You didn't show this morning though, I do know that. Daddy was so upset with you–, he had me to stand in at the last minute." She paused, looking down at the floor then back up at her sister. "How do you ever expect him to be proud of you when you work so hard to disappoint him?" Donna scolded her older sister. "You have always been Daddy's favorite and you do everything you can to disappoint him. I wish he was even half as proud of me as he is of you. It just isn't fair, you're gonna break his heart. You don't even seem to care." She stood, walking over to the door to stare out the window so that Brenda couldn't see the hurt tears forming in her eyes.

The double doors swung open allowing Larry Joe back into the Waiting Room. He crossed directly to his wife, sitting in the chair just vacated by Donna. "Baby, it looks like your dad will be alright. Have you talked to him at all?" He gave her a questioning look. "Do you have any idea what happened? All he would say was that he couldn't say what happened." As he spoke he wrapped an arm across her shoulders, drawing her close to him while sobs shook her entire body. "I should have looked until I found you last night. I'm so sorry."

Chapter 2

Smoke was rolling unnoticed out of a first-floor window. Anthony Payne was leaning into the open window of the Lincoln Town Car parked in his drive, talking to the passenger. When his cell phone rang, he straightened up turning toward his house as he answered it. He saw the smoke at the same instant. "This is Tony. Oh shit! I'll call you back, my damn house is on fire." He was sprinting for the back door as he spoke.

The air in the kitchen was thick with smoke. Anthony had been cooking when the men showed up at the house. He hadn't expected to be outside long when he left the burner on. Flames were engulfing the top of the stove by the time he rushed into the house. First throwing flour on the surface of the stove, he grabbed a heat proof oven-mitt from the granite counter by the stove, jamming his hand into it before he picked up the flaming skillet. After quickly looking around the room, he went to the open back door tossing the skillet into the yard. "So much for lunch." The two men from the car had followed him to see what was going on.

After the laughter stopped the taller of the two men spoke. "It looks like it ain't your day man. I can't believe you let the merchandise get away. The boss is gonna really be pissed. That him on the phone?"

"Let's step on out here in the yard away from the smoke. Damn! Yeah, it was him. I'm going to have to call him back." He punched the side of the house. After he spit, he started rubbing the knuckles on the hand he had used to hit the building with. "From what Ben told me she shouldn't have had anybody checking up on her. She wasn't supposed to have any family. I couldn't believe her ole man showed up. If he hadn't keeled over, I think I could have got her anyway."

"You know what's gonna happen if we don't deliver in a couple days. You got anybody else lined up?" The taller man spoke again.

Anthony grinned. "Here in Hicksville? You know it ain't hard to find all you want. It's like fishing and I got all the right bait. If you don't believe it, just look around." He boasted while making a sweeping motion with his right arm.

The shorter man spoke for the first time. "You are one conceited asshole. All I can say is, you better not screw it up again. The boss man don't like mistakes. Hell, he don't like you much to start with. It wouldn't bother him to put a bullet in your black hide. Don't be a liability, hear me? I'd hate to have to make you disappear." The man didn't crack a smile as he delivered the warning with a deadly edge to his voice. "We'll be in touch." The two turned, heading back to their car without a backward glance. Anthony knew that the man would really love to kill him, no questions asked.

There was something worrisome about this particular target. Not only was Anthony troubled about his attraction for the woman and the fact that he acted on it, but he knew he had been lied to about all the information connected to her.

Tulips were bursting out in a riot of colorful blossoms against the green backdrop of new spring grass, just starting to form a lush carpet over the ground. Green onions had sprouted up overnight dwarfing the crocus which were blooming their last blooms of the season. Anthony didn't notice any of that or the robins playing in the yard. He knew he had made a mistake that could cost him his life. He wasn't sure why he had been given misleading information, or how much. All he knew was that he would have to deliver, soon.

Bad Leroy Brown sounded as the ring tone announced an incoming call. Anthony winced when he read the anonymous printout for the caller's name. "Hey Boss, sorry about hanging up on you. Had a little house fire I had to take care of. The boys were here when it happened." He thought it couldn't hurt to validate the episode to help temper the caller's anger.

There was a brief silence before a voice was heard. "I already heard all about it when I spoke to Bud. I just wanted to ask you how the knees are doing. You haven't forgotten how accidents can just up and happen have you? I expect delivery." Silence followed the click.

He stood with the silent phone to his ear, remembering the pain. Kitchen duty at the prison hadn't been bad. Anthony preferred that to working in the laundry any day, until the day he was attacked. Mr. Arnold was one mean man. Anthony had gone to prison because of him. There had to be a way to get out from under his control, if he could just stay alive long enough.

As a teen living in Elgin, Illinois, Antony ran errands for Mr. Arnold. When he got older he distributed drugs, handled some of the prostitutes, and helped launder money. Anthony came home one day to find his younger brother Raymond dead. Raymond had been badly beaten; but, his death appeared to be from an overdose.

Raymond hated the thought of what drugs had done to their mother and to some of his friends. He had begged Anthony to stop helping get them into the hands of the kids in the neighborhood. Anthony knew his brother had not willingly taken the drugs that caused his death. After finding numerous fresh bruises on his brother's lifeless body, Anthony went to Mr. Arnold. His boss explained that he had asked Raymond to help him with something and Raymond refused.

Mr. Arnold wasn't happy when Anthony confronted him, threatening to turn him in for the murder of his brother. He told him he quit and stormed out of Mr. Arnold's office. Shortly after that, there were drugs found during a police raid on Anthony's apartment, along with a gun used in a gang related hit. The information came in the form of an anonymous call to the Chief of Police. Anthony had been set up. He went to prison. A few months before his release he was badly beaten. The beating was a message from Mr. Arnold.

Fifteen years had gone by since he had been on the outside of the prison walls. A long limo pulled up outside the gate when Anthony walked out. The window slid down a crack and the voice that greeted him was one he would never forget. "Well, boy, are you ready to go back to work?" The nightmare was starting again, or had it ever stopped? The smell of damp dust in the air said rain wouldn't be long in coming. Until the vehicle's window opened he had felt darn good about being on the outside. "I got a job for you." Hearing those words, he realized how cold and overcast it really was.

The car door opened for him to get in. He knew to disobey would cause his death by nightfall. "It's been a long time, Boy. I've had people keeping me informed about you. They told me you kept yourself in good shape. Glad to see you're not limping. I made sure the boys knew not to break you up too bad when they delivered my message."

He had aged some, but in a good way. The streaks of grey in his dark brown hair lent an air of sophistication to the man seated across from Anthony. With one leg crossed casually over the over, he had an arm resting across the back of the seat. Steel grey eyes matched the expensive tailor-made suit he was wearing. The light blue shirt did nothing to soften the daggers coming through the amused stare. "The women seem to like your kind now. That will be in our favor." Looking down long enough to brush at a piece of imaginary lint on an expensive Italian made loafer, he continued. "We have expanded into something a little more profitable. You should enjoy it." The smile didn't quite make it to his eyes. "After all, you have been locked up for a few years. My informants tell me you haven't turned to men so you can make up for lost time. I know you never did care for the prostitutes."

"Doesn't look like I have much choice in the matter. Does it?" By working in the kitchen, Anthony's diet had been better than most of the inmates. Every spare minute was spent working on his mind or his body. He had managed to get degrees in business and economics among other things, thanks to the extensive libraries and online classes. All six foot six inches of body was rock hard muscle. The slight scar on his left cheek gave him character. "What do I have to do?" He gave the man sitting across from him a look of revulsion mixed with a healthy dose of hatred. Mr. Arnold laughed quietly as they sped away.

Over the next four months, meetings were held in a condo in the city of Arnold, Missouri. Anthony was outfitted in expensive clothes. He learned more about international business than he thought was necessary at the time and learned all about the likes and dislikes of the clients he would be supplying. When he had the information memorized, he was moved into a house in an exclusive area just outside of Dexter, Missouri.

Large trees lining the drive led to the most impressive home Anthony could ever remember seeing. What made this house even better was the fact that he held the title in his hand. Sitting on ten acres of rolling hills, the house was two stories tall. A fountain backlit with a rainbow assortment of light sat in the center of a small lake situated down the hill in front of the house. The columns decorating the front entrance of the structure were two stories tall. Light poured from the arched windows of the upper story, cutting through the light fog, it looked almost like a halo around the entire house. The house appeared to angle toward the lake on each end with the center being taller than the sides. A circular drive in the front of the house was outlined with manicured evergreen shrubbery.

"It's a dandy ain't it boy?" Wilbur, Will Wilkerson, turned to look over the back of the seat at Anthony while he spoke. Will was a downright disagreeable man to start with. He was five foot ten but due to his stocky build, with a neck like a bulldog, he didn't look that tall. His hands were broad palmed making his stubby fingers look like nubs. He enjoyed making people squirm, almost as much as he enjoyed inflicting pain. Right now, he was attempting to get a rise out of the passenger he and Bud Lowe had in the backseat.

Seeing his new home, Anthony was in a pretty good humor. Over the last four months he had learned to ignore most of the verbal jabs thrown his way by Will. "I tell you what Wilbur, if you call me Tony instead of boy, I'll call you Will instead of Wilbur. How does that sound to you?" His face split into a grin when he saw the effect his comment had on his adversary in the front seat. When Bud chuckled, it made him feel even better.

"Alright smartass, I'll call you Tony." Slightly flushed with anger, he turned to face the drive again "Wait 'til you see the inside of this shack boy,–I mean Tony. Me and Bud are gonna be staying here when we gotta come down here for pickups, so we wanted to make damn sure it was good enough."

Knowing Wilbur was working up to something, Bud cut in "The Boss knew what you needed for the job. We'll show you around before we take off. I think you're going to like the toys in the basement." Bud looked like a tall lanky nerd with curly brown hair. Looks can be deceiving and when it came to Bud they were. He was an electronics genius, but, he was deadly with any weapon he got his hands on. Another thing about Bud was that he was fast and deadly with his bare hands also. There are those people you instantly feel comfortable around, Bud was one of those people. Reality of it was, Bud's mind was twisted and he had no conscience. He could be friendly, talking to you, laughing and sharing jokes, right before he cut you into tiny pieces, while enjoying every scream.

Bud pulled the car into the four-car garage, at the back of the house. While the door slid down, Anthony looked across at the next bay seeing the cars he had been given to drive. He let out a low whistle when he saw the 2013, deep maroon Bentley convertible. "Luxury from start to finish." Opening the door, he spoke over his shoulder to the two men as he slid out of the back seat. He went to inspect the dark mesh-style grill, flared fenders, and chrome-accented tail lamps, before looking at the diamond-quilted leather interior. Rich mahogany wood trim on the dash and doors stood out even in the inadequate lighting of the garage. "I didn't think these would be on the market this early."

"You know things can be got early for the right price. The boss knows what bait it takes to get what he wants-Tony." Wilbur intentionally hesitated before calling Tony by his name. He intentionally emphasized Tony, to let him know he still thought him to be a lesser person. "You won't have forgotten that though, will you Tony?" He snickered loudly causing Bud to look at him through squinted eyes.

Anthony ignored Wilbur, instead of rising to the implied insult. He walked from the Bentley to the next bay. Bud flipped a switch, causing the garage to be bathed in bright lights. Parked in the third bay sat a 2012 Range Rover. He liked the black exterior with the darkly tinted windows. Twenty-two-inch 5 Split Spoke alloy wheels finished out the look. Without looking, he knew the inside would be just as nice. He couldn't help thinking to himself that, no matter how grand, all of this couldn't pay for Raymond's life. "These will do. Now, who has the keys?"

Bud held the keys up over his head as he turned, heading for the door. "Let's go on in. We can order something delivered, we have work to do. No time like the present to start getting you known around here anyway. Delivery people talk." Entering, he waited for the others to go through the door. Cracking a half smile he shrugged, closing the door behind them. "You make the call. Make sure to tell them they need to bring change for a hundred. After that change into lounge pants, no shirt, be barefoot. Your clothes are already in your bedroom. Hopefully a female delivers." He gave a sly half smile and a slight nod, to get his point across. "Have the food brought in through the living room to the kitchen. These hicks will be talking about you before you know it."

Walking through the house, he understood what Bud meant. The living room had wood floors polished to a high shine, a high vaulted ceiling with a chandelier, and overstuffed leather furniture sat around antique, hand-woven, wool Persian rug. The main focal point was an enormous field-stone fireplace with a thick mahogany mantle. The fireplace went up the full two stories, dominating that side of the room. There was a ten-foot fish tank filled with brightly colored tropical fish. It was tucked between twin mahogany bookshelves against another wall, with a mural depicting an ocean as the backdrop. He rushed up the curved staircase to change, hoping he would find the right bedroom quickly. On the way he noticed several oil paintings lining the stairwell. He wanted to take a better look at the paintings but that would wait until later.

Anthony finished dressing the way Bud told him to. Hearing the door chimes, he surveyed his appearance in the mirror, satisfied it would have the desired effect, he went to answer the front door. As Bud had hoped, the delivery person was female. Tony told her to take the boxes on into the kitchen, which could be seen through an arched doorway, while he got his wallet. He already had the money in his pocket, but he stood just out of sight to watch her as she looked at her surroundings. Built-in stainless-steel appliances trimmed in black, surrounded by granite countertops, gleamed and sparkled. The pizza boxes were sat on the matching island, which had a lighted utility rack filled with top of the line cook ware hanging overhead. Her expression said how impressed she was, as she bent down to run her hand across the marble tiles that covered the kitchen floor.

To draw her attention to his entrance, Anthony lightly slapped the wall before he entered the kitchen. His movements were fluid, sensual, and seductive as he slowly walked into the room in order to give her time to look him over before stopping in front of her. Reaching into his pocket he grinned down at her. "Hope they told you to bring change. The smallest thing I've got is a hundred-dollar bill," he drawled as he leaned casually against the counter.

The young woman caught herself looking at the rock hard, corded abdominal muscles just above the V at the top of his low riding lounge pants as she stood. She appeared to be about five foot tall, eye level below the center of his massive chest. When she realized she was staring, her cheeks turned bright pink as she fumbled, dropping the change which rolled across the floor. "I, I'm sorry sir." She was almost stuttering as she bent to chase the rolling coins. "I brought change, they told me." Tripping, she almost went sprawling across the floor herself. Anthony caught her before she could hit the floor.

Laughing, he made a motion for her to stand still while he retrieved everything she dropped. Handing it back to her, he was still chuckling when he spoke. "Young lady, I appreciate you bringing this out here so fast. You keep the change for your trouble." He held her hands in his, while wrapping her hands around the money she attempted to give back to him.

"But that, that's over fifty dollars." She stammered.

"It's well worth it. I just moved in and didn't want to have to go out anywhere. With nobody to cook for me, you have just made my day so much better than it would have been. Now, you keep it and have a good night." He smiled seductively while slowly releasing her hands.

Still looking shocked, she quickly pocketed the cash. "Thank you. Gosh, thanks a lot. Anytime you need a delivery just ask for me." She held up her name tag, blushing again. She almost tripped over her own feet as she hurried out through the front door.

Bud and Wilbur had been watching what went on in the kitchen on the monitor in the basement. After the girl sped away from the house they came upstairs. While Wilbur was seething with jealous rage, Bud was amused. "Talk about making an impression. That gal will be doing good to get back without having an accident. Looks like the boss was right. You got what it takes, eye candy for the ladies, plus the bucks. She will be talking." Bud made a sweeping gesture with his hand as he spoke, before dipping into a low mock bow in front of Tony. Both Tony and Bud burst out laughing, while Wilbur did a slow boil. If looks could kill, Tony would have been a dead man.

Wilbur stomped toward the door leading to the garage. "I don't want no damn pizza. Let's get the hell outta here. We can come back in the morning to give him instructions on the gear. I wanna drink." Bud knew the word bigot was too mild to use when it came to the way Wilbur felt about anyone that wasn't lily white in color. "Thought you wanted to stay here tonight. Wasn't it you that said you wanted to finish up? Did your lady fair dump you again? Is that why you aren't in a big rush now to get done so we can head back home?"

At the tender age of fourteen, Bud castrated his favorite uncle. During a card game his uncle jokingly accused him of cheating. Bud didn't act upset at the time. Later that night he waited for his uncle to pass out before he slipped into his bedroom with a filet knife. First he slit his uncle's throat, then he castrated him before cutting out his heart. Bud cleaned everything up, removed the bedroom screen from the outside, and went back to bed like nothing happened. Although he carried on like he was grieving, he felt no remorse when he was told his uncle had been murdered. The testicles were found shoved deep down the dead man's throat during the autopsy. Bud cut the heart into bite size pieces for the neighbor's dog. The murder was never solved.

If he didn't need Wilbur for this job, he wouldn't put up with him. As it was, he just enjoyed pushing Wilbur's buttons to see him squirm. He followed Wilbur to the door. Before he went out he turned to wink at Tony as he spoke to his partner. "Man, you know I have a couple of lookers waiting on me whenever I decide to share myself with them." You could hear his laughter as he pulled the door closed behind him.

Tony was exhausted. He ate part of the cold pizza, washing it down with a beer, before putting the pasta in the fridge for later. Exercise would have to wait; he was too tired. Padding barefoot up the stairs, he slowed just enough to appreciate the original oils hanging on the wall. He thought once again that no matter what all this cost, it wasn't enough to pay for Raymond's death. He would give anything to have his brother alive and well but it was too late. By putting a stop to the organization, he would be avenging Raymond.

Sitting straight up in the king-sized bed, he looked across the room at the digital clock. It was three in the morning. He hadn't been awakened like this since shortly before his release from prison. The form of a man slowly manifested itself in the sturdy brocade chair across the room. Dim light filtered in through the windows from the pole light outside making the figure look like a real person. The ghost appeared to be around six foot four inches tall, slim lanky build, with dark hair. He had to be in his early forties. His clothing was always a dark vested suit with either a neck scarf or bow tie.

"Why can't you leave me alone? I know I'm not crazy, just like I know you aren't real." When Tony first started having these unexpected visits he had tried grabbing the figure, only to have his hands pass through thin air. Other times he had repeatedly opened and closed his eyes only to find the figure didn't disappear. "What do you want from me? I know who you are supposed to look like, but not why." He almost shouted.

Tonight was the first time the ghost had communicated with him. He didn't speak but Tony heard the words in his mind. "In time son. In time, things will become clear. You're not ready yet. Take a good look at me then look at yourself in the mirror." The image smiled at him before he continued. "You have to believe first. Just remember one thing-be true to yourself. I'm here to help if you need me. What you are doing is a noble thing. Just don't cross the line so far you can't come back." Tony looked toward the large mirror over his dresser. When he looked back the chair was empty. He could still hear the soft voice, "Many times I walked slowly, but I never walked backwards."

"What the hell is that supposed to mean old man? I don't know who you are or were. Why are you picking on me? What has the mirror got to do with all this? Come back here and explain." He shouted toward the now empty chair while he threw his legs over the edge of the bed. After going to the bathroom, he fell back into bed, asleep almost immediately when his head hit the pillow. The first few visits from this ghost had caused him to lose sleep, not anymore.

Chapter 3

Slamming the front door behind her, Donna made herself at home dropping her purse on the sofa, tossing car keys on the kitchen counter. "Brenda Lou, where are you?" Donna called out in a singsong voice as she made her way farther into the house. "Don't you ever lock your doors? You don't know who might decide to come in here." She grinned down at her sister who was bent over scrubbing the bathtub. "I don't know what's got into you, but the house looks good. Got any tea made?"

Pulling herself up to sit on the edge of the tub, Brenda gave her sister a rather bland go to hell look. "Out slumming? I know you don't like coming to Malden." She rose, heading for the kitchen. "I need a break any way, I'll get you a glass of tea. You normally get it yourself. What's up?"

"Nothing much." She took the glass Brenda held out for her. "Just thought I'd fill you in on how daddy's doing today. I spent the morning at their house." She sat down at the kitchen table. "How long before you start re-doing this room?" Looking around the room, her nose wrinkled up like she smelled something bad.

Taking her own glass to the table, she sat down across from her sister. "I talked to daddy earlier today, Donna." Turning in her seat, she grabbed a bag of cookies off the counter behind her. She extended the bag toward Donna. "Have some, you need to gain a few pounds. I would have gone to Momma and Daddy's; but, some of us have to work. My shop doesn't run itself."

Rolling her eyes, she opened her mouth to say something, then changed her mind. Looking directly at her sister, she curled up her lips while squinting at Brenda's hair. "Just cause you have a beauty shop doesn't mean you have to look like a clown. Why do you want to look like that? You're not a teenager anymore you know."

"Donna Mae, did you just drive down here to make me feel bad or is there another reason?"

Taking a bite of cookie, Donna grinned. "These are really good." When she took another bite she looked her sister straight in the eye. "What all really happened night before last?"

"What do mean? Larry Joe and I were supposed to go out but Daddy called. He got tied up and didn't make our date. Is that what you're talking about?"

"Oh, come on. I know about Larry Joe helping Daddy with the suicide call. That's not what I'm talking about and you know it." She rose from her chair to refill her glass. After she sat back down she glared at her sister. "What about the black man? You know, the hunk! The one at that dive you ended up at outside of Bloomfield! That's what I'm asking about." She was leaning across the table watching her sister's face.

Brenda was already pale. Her sister's words caused her to turn deathly white. She started coughing after choking on the tea she was in the middle of swallowing. "Did Daddy say something to you?" Picking up a nearby dishrag, she mopped up the tea that spewed when she coughed. Trying to regain her composure, she looked up at her sister. "How about you tell me what you heard."

Donna enjoyed telling her sister everything she heard. Smirking, she told how Brenda Lou was all dressed up when she got to the bar. She said some of the people there thought she was a call girl the way she waltzed in to claim a stool right up in the front, like her name was engraved on it.

Brenda listened closely, hoping she could remember what happened, while Donna happily obliged her with more details. She remembered several drunks trying to buy her a drink. Anthony came up to her, introducing himself and told her he was new in the area and asked if he could sit beside her. She knew she told him it was a free country; he could sit where he pleased. While they were talking, she didn't pay attention to how much she had to drink. She was upset but didn't think she had drunk that much. After the fourth man's attempt to drag her onto the dance floor, Anthony suggested they move to a table to escape the unwanted attention aimed at her. He had appeared to be a gentleman, so she didn't think there would be any harm in sitting with him.

"I heard you was crying and sitting all huddled up with that black man. Is he as tall and handsome as they say? Brenda Lou, what on earth were you thinking? Did you really leave with him?" Donna was shaking her head making little tsk-tsk noises. "Better yet, what is Larry Joe gonna think when he hears?"

"Is there any other gossip you want to share? Girl, I am the one working in a beauty shop and I don't hear near as much crap as you do. At least when I hear bull crap, I don't believe it. I sure don't go around spreading hurtful gossip as truth!" Standing spread legged with her hands on her hips, she looked down at the floor as she shook her head. Brenda Lou was so angry her face was red. "I was at the same table across from him. I was not huddled up. You are my sister for Pete's sake. Did you at least defend me?" The tears sliding down her face were as much from anger as they were from hurt.

Donna Mae stood sputtering, unable to speak for a change.

"I'm glad I told Larry Joe that Anthony helped me out by driving me home. Good grief. I was upset with Larry Joe over him missing our date. I had a couple drinks and didn't want to run the risk of having a wreck. End of story." She turned to walk out of the room but changed her mind. "I am really glad my husband trusts me. It's people like you break up marriages. Go home before I say something I'll regret."

The surprise she felt at her sister's outburst was wearing off, Donna looked up wide eyed and innocent. "Does this mean you don't want to tell me what you know about the black guy? At least tell me if he's as good looking as the girls said." Then she smiled, looking like the cat that ate the proverbial canary.

Brenda Lou was really ticked off. She was gritting her teeth as fresh tears filled her eyes. She raised her arm pointing her finger toward the door. "Go, get out!" As the door closed behind her sister, Brenda Lou let the tears flow. She dropped back down into her chair burying her face in her hands as she sobbed, still ignorant of the details.

Fifteen minutes later, she looked at the clock. Larry Joe would be home soon. After what her sister had said, she didn't know what to expect from her husband. There wasn't any way she could have slept with another man, she told herself. Her body told her differently, she ignored the obvious. "How did he end up in my bed?" Brenda Lou raised her hands toward the ceiling as she shouted into thin air.

No matter how loud the volume, the Duffy CD couldn't drown out the voice in Brenda Lou's head telling her what a bad person she was. Browning ground beef simmered on the gas cook stove while she chopped the vegetables to be steamed. A box of Hamburger Helper sat on the counter, forgotten for the time being, while Brenda Lou was busy mentally beating herself up. Sounds of the front door slamming shut brought her back to the task at hand. When Larry Joe walked into the kitchen the sight of his wife draining the grease from the skillet caused him to stop. He leaned against the door facing to watch her work.

When she looked up at him, Larry Joe grinned a lopsided grin as he started walking toward her. "How did things go today?" He wrapped her in his arms, holding her close. "I hope you're over being upset over the choir thing and your dad. I wish I hadn't fouled things up the other night to start with. I'm so sorry baby."

Snuggling into the warmth of her husband's arms, Brenda Lou stayed silent. She was so afraid her father had told him what he saw, she couldn't believe what she was hearing now. Her thoughts were whirling in several directions all at once. While she held Larry Joe close, she said a silent prayer he would never find out about Anthony spending the night.

Still pressing his face against his wife's hair, tears made a slow path down Larry Joe's face. "I was glad they said your daddy just hyperventilated causing a panic attack or something like that. I never knew of anybody passing out from that. Me not letting you know what was going on, – well, it caused so many problems. I should of came on back home and waited on you. I should never have just assumed you would go back to your parents' house." He paused again for a minute, letting his tears moisten his wife's hair. "I knew how much leading the choir meant to you. That hurt you and your daddy both. You are my whole world Brenda Lou. Can you forgive me?"

Brenda Lou had started crying too. Her tears were tears of relief, plain and simple. She pulled back to see her husband's face. "Let's just forget the other night ever happened, okay? We were both in the wrong. I love you so much. You know that don't you?" She searched her husband's face as he smiled upon hearing her words. Giving him a hug, she remembered what she had cooking. "Oh no, supper's burning." She rushed back to the stove. "How about you get a bottle of wine out of the cabinet? I don't think it burned too bad." While she spoke she stayed busy putting the meal on the table, thankful her husband had blamed himself instead of questioning her.

Sitting down to the table, Brenda Lou broached the topic of her sister. "Donna Mae came by this evening. I'm afraid I wasn't too nice. I was still upset and, well, I kinda kicked her out." She looked a bit squeamish as she told him. "Tomorrow, I'll go see her when I have a break. Judy is working so I can have her take the walk-in customers while I'm gone. If I don't apologize Momma will get all bent out of shape. Donna was gloating. She sure knows what buttons to push to get me going. She's still such a brat, but she's still my little sister. I love her to pieces but there are times I would like to strangle her half to death or at least beat some sense into that head of hers."

Larry grinned at the thought of his wife kicking her sister out of the house. "She's jealous because you're your daddy's favorite. Another thing, she was babied so bad cause she was sickly that she never will grow up. I think I got the pick of the litter." He teased taking another bite. "And, you can cook." Larry didn't like Donna Mae, he only tolerated her because of her husband

and his wife's family. Each passing day it became more difficult for him to keep up a pretense. He thought she was too nosey for her own good.

The next day before noon Brenda made the trip to Dexter to see her sister. She knew Donna thought she was better than her, that her house was better, that her husband was better, thought her whole life was better. Donna didn't have to work because her husband made a lot more money as a lawyer than Larry Joe did as a salesman. The Hester family could afford to be members of the Country Club, Brenda Lou and Larry Joe couldn't. Donna made sure to remind Brenda every time she had a chance. "Who wants to belong to a club like that anyway? All those stuffed shirts running around with their noses in the air talking about other people, I would rather be around real people. Give me a float trip over a cocktail party any day of the week." She said aloud, patting the dash of her Nissan Z350 convertible. "Grey Ghost, not only are you paid off; but, you don't give me any problems and I like you."

Pulling into the drive, she parked beside her sister's Saab. Marvin (Mac) wasn't there or his car would have been in the garage with the door open to show off his BMW. It amused Brenda Lou the way both her sister and her brother-in-law worked so hard to show off all their toys. Parked by the curb was the pickup truck the cleaning lady drove, so she knew she would get to hear Donna talk about how bad her housekeeping was.

Loving someone and liking them are two totally different things, she thought. Brenda loved her entire family; but, she had a hard time when it came to liking her sister sometimes. Donna was self-centered, opinionated, condescending, snobbish, and at times, a mean-spirited gossip. Brenda didn't like it when she was the object of Donna Mae's attention. Her sister had the ability to hurt her feelings worse than anyone else could hope to. Donna had never worked a day in her life; but, she loved to talk about other people being lazy. Brenda Lou put in long hours at her shop, leaving her little time to clean house. Even if she wanted to, most evenings she was too tired to try.

Brenda was on her way to the door when her sister came jogging up the sidewalk. She stopped to wait until Donna made it to the house. When Donna came up to where she was she stopped, bending at the waist with her hands on her knees, she was breathing hard. Donna was wearing a lime green jogging suit with white stripes, new white Nike's, a matching lime green ribbon held her hair in a ponytail. "Darn Donna Mae, I haven't seen you this outta breath since you were chasing Mac. That's been what, nine years?" While Donna rolled her eyes at her sister, Brenda continued. "What's the occasion?" she joked.

Donna straightened up, stretching with her arms up over her head, Donna gave her sister a very pointed look. "No occasion, I just don't want to get fat. You should try it." Turning toward the house, she called out over her shoulder as she headed for the door. "You might as well come in, you're here. Why aren't you at work?" She went on in the house leaving the door open for Brenda to follow. "Don't you look put together today? Is that outfit from the new resale shop in town?"

Brenda Lou had taken special pains to dress nicely before going to see her sister. She was wearing a good fitting pair of new jeans with a smart, light weight pastel sweater and a matching jacket. Her new boots were good leather with a two-inch heel to make her look slimmer. One of the girls at her shop had helped with her hair and makeup, it was flawless. Ignoring the pointed barbs, she addressed her sister. "You sure are in a good mood today Donna Mae. I came to apologize for the way I acted. I was just so upset about Daddy to start with–. It wasn't right of me to talk to you that way. Too many things happened too fast, I'm sorry."

Donna turned to face her sister. After giving her a scorching look, her face relaxed. "You want a glass of tea? Come on in." She led the way past an oversized overstuffed sectional sofa; the thing was enormous. The room could have been beautiful; but, it was too full of expensive furniture, pictures, paintings, and nick-nacks. The heavy brocade drapes were oversized, sweeping the floor making the room look even gaudier than it already did.

Brenda Lou followed Donna through the formal dining room into the kitchen. "Do you have unsweetened?" She sat down looking around the room while her sister got them both glasses, bringing the pitcher to the table with her. "Thanks Donna Mae." Brenda Lou couldn't help but notice that Donna had bought even more expensive trinkets to add to the already overcrowded countertops. "It must be nice to have someone to help with the dusting. I do good to keep the top of the fridge wiped off. I'd never be able to keep up with this."

Plastering a fake smile on her face Donna looked across the table taking a sip of sweet tea. "Sorry, no unsweetened." She looked smug, holding her glass up to make sure Brenda Lou had a chance to get a good look at her new diamond ring. "It's nice to have a husband that brings home enough to hire help. He says I'm worth every penny. We go out to dinner so much that I don't even need the appliances, but they are all top of the line. The kitchen would look funny without a stove, plus the fridge comes in handy for ice anyway." She paused for effect. After taking a long swallow, she jiggled the ice cubes. "What did happen the other night anyway? Momma and Daddy told me Larry Joe spent the night at their house. Did you piss him off that bad?"

Sighing, Brenda looked up at her younger sister. It wasn't easy to bite her tongue when she wanted to lash out at her. "No, it was just a misunderstanding. We were going out, but Daddy needed him. When I stopped in to ask how long he would be I didn't see Daddy. The person that called for help was a good-looking woman. Daddy was there; I just didn't see him. I got my feelings hurt. Once again, I made a fool of myself. I'm thankful there was a trustworthy, sober man there to drive me home. You know I love my husband, Donna Mae. I would never intentionally do anything to mess up my marriage. You know that."

While listening to her sister, Donna couldn't help thinking about how often Larry Joe upset Brenda. She thought he was self-centered and completely inconsiderate toward her big sister most of the time. In her opinion, the only time Larry Joe treated Brenda Lou right was when he wanted something.

At the mention of someone driving her home, Donna perked up like a Beagle pup on the scent of a rabbit. "So, spill. I've heard all kinds of things about that man. I finally got a chance to see him at the club, but never talked to him. Is he really as rich as they say? Nobody knows if he is attached or not. They say he has some kind of international business or something. It would be great if Mac could handle his legal work. Do you know him well enough to suggest that?" Donna's eyes were wide with excitement. She stopped just long enough to breath. "How did he get home, or did you have to go back to get your car?"

"Hold on. That's way too many questions at one time." She fiddled with the water ring around her glass for a moment, wondering how many more times she would have to recount the story for her sister. "I knew enough about him to know it was a lot safer to let him drive me than to drive myself. Like I said before, Larry Joe already knows all about it. I drank too much wine. Anthony drove me home and someone picked him up. We didn't talk about anything personal, so, I don't know if he is attached or not. I have absolutely no idea about his finances let alone what he is worth. He's a nice man. I think he's from around Chicago. That's all I know. I don't even know where he lives."

"He doesn't live too far from here, is where he lives. That house about a mile on out that looks like a mansion is where." Donna's arms were gesturing toward the direction of Anthony's house. The more excited Donna became, the more her voice rose.

"Whoa, the point is, I don't care where he lives Donna Mae. I am married, so it doesn't matter to me. Like I said, he is a nice man who is pleasant to talk to. I never met him before and will probably never meet him again." She shook her head then grinned. "I could just see Daddy if one of his girls ended up with a black man. What do you wanna bet he would resign from the church? I know he's not prejudice, but you know how well he likes that part in the

Bible about where God makes the soldiers take those women back to their people. He thinks mixed marriages cause confusion, along with problems for the children that come from them." She knew better than to bring up what her mother acted like when it came to mixed races. Donna got bent out of shape every time she said anything about it to her.

"I never said you should dump your husband to go after Mr. Rich and handsome. It's just that if a man could provide well enough, I think dad would get over it if one of his daughters married a man of a different race, if he made her happy. Look how many hours you put in at that shop, and then there's what you do to your hair. Larry Joe couldn't do better if he wanted to. If you would of tried you could have married someone with money like I did." Donna studied her sister before glaring at her. "You know, the way you let yourself go, stay depressed, and mope around instead of standing up to him, maybe it would have been better for Larry Joe to marry someone else."

Donna Mae as well have slapped her sister. Brenda's guilt was so high and her self-esteem so low, her feelings were hurt because she thought Donna meant Larry Joe married beneath him when he took Brenda as his wife.

"I married who I wanted to. We don't need to be rich. Donna Mae, knock it off. I didn't trick someone into marrying me. I pursued an education while you pursued Mac. I got my associates degree and you got pregnant. My diploma hangs on the wall while you can't even carry a child to term. No wonder Mac is on the prowl." Catching herself, she realized what she had said in anger. Shocked at herself, she covered her mouth with her hands but the damage was already done. "Oh, Donna Mae, I'm sorry. I didn't mean it. I'm so sorry, please forgive me." She watched as her sister's face went through a series of emotions. Finally, Donna Mae burst into tears, running from the room.

Brenda stood in the empty room feeling miserable. She was shocked that she had said the things that came out of her mouth. There was no way for her to retract the terrible things she had said.

Her intention was to mend fences with her sister, not blow up the family.

She drove toward her parents' house hoping to head off a major disaster. On the way, she briefly considered how different Anthony was the morning after he spent the night with her than he had been when they were talking the night before. Brushing it aside, she told herself it didn't matter because she would never see him again. Not knowing what to say once she arrived at their house, she sat outside thinking. Her car window was down; but, she was oblivious to the birds singing or any of the other sounds of spring that surrounded her. After about fifteen minutes, her dad surprised her when he tapped on the roof of her car causing her to jump.

Smiling down, he leaned his arms on the door to bring himself eye level with his daughter. "I know that look, what happened?" Brenda briefly looked up into the worried eyes of her dad as he spoke. "Baby Girl, I don't know what happened Saturday night. I never should have allowed myself to get as worked up as I did. I'm so sorry for the things I said to you. Whatever was going on is your own business. It isn't any of my business so I won't ask. You don't have to worry about me saying anything to Larry, if that's what that look is about." He waited patiently for a while. After his daughter continued to sit silently staring at her hands, he tried a different approach. Reaching out, he opened the car door, extending a hand toward her. "Come on Brenda Lou, let's you and me go for a walk."

Reverend Perkins loved all his children. He and his wife were blessed with three daughters and a son. Walter worked as a mechanic for a motorcycle dealership while living in Cape Girardeau, Missouri. He attended classes at the college there part time, working on a degree in Mechanical Engineering. Patty Sue was working on getting her Bachelor of Science degree at the college in Columbia, Missouri. Donna Mae married a lawyer, dropped out of college, and they live in Dexter. Brenda Lou, their eldest child, worked the hardest for her education, completing her Associate's degree before going into business for herself. Brenda married Larry Joe Green and lives in Malden, where her business is located.

Out of all the children, (Reverend) Chet Perkins was closest to his eldest daughter. The two walked in silence through the front yard around to the big old Redbud Tree, which was just starting to bud out in the back yard. There was a circular wooden bench built around the base of the tree. On a hot summer day, it made for a good place to sit in the shade, under the umbrella formed by the leafed-out branches. Sitting down, he patted the seat beside him indicating that he wanted his daughter to sit with him. Looking at her troubled expression, it was obvious that she wanted to cry.

After standing a bit longer, Brenda sat down. "I'm glad you're out of the hospital." She buried her face in her hands while looking down at the ground. "Oh Daddy, how can one person try so hard to do right and still end up doing everything wrong? I have just messed my whole life up and don't even know how bad because I don't remember what happened. On top of that I hurt Donna Mae. I hurt her feelings real bad this time." As hard as she tried to keep from it, she had started sobbing.

"How about you start from the beginning?"

When she started talking, she told her dad everything that she could remember about Saturday night, right up to the headache. She explained that while she was at the bar she took a pill Anthony Payne gave her for her headache. "The headache started while I was driving around looking for Larry Joe. My head started spinning, then the next thing I knew you were at the house. Daddy, what if I had sex with him? I think I did but really don't remember a thing." She stopped to wipe her eyes and blow her nose. "Then Donna Mae came over after I got home from work, it was so bad. Larry Joe was still at work. I hadn't got over being afraid I had almost killed you, not to mention wondering how I ended up in my own bed with another man. I ran her off. That wasn't the worst of it with her either. Right before I came here, I just went to tell her I was sorry for that, and screwed that up too." Her dad sat quietly thinking, giving her time to compose herself before she finished. "Daddy, I said some horrible things to her that I didn't mean. I am afraid I spilled the beans about Mac's woman chasing too. I just wish I could find a hole to crawl in and never come out." She had started sobbing again.

Chet let everything soak in before he spoke. There were a few things that didn't fit right about that night. "First off, I'm proud of you. I'm sorry I yelled at you. I never should have jumped to conclusions or said the things I did. I didn't have any right to be that upset. Will you forgive me for busting into your home, using the kind of language I did? God only knows how sorry I am. Then next thing, it sounds like you didn't drink enough for things to go the way they did. On the one hand, you may very well have been drugged. On the other hand, you have been so stressed out and worried about too many things lately that you may have drank more than what you realized. You hadn't had anything to eat in how long before you had something to drink? As upset as you were you were probably hyperventilating, you know you tend to do that. I think I better ask around about that man."

He paused, hugging his daughter. "Don't worry about your sister, she'll come around. I've watched how she treats you and she shouldn't do you the way she does. I don't know what drives her but it worries me at times. Don't worry about what she'll tell your momma either, I'm going to tell her the strait of it before Donna Mae has a chance to try to twist it." He hugged her close, kissing her forehead. "We're all just human Baby, we're all just human. Nobody goes through life without making mistakes. I've made some pretty big ones my own self." He stood up smiling, motioning for her to rise. "Come on over here, I got something for you to see." As Brenda stood to follow her dad, he added. "Next time Larry Joe offers to help, I'll make sure you two don't have plans first."

There behind the shed in the backyard was a new dog pen. Brenda followed her dad around the side of the shed in order to get a better look. There on a blanket covered in straw were eight tiny Cocker Spaniel puppies. "Lady Bug surprised us last week." Chet stood watching his daughter carefully inspect the tiny creatures, then it dawned on him, why had Larry Joe told his daughter he had been asked to help? Something about the time frame was off also, he just couldn't put his finger on it right then.

Putting an arm around his daughter's shoulder, Chet pulled her close, pointing to the puppies. "Before long those little things are going to be scrapping like you and your sister." His face split into a grin, when Brenda looked up at him. Thinking about the puppies playing, mixed with her father's grin, lightened her mood.

Chapter 4

(June 2013)

For the last two months things had been so hectic at the shop that Brenda Lou barely had time to breathe. Things were just starting to calm down before the next big rush. From the looks of things, teenage girls spent more money each year for prom and pageant dresses, including the accessories to go along with them. This year she was amazed at the number of girls that wanted to have dark tans, hair extensions, colored highlights to match their gowns, fancy manicures and pedicures. Business had been so good, she had been booked solid for almost three months straight. She was glad to be able to take a day off for her annual checkup before the Fourth of July customers started to mob them.

Brenda heard the bell over the door tinkle before her sister's voice reached her. "I hope I'm not late." Donna was rushing toward her. "I really tried to get here faster. I need this makeover. Mac needs to drool and beg. Actually, he needs to get down on his knees, or crawl on his belly, begging for my forgiveness. For now, I want to make him beg for sex so I can turn him down. I intend to make him sorry he ever crossed me." She was so animated it caused all the women in the shop to giggle or laugh out loud while cheering her on.

"Sister you are so bad you're good. I just love it." While they spoke, Donna dropped several bags on the floor. Brenda noticed the names of the boutiques on them. Pointing to the bags she started laughing.

"Expensive new wardrobe too? Looks like he is paying in more ways than he knows."

"Just you wait and see. I never wore clothes like these before. Mac won't know what's happened. I will look like a million and cost almost that much before I'm done. You're right, he's already paying and doesn't have a clue, – yet." She had such a pleased evil grin to go with the singsong sound of her voice that the other women in the shop applauded when she held up the credit cards.

Things had been rocky in her relationship with Donna, but were smoothed out now. After their blow up, Donna said she had caught her husband with one of the town whores. Donna loved her husband; but, she had always said that if she wasn't enough woman for him he needed to let her know before he went out looking. If he was going to play dirty so would she. She was already tallying up what her divorce settlement should come to, and trying to get Brenda to help her get pictures, before the filing. Of course, Donna neglected to tell Mac she saw his naked backside through that motel window when she tracked down his car. She said he didn't have enough sense to make sure the drapes were closed all the way or hide the car, because she saw his car sitting in plain open sight out front. Brenda felt obligated to help her sister since she was the one to spill the beans on him in the first place. She knew her sister would make out like a bandit, she always did.

Patty Sue was home on break from college. The three sisters had a big outing planned. It had been several months since they had been able to get together to just hang out. They were picking their parents up on the way to Cape Girardeau, to surprise Walt with a birthday dinner at the steakhouse he liked. Patty was the one elected to call him, with a made-up story about needing his advice, to make sure he would be home alone.

Brenda hadn't been feeling well for a couple weeks. She wanted to make sure she kept her doctor's appointment on Friday morning. That would leave her the rest of Friday plus all day Saturday and Sunday to spend with her family. She looked forward to catching up on what was happening in their lives. It would help her relax while getting some rest she so badly needed. She chalked up feeling tired to gaining a couple more pounds along with all the hours she had been putting in at work. There were too many sweet treats kept in the break room to tempt her weakness for them. She hadn't taken time to eat regular meals for a while.

Larry Joe came home in a good mood Thursday night. He said he was late because there was a big sales promotion taking place at the dealership where he worked. He brought home a surprise. "You need to come outside with me. Cover your eyes, I'll lead you." He took his wife's hand pulling her out the front door.

Brenda was having difficulty keeping up with him. Her eyes were covered and he was pulling her so fast she was afraid she would trip. "What is it?" Brenda had a hard time waiting even a few seconds when it came to surprises.

Once outside Larry Joe dropped her hand. "You can look now." He stood off to one side watching her as she examined the new Cadillac parked in the driveway. "Well Baby, what do you think?" There sat a 2012 Pearl White Cadillac with soft, tan colored, leather seats. It was the most beautiful vehicle Larry Joe had ever brought home. "With the money that's coming in from your shop now, we can afford it. They let me have a good discount since I work there, and we had a great down payment in the savings account."

Brenda stood in stunned silence for a couple minutes before answering. "It's beautiful Larry Joe; but, I thought we agreed when we bought another vehicle it would be a van or station wagon. Remember?" Brenda felt like someone had punched her in the stomach, and it showed on her face. They had agreed it was time to start a family. She had been putting all her extra earnings into their savings account for that purpose. Larry Joe normally drove a demo from work which helped them save on payments and insurance. "We agreed to keep expenses down after the remodeling so we could afford to have a baby. Tell me you didn't use the money I put into that account for this car."

Larry Joe didn't say a word. His face, contorted with anger, turned bright red. After walking around the car twice, he aimed a hate filled look in her direction, and got in slamming the car door, before he sped out of the driveway. Brenda hoped he was returning the car to the dealership. She couldn't understand how he could do something like that without talking to her about it first. It was close to midnight before he returned home.

To say that Brenda was conflicted would have been putting it too mildly. She thought her husband was sincere when he told her he wanted a baby. They talked about what they wanted, about remodeling the house while they waited, about getting another inexpensive vehicle that would be good for traveling with all the things a baby would need. The baby had been Larry Joe's idea. Starting the savings account for that purpose was his idea also. It didn't take long for Brenda to start looking forward to having a baby.

Larry Joe knew she was putting in all the hours she could to help make their plans work financially. She had signed for the loan to redecorate the house, at his insistence, because they would need a nursery for the baby. He convinced her, because she had the higher income, it would be easier to obtain the loan. The finance company wouldn't loan him any more money. She wondered how he had gotten the car without her signature.

Channel 12's late news was depressing; they showed pictures of another missing woman. Brenda wondered how many more were missing. The week before they found the mutilated body of one that had been missing for nearly a month. This wasn't new. A few years ago several women in the surrounding area had gone missing. The abductions had stopped for quite some time. It looked like they were starting up again. This one disappeared from the casino at Metropolis, Illinois. She couldn't help wondering how that many women could just vanish without a trace.

By eleven that night Brenda Lou was exhausted. When she went to bed, she cried herself to sleep wondering about her husband's motives. Her doctor's appointment was first thing Friday morning and she didn't feel she could miss it. She didn't hear a sound when Larry Joe slipped into the house to sleep on the sofa.

It was hard for Brenda to get out of bed; she'd had a hard time sleeping. She was afraid her husband might be starting to go through a mid-life crisis. What else could cause a normally sane man to act the way he had, she asked herself. That he would go out and buy such an expensive vehicle without her knowledge troubled her.

"Mrs. Green, we have the results of your lab work back." Brenda was sitting on the exam table wearing a paper gown. She had already counted the green and white floor tiles a couple times before counting the ceiling tiles while wondering how long the wait would be. Dr. Riley entered the room, standing in front of her reading the chart in his hand, he spoke before he looked up at her. The nurse was standing beside the doctor, with a big grin on her face. "Brenda Lou, you're slightly anemic, so I'm putting you on a pre-natal vitamin with minerals. You know you're pregnant, right? It will be good for you and the baby." He looked up grinning as he teased her. Dr. Riley knew Brenda had gone off her birth control pills several months ago. She told him she wanted to have a child. "You are going to have to cut back some on work; but, I would advise you to start walking for exercise. We need to try to keep your weight down." The doctor watched her face go through a range of emotions. There was the initial smile he expected, then a blank look followed by a look of fear. "Brenda Lou is everything alright? Is there something you need to ask or talk about?" He was concerned about her reaction to the news she had been hoping for the last time she had been in his office. He had been her family physician since she was in her teens.

Brenda shook her head no, before she remembered to ask how far along she was. After telling her the due date, the doctor and nurse both left the room. Brenda had time to dress before the nurse came back into the room with pamphlets and an appointment card for her next office visit. Leaving the office, she wandered around in a daze for over an hour before going home.

She asked herself how things could have changed so fast. She was determined to find out what caused her husband's drastic change in behavior.

The white Caddy was sitting in the drive when Brenda arrived home. Larry Joe was in the kitchen, heating a cup of coffee in the microwave, while the back door stood wide open. There was already a steaming cup setting on the counter beside the microwave. "This is a surprise. I thought you would be at work Baby." Larry Joe said.

He was barefoot, his shirttail wasn't tucked in, his hair needed combed, and he was fidgeting. It was obvious he had just gotten out of bed. "I didn't feel so hot so I came home after a couple hours this morning." He looked, with concern, at the expression on his wife's face. "Is something wrong?"

She looked at her husband, seeing him for what he was for the first time since she had met him. "I see the car is still here. I really hoped you would return it. You were supposed to go to the doctor with me this morning. I went by the dealership; you didn't go to work." Before coming into the house she had looked through the car. Adding to the distress she already felt, there were women's panties sticking out from under the seat. Beside the extra coffee sitting on the kitchen counter was a tube of lip gloss. It hadn't been there when she left that morning. It wasn't even a brand she would use. "Are you having an affair?"

While Larry Joe was gone the evening before, Brenda Lou had a talk with her dad. She found out that Larry had left right after she did the Saturday night before Easter. He hadn't been where he claimed to be. After she spoke to her dad, Mac came by to drop off some papers that Larry Joe had left in his car when he borrowed it. While talking to Mac, she found out that Larry Joe had been using his car fairly regularly while she was at work. Brenda was shocked at what she found in the folder after Mac left.

Before Brenda Lou came home from the doctor's office she picked up the mail. Normally Larry Joe picked it up, but she was going by the post office, so she took care of it. She couldn't believe the unpaid bills she found in the mail. From the post office she went to the bank. There was very little in her checking account and the savings account was wiped out. Larry Joe had even been into her business account. While she was there she was approached by one of the loan officers, asking when she could make a payment on a couple loans she knew nothing about.

Larry Joe didn't look alarmed. "Baby, how can you even think that? You know I love you. I could never do anything like that Brenda Lou. I can't believe you would even think such a thing." She noticed that after he passed by the area of the counter where the lip gloss had been, it was gone. He came to stand near her. "Either you asked someone that just didn't see me this morning, or it was one of the men that's jealous of me. You know how some of them are." He hugged her then headed toward the bathroom. "I'm feeling better now. I guess I'd better get ready to go back to work."

When Larry Joe shut the bathroom door, Brenda looked out the front window at the Cadillac. Barely visible above the dash was the top of a woman's head. The woman had been in her home only moments before, leaving the backdoor open as she hurriedly exited the house upon Brenda's arrival.

Brenda found herself hearing what her sister had said when they thought that Mac was running around. She had learned a few tricks while helping Donna spy on Mac. Not letting her emotions cloud her actions, she took out her camera. After taking pictures from inside the house, she went out the back door, slipping around her neighbor's house where she stood unnoticed, getting a few good pictures of the side of the car. The woman was more visible in those.

When Larry Joe opened the door to get in, she got a few good clear shots of him as well as the woman trying to hide inside. "You sneaky, fat, little bastard. Let's see you try to talk your way out of this." If ever there was the intonation of righteous indignation in anyone's voice, it was present in Brenda Lou's. She wasn't speaking loud enough to be heard by anyone else. "I don't know what all you are up to but you are not going to get by with whatever it is."

Now that her husband was away from the house, Brenda called Donna. If anyone knew how to catch someone, it was Donna. "Guess what I just found out? Donna Mae, Larry Joe is the one that made it look like Mac was messing around." Choking back tears of hurt anger, she continued. "I so apologize. The bastard set your husband up because he doesn't like you and I believed him. He tried to drive a wedge between us so he could get by with murder, or whatever he is trying to do to me financially. The only thing I know for sure is the fat little turd bastard is dipping his wick in other women. I need to see the pictures you took, thinking it was Mac, at that motel. Good news for you, it was my husband instead of yours." Not giving Donna a chance to get angry or gloat over the situation, she rushed on. "How would you like to get even with him?"

Before the call Donna had gone through emotional ups and downs. Some days she wanted to make Mac pay for every bad deed ever done to any woman alive. Other days she wanted to kill her husband with her bare hands. There were times she just cried until there weren't any tears left because she loved her husband more than she wanted to admit to anyone, even him.

Now that the shoe was on the other foot, Donna jumped in with a vengeance. This would give her a chance to get even, plus give her something good to spread at the same time. She had felt sorry for some time for letting her sister think that she meant Larry Joe could have done better in picking a wife. "You know that I never did like him. It always amazed me that you would settle for someone so inferior when you could have had anyone you wanted. Big sis, I'll be happy to help! How soon can you get here?" If there was one thing Donna was really good at it was revenge.

Brenda had already made arrangements to be off the whole day. For the first time in a long time, she didn't feel the need to answer questions about where she had been. Larry Joe thought she would be at work.

Pulling up to Donna's house Brenda chastised herself once again. Her doubts about Larry Joe had eaten her alive until Easter. She let herself be blinded by guilt, accepting whatever he said as true, convincing herself her husband loved her. At one point Brenda had been fed up with her husband's actions, or lack of, toward her. During that period, she considered divorce when she realized she didn't care if he came home anyway. When he started paying attention to her again, and wanted to start a family, she knew she had convinced herself things were back on track because she had been raised to believe that marriage was forever. The truth was, Larry Joe had killed the love she felt for him a long time ago.

Brenda picked Donna up on the way to meet the rest of her family. During the drive, they compared notes and started plotting. Sitting around the table at the steak house, the entire Perkins family heard the details of what the eldest daughter had discovered about her husband. It wasn't good. Donna enthusiastically went into detail about how he had tried to set her husband up too.

Lou sat quietly during the meeting. Thoughts running through her head couldn't be voiced in polite company, especially in front of her family. When she did speak her voice had a cold deadly, hate filled, edge to it that her children had never heard before. "We accepted him as part of the family. He will pay dearly for what he is doing to Brenda Lou and what he has done to the rest of this family."

After the first shock wore off, Brenda let them all have time to think about what they heard before she told them she just found out she was pregnant. She knew she needed help gathering all the information she could get her hands on. Her family didn't wait to be asked. The first step in the planning started with Walter volunteering to get a GPS to track Larry Joe. Donna already had several pictures with a date/time stamp of Mac's car at different motels and restaurants, along with the picture of Larry's naked backside in that motel room.

The weekend went by in a blur. When Monday morning rolled around, Patty Sue was back on campus with samples of Larry Joe's DNA. Larry Joe's fingerprints were being sent to be checked against those in a data base of wanted individuals. Brenda left for work with Larry Joe in the shower, stopping on her way out the door to hide the tracking unit on the Caddy. Walter had several friends scattered around the Dexter area, not to mention his retired friends from Cape. Several of the retirees he met through the motor cycle business had nothing but free time. He knew they would enjoy playing detective. Walter made sure his friends were in place to follow Larry Joe when Larry Joe left the house. Donna had her phone in her pocket and her camera handy.

When Mac found out that Larry Joe had been using him, he was livid. "To think, I felt sorry for that slimy little bastard. I believed his sob story. He had me convinced he was looking for a better job." First thing Monday morning, Mac was on the computer helping his sister-in-law try to run a background check on her husband.

Chet went to the bank with signed forms in hand for the loan officer to get copies of any loans that were supposed to have his daughter's signature on them, while Lou explained the situation to the bank president. Larry Joe wouldn't be allowed to take any more money from Brenda Lou's business account. The joint account Brenda had with Larry Joe was closed and Brenda opened one in her name only. Brenda sent along a letter instructing all bank personnel to contact Mac if they had further questions.

It didn't take long to start getting results.

Larry Joe had been sucking up to Chet in an attempt to get his hands on the church funds. So far, there hadn't been too much damage done there. Unfortunately for Larry Joe, he hadn't taken time to find out too much about his mother-in-law's family. Lou's second cousin was a Supreme Court Justice, while one of her nephews worked as a U.S. Marshall. Lou had a good long conversation with them both over the weekend. Brenda had been an adorable baby and was favored by both of the men. Hearing what her Larry Joe was up to, they agreed to help in any way they could. The other side of Lou's family agreed to help in less visible ways.

Information started rolling in. The DNA analysis went through the crime lab at Columbia, matching up to several unsolved crimes.

There were multiple alias matchings for his finger prints. Larry Joe Green was not who he claimed to be. He had been a con man most of his life, living off unsuspecting women. At one point he was caught on a rather minor charge of stealing. While on probation he skipped out. Going by a half dozen different names, he ended up in the college town where he met Brenda Lou.

That evening Brenda was busy in the kitchen when Larry Joe came home. She composed herself before he entered the room. "Baby, it's been a day. Things have been so busy, I'll be glad when this sales promotion is over. I'm exhausted." He came up behind her, wrapping his arms around her. "I think I'll go to bed right after supper." He brushed a kiss on the side of her neck. "I have some paperwork to finish up. Call me when dinner's ready."

"It will be a few minutes yet. My day has been rather interesting ...." She realized he had already left the room, leaving her talking to thin air. She turned glaring at the doorway he had left through. In a way she felt relief, she wouldn't have to act as if nothing was wrong. "You don't know it yet; but, you're goose is already cooked mister."

Later that night after Brenda was ready for bed, she stood looking at her sleeping husband. He looked so peaceful and innocent. As she observed him, she wondered how she could have fallen for such a plain looking, chubby, little man. He had the look of baby-faced innocence with his chubby cheeks and boyish charm. He had known all the right things to say to make her feel better about herself from the start. The man she married didn't even exist. This man sleeping on the sofa made him up.

"You can't lose something you never had to begin with." she told herself as she slipped into bed alone. She had gladly left Larry Joe, or whoever he was, sleeping on the sofa.

***

When Brenda left home after high school it was the first time she was responsible for herself. After moving to a college town, she soon found herself broke. Instead of attending classes, as she had planned, she went to work to support herself attending classes part time at night. Larry Joe came into her life just before she completed her Associate's degree. Her issues with low self-esteem were compounded when she found out her younger sister was to be married to an attorney and worsened further when she was told Donna Mae was expecting a child. Donna gladly pointed out Brenda's short comings to her every chance she got.

Larry Joe was a boost to Brenda's moral, making her believe in herself, inspiring her to start her own business. He claimed to be an only child, stating that he grew up in a large city. According to him he had been raised by an aunt that begrudged his very existence. Listening intently to Brenda whenever she spoke of her family, Larry Joe told her how fortunate she was to have grown up the way she did. He found out all he could about her before he proposed, claiming he wanted her for his wife, acting excited to be a part of her family. He made her feel both loved and wanted. It was the first time in her life she felt pretty.

Larry Joe lived in Jonesboro, Arkansas for two years before meeting Brenda. His boss, Mr. Ronald Arnold, had him involved in the trafficking of human flesh and drugs. His work was mainly out of the Memphis and Little Rock areas. With the casinos so close to Memphis it made things much easier for him to come into contact with people from an even greater area. Due to him looking so young, Larry Joe blended in easily with the college crowd.

The first time he saw Brenda Lou she was sitting alone in a booth studying for a test. He noticed she looked both lonely and depressed. The bleached blonde hair, along with the amount of cleavage showing, drew his attention. When she looked up off into space, he noticed her striking emerald green eyes, set in an oval face with cupid lips. Dressed the way she was, he thought she could be easily seduced. While he sat watching her, he couldn't help notice her figure when she got up to go to the ladies' room. He thought to himself that she had the kind of body every man dreamed of. Deciding he wanted to get her into his bed, he felt himself grow hard with arousal.

Larry Joe made a point to bump into her when she started back to her table. He apologized before taking a seat at the empty table beside the booth where she sat. During her absence he looked to see what subject she was studying. He lied, pointing to her book, he stated that happened to be the subject he was majoring in. Before long he was offering to help her with her studies. She accepted his offer. It took him two months of hard work to get her into his bed.

While Larry Joe was working on getting Brenda into his bed, Mr. Arnold decided it was time for Larry Joe to make a different kind of move. Ronald Arnold didn't think it wise for one of his men to stay in one place too long without a proper cover. He did his research on the female his employee was dating. By the time Larry Joe was ready to dump Brenda and move to greener pastures, she told him something that made her look too good to Ronald Arnold for Larry Joe to leave behind.

Brenda would be opening her business in the area Mr. Arnold wanted Larry Joe to relocate to. Ronald Arnold was ecstatic when he found out that Brenda's parents were the good Rev. and Mrs. Chet Perkins. Larry Joe was told being part of Brenda's family was the perfect cover for him. Larry Joe had his boss's blessing even if he wasn't happy about it.

Chapter 5

Things worked out well for Anthony over the weekend. Mr. Arnold was pleased with the number of women Anthony supplied him with since his arrival in Southeast Missouri. Benjamin Orr, aka Larry Joe Green, had been in the area long enough to set things in motion for someone like Tony to step into. Ben had been supplying a few women, along with all the needed information to set up the operation.

Ben was to continue moving drugs and guns in the area, while Mr. Arnold intended to turn the human trafficking over solely to Anthony. Ronald Arnold decided to pull Ben out of the human trafficking branch of his operation because Ben started getting sloppy. Too many of the women Ben had been abducting were being reported as missing, and he wasn't happy when the mutilated bodies started surfacing.

Ronald Arnold really wasn't pleased when told Ben quit his job as a car salesman. Ben was becoming a liability to the organization. He was afraid it would draw unnecessary attention from the family Benjamin married into if they found out he was no longer employed. Up to now Ben had the perfect cover to help him blend in. Ronald Arnold couldn't afford to have his boss pissed off at him because of Ben or anyone else.

Ever since Anthony made the mistake with Brenda Lou Green, he was more careful about doing his own background checks on the women. He needed to make sure the women he picked up had no ties that would cause someone to try to find them. Now he also made sure the women weren't married and had been telling people they wanted to leave the area where they were living. At first he blamed Ben for telling him Brenda Lou would be a good mark to pick up. It hadn't taken long to see Ben lied about her. The more he thought about it, he could see that Ben was up to something much bigger than getting rid of someone's wife for them. What worried him was being blamed for the consequences of the outcome.

Bud and Will came back into the house after making sure the woman was well hidden in the trunk of the Town Car parked in Anthony's garage. "She's good to go. That stuff won't wear off until she is half way across the ocean." Bud told Anthony as he patted him on the back. "Where'd you say you found that one?"

"I picked her up in Paragould, Arkansas. She said she was from Green High, Arkansas. It sounded like she lived there for a long time." Anthony talked while putting papers into a manila envelope. After he sealed it, he handed it to Bud while Will got a bottle of juice from the refrigerator. "Here's all the information I have on her. She's a cute little thing. This one will do nicely for the buyer."

Wilbur walked back to stand beside Bud. He had a bottle of juice in one hand and a thick ham sandwich in the other. He took a large bite then tried to talk around it. "You're one lucky asshole. How much pussy you get that stays around to tell about it? Hell, we're not allowed to touch them girls once we pick them up." Belching, he glared at Anthony as he continued to chew the food he had just taken from Anthony's fridge.

Anthony tried to ignore Will. Looking back at Bud he faked a lopsided grin. "What can I say? Boss's orders. I hate to rush you off; but, I need to get to work. I think I found the kind of merchandise our most particular customer wants. The young woman lives in a place called Aquilla. I want to double check all of her information before making contact. If everything goes as planned, I'm going to have you make the pickup at a motel in Cape Girardeau. I'll call later with more information." He was maneuvering them toward the door to the garage as he spoke.

When the Town Car pulled out, Anthony closed the garage door. Once inside the house, he leaned against the kitchen door. Closing his eyes, he wished the whole operation was over and done with. Being around men like Wilbur, Bud, and Ben made him feel ill.

Ronald Arnold was not to be trusted under any circumstances. The man was crazy mean. Anthony felt like he was walking on eggshells, expecting a knife in his back at the least provocation, whenever he had any contact with him.

He planned to take a nap before getting ready to go to the gym. While climbing the stairs on the way to his bedroom, his thoughts were of Brenda. Several times over the last two months he wanted to pick up the phone to call her. Her marriage was a disaster but she still held on, hoping things would change, and he couldn't understand why. Anthony still had a hard time with the fact that, according to Ben Orr, her own husband tried to have her sold. All the information Ben had given him about her was wrong, except the part about her being married. Anthony wondered why.

It upset him when he thought over everything that happened the night he was supposed to pick her up. He kept picturing her sitting across from him, her beautiful face streaked with mascara from the tears she shed over the man that tried to sell her. He knew he allowed things to go too far. Never before had he felt so drawn to any woman. Never before had he crossed that line. He hated himself for having sex with a woman he was supposed to protect. She stayed with him in his thoughts, always.

***

"What now? I wish you would leave me alone. You know you're dead, right?" Anthony had almost drifted off to sleep. The window shades were drawn so that a small shaft of light made the chair visible in the darkened room. When Anthony felt the presence of the ghost, he sat up straight in the bed, looking toward the chair that the ghost seemed to prefer. "Why are you picking on me?"

It looked to him like the ghost smiled at him before he heard the unspoken words. "You need a dog. You always wanted one. Now you have the room. I had lots of animals. There was one dog that was very special to me, named him Fido."

"You mean to tell me you're making my life miserable to tell me I need a dog? How would you know if I wanted a dog or not?"

"No, no, no, no, I'm not the one making your life miserable. Think about it." There was a long pause before the ghost seemed to smile. "My first love was a beautiful black woman. Then, that shouldn't surprise you. Everyone knows how I felt about slavery. We were so young, and dirt poor. Her master beat her awfully bad when he found out she was with child. I loved her, but couldn't afford to buy her. He sold her along with my unborn child. It almost killed me. I had a hard time finding out where they ended up. Slavery is wrong, no matter what. At first I felt bad about telling those whoppers. If I hadn't led some of them to believe I really thought slavery was alright I would never have been elected."

"So, are you here because of the women?"

"No, son. I'm here because of you, among other things. This thing you are involved in? I do understand why you have to hide your true feelings. As for those women, you're sending them to places where they will be better off. Before you pick them up they are given options, not enslaved. Those women will have the opportunity for a better life with a decent future because of the work you are involved in." The voice softened. "You're a bright young man. There may be a reason you can't get that girl off your mind. Mull it over."

Glaring at the ghost, Anthony took a deep breath before speaking. "I wish you would stop talking around everything. Just tell me what you have to say."

"We used to take part in séances, the Mrs. and I. She wanted to contact our deceased son. In all honesty, I did also. It never worked. Until his death she had no desire to join me in one. You see, I had already been trying to contact my first love to find out about my son that was born into slavery. My wife understood. I think she was a little jealous that there were others before her. It didn't bother her that the first was a black woman. She was a very understanding woman. It hurt my heart to know people thought her crazy for trying to contact our son."

The ghost appeared to be lost in thought momentarily. "It still bothers me that she was locked up, people turned against her, I feel responsible. I should have throttled that boy when he was young. Who would have ever thought he would turn on his own mother! He was a greedy one, he was. Sometimes you can't trust your own kin. She protected me. No one knew about my involvement in the séances." Still looking upset, Abe's ghost started fading away.

"Hold on. You started this. At least answer my questions." Anthony was talking to thin air. The ghost was gone again. He tossed and turned several minutes while he wondered what the ghost was hinting at. Going back over the conversation, Anthony slipped off into a troubled sleep.

***

It was the middle of the morning when sounds from outside woke Anthony from a sound sleep. He lay listening to see if he had heard someone inside his house. The sound of glass breaking brought him out of the bed. He reached into a hidden panel in the headboard for his gun as he rolled out from under the covers. Creeping down the stairs careful not to make a sound, Anthony approached the kitchen as the door leading from the garage to the backyard, slammed shut. Rounding the corner into the kitchen, Anthony saw his cat on the counter with the empty juice bottle laying broken into tiny bits on the marble tiles of his kitchen floor. Glancing through the window, he saw a fleeing figure dart behind the tree line and disappear into the fence row.

"Okay, I'll get a damn dog! Will that make you happy?" Throwing his hands up, he was shouting at the ceiling. Hearing no answer, he sat about cleaning up the broken glass.

The gym wasn't crowded when Anthony arrived. He went directly to the weights. Putting on headphones to drown out the voices and sounds made by the equipment being used by the others working out, he was able to think. By the time he made his way to the tread mill, he had worked up a sweat. Running hard for several minutes, sweat was pouring off of him, he still hadn't come up with the answers he had hoped to. He decided it was time to knock off. When he looked up he saw that the others had stopped what they were doing to watch him, the men with a look of astonishment and awe, the women's faces held looks of pure lust.

After leaving the gym, he went home to shower and change. There was still time to see Ben before checking on the information he received concerning the woman from Aquilla. When he arrived at Ben's address, Ben wasn't home. Anthony was shocked to see where he lived. He had been in this house before. After rechecking the address to see if he was at the right house, things started falling into place. Larry Joe Green and Benjamin Orr were the same person. "That bastard isn't trying to sell someone else's wife; he's trying to sell his own." Gripped by fear for Brenda's safety, he knew there wasn't time to waste in removing her from the area.

Anthony had seen Brenda in the grocery store a few times without her being aware he was there. He loved watching how she interacted with other people. She seemed to be an honest, open, caring person. The more he saw her, the more he had to admit to himself he had feelings for her. There was no doubt in his mind that she thought she was in love with the poor excuse of a man she was married to. From what she told him, he knew she wondered if her marriage was solid. He was puzzled though because he remembered how she had known who Anthony was when she kissed him. It was Anthony's name she used when she said she wanted him. He wished the situation were different. He wondered if she really loved that man or if she was fooling herself because of her upbringing. Even then, he wanted to tell her what her husband was trying to do. He couldn't.

On two different occasions he caught himself outside her business, watching her through the window. He was afraid if she saw him watching her she would think he was stalking her. Each time he told himself, although she needed to know, he couldn't be the one to hurt her again. Another problem with that would be it getting back to Mr. Arnold. If she confronted her husband with the information that would surely happen. While he had thought her husband was some jerk off the street, he told himself, the man would be afraid to try something like that again. Now he knew Ben was behind it, the danger was real and possibly worse than anything he could imagine. That thought chilled him.

While Anthony stood staring at the name on the mail box, he realized just how great the danger to Brenda was. He knew also she would never listen to him if he tried to warn her, he had seen to that. The morning, he woke up in her bed, he needed to make her believe he was a horrible person. Now, there wasn't any way in the world he could tell her the whole truth without giving himself away right along with Ben (Larry Joe) or whatever else he called himself.

Ben Orr had abducted and raped more women than anyone could keep track of. If he damaged them too badly to sell, he kept them long enough to rape, torture, and have fun with for a while before disposing of their bodies. He had enjoyed his work too much.

Ben wasn't home. Anthony had tried the doorbell before he knocked, but no one answered. He turned, went back to his Bentley and drove away, unaware his picture had been taken by a camera hidden in the bushes near the house. He called Mr. Arnold to let him know he wasn't able to reach Ben about the shipments of drugs, guns, and electronics. Mr. Arnold wasn't happy.

The conversation with Mr. Arnold left Anthony with an uneasy feeling. At the sound of the dial tone, he immediately called to see if he could make an appointment with an attorney from one of the law firms in Poplar Bluff. A receptionist told him they could work him in if he could get there within the hour. He was in Malden already, so he cut across J Highway to make a stop at Bader's Orchard on the way. He wanted to pick up some of the peaches

Campbell is famous for enroute to Highway 53, which would take him into Poplar Bluff. After leaving the attorney, Anthony went to speak with one of his contacts from prison. They had lunch at Ryan's while they discussed the predicament Tony found himself in.

Driving east bound on 60 Highway toward Dexter, he noticed a dog playing in a yard along the way. "Damn it, if I want any peace I better do something about that. I must be nuts to be keeping a promise to a ghost." He smiled, shaking his head at the thought of what he was about to do.

"What the devil is that monster?" Will asked, hurrying past Tony to get to the house without getting close to the beast. Bud stopped to pet the enormous mixed breed dog Tony had rescued from the pound earlier in the evening.

"If it tries to bite me I'll shoot it. I don't like dogs." Will threatened, looking away from Tony. He stared at the dog, which by now was growling at Will.

"Looks like he don't like you much either." Bud laughed while he scratched the dog under the chin and between the ears. Turning his attention to Tony, "I think he likes me. What's his name?" he asked. Picking up a small limb that had fallen from a nearby tree, he tossed it, delighted when the animal ran to bring it back to him. "What did you do, steal some kid's pet?" He teased Tony while enjoying the game of fetch.

Ignoring Will, who was cowering behind him, Tony struck up a conversation about the dog with Bud. "I'm naming him Bowser. I never had a dog before. What kind do you think he is?"

"Looks like he has a lot of Mastiff in him with the massive shoulders and stout body, I'm not sure what else. Look at that coat, I'd say as ugly as he is, he has some Irish Wolf Hound in the mix too. He'll make you a good watchdog. That breed is supposed to be fiercely loyal and gentle as a lamb. He's big as a horse. Look at the size of those feet. I wonder if he is still growing." Bud alternated between laughing at the antics of the large creature and being intensely serious. The whole time he spoke he was busy inspecting the animal. He ran his hands over the dogs' body, cupping the chin in his hand while he knelt to have a closer look at the structure of the head. Looking in its mouth, he found the gums and teeth to be in good shape. When he was finished, he playfully roughed up the fur. The beast loved the attention. "He's still young. Just watch him, he has character and some training already. He isn't pretty but he will make a handsome fellow when he gets his growth. There is just something about him." Bud looked like he was in awe of the creature.

"He gets along good with the cat. That surprised me." Tony laughed, watching the dog lap up the attention it was receiving. Still speaking to Bud, Tony cut his gaze toward Will. "Did you see how he was high stepping, or was that dancing?" Both of them laughed while Will glowered at the dog.

"I once killed a man for kicking my dog. Buried what was left of the dude in my backyard. Nobody ever did figure out what happened to him." Bud was laughing but Tony knew he was serious. "I cut him up and let the dog eat most of him, kept the pieces in the fridge out in my garage. It took a while for the dog to finish him off, then I started buying dog food again." Bud looked pointedly at Will while telling what he had done to the man for mistreating his pet.

Wilbur Wilkerson wished he hadn't threatened the dog. He swallowed hard as fear raced through him. He had seen first-hand what Bud was capable of. Although he didn't want to admit it, he was afraid of the man that appeared so easy going. He had worked with Bud long enough to see how much he enjoyed torturing anyone who crossed him. "Let's get to work. The boss needs some things done, that's why we're here. We're not here to play with the animals." He started to step into the house but stopped short when he heard barking coming from inside the house too. "Tony, go ahead we'll follow you; we need to go to the basement." Will paled and Bud exchanged a look of pure humor with Anthony.

During the night dreams of Brenda Lou kept Tony tossing and turning. There was something about that woman he couldn't put out of his mind. He knew she was off limits to him but he wanted to see her again. No, he needed to see her again. He told himself the man she was with wasn't really married to her; besides that, he was dangerous. She had no idea what she was messed up in just being near him. He asked himself how someone like her could possibly ever love someone like Benjamin Orr, no matter what name he went by. Somehow, he had to keep her safe; but how, without giving himself away? Her life depended on him. Desperation, fueled by fear, gripped his heart.

Ben wasn't happy. Ever since they brought Anthony into the picture things had been changing. Ben missed being the one to procure the women. He detested being told what to do. If Ronald Arnold hadn't insisted, he would never have married anyone. Now that his part in the operation had changed he was bored. He was tired of being married to Brenda. He planned to have her not only disappear; but glean sympathy in the process while coming out ahead financially. When his plans came into fruition, he would walk out on Mr. Arnold to start his own business in South America. All that was left to do before he could be free of them all was to have his wife sold. The only thing he hadn't been able to accomplish was getting access to the church funds. He was still trying to figure out that password. If he could do that, he could deplete the accounts for the missionary funds also. It would be an added bonus. The thought of getting his hands on the church funds brought a smile to his face. He figured they owed him for putting up with their daughter anyway.

Chapter 6

Mom, are you sure you don't want to come stay with me for a while?" Walter teased, throwing an arm around her. "I'm your baby boy. Don't you worry about me being around all those wild city women? After all, Cape Girardeau is a big ole city compared to where I come from." He laughed as his mother playfully jabbed him in the ribs.

After finishing breakfast, he helped clear the table and load the dishwasher. "I haven't had a meal like that in months, biscuits, gravy, hash browns, your homemade sausage, farm fresh eggs. I like the way you spoil me." Sitting down at the cleared table, Walter took a sip of coffee, letting out a sigh of satisfaction. "Nobody cooks like my momma."

Lou gave him a big hug, she was laughing. "You are my only boy. I'm afraid your dad would be lost without me. Maybe you haven't noticed, he never did learn to mate a pair of socks, not to mention use a toaster. He would starve to death without me here. Aren't you glad I taught you to cook?" After dipping a dishrag in the sudsy water in the sink, she wrung it out then threw it to Walter. "You don't mind washing off the table to pay for your breakfast do you?"

"Your wish is a demand, I mean my command." He laughed at his own joke while wiping the table. "I love this place. Maybe someday I can find a girl even half as good as my momma, you'll have to teach her to cook. I never really was able to master the art." He winked at his mother.

"Walter Perkins, I am not teaching one of your wayward women to cook. When the time comes that you settle down with one girl, then we can talk about it. Until that time, you can come here for a home cooked meal any time you want to. Your dad and I enjoy having you around. The last time you were serious about a girl, if I remember right, you were about fifteen. How old was she?"

"Actually, it was her car I was serious about and she was eighteen. She wanted daddy to give her a reference for that college she wanted to attend. It didn't bother me to be used; I got rides to school. It beat taking the school bus, plus the rest of the education that came along with it wasn't bad." Winking at his mother, he chuckled taking a bite out of the biscuit he had put a large piece of sausage on.

"You're still my baby boy and still a big mess." Lou's expression took on a more serious look as she thought about the reason her son was there. "Have you seen your dad yet?"

"I called him before I came in, he'll be here soon. That Ben has been one busy fellow. I'll tell you all about it when Daddy gets here. You're not going to like it, that's for sure. That's one nasty piece of work my sister married."

"After what we've been finding out, I thought as much. Poor Brenda Lou." She started for the back door with a bowl of scraps in her hand, thinking to herself, she wished she had personally checked the man out before her daughter married him. That was one mistake she did not intend to repeat. Turning back to face Walter she asked "Are any of the girls going to be here today?"

"Mom, I think Brenda Lou is taking off work to come up, and you know Donna Mae wouldn't miss it for anything." He grinned at the thought of his nosey sister's involvement, knowing how much she loved getting the dirt on someone else.

Donna Mae was grinning as she wheeled her Saab out of the parking lot beside her husband's law practice. Not only did she like the way it handled, there were the looks of envy that gave her a rush. She was supposed to meet Brenda at her house; but, called telling her something had come up so she would meet her at their parents' house instead. Hanging up she went back over what came up, in her mind.

Some of the reports on Larry Joe had been delivered to Mac's office. When his wife went by to pick them up, the information was so good the two wanted to celebrate. "Before we discuss Brenda Lou's husband, is there anything you want to share with me?" Mac studied his wife's face before continuing. "I know we agreed to wait for ten years to have a baby. When did you plan on sharing that news with me?" Mac was attempting to keep a stern expression on his face while looking at his wife over the top of his glasses, which had slid down his nose. "I know you well enough to know that when your sister started talking about trying to get pregnant, you would have to beat her to it. Am I right?" After several seconds of silence, Mac couldn't help breaking into a grin at the condescending look his wife was giving him. "Well?" He waited, crossing his arms over his chest, while she glared at him. "Come over here and sit on Daddy's lap. I already know the answer. When I found out that Brenda Lou made you cry, that was a dead giveaway. Nobody can make you cry. You had to be pregnant." He was laughing out loud as he pushed his chair back from his desk, patting his leg for her to sit. "God, Donna Mae, I love you. You are just as bad as I am."

She knew her husband was telling the truth when he said he knew she was pregnant. "You do know me well." With her head bowed, eyes glaring up at him, she walked slowly toward him. Giving him a sudden lopsided grin, she plopped on his lap. "We're going to beat her by about three weeks." She threw her arms around his neck, giving him a loud kiss on the cheek. Looking straight into his eyes she asked, "What do you think about that?"

"Do I get to pick out the nanny?" He joked. He looked lovingly into his wife's eyes. "Seriously, it will be great. I don't care if it's a boy, or a girl, or both. We will spoil our children rotten. I'm looking forward to it. To think, I'm going to be a daddy. Donna Mae, you make me feel like a king."

"Not only do I love you, I think you're great. If I hadn't been watching what you were up to, I would have suggested it myself just to make you happy. I still can't believe that little dip shit used my car to do his running around in. You were brought to tears because of him. He is going down!" Holding her by her upper arms, Mac held her out from him enough to see her face while he spoke. "I still remember when we married." He paused for a moment with a sly half grin on his face. "I was going to ask you sooner; but, when you pulled that fake pregnancy I wanted to make you squirm. We went to Peach Tree Lane to park, remember? I already knew you well enough to know you were up to something that night. The reason I picked that place to park? I knew there would be other cars there already. When you said you had to pee, I handed you a bottle to use I had brought along for that purpose. I'll never forget the way you looked at me. I never told you I had a friend do a pregnancy test on it. You've always been as devious as me; but, I was one step ahead of you. That's one of the things I love about you." He was trying to keep a straight face but his dimples gave him away.

"I had already planned on asking you to marry me. When you made your announcement, you thought you had me trapped."

"You scoundrel! You knew all these years there wasn't a baby back then? I ought to hit you." He had released her arms and she threw them around his neck. "Why didn't you ever say anything?"

"I wanted to see how far you would take it. Besides that, it saved me a boat load of money I had planned on spending on a big wedding."

"Your poor daddy believed you were pregnant, and your momma. She got so upset when you told her you lost the baby. I believe you told them it happened during the two weeks I was away with the National Guards." He paused watching her smiling face. "I felt so sorry for them that I almost told your daddy the truth. You were loving the sympathy so much I couldn't bring myself to do that to you."

"What would I ever do without you?"

"Let's not find out. Where else would I find a woman enough like me to make me happy? We were made for each other. You're so bad you're good." He was unbuttoning her blouse while he pushed the intercom button to tell his secretary he needed her to run to the post office for stamps, and to lock the door on her way out. When he heard the click of the lock he pushed the button so the sound of Charlie Rich's voice filled the air with the song Behind Closed Doors. "Now, for another reason I love you-." His words were lost in the kiss, as Donna covered his mouth with hers.

***

Hearing a car door slam brought Chet around to the front of the house with Walter following close. Brenda was already on her way to the front door, clutching a folder to her chest. "Looks like you got the papers Patty Sue said she was sending." Walter looked pleased. "Where is Donna Mae? I thought the two of you were riding together." Walt could hardly wait to see the papers. He approached his sister with an outstretched hand to take the folder she held, before greeting her with a hug followed by a peck on her cheek.

"She said something came up; she will be here pretty soon." After handing the folder to her brother she turned to her dad. "Have you said anything to Tom yet?" She had dark circles under her eyes. Her dad, seeing her appearance, worried what all this would do to her health before it was over. He felt his heart would break for her, knowing the anguish she was going through.

Chet's friend, Tom Smith, was a police officer working out of the Dexter Police Dept. He recently took over as Chief of Police there. The two men became close friends when Tom took time off from the Dexter Police Force to do undercover work for a state task force. Due to the nature of the crimes, he investigated at that time, Tom sent a few of the victims to local churches for counseling as well as help becoming reestablished in their communities. Now Chet turned to his friend of many years for help with a problem within his own immediate family.

"Yes, he should be here shortly. I thank my lucky stars for having a man like that on our side." Chet became silent thinking back five years to performing Tom's marriage ceremony. Tom married the widow Liz Kelly, after the death of her mother and the discovery that Robert Moffield was her biological father. Chet was delighted for his friend's good fortune. Tom went from being a bachelor of many years, to being part of a very large, loving family. The change was good for Tom, and it showed.

The door barely closed behind Chet, Walter, and Brenda, when they heard the sound of loud music approaching followed by the sound of a car on the gravel road in front of the house. "Looks like Donna Mae finally got here." Lou called from the kitchen. "That girl will be late for her own funeral."

Lou came through the doorway wiping her hands dry on her apron. "I just took a batch of rolls out of the oven. There is fresh coffee, lemonade, or tea, for whoever wants it. We can sit at the table in the kitchen. There's more room in there." As the group started for the kitchen, the front door opened. Donna entered with Tom Smith holding the door. He was carrying a stack of papers, along with the pictures, she had brought along. No one heard Tom's car arrive over the noise made by the music Donna was playing. "Come on in. Momma has things all ready in here." Chet gestured for them to follow. "Tom, I don't know how to thank you.

I think my girl may be in way over her head." The look he sent Brenda was apologetic while at the same time filled with love.

"From the looks of it, you have all been pretty busy." Tom was looking all the stacks of papers in front of Walter and Brenda. They were all as thick as the one he carried in for Donna. "Where should we start first?"

Lou finished seeing to it that everyone was served what they wanted. When the group looked comfortable, she stood up taking charge. "I've been going over some of what is in those reports, and I spoke to Patty Sue." She looked directly at Brenda. "Baby, I hate to tell you; but, that man of yours isn't who he claimed to be. Your sister ran his DNA and sent that along with his fingerprints to my cousin. They will see if there is anything else in his record we don't already know. Larry Joe's real name is Gregory Wayne Johnson. He was born in Louisiana forty years ago." Her heart went out to her daughter when she saw the look of hurt disbelief cross Brenda Lou's face. Lou had taken time to read every word contained in the information several times. Her composure was painstakingly controlled. No one could tell that her seething hatred, growing like a wildfire, every time her daughter's husband came to mind, existed. Although she hid it well, she felt as betrayed as her daughter. "It's all in the fax here." She tapped the paper laying in front of her. "Walter, what have you got for us?" Lou sat down and looked over at her son.

Walter spread the papers out in front of him, some of which had photos attached. "My friends are enjoying the cat and mouse game." He chuckled. "They feel like private eyes. It is keeping them busy. Larry Joe, or whoever he is, doesn't sit still."

Walter had details of almost every move his brother-in-law made. There were pictures of him with several different women, two of which could fit the description of his sister. With information already gathered on most of the shady deals Larry was involved in, it was obvious he was setting his wife up to take a financial fall. Larry Joe was passing these women off as Brenda to obtain large loans all over the tri state area. Unknown to those around the table, the body of one of the women in the pictures had just been pulled out of an area lake. With the exception of Anthony Payne, no one appeared to recognize any of the men in the photos with Larry Joe.

When Donna Mae saw the photos of Anthony she hurriedly dug through her papers, producing her own pictures of him. Donna brought along pictures of Anthony taken outside of her sister's house as well as outside Brenda's Beauty Salon. Seeing all the photos of Anthony, Brenda Lou turned white as a sheet. Chet looked up at his daughter with real concern, remembering what he had walked in on that Easter Sunday.

Donna cut her eyes over at her sister. Smiling like the cat that ate the canary, she spoke directly to her sister. "Mac had a little help finding out about your hero there." She said pointing to Anthony's image in one of the photos. "Seems like he might be a legitimate businessman; but, maybe not. We need to find more out about him. What we did find out is that he was in prison–," She let her voice trail off before continuing. "and–, that isn't his right last name he's using." It was obvious she was gloating from the tone of her voice and her too innocent eyed facial expression. "He goes by the name Payne when he is out and about but his real name, the one he does business under, is Taylor."

Donna sat down, watching the stunned face of her older sister. She loved her sister, would do anything to help her; but, she just couldn't help herself. She had to gloat, it was in her nature.

Chet felt relieved to see his wife appeared to have missed the exchange between his daughters. Lou had her back to them refilling drinks at the counter. Shocked by what she just heard, she took a moment to calm herself so her family wouldn't see how it had affected her. Chet turned his attention back to Tom. "Things like this just don't happen around here. I'm worried about my girl. What can we do Tom?"

Tom had been sitting quietly listening to what everyone had to say while watching Brenda's reaction to it all. He knew there was something being withheld, he would have to ask Brenda Lou about it later. He couldn't tell this family he cared about so deeply, what he was afraid they were involved in. "Tell ya what. First off, you can't be following that Payne fellow no more." He scanned the faces of the people sitting around the table to make sure they understood. "If he comes to your house that's one thing; but, other than that—it's a free country. Understand?" Maintaining a stern expression he hoped didn't show the fear he felt for them, he looked slowly from one face to the next to make sure they did indeed understand they had to leave Anthony alone. Police Chief, Tom Smith knew a lot more about Anthony, none of which he could share with anyone at the table.

"Brenda Lou, I will need to speak to you when we're done here." Tom selected what he could tell them from what he knew he couldn't mention.

"You all have to keep this quiet. Go on like you don't suspect Larry Joe of anything. Let him go on believing you think he is still employed. There is a Federal Judge I know who lives in Dexter. I'm going to see if he will let me put a tap on Brenda Lou's phone. If she agrees, it will make things easier." As he looked over at her, she nodded her agreement. "Do you have copies of all this, or are these the originals?" He asked, scanning the faces of his friends.

Lou spoke up. "We have copies of everything." From her grin, Tom knew there were multiple copies. She reminded him of a mother hen ready to defend her chicks. He had never seen anyone look as formidable as the woman standing in front of him. He told himself he hoped to never cross her path the wrong way.

"Good thing. I need to take these with me then. I want to make sure that Brenda Lou doesn't have any of this at her house or her shop. It would be a good idea if none of you did. Put your copies somewhere Larry Joe can't get access to, which includes Mac's office too." He pointedly looked at Donna. He had been around her family enough to know that when she got an idea in her mind, she wouldn't let go. "Donna Mae, don't take any chances. You hear me young lady? Don't leave anything in your house, cars, or at Mac's office. Alright? And, don't you follow any of them. If they see you, well, it could be dangerous for you. It might even get you killed."

Tom leafed through a few more photos that Walter had handed him. "Looks like Walter's friends are doing a darn good job. They don't know any of them, so Larry Joe won't think anything of seeing them out on their motorcycles." Tom scratched his head, running his fingers through his hair, giving himself time to think. "I wish none of you would keep any of this. Like I said, Walter's friends are one thing, but–, well, don't none of the rest of you be following anybody. I'll put some people on it. I don't want to see any of you getting hurt."

Due to the thoughts racing through his mind, a worried look crossed his face. Tom knew it wouldn't do any good to tell this family not to do anything if he couldn't explain everything to them. Warning Anthony about this would be his top priority. Also, he intended to talk to Brenda first thing in the morning.

Chapter 7

It was a typical Monday morning. Brenda was getting ready to go to work with the morning news blaring away in the background while she fixed breakfast. What she heard almost caused her to drop the hot skillet she was frying bacon in. The newscaster was showing pictures of several women from the area that had gone missing over the last three years. She rushed into the living room in time to see a picture of the latest woman that seemed to disappear without a trace. Glued to the spot, she looked at a woman that could have been her. It was one of the same women from the pictures that Larry Joe had been seeing recently. Up until now, it had been hard enough to pretend that nothing was wrong when she was around him. Knowing she couldn't face him after what she saw on the news, she hurried to leave. Rushing out the door yelling good-bye, over her shoulder, she left her husband's breakfast on the table.

The night following the meeting at her parents' house, Brenda told Larry Joe that she was pregnant. All her family members already knew. They all agreed she should tell him before someone accidentally let it slip. One of the women she knew told her that her husband was such a good liar the only way she could tell he was telling the truth was to watch his eyes when he spoke. She told Brenda that his pupils would get really large when he lied.

Larry Joe just came into the house, heading for the aroma of food in the kitchen. "Hi Baby." He wrapped his arms around his wife, kissing her on the side of the neck. "Tough day. I'm looking at a pretty good commission this month. We should be able to go ahead with the new appliances in a couple months. What smells so good?"

It was getting harder and harder for Brenda Lou to pretend to believe him. She kept her back to him as she spoke so he couldn't see her face. "I know how hard you work. Poor thing, you must be exhausted. Go on, sit down and I'll bring you a beer." She turned opening the fridge. After handing him the bottle, she went around the table to sit where she could see his face while she spoke. "I'm fixing you that beef and gravy you like so much. With that, I'm making steamed green beans and mashed potatoes." Knowing she had his attention she continued while watching his eyes. "We have something to celebrate." She couldn't bring herself to call him any kind of endearment; but, kept her voice sweet. "You're going to be a daddy. We finally got pregnant." She smiled sweetly while watching his expression.

"I'm so happy Baby. I was beginning to wonder if it was going to happen." He seemed genuinely happy. Before he could say anything else his cell phone rang. Looking at the caller ID he started rising from the table. "I'll be right back, business." Putting the phone to his ear, he quickly disappeared into the other room.

After Larry Joe left the room, Brenda Lou puzzled over her husband's reaction while she sat the table. By the time he came back, several minutes later, she had everything ready. She took a sip of tea while he sat down. "That took longer than I expected. Is everything alright?"

"I called my momma after I finished with that first call." She watched while his pupils started to dilate. "Baby there's something I got to tell you that might make you want to get an abortion." Now his pupils were as large as saucers. His attempt to look sincere didn't quite make it. He knew her well enough to know that nothing in the world could or would cause her to want to kill her unborn child. She didn't know what he would say next. Her thoughts were racing everywhere. "My momma just told me that my grandma from Louisiana had tainted blood. Sounds like her momma was part black. Baby, I didn't know. I never met her. If our baby comes into this world black–well, you know how damn racist your daddy is." Of all the lies he had been telling her recently this was the biggest line of bull he had dished out yet, at least that she knew of. "We'll think of something."

He reached for her hand. She drew it back before he could touch her. Lowering his head momentarily, he fought to keep from showing the anger caused by her rebuke.

She knew she looked stunned by his remark. After she regained her composure to a small degree she answered her husband. "An abortion? You want me to kill our baby?" She raised her voice almost to the point of yelling. "You know my daddy isn't a racist. He's not a bigot, or prejudiced in any way. I don't know who's worse about judging him in that, you or Donna Mae. I know you have heard him say he didn't want his children dating someone of another race. It is simply because he is afraid there would be trouble for a child that came from a mixed union. Daddy never holds the color of someone's skin against them; he never has and never could. He gauges people by what's on their inside as opposed to their color or where they came from. You know, love thy neighbor? Well, Larry Joe, he is one person that really does live by that!" Stabbing at a piece of meat, she continued. "It wouldn't matter to Daddy if one of his kids brought home somebody black, green, purple, or blue, if that was the one that made them happy." She looked up at Larry with tears starting to well in her eyes.

"I didn't mean to upset you. You know, we could always move away from here. That way we don't have to worry about what anybody thinks. The house is in good enough shape to sell out now. We could be reestablished before the baby's born." The expression on his face, the look in his eyes, the sound of his voice, this was what he had been planning all along. This was why he wanted her to get pregnant. Why did he want them to move? She asked herself, what then?

"I have a business to run, have you forgotten?" She snapped at him before she caught herself. "I'm sorry. I didn't mean to sound like that, I'm just tired. How about we sleep on it? We can talk about options tomorrow." Rising from the table, she knew she had jumped to her dad's defense too fast. She couldn't let on that she knew he wasn't what he was supposed to be. She mentally kicked herself while she started clearing away and cleaning up, she would have to be more careful. She thought about how happy he was when he started talking about selling out to leave. He was using the baby as an excuse.

What he didn't know was that the baby she carried may very well be black, she wasn't about to tell him that. She also knew her mother's bad feelings about mixed races. She remembered how her mother had drilled that into them from the time they were small children. There was no way she would tell him that either.

***

Tom Smith had been careful when he spoke to Brenda Lou. He had known her family for years and didn't want to frighten any of them. He knew there was some kind of a sting operation being set up in the area and Anthony Payne was somehow involved. After going over all the information her family had given him, he did some investigating on his own. Tom's talk with Brenda Lou hadn't gotten him anywhere. It looked like this family was right in the middle of what was happening. Since Lou's cousin was a U.S. Marshall he planned to set up a meeting with him and an old contact of his, still active in the F.B.I. He was afraid his friend's daughter was in more danger than any of them could imagine.

After seeing the news that morning, then reading the newspaper at work, Brenda was frightened. She could see how important it was for her to play dumb. She had already told Tom she would do what he asked of her. If she had any doubts before, she didn't after seeing the act her husband put on at their table when he learned of the pregnancy.

It was the wee hours of the morning when Anthony awoke consumed by fear. He had tossed and turned most of the night. When sleep did come, so did the dreams. He dreamed of the night he spent with a woman he had been asked to get rid of. She was the kind of woman every man desired and searched for most of their lives. The woman was beautiful, full figured, sweet natured, caring, gentle, hardworking, and every man's fantasy in bed. It was bad enough he caught himself thinking of her during the day, now he was reliving the time he spent with her in his dreams too.

Looking around the room, he couldn't believe his ghost was back. He took a deep breath letting the feeling of fear pass before speaking. "Okay old man, I got the bloody dog. As a matter of fact, I got two. Now what?" He laid back onto the expensive Egyptian cotton sheets, pulling the cover over his head, closing his eyes. It almost sounded like the ghost chuckled, causing him to yank the covers back down enough to glare at the image.

"I had a son named Anthony once. Oh, how I loved that woman. I was too poor to buy her while she carried him. Later, when I could afford the price for him, they refused to let me purchase him." The ghost looked sad. "By then she was already dead."

"I know my history. Nobody said nothing about you having a son by that name." Shaking his head in disbelief, he continued. "If you are who you want me to believe you are, you didn't have no black children or the historians would have found out by now. They found old Tom Jefferson's."

"Anthony, it hurt too badly to talk about. Why do you think I pushed so hard to have him freed? I kept up with where he was, with his entire short-lived life. He was such a good-looking young man. Gentle, kind, good natured as anyone could ask for. Had I told anyone about my reasons for an end to slavery–. Times were different then. I couldn't be seen as having any connection to any slave or there would not have been an end to it. At least not in this country during my lifetime. No one would have listened to me."

"Why should I believe you? You're a figment of my imagination."

"You know better, Anthony." He was now looking very sad as he rose from the chair, with his hands clasped behind his back he started pacing the floor. "You're going to be a father. You don't want your son's mother to be a slave, or worse. You are going to have to protect her from those she loves." He stopped pacing to look directly at Anthony. "Remember the conversation you had with that man yesterday? That child she is carrying is your child whether you want to believe it or not..." The image merged back into the air in the room leaving Anthony staring after it.

"What a way to start a day!" Anthony's feeling of self-loathing was bad enough before. He despised himself for being weak enough to sleep with Brenda to start with. After this conversation those feelings increased tenfold. He was more confused than ever.

The whole time the encounter with the ghost took place, the dog lay near him on the bed watching. Now it jumped up on the bed beside its new master, cheerfully licking his face before it started jumping around in an attempt to get him up to go out to play.

Anthony was trying, without success, to push the dog from the bed. Every time he managed to get part of the huge animal to the floor, it sprang right back up. "You got a dog door, go use it." He once again pushed at the enormous Mastiff mixed breed he now shared his bed with. No matter what he tried, he couldn't keep it off the bed. "I'm changing your name to Jumper. Damn you, how am I supposed to sleep with you shaking the bed to pieces and the house right along with it?" Fully awake, he started to laugh as the dog practically bounced him out of the bed. "Okay, okay, I'm getting up. You have a nice new doghouse; why do you think you're going to take my house over?" He laughed at his new best friend as it raced in circles around him. "The cat won't like this."

Barefooted, dressed in only sweatpants, he made his way across the marble tiles of the kitchen floor. Enjoying the way the cool tiles felt, he marveled again at the thought that he owned such a house. "Raymond, I wish you could be here. This is going to work; he won't get away with it." To anyone who might watch the tape later, it looked like Anthony was talking quietly to his dog while he poured food into the bowl.

After filling the dogs' bowls, he filled one belonging to the cat before placing it on a shelf he had cleared for that purpose. "Come on Puss. He can't get at you here." The cat leaped from the top of the fridge onto the wide shelf. "I see you found a new place to sleep. Sorry sweetie, but we have to keep him." He stroked the soft fur while his cat rubbed against his arm. "I think you two will become good friends if you give him a chance." Bad Leroy Brown played as the ringtone signaling an incoming call from Mr. Arnold.

"Morning Boss." That was all Tony had a chance to say. The one-sided conversation was short and to the point. Mr. Arnold informed him that Bud and Wilbur would be in town. When he was finished, he ended the call. Tony was left staring at the phone wondering if it had anything to do with the articles that ran in the papers the day before. There wasn't any speculation as to what might be happening to the women, so he doubted that was what the call was about.

Tony looked up in time to see a tiny rag mop of a dog come flying across the kitchen. "Hey buddy, where have you been hiding?" The little thing stopped, cocked its head in his direction, before continuing on to the dog dish. Jumper was already in the process of emptying the dish, but when the little ball of fur growled, Jumper backed up whimpering. Tony burst out laughing at the sight. "Looks like we know who the boss around here is." Reaching down, he scooped the small dog up. "I wish I knew where you hide all day. The only time I see you is when it's time to eat." The little thing let him pet it for about a minute before it licked his face, then started squirming to get down. After it finished eating it took off in the direction it came from, letting Jumper get to the food dish once again.

Finished with his breakfast Anthony went to get dressed, dreading the arrival of the two men Mr. Arnold was sending to his house. While he showered he went over his conversation with Ben (Larry Joe) once again. He knew Ben was up to more than just getting rid of an unwanted wife. What did he hope to get out of her disappearance other than the little bit of money she would sell for? Why would he risk being investigated when a divorce would be an easy way for him to be free of her? There had to be more to it, too many things that just didn't add up. He was worried for Brenda's safety. "Cotton Candy, you're going to see me again." He mused aloud. "You may not want to, but you will."

Chapter 8

There was a loud, persistent pounding on the door. Opening the front door, Anthony was surprised to see Will standing there without his partner. "Where is Bud?"

Pushing past Anthony, Will stomped into the house. "He ain't here." Without slowing down, he went straight into the kitchen. He threw open the refrigerator door with enough force, bottles coming close to being thrown out, rattled loudly. Rummaging through the shelves, not caring what he spilled, he turned toward Anthony. "Don't you keep any real food, asshole?" He demanded with a smirky grin that looked more deadly than friendly.

"I have a lot of real food in there, just not greasy, sugary garbage. Had I known you were coming for breakfast, I would have gotten doughnuts or pastries." Standing with feet planted at shoulder width apart, hands on hips, Anthony answered Will with an edge to his voice, and an expression on his face that would have caused a wiser man to tremble.

Will ignored Anthony's building anger. "Yeah, yeah, yeah, I bet you would of." He slammed the door, taking a banana from the bowl sitting on the island. "Bud had things to do. Ever hear of a place called Wilhelmina? You and me's going there, boss's orders. We gotta find out if they still have their fish fry, picnic, the tavern, stuff like that. Looks like he wants to expand in that direction." The lopsided, authoritative grin caused Anthony to wonder what Wilbur had planned. Wilbur's antagonistic demeanor put Anthony on guard. He knew if Mr. Arnold wanted him to do anything like that, he would have spoken directly to him. "Let's go." Wilbur commanded, heading out through the door leading to the garage.

The windows of the Range Rover were tinted dark enough that the men didn't have to worry about being seen. Anthony slid in under the steering wheel, pushing the button to open the garage door. Watching Wilbur light the stub of his cigar, he knew the new car smell wouldn't last long. "You're going to have burn holes in the leather. Put that damn thing out."

"Mind your own damned business. Just shut the hell up and drive." He intentionally flicked ashes onto the carpet leering at Anthony, daring him to say something. "We got a lot of miles to travel, boss's orders."

"It is my business. I can't have this trashed. You know I have to keep it in good condition for the job, boss's orders." He spat out his reply.

As hard as it was, Anthony ignored the other taunts from his unwanted passenger as he backed out. Putting the vehicle into drive, he took a deep breath to keep from saying something he would regret later. Wilbur gave him a rundown of the area they were supposed to scout out on the way to Highway 25.

From Dexter they drove down 25 Highway to Bernie. Making a right turn onto U, Anthony enjoyed the silence for a few minutes. A couple of miles before they reached Powe, Wilbur started complaining of hunger. When they reached the community of Powe, they stopped off at the little crossroad grocery / gas station, so Wilbur could get something he considered real food to eat. Anthony had been there before, he liked the selection of lean, baked sandwich meat they offered.

A rather frumpy, middle-aged woman was working behind the meat case. When the two men entered, she gave them each an appraising once over. Not too many area black men were as well dressed as the one she saw standing in front of her. Not many white men looked as mean or dangerous as the man with him. Looking out the window, she saw what kind of vehicle they were driving. Wondering if they were drug dealers, she was considering placing a call to the sheriff until Anthony left the biggest tip she had ever received.

Money in hand, she forgot all about making the call. She let her eyes roam over Anthony again, winking she told him to stop by again soon.

With his appetite satisfied, Wilbur's surly mood improved to a small degree. Crossing the St. Francis River, Anthony noticed the water levels were starting to improve after the bad drought of the summer before. He found himself worrying more and more about the economy of the area because of the effect it had on some of the people he now considered friends.

Reaching CC Highway, they decided to take it down to 53 Highway West, to Qulin. They stopped in at a dollar store there to ask a few questions about the small town before heading off to the Southeast toward Glennonville. At Glennonville they went back up 53 to Poplar Bluff where they turned onto Highway 160.

Following 160 South through Fairdealing to Doniphan, Anthony marveled at the beauty of the countryside while Wilbur complained about the lack of civilization. Touring Doniphan, they drove around the courthouse square on roads which were almost empty of other vehicles. From all appearances, it was another small town in the process of dying out. Tourist season brought in campers, divers, and people who were there for float trips on Current River. Hunting season was another reason the town stayed alive, drawing hunters from all over the country. There were several rental cabins scattered around the area that remained vacant most of the time.

Wilbur protested when Anthony told him they were going to make a stop. He wanted to see Current River while they were so close. "What the hell do you want to look at a bunch of rocks and trees for? Let's get out of here before mosquitoes have us for lunch." Anthony parked the car near the river. Getting out of the car, he walked to the water's edge where he sat down on a fallen tree to remove his shoes. After rolling up his pant legs he walked out onto a gravel bar. Stepping into the shallow ice-cold water, he looked around in awe. The beauty surrounding him was mesmerizing. Closing his eyes, he inhaled deeply, engrossed in the smells bombarding his senses while the sun warmed him. A serene peace wrapped him in a cocoon, filled him, easing his troubled mind.

Anthony opened his eyes when he felt a tingle on the back of his neck. The only time he had ever had that feeling was when he was a boy and Raymond was staring at him. Not just any stare, but the kind that said he had a really good secret that Anthony would have to find out on his own. Startled he looked around. The only person he saw behind him was Wilbur, who wasn't paying any attention to him.

It was easy to see how the river got its name. Standing there he could feel the power of the current as the water raced swiftly across his bare feet in the shallows. Looking farther out, he saw a large tree being carried down river at an amazing speed by the swift current. It crossed his mind to dump Wilbur into the freezing, fast moving water just to see his reaction. That thought amused Anthony. He pictured Wilbur gasping from the shock of the cold water, arms flailing, while the current carried him away leaving behind blessed silence from all the bitching and complaining.

While he watched the water, a group of divers broke the surface just a little downstream from him. There were six wetsuit clad individuals exiting the swift water. Each one had a wrist lanyard with a garden hand rake attached to it. They were joking about pulling themselves across the bottom of the river while using the rakes to keep the current from carrying them away. It didn't take much imagination to see that they really did use the rakes to keep the current from carrying them away. The group was a scuba diving club called The Bottom Scratchers according to the logo on their tanks. They had been removing monofilament and lost lures from the river, along with broken bottles, cans, and other debris. The net bags attached to their BCs were all full of objects removed from the bottom of the river.

"Well nature boy, had enough? We need to get going. Don't want the boss pissed." Hearing Wilbur's loud, obnoxious voice brought Anthony out of his fantasizing. "Come on pretty boy, move your ass."

Walking back toward the car with his shoes in his hand, Anthony paused a moment taking another deep breath before reaching Wilbur. "Man don't lean on the vehicle. You scratch the damn paint, you pay for it." Giving Wilbur a pointed look, he sat on a large rock to put his shoes on while talking. "Know what that minty smell is that's mixed with the Honey Suckle?"

"I don't give a damn what it is as long as it doesn't cause me to break out in a rash. I'm allergic to country." He snarled slamming the door. "Let's get a move on before a snake decides it wants a ride."

From Doniphan they continued on 160 to Alton, where they picked up Highway 99 heading north. Crossing Eleven Point River bridge, the speed limit slowed coming into Thomasville.

Anthony wasn't too surprised when he looked over to see Wilbur, holding a gun pointed right at him. "Somehow, I didn't think the boss wanted us to go on this little scouting trip. Am I right? Can I ask what you plan to do with that?" They had been discussing the missing women that had made the news recently. Wilbur made multiple remarks about his displeasure with the boss's decision to use Anthony as bait to lure the women they needed for their trade. "If you use that thing the boss won't be happy." Anthony knew Wilbur didn't like him, would like nothing better than to see him dead.

"Things was better when Ben did what you're doing now. Looks like I'm in charge now, don't it boy? I'm going to shoot you in self-defense, pull off down by the river over there." Wilbur spit the words out while he waved the gun in the direction he wanted Anthony to turn. "You brown nosing black sum bitch. How ya like that, boy? The boss will believe me cause I'll be the only one left to tell what happened." Wilbur laughed waving the gun at Anthony.

"Are you out of your mind?" He accelerated taking the curve North of Thomasville at a speed way too fast for the road. It threw Wilbur off balance just enough for Anthony to reach for the gun. At the same time, he jerked his arm up, Wilbur was thrown toward him with his head turned toward Anthony. Anthony's elbow made contact with Wilbur's throat, forcibly throwing Wilbur's head back and to the side at an unnatural angle. The dull hollow, popping sound followed by the spasms of his body told Anthony that Wilbur wouldn't be shooting him or anyone else. A couple miles north of Thomasville, he pulled the vehicle off onto a little used service road. Looking around the heavily wooded area, he noticed a sharp drop off by the road. He didn't see any houses to worry about.

Getting out of the Range Rover, he carefully made his way around the vehicle, watching for approaching traffic. Not seeing any headlights in the dusk of evening, he opened the passenger door, unfastened the seat belt, and let Wilbur's body hit the soft cushion of leaves on the side of the narrow road. Anthony patted down the body, taking everything from the pockets while he watched to make sure he wasn't seen. Before getting back into the vehicle, he gave Wilbur's lifeless body a push to send it rolling about five feet down an incline into the underbrush by the side of the road. Looking down, no trace of Wilbur could be seen. He knew it wouldn't take scavengers long to start working on the body. In no time it would either be drug off or consumed.

Anthony put Wilbur's wallet in the glove box, along with the other contents from his pockets. The Rossi 351 .38 special Wilbur pulled on him was put into a hidden compartment under the seat along with a knife he found strapped to the dead man's ankle.

Continuing north on the narrow highway with all the hills and curves, Anthony breathed a sigh of relief as he reached Highway 60 in Birch Tree. Even with the one brief stop he had to make before he left the area, he knew he could make good time going back to Dexter. There would be a couple small towns with reduced speed limits to pass through before he reached Poplar Bluff which wouldn't slow him down much. As he circled around getting back onto 60 East at the junction in Poplar Bluff, he knew it wouldn't take long to be home. He quickly made two calls before he got into the gently rolling low hills and curves, where signal strength causes problems with cell service.

Once he had a scenario down pat for why Wilbur wasn't with him, Anthony's thoughts jumped to Brenda. As hard as he tried, he couldn't keep her out of his thoughts. No woman ever had this kind of effect on him before. He wouldn't let himself believe she was carrying his child, no matter what his ghost said to him, it would be far too dangerous if it were true. He made up his mind to warn her about her husband's plans. Now, he would have to figure out how to get her to listen to him without giving away his cover.

He mentally went over everything that happened the evening he met Brenda. Ben had everything set up to make it look like an accidental meeting. When Tony was first contacted, Ben told him Brenda's husband had arranged for a fictitious suicide call to go to her father. Ben, aka Larry Joe, then called Chet after he knew the call had been placed. He, Larry Joe, insisted on helping with the person that was supposedly suicidal. A tracking device had been placed on Brenda Lou's car making her easy to follow. Anthony entered the bar right after she got there. From the information he was given, he expected to find a woman who made a habit of running the bars to pick up men. He had been led to believe that Larry Joe Green was a man driven to madness by an unfaithful lush of a wife, with no family that would miss her. Anthony was told the woman's family would be glad to see her out of their hair. Now he understood Ben was trying to set him up. He knew if Brenda had disappeared, it would have looked like Anthony kidnapped her. Ben wanted revenge against Anthony for taking what he considered to be his position in the organization.

Anthony sat watching Brenda turn away first one man then another before he sat on the stool beside her. He stayed there for a few minutes before trying to strike up a conversation. While sitting there he noticed she was doing more crying than drinking. When she went to the bathroom, he put something in her drink to help her relax so she would speak openly to him about her relationship with her husband. He learned that she was worried about her husband's lack of interest in her. She told him she wondered if he had ever loved her. She said she loved her husband. She told him how upset she was because it was supposed to be a special night for them to reconnect; but, she had seen him in a bar holding hands with another woman.

Seeing how hurt she was had caused him to be suspicious, so Anthony wanted to hear her side of things. There were so many interruptions he suggested they move to the far end of the room where other men would leave her alone. Finding her fascinating, he listened while she talked. He was repulsed every time he thought of hearing Ben laugh and tell him, "With the right attention along with the right drugs, any woman could be persuaded to do about anything". Anthony hated to think how many women Ben had treated that way and worse.

It was late, Brenda thanked him for listening and for being a gentleman. When she attempted to stand up to leave, the room started spinning. Anthony jumped up and caught her when she almost fell, offering to drive her home. During the first hour he spent talking to her, he learned she was nothing like he had been led to believe. First, she tried to call Larry Joe again, but he didn't answer. She had already made repeated attempts to reach him. Afraid to drive, she accepted the offer of a ride from Anthony, who drove her to her house in her own car. He already knew her husband had no intention of showing up at their house. After spending a couple of hours listening to her speak, he wasn't about to abduct this woman.

From what he had seen, Brenda hadn't had anything to eat since having an early light lunch. She had been emotionally distraught, to the point of hyperventilating for an extended period of time before consuming a few drinks. It was easy to tell she wasn't used to drinking alcohol. On top of everything else, he had given her something to help her relax. Seeing how badly she needed sleep, he intended to see her home safely, then leave. He would think of something to tell Ben later.

Normally, if a woman was to be taken, her vehicle was left where she was abducted. Occasionally, the victim was driven to a remote location using the ruse of finding a parking place along a ditch bank or riverbank, where the vehicle would later be found. From the abduction point, she was taken directly to a location to be held for shipment. On occasion the victim's vehicle would be sold to an out of state chop shop and Ben would pocket the cash.

Things Ben told about enjoying the abduction of small children sickened Anthony. Ben loved the feeling of power he got from taking that kind of a risk, while claiming it was easier because there wasn't a vehicle to worry about disposing of. Anthony had seen a lot of mean and sick-minded men in prison. Ben wasn't just mean, he was the most evil, sick, twisted person he had ever seen.

To Anthony, Brenda wasn't only beautiful to look at, she was sweet, naïve, and completely blind to how wonderfully unique she was. He was drawn to her. By the time they reached Malden, she was in such a sleepy fog that she was calling Anthony by Larry Joe's name.

He helped her into her house, thinking it didn't take a rocket scientist to see that her husband had blatantly lied to get rid of his wife. The fresh night air seemed to wake Brenda somewhat. He intended to leave her at the door, until she kissed him. Knowing how wrong it was, he couldn't stop himself. He was taken by surprise and as soon as her lips met his, his mind went totally blank and instinct took over. He kissed her back. Sliding her hands around the back of his neck, drawing him to her as he tried to pull back from her, she called him by name. Never in his life had he experienced such a powerfully urgent need to possess someone. It was a primal need he had no control over. As she urged him to the bedroom he half followed, half helped usher her to the bed.

Laying Brenda across the sateen sheets, Tony pushed the bedspread to the floor. Driven by an instinct that left no room for conscious thought, need dictated their actions. Between the pill and the small amount of alcohol Brenda had earlier, the normal anxiety she felt about her naked body vanished leaving her without any inhibitions. Unaware of how they became naked, neither cared as long as they satisfied the overpowering hunger burning inside.

Bodies locked together, they each explored the other. Brenda gently raked her long fingernails down the length of Anthony's back to his buttocks while his caressing fingers traveled over her body. The smell of her hair and skin imprinted somewhere in the recesses of his brain while she moaned, arching in to mold her body with his.

The sound of his phone ringing brought Anthony out of his thoughts. "Hey Bud, what's up?" He asked, before disclosing his location in answer to the questioning, "I'm coming into Dexter now. I should see you in a few minutes."

Anthony pulled the car into the garage with Bud following on foot. Jumper was right on Bud's heels with a football in his mouth. He stepped out of the car as the garage door slid down. "Jumper boy, Bud looks upset. What have you been up to? You didn't pee on his leg or eat the cat before I got here did you?" He laughed, cupping the dog's massive head in his hands, speaking to the dog. After roughing the dog's fur, it took off into the house through the doggie door.

"What? You talk to the dog now and ignore me?" Bud made a joke out of the remark, but it was clear from the tone of his voice that he wasn't happy about being ignored. "Where is Will?" This time it sounded more like an accusation than a simple question.

"Sorry man, I don't know." Anthony opened the door leading into the kitchen, motioning Bud in after he stepped from his car.

"He left with you this morning." Bud was watching Anthony a little too closely, while stating the obvious. Anthony could tell that Bud already knew what Wilbur had planned.

"I was surprised to see Will without you. He told me we were supposed to go down to some little hole in the wall community. Said he knew how to get there. We drove around down Southwest of Malden without finding the place. After a while he had us lost. Looks like he should have written the direction down. He got pissed; told me it'll keep for another day. He wanted to come back, so I brought him back." Grinning at Bud, he shrugged his shoulders. "He's a puzzle sometimes. Want something to drink?" He asked, turning to the fridge to open the door, hoping Bud bought the line he just delivered. "What have you been up to?" Pulling out a bottle of sports drink, he offered it to Bud.

"How about a beer?" He said looking disdainfully at the sports drink. Tony handed him the beer; he seemed to brighten somewhat. Sounding less skeptical, "Where is Wilbur now?" Bud asked, believing Wilbur decided to wait a while before eliminating Anthony. Sensing Bud was buying the story, Tony relaxed. By Bud using Wilbur's given name it was apparent the agitation had transferred from himself to Wilbur. "When we got back he had me drop him off down town. He was acting kind of funny, even for him. Is there some gal he's taken a shine to?" He leaned against the island with his arms crossed over his chest, waiting for Bud to answer.

"Who knows what goes on in his head." Looking thoughtful, he paused for a moment. "I had some errands to run for the boss so he came without me. Where have you been if you dropped him off that long ago?"

"I thought I'd take care of some other business while I was out. I have to look legit, remember?" He knew he sounded convincing. "Have you been here long enough to check around for him in the house?" Tony asked "I hope that idiot didn't bring some female here to screw!"

"Relax man, he isn't here. He might be holed up in some no-tell motel room. I'd better go find the idiot. He isn't answering his phone." Sitting the empty can down, Bud headed for the front door. "If that asshole shows up, have him give me a call."

When he was alone, Anthony breathed a sigh of relief. Bud believed the story. He went out to the back yard to make a call where his conversation wouldn't be picked up by the bugs in the house. He had to pass on the information about Wilbur's death.

Ending the call, he wondered how he could find out if Wilbur had been ordered to kill him. Even knowing how much Wilbur hated him, he didn't think he would try something like that without being ordered to unless Wilbur and Ben had cooked up some kind of a dumb plot to try to sell Ronald Arnold after Wilbur killed him.

Anthony knew he would find out soon enough.

Chapter 9

Tom Smith was sitting at a table in the back room at a family restaurant in Dexter, along with three other men. At the table were a State Patrolman, a detective working for the county, and another man dressed in a suit. Anthony didn't recognize the man in the suit. Tom got up motioning for Anthony to take a seat while he shut the door. "We're still waiting for someone else. It's someone you know. When your old buddy gets here we can start." Nervous to start with, Tony saw the grin spread across Officer Smith's face and wondered who they were waiting for.

The man in the suit stood up, extending a hand to Anthony. "It's a pleasure to finally meet you. I'm Special Agent Allen Burner with the FBI; we've spoken several times over the phone. I just flew in from Langley to meet you. These gentlemen told me you're doing a good job for us. It will be interesting to hear the new information that brought about this meeting." Before Special Agent Burner had a chance to sit down the door opened again.

A bearded man in bad need of a haircut stuck his head in the door. "The gal is bringing coffee. Anybody want anything else?" Looking around at the shaking heads, the man yelled over his shoulder to the waitress before entering. He made his way across the room to Anthony. "Tony my man, long time no see." When Anthony stood he was immediately grabbed in a bear hug.

It took a couple seconds for Tony to recognize the man behind the beard. He knew the voice was familiar; but, the last time he had seen James Trout he was clean shaven, short haired, and wearing a prison uniform. "I can't believe my eyes. Man, what are you doing here? The last time I saw you they were hauling you away after you saved my hide." Tony returned the hug and patted James on the back several times before leaning back to take a good look at him. "Aren't you a sight? What are you doing wearing clothes looking like they should have gone out with the trash?" He was glad to see his old friend, so much so, he was having a hard time speaking due to the surprise. "If it hadn't been for you those assholes would have messed up my pretty face. I never got a chance to say thank you before they hauled you off. So, thanks man. Looks like you were the contact on the inside all along. I never was able to figure that part out."

"Somebody had to save your sorry butt. Well, now you know who is attached to the voice on the other end of the phone when you send your women away too." The dark-skinned man that posed as a buyer from a Middle Eastern country was the same man that had rescued Tony from being beaten half to death by one of Mr. Arnold's men in prison. "If you haven't heard, you'll be glad to know the women are all safe and still willing to testify. Most of the ones that aren't at the farm are taking college classes or job training classes while they wait. After this is over, remind me to thank Arnold for recording everything. I have some really detailed recordings of him haggling over prices with me. From what I've seen, the films are damned good too." James grinned as he motioned for the coffee decanter, then put on a thick Middle Eastern accent. "How do you like my accent?"

Burner cut in "Sorry to cut in on old home week; but, we need to get down to business. Please take a seat gentleman." The agent had a stern demeanor to start with, now he almost looked angry. "I have been informed, Arnold will be bringing in another man to replace the one that Mr. Payne disposed of yesterday. We arranged for someone to happen onto the remains earlier today, so Arnold will see Wilbur's picture on the Evening News." While he spoke, he was busy handing out photos of criminals that might be potential replacements for the now deceased Wilbur Wilkerson. "We're not sure which of these men will be sent down here, but we think it will be one of these three. He always has a team paired up for certain jobs, so we know he will be replacing Mr. Wilkerson soon."

Once everyone had a chance to study the pictures, James Trout looked at Tony. "Buddy, I get to spend the night at your place. Wait 'til you see me in a turban, you already heard my accent. I'm meeting that asshole Arnold there in the morning. We are going to tell him I'm there by invitation from you. You're going to have some help tonight picking up a couple of the women you've been staking out. The story is that I'm there to choose between the two, but I will end up taking them both. All the negotiations over price will take place in the kitchen. The videos pick up better sound there than anywhere else in the house. I've had a chance to see some of the tapes, but I'm dying to see the way it's set up in your basement. I'm a tech junkie at heart. From what I hear, I'm going to feel like I died and went to heaven."

Officer Tom Smith had been sitting quietly listening to everything while he watched Anthony, hoping to get a better idea of what he was really like. The photos shown to him by Chet's family, of Tony outside Brenda's house and place of business, caused him to feel uneasy about Tony's intentions.

During the conversation that followed, Tom learned what time the State Patrol had dispatched someone to the Thomasville area to accidentally stumble upon Wilbur's body. They would show Wilbur's mug shot on the news asking for information from witnesses. The detective filled everyone in on Larry Joe Green, aka, Benjamin Orr, aka Gregory Wayne Johnson. Hearing how Anthony was connected with Ben Orr because of Ronald Arnold put all the pieces of the puzzle into place for Tom. Learning what part Larry Joe played, along with the information Brenda's family gathered about his actions, Tom realized how close his friend, Chet was to losing his daughter.

Listening to the information about Larry Joe, Anthony started to pale. Tom noticed. To Tom, it looked like more than passing concern when Brenda's name came up.

Anthony knew that the man he had known as Ben Orr had been grabbing women and children for Mr. Arnold's flesh trafficking for a long time before he came along. The government had been building this case against Ronald Arnold over a period of several years. Just about every government agency imaginable was involved in one way or another. They already had enough to put him away for arms trafficking. The supply route for his drug trade had been located and was currently under surveillance. The person providing weapons to his arms dealer was close to being run to ground. This meeting would help put the last nail in his coffin for his trade in human flesh.

After Arnold was behind bars his prostitution business would disappear on its own, without him being able to watch over it personally. No more trucks carrying electronics would be high jacked by Arnold's operatives either.

While Anthony listened to the conversation going on around him, he was trying to think of a way to get Brenda to speak to him. He feared for more than just her safety, he feared for her life. Tom had been thinking about how to protect her himself, ever since the meeting at her parent's house. Watching Anthony Payne's reaction to the information gave Tom an idea.

The meeting was breaking up. James Trout told Tony what time he would arrive at Tony's house before leaving through the back door. "Mr. Payne, hold up a minute." Tom called to Tony before he could follow his friend out. "I need to talk to you about something concerning my friend's daughter. From the pictures I saw, looks like you probably know Brenda Lou Green."

Tony didn't know what was to come next, he thought he was in for a major dressing down. He had no idea that Tom Smith had any connection to Brenda's dad. Now, he wondered what Chet had told him of the incident on Easter morning. Looking sheepish, with his head slightly hung down, he jammed his hands deep into his pockets, he swallowed hard before answering Tom. "Yes Sir, I've met her. Why do you ask?"

The conversation that followed wasn't at all what Anthony had been expecting. Tom told Tony everything Larry Joe had been doing to destroy

Brenda's finances, while building up a tidy nest egg for himself. He was delighted when Tom told him of her family's response to what was going on, along with Brenda's participation in it. Tony knew how she felt about her husband the night he met her. He also knew her husband had been trying to have her sold. Now Tony realized she not only had good sense but also a strong survival instinct along with all her other admirable qualities. Without hearing the details, Tony agreed to help Tom protect Brenda. He told Tom the condensed version of how Larry was trying to get rid of his wife for a profit.

Anthony did not tell Tom what happened after helping Brenda home that Easter weekend. He intentionally left out the part about meeting Chet. From what Tom told him, Brenda now knew her husband wasn't the man she had believed him to be. He was surprised to feel how much it lifted his spirits to know Brenda wanted out of her involvement with Ben.

After a lengthy conversation the plans were agreed upon. Tom had several things to do before meeting the two men at Tony's house that night. He headed home to talk to his wife, Liz, about sending Brenda Lou to New York. He was sure his wife's sister would welcome someone to help with her children for a couple months. Tom told Liz an abbreviated version of what was going on before they called her sister, Susan. Susan having heard part of the story agreed immediately to have Brenda stay as long as needed. Tom's next stop was Bloomfield. As expected, Chet thought the idea his friend came up with was wonderful. Chet had no idea it was to be the same man he had seen in his daughter's bed. Everything was set. The only thing left to be done was to pick Brenda up before Larry Joe got home.

By noon, Anthony had everything caught up connected to his own business. Being distracted by worry over Brenda's safety, he hadn't been paying enough attention to it lately. He was pleased when he noticed it had started growing so fast, with an added plus, it almost ran itself. He was glad he had a reliable person in his employ to oversee things for him. Since the night ahead looked like it would extend into the next morning, Tony decided to grab a couple hours sleep before the others showed up.

Tom picked Chet up at his house so the two of them could speak with Brenda. On the way from Bloomfield to Malden Chet called Brenda first, then Donna. They agreed to meet at the Mexican restaurant in order to have a room where they could speak without being overheard. To anyone watching it would appear to be just a friendly get together for lunch. Tom's wife, Liz was joining them to get the details in order for her to pass necessary information along to her sister.

Once everyone arrived, they placed their orders before discussing details of the hastily put together plan. Donna's husband, Mac, couldn't get away so Donna was there to pass on what he needed to know. They would be responsible for seeing Brenda's business ran smoothly in her absence. She would need the income when she returned. No one knew how long it would take to straighten out the mess Larry Joe had made of her finances.

"Well now, tall dark and handsome is going to help my big sister. If it weren't for the reason behind this it would be romantic." Donna shocked everyone with her remark.

"Donna Mae, that's enough of that." Chet chastised his daughter. He still hadn't said a word to anyone about what he witnessed, the secret he kept about Anthony and Brenda. "Your sister's life is in danger. It isn't something to joke about." Knowing what his daughter had confided to him, mixed with what he had seen, he didn't know where his own feelings were when it came to Anthony Payne. His thoughts about the man's character were conflicted. He was glad she would be leaving the state with Tom's sister-in-law instead of what was originally planned.

Even with her fair coloring, Brenda looked pale. She didn't like the idea of being thrust into the hands of Anthony Payne for protection. Not being able to remember what happened when she was with him was one thing, but she might be carrying his child and she had been dreaming about him. This was the first she had heard about him being one of the good guys in the whole mess that was going on. Appearing distracted she said, "Well, what I just heard explains why he has been lurking around my house. Is there any other way to go about this without involving Anthony?" Brenda knew she was grasping at straws, but it didn't hurt to ask.

Tom was the one to answer. He now explained facts that hadn't been disclosed up to this point. "Brenda Lou, I'm sorry to tell you this on top of what you have already found out about your husband. You know his real name isn't Larry Joe Green. The man has used at least two other aliases that we know of. While he was in prison his name was Gregory Wayne Johnson. We think that may be his real name. He has been trafficking in some pretty bad things like drugs and firearms. He's involved with prostitution rings, and he also has been kidnapping people to auction off to the highest bidder. It hasn't just been women either. He was in the human trafficking business long before you met him. What makes these arrangements so important to us is that he has tried to have you sold." There was a pause to let this sink in. While he watched her face he could tell when she accepted what she had just heard as true. In an attempt to lighten the news, he smiled before he continued. "Young lady it looks like you are about to have an all-expense paid vacation to the Big Apple. A private jet will come to whisk you away for a stay in beautiful Manhattan, New York."

Chet squeezed his daughter's hands in his while he watched for her reaction. His expression was grave giving away how concerned he was about all his daughter was going through. "Baby girl, Liz's sister lives there. You probably remember Susan. They have a grand place with room for you to stay as long as need be. You'll be safe, that's what's important to us all. You met Susan and Abe when they came here to visit. They are darn good people."

Brenda sat a moment absorbing all of the information coming at her so fast. It was overwhelming. She knew at this point things were already out of her control. She didn't have a choice if she wanted her life back. This would be the only way to fix the mess Larry Joe created. She didn't know how else to keep herself and her unborn child safe. "Yes Daddy, I remember them. I did Susan's hair once when she was here. I like them. It could be a lot worse. I don't know what else there is for me to do under the circumstances. Count me in." Looking up, she saw her sister sitting across from her batting her eyelashes and grinning. The stark fear Brenda had been feeling was replaced with a feeling of morbid humor at the whole situation. The two young women bust out laughing, leaving the men wondering about their temporary sanity. While Liz watched the exchange she thought of her own daughters and grinned.

Everyone knew what their job was and there wasn't much time to spare. The detective was to wait, in a building that shared the parking lot with Brenda's business, until she went into her shop. Once she was inside, he would slip out and slash her tires. Donna would meet Brenda at her beauty shop about an hour after her arrival to go over the financial arrangements needed for Donna and Mac to keep the business running in Brenda's absence. The way things were set up the other girls at the shop would see Brenda appear to be abducted by strangers shortly after Donna's departure.

Chapter 10

Someone was alternating between ringing the doorbell and pounding on the door. Anthony jumped out of bed, looking at the clock. He had overslept. It was already a quarter before six. "Hang on, I'm coming. Alright, alright, I'm coming." He was upset with himself for oversleeping. His disposition didn't improve when his foot made contact with a pile of dog crap, in the middle of his antique, wool, hand woven, Oriental rug. He didn't have time to stop to clean it up. Looking down at the mess, he decided it could have been worse. "At least it's not mushy, he filled up on the cat's food before he left that surprise for me." He continued on to the door, grimacing he made a mental note to take the dustpan and a whisk broom with him when he went back to the room.

He had to maneuver around Jumper on the way to the front door. "Damn dog, what did you do that for?" Jumper knew he was being scolded. The poor giant beast lowered its massive head, cutting sad eyes up at Tony, while it almost belly crawled toward him. It stopped about a foot in front of him putting its massive paws over its nose while it watched for his response. "Is this how you ask to be forgiven?" He almost laughed at how pathetic the dog looked lying there at his feet. As soon as the door opened Jumper shot out like a flash looking for a place to relieve himself. "I'm glad you didn't do that in there too." He said under his breath.

When Tony threw open the door there stood Agent James Trout. The man was muddy, bloody, and the clothes he was wearing were badly torn. He looked a major mess while grinning like the cat that ate the canary. "She's in the car. You wouldn't believe how those beauticians can fight." He was looking around Tony while he whispered. "Is it safe to bring her in?"

"Good grief man, you look like you got ran over by a Mack truck then drug down the road. You saying girls did that to you? Girls! Pull on in the garage. I have got to hear this." Reaching out, he took James' chin in his hand to turn his head back and forth while he inspected the damage. "If that nose isn't broken it will be a miracle. Go on, I'll look at it better under the light." He stood there with a disbelieving half grin, shaking his head as the other man got back into his vehicle.

Before he got to the back door he saw the cause of Jumper's accident. The stool that normally sat beside the door was turned over blocking the dog door exit. The cat's food bowl/water dish was lying in the floor. There was only a small amount of food that Jumper had missed lapping up, but the water was splashed halfway across the kitchen. The poor cat was hiding as far back as it could get on the top of the fridge. Jumper was trying to get back in through his door and looked to be tangled up in what was left of the stool. Tony started laughing at the sight. "Damn dog."

After moving the stool, Jumper came crawling in through the hole, then bounding across the room. Anthony opened the door for Agent Trout. "Be careful, there's water all over the floor. I don't need you having a broken leg on top of whatever else those poor little girls did to you."

"Yeah, and the horse you rode in on too. You should see the poor guy that helped me. They almost killed him, it's gonna cost extra for this job. Come on, give me a hand. That stuff I gave her has her pretty much knocked out." Knowing every move was being filmed, every word recorded, the two men were careful to make the abduction as realistic as possible for Mr. Arnold's benefit.

Brenda's hands were tied behind her back. There was a thick piece of tape over her mouth, with a blindfold over her eyes. Agent Trout had her to put on thick skin cream before he taped her mouth to help when it was time to remove it. The rope and blindfold were both loose enough for comfort. He had told her he wouldn't tie her ankles if she acted like she was totally out of it, allowing them to drag her through the house. On the way to Dexter, he had filled her in on what to expect before he gave her something to put her to sleep. Due to her pregnancy, they hadn't wanted to give her anything; but, they couldn't risk her life. It had to look real. They gave her a very mild sedative that had been suggested by their medical advisor.

After getting Brenda safely tucked away in a bedroom until she could be moved, the two men went out into the back yard, where they could speak freely. They discussed how they would handle the pickup of the other female, then the transport.

About halfway into setting the plans, Tony's phone rang. The voice came across loud, mixed with excitement. "Hold on. Slow down, Ben. You're running over your words." While Tony listened to the message that he was taping, he put it on speaker for Agent Trout to hear.

Without realizing where they were standing, Tony spoke in his normally loud phone voice. He had the phone on speaker to allow agent Trout to listen in. "Yeah Ben, we got her. That was what you wanted wasn't it? The buyer has business here in the states, so he will be doing his own pickup later tonight."

"What about my money?"

"Don't worry, Ben, you'll get your cut from Mr. Arnold. Since the buyer brought his own plane down here, the boys won't get their normal amount.

Ben sounded excited. "Who, Bud and Wilbur? They'll be pissed." He rushed on before Anthony could speak. "How much am I getting?"

Do you know where Wilbur is? We haven't seen him, but, Bud is going to be pissed. We had to use somebody else for the grab because of Wilbur. Yes, your cut will be better."

"Hey man, it's my ole lady. I should get most of it."

"What are you saying? Ben, you weren't straight with me. You told me she was married; but, you said she was married to someone else. It complicated things. We had to get her in broad daylight. Because of that, there were more chances of being caught. You should see the poor guys that grabbed her, those gals that work for her beat the hell out of them. We're all taking a bigger risk with her." Anthony waited a couple seconds before continuing. "Damn it. Why the hell did you lie you asshole?"

"That don't matter, it was my idea."

"Look man, to start with she's older than the buyer likes. Just be glad he is agreeing to take two this time, if the price is right. Shit, she told the boys she's pregnant. You know that's going to lower the price too. Why didn't you tell me she was pregnant? That was an important little detail to leave out." Anthony didn't have to pretend to sound disgusted with Ben, he was. "Oh, just forget it. It's too late now. Take it up with the boss your own self. The buyer is meeting him here to negotiate after we pick up the other one." Tony paused for a moment as an idea took form. Grinning at Trout he continued, "By the way Ben, I saw where they found two of the bodies you dumped. I never was straight on how many of them sold and how many you kept to play with. I know they turned up the body of one a while back. How many does that leave?"

"You talking about around here?"

"Yeah."

"I think all but about twenty sold. Getting rid of bodies around here ain't hard to do. I love these rivers and bayous. You should see the size of some of the catfish in the Mississippi River. Those things can eat somebody in a hurry." With a sick sounding laugh Ben Orr, aka Larry Joe Green, hung up. He started whistling again looking at the suitcase he had already started packing. He was preparing to flee the country.

"Anthony, you have enough to put that sick bastard away. Too bad we couldn't get you down here in time to save more of them." He whispered under his breath, so that it wouldn't be picked up on the recording.

Shutting off the phone, he shook his head in disgust. "I wish I'd known that Ben Orr was Larry Green a few months back. Oh well, like my grandmamma said, = don't cry over spilt milk, get your ass up and do something about taking care of the mess." He responded.

"Sounds like a smart woman, Tony."

"The greatest. Come on, we still have a lot to do." Anthony motioned for Trout to follow him to the garage. It was important they have things ready for what lay ahead. Walking away neither man noticed the window they were standing under was open just a crack.

***

Brenda was on the verge of hysteria. In her half coherent state, the voices coming through her partially opened bedroom window caused her to conjure up something totally different from what she heard in her still drugged, partial sleep. She had listened to the men discuss detailed descriptions of the women's bodies that had been found dumped. Unable to place where she was, or how she got there, panic took over. The inevitable fight/flight response kicked in causing her to struggle in an attempt to get away. The more she struggled the more the ropes tightened, burning into her wrists. Her feet became tangled in the covers binding her further. She began sobbing, causing her to choke. Never feeling so helpless in her life, unable to think clearly, she thought she was to be the next victim to die at her own husband's hands.

A sound made its way through her panicked mind. She stopped struggling long enough to listen. The blindfold had slipped enough for her to see the shaft of light from the window partially illuminate an area of the darkened room. Listening carefully while looking around the room as much as she could, she recognized the tune. Her grandmother used to sit on her bed when she was afraid, humming the very song she now heard. Wondering if she were dead already, she lay still listening.

A soft voice filled her head. "You're safe child, nobody gonna hurt you now." Brenda told herself instead of being dead, she was going mad when the side of the bed felt like a person sat down beside her. She was able to see enough to know no one was there. "They gonna take good care of you. You can't be getting so upset, it don't be good for the child in you." The female voice seemed to say.

The humming started back up along with the feeling that someone was sitting there rocking. Shortly, she felt someone gently stroking her hair in a very motherly way. It felt like the hand of an elderly woman. The humming stopped to be replaced with a crooning voice. "He's a good boy, that man is. What he did weren't right, him thinkin' you were married to another man, but he's a good man. He loves you. He don't know it yet, but he does. Thing is, it be drivin' him powerful knowin' you're carrying his son. He don't want to believe it yet, but he know it deep down."

There was a sound of a soft chuckle. "Girl, you done hit him hard, you did. Rest child. It all gonna work out fine. It gonna work out real fine." The soft humming picked back up. Now feeling like she was wrapped in a soft, silken, comforting cocoon, Brenda Lou relaxed slipping off into a deep restful sleep.

Chapter 11

Police Chief Tom Smith and his wife Liz, lived in the old Robins' house in downtown Dexter. The large two-story house had been the childhood home of Liz's mother before her. The house was about to be a beehive of activity as plans were being put into action. Liz Smith, Tom's wife, called her daughters to let them know what was about to happen. She knew they would jump in with both feet to help out. After speaking with her daughters, she called her dad. If Liz's sister Susan came to Missouri without Robert being told it would break his heart.

Susan and her husband were already in the air, flying to the Malden Airport, since they needed to bring the larger plane they wouldn't be able to land at Dexter. Abe and Susan Fields were bringing all five of their children with them. They had a set of twins age four, a set age three, and a baby. Liz's dad, Robert would pick them up in his van for the trip to Liz's house. From there he would take them to his farm. Along with all their children, Dr. Fields was bringing extra equipment with him in case it was needed, due to Brenda's pregnancy.

Liz's oldest daughter, Mari lived near Cape Girardeau with her husband Doug and daughters Issa and Rosie. The big old Robin's house was called home to Tom and Liz along with Liz's younger daughter Linda, her husband Joe, and their baby girl Casey.

Linda helped her mother get a room ready for Brenda. Brenda needed to be examined by the doctor before she went to Robert's farm. When Robert heard what was going on he insisted it would be safer for her to stay there than in town, while she waited to be flown to New York. He was afraid she might be spotted by Larry Joe. Tom agreed with his father-in-law's logic.

As quick as Liz's dad got off the phone with her, he called Henry and Eula. They were well into their eighties and had been as close as family to Robert for over sixty years. Their own granddaughter had been abducted in 2009. Everyone thought that Ronald Arnold had something to do with her abduction, but it could never be proven. Robert tried, without success, to help locate her while she was missing. Now, he wanted to let Henry know that he thought the man was about to be brought to justice. While on the phone with his friend, he told them that his daughter, Susan, would be flying in for a visit.

Earlier it was decided Anthony would pick up the woman in Aquilla, a little town in Stoddard County. Due to all the activity that would be taking place in the area that evening, a different course of action was set into play. A woman from Tallapoosa would be targeted for abduction instead. With Wilbur out of the picture, Anthony called Bud to help him with this staged abduction of the woman. It would look more realistic if Anthony used one of Mr. Arnold's men in this second abduction. The plan was for Bud to be detained at Anthony's house while the alleged buyer arrived to look over the merchandise. Ronald Arnold would show up while Brenda Lou was being inspected; then, Anthony would send Bud on his way so they could discuss the price. Anthony felt like a nervous juggler, knowing everything had to work perfectly.

Bud showed up right on time. Anthony checked in on Brenda to make sure she was still asleep before answering the door. "Come on in, I'll just be a minute." Anthony headed for the stairs when he saw a flash of fur streaking toward Bud. Dashing back just in time to catch the growling little creature before it attacked, Tony couldn't believe what he saw. "Shit! I've never seen it do that before. I thought it liked you. I still haven't found where it hides out." He swooped the dog up right before it reached the startled Bud.

"It's too small to be a dog. What the devil is it? Does it have a name?" Bud stared at the little creature before he smiled at its antics. He found himself amused at its furious behavior. He laughed aloud at the thought of such a tiny fur-ball protecting a territory. "Damn, it has a big attitude for such a tiny thing."

Anthony was trying to hold the dog like a football while it crawled up his chest to lick his face. He couldn't keep from laughing. "I haven't seen enough of it to even give it a name." He turned, walking to the bedroom where Brenda was. Opening the door, he put the dog down. Before he had the door closed he saw it leap onto the bed with her, curling up by her on a pillow.

When Tony started back to the stairs, Jumper came galloping into the room. The beast flopped down in front of Bud, rolling over so Bud would rub his stomach. "That's more like it. A true guard dog if ever I saw one." He laughed as he bent down to play with the enormous animal while Tony ran up the stairs.

Tony was back in a flash with a Western jacket and cowboy boots.

"Bud, if you're ready, let's get going."

"Which vehicle?"

"I think we can take the Bentley for this one. It's going to be dark enough, no one can see inside." He was afraid there might be some trace of Wilbur left in the Range Rover. "We'll go in style tonight."

Bud grinned as he pulled the door shut behind him. "Anthony my man, you won't hear any objections from me. Since I'm heading back to Chicago tomorrow in the Ford, it will be nice riding in style tonight."

Anthony headed the car south, leaving Dexter by AF Highway enroute to 25 Highway. They turned heading South on 25 until they passed through Malden. When they came to the Clarkton exit, they turned east toward Gideon. Anthony knew the woman they were to pick up would be at the little bar there. As they pulled into the parking lot, they could hear the music spilling out of the small building before they got out of the car. "How do you find these dives?" Bud asked, shaking his head in bewilderment.

"Dives? This may not look like much, but it's a real hot spot. They normally have a decent band. Believe it or not, some pretty high-class people hang out here." He opened the door to allow Bud to enter the smoked filled room ahead of him. Once inside he waved at the woman taking the money. "I've got this, I'm paying for my friend too." He handed the woman money for the cover charge plus a bit extra, getting a wink in return. She didn't take her eyes off of him until he caught up with Bud.

Selecting one of the few empty tables slightly away from the dance floor, Bud gave Tony an amused look. "Beer, country music, cowboy boots, and loose women, what more can a man ask for?"

They had a drink and danced a couple dances while watching for the woman Anthony had targeted to show up. Nodding to Bud, Anthony pointed her out. "Over there. That's her. She is just what our client ordered." Bud turned to look at their mark. She was around five foot six, slim built, shoulder length blond hair, fair skin, full breasted, and beautiful. The plunging neckline showed off her ample breasts, while the short denim skirt showcased her shapely legs. Tony waited ten minutes before ordering a drink for her.

The waitress that brought their drinks to the table tried to strike up a conversation with Bud. At first he ignored her. When ignoring her didn't seem to work, he told her he was interested. Smiling at her, he explained there was a little medical problem. He said he thought it was only fair for her to know he had AIDS before he had sex with her. She left in a hurry. Tony burst out laughing when she was out of ear shot.

Dropping the drug into the drink, he headed for the table where their victim sat. She asked him to have a seat, accepting the drink he offered, knowing what was to follow. He sat with her making small talk for a few minutes, waiting for the pill to kick in, before inviting her to join them as planned. A short while later no one noticed Bud and Anthony were half carrying the woman they were escorting out of the bar.

The men had their merchandise tucked into the back seat sleeping peacefully. When they pulled out of the lot, Bud turned to Anthony, "The boss had it right when he said you're a natural. I worked with that damn Ben several times, not once was it this easy."

"Ben acted on impulse too often. I plan and do my homework. That's why Arnold uses me. She shouldn't come around until we have her in the house trussed up like a Christmas turkey." Anthony answered, pointing to the woman in the backseat. They both laughed.

Just over thirty minutes later, they pulled into the garage at Anthony's house. After maneuvering the woman into a bedroom, they tied her hands together behind her back and tied her to the bed by attaching a rope from her ankle to the bedpost. With that done they went to the kitchen for a drink while waiting for the buyer to arrive. Bud got out the whiskey while Anthony made himself a weak screw driver. Halfway through his drink, Anthony excused himself to go check on Brenda. When he opened the bedroom door to check on her, a flash of fur flew by him heading straight for the doggie door.

The sight of her safe, laying there sleeping warmed his heart. Knowing she was bound, and the reasons behind it, disturbed him. Watching her sleep, his anger fueled a powerful hatred for those responsible for the dangers she could have faced. Anthony closed the door, going back toward the kitchen. A flash of fur caught his eye as the tiny dog flew back past him to scratch at the bedroom door. Going back, he opened the door allowing the small creature back into the room. "Well you little beast, you have good taste." He stood for a moment watching as the dog reclaimed its place, curling up on the pillow close to Brenda. She seemed to visibly relax when she felt it near once more. He quietly closed the door to return to the kitchen, wondering what it would be like to have her this close on a permanent basis. When he realized what he was thinking he wondered if he had lost his mind.

Right on time, a long black limo pulled around the circle drive in front of the house. Anthony was shocked when he opened the door to find a very old black man dressed as a chauffeur. The man was glaring at him. It was hard to guess just how old the man behind the wizened face was. Along with the kinky white hair, his shoulders were rather stooped with age; but, his eyes were sharp. If looks could kill, those aimed at Tony would have done the job. Hands holding the chauffer cap in front of the old man were covered in wrinkled, thin skin, but looked strong and steady. When the man continued to stand there glaring a hole through him, without speaking, Anthony began to feel ill at ease. "May I help you?"

Giving Anthony a pointed look of disgust, the man finally opened his mouth to spit out his response. "The sheik is here, sir." There was a sound of distain clearly emphasized on the word sir.

"Won't you have him come in? You can come in too, if you like." Anthony heard Bud approaching from the other room.

When the old man started walking back to the car, out of ear shot, Bud chuckled. "There for a minute I wondered if he spoke English or if he was here to gun you down."

"Me too." Anthony gave a shudder at the thought. "You get to take him to the kitchen for refreshments. Lucky you. I have to take the sheik to inspect the merchandise."

"I could trade places." Bud raised an eyebrow, nodding toward the bedroom where the younger of the two women was being held. "It wouldn't bother me a bit to get a closer look at that one."

"Not on your life. You know the rules." Tony grinned at Bud before turning to the door at the sound of two men approaching. "Can you try to keep Jumper in there with you?" He nodded toward the kitchen. "If not, I'll have to put him in the garage and we can listen to him howl."

"No problem. At least I'll have him to talk to while I entertain Mr. Personality." Bud turned toward the kitchen, patting his leg so Jumper would follow. "Tell him to come on in, I'll see what you have in the fridge."

Everything was running like clockwork; the only disconcerting thing was the limo driver. Anthony had never seen so much as even a picture of him. He wondered who the old man was. Under the circumstances he wasn't in any position to ask his friend. He couldn't risk doing or saying anything to give away the real identity of the sheik.

While the chauffer was in the kitchen with Bud, Anthony took Agent Trout, disguised as the sheik, to have a look at the women. Both women appeared to be asleep. Taking their time, the two men played it up big for the surveillance cameras. Anthony had a feeling that Bud would slip away into the basement, so he could watch the inspection. If there was something that didn't look right to him, Bud would report back to Ronald Arnold immediately.

Anthony kept a close watch on the time to insure they would be back in the kitchen when Mr. Arnold arrived to discuss the price. He wasn't surprised when the boss showed up a few minutes earlier than scheduled.

With Mr. Arnold seated in the kitchen, Bud gave him a brief rundown on how well Anthony handled the abduction of the woman at the little bar near Gideon. After listening to the report, Mr. Arnold told Bud Lowe he needed him to drive him back to Chicago. Anthony entered the room in time to hear part of the conversation. A muscle twitched in Bud's jaw, along with a slight reddening of his face indicated Bud's displeasure. His facial expression didn't change and if Tony hadn't known him so well he wouldn't have known how angry he really was.

Anthony wondered what had happened to cause the change in plans. He didn't have to wonder long. "Mr. Lowe, when we leave here, I need you to help with a problem that has been brought to my attention. We will be going to Malden before we leave for Chicago in the morning. I think it's time to speak to Mr. Orr."

Bud perked up. There could only be one reason for them to go down to Malden. "Boss, it will be my pleasure to take you to see our friend."

To say that Bud was disillusioned by Ben's behavior was an understatement. He wasn't upset that the women had been raped or the fact that they had been so badly mutilated. It was simply because Ben's actions jeopardized their operations. When the women's bodies started turning up, Bud wanted to get rid of Ben immediately. He wondered why the boss hadn't done something sooner. "Want me to hang around for a while or are you going to call when you're ready to go?" Bud was so happy with the news, it was hard for him to stay still.

"If you can't stop fidgeting, go run off some of that energy. You're making me nervous. I'll call you when I'm done here." Dismissing Bud with a wave of his hand, Mr. Arnold turned to Agent Trout. "Are you ready to discuss price?"

"The one woman is too old. Not only is she too old; but, it is apparent she is with child. I don't really want her. Still, I will consider taking her off your hands if the price is not much. She could be used for a wet nurse. I will give you full price for the other if you take off the price for delivery." Agent Trout kept a straight face while speaking with an accent that sounded like the real thing. Mr. Arnold believed he was who he claimed to be. With the elderly black man standing at rigid attention it was obvious there was a bulge that could only be from a hidden weapon. The stoic demeanor bespoke of his willingness to use the weapon if necessary. Ronald Arnold got the impression the old man would shoot him without question, all the sheik had to do was give the word.

Choosing his words carefully, Mr. Arnold came back with a countered offer. "I will agree to deduct the pickup and delivery charges because you are handling that yourself. As for the older woman, I will have to have half price, that's only fair. My boys went to a lot of trouble and expense to get her. With her you're getting two for the price of one. American children bring a pretty penny in your country." He watched the sheik's face for any sign of acceptance while he spoke. He wasn't able to read any change in the bearded man's expression.

After what seemed an eternity, Agent Trout, the sheik, came back with a counter offer. "Either the woman or the baby or both could die during the birth. When I made this trip, it was with the belief there would be two prime specimens. I will give you one quarter the normal price for the older one, minus the other charges on the good one. Take it or leave it."

Mr. Arnold stood, extending a hand. Agent Trout merely nodded, ignoring the offered hand. Trying hard not to show the anger he felt at the snub, Ronald Arnold dropped his hand to the table top. "Well then, it looks like we have a deal, do you have the cash with you?"

Agent Trout motioned for his driver to bring the briefcase containing the cash. After the old man counted it out into stacks on the table, the phony sheik turned to Anthony. "Are you ready to prepare the women for transport? My plane is waiting." Turning back toward Mr. Arnold, he dismissed him. "We are finished with our business now. When the time comes, I will contact you." Addressing Anthony, Agent Trout made a waving motion of dismissal toward Mr. Arnold. "Come, let us get started."

Ronald Arnold was not used to being treated as if he were an underling. He was furious as he made the call for Bud to come back for him.

Chapter 12

While things were falling into place in Dexter, Missouri, Dr. and Mrs. Abe Fields were nearing the Malden Airbase. Their flight was smooth, weather was good, and the children were behaving. Susan enjoyed being able to remain up front with Abe while he flew the plane.

***

Bud was driving Mr. Arnold to meet with Ben Orr. There was a smile on Bud's face, as he pictured how he wanted the meeting to go. Ronald Arnold sat quietly in the backseat, still seething with anger at the way he was treated.

Ben wasn't idle while waiting for his boss to bring his cut of the payoff. As soon as he received the call telling him his wife had been abducted, he finished gathering everything he wanted to take with him. He had already cleaned out the safe deposit box, booked his flight, and then packed the clothes he planned to take. Everything was stowed in the trunk of the car, waiting for him. After having double checked all his plans, he turned on his CD of Island tunes. He was having a hard time staying busy while waiting for the cash from the sale of his wife.

He danced around the house singing a song he made up, as he went along. The lyrics were about leaving his life behind to find his own paradise. His mind jumped from one thing to another before settling on memories.

Fingering the belt he wore elicited a sadistic smile along with a feeling of sexual excitement. This belt was made of human skin with cross sections of human bone as adornments. In place of leather, the metal buckle was covered by tiny strands of braided human hair. He thought to himself, how well the hours he spent reading about the Nazi experiments had paid off for him. The memory he enjoyed most was of the first woman he took on his own, just to play with before he discarded her. He wore the belt he had tanned by himself, in memory of her. Without the contributions from her, there would not have been a belt.

The weather in Memphis, TN. was warm with a slight feel of rain in the air. Gregory Wayne Johnson had only been to the city twice before. This time he was going to be paid for making the trip. His boss sent him to Memphis to pick up a few women and children as merchandise for an auction to be held in California. The room booked for him was better than any he had ever stayed in. On his way to the mall to shop for a couple good suits, groceries, and other necessities, he thought about the plush accommodations and the pocket full of cash his employer had provided, along with a fancy red convertible.

Greg had just turned twenty-one. He wasn't very tall, so having a baby face and blond hair, he could pass for sixteen. Wheeling into the parking lot, he saw the most beautiful woman he had ever seen in his life getting out of a brand-new Cadillac. Parking beside her car, he followed her into a shop trying to speak to her.

He approached the woman with a smile on his face. When he said hello she turned, ignoring him. She acted like he wasn't there as she walked away. While he stood there watching her, she walked up to another man and started flirting. They left together, arm in arm speaking in hushed tones while laughing.

Humiliated, he came to the decision that she would regret treating him the way she did. He went back to his car, picked the tool he wanted to use, and squatted between the two vehicles. It only took a minute to puncture her tire.

Greg was sitting in the parking lot with the top down speaking on his cell phone when he was interrupted. "Excuse me young man. I hate to bother you; I seem to have a flat tire. Would you be an angel and call someone to come fix it for me?"

"Mr. Arnold, I'll have to call you back tomorrow to make the final arrangements. It looks like I have a damsel in distress that needs my help." He watched the woman smiling down at him while he ended the conversation with his boss. After waiting almost forty-five minutes, his patience was about to pay off. "How about if I see if I can do something about that? Let me get my gloves on." He reached into the glove compartment and nodded in the direction of her car.

When he got out he rounded the car to where the woman squatted near the flat tire. He watched her brush her long flaxen hair away from her face as she rose. She turned to him with her hand extended. "I don't know how to thank you. My name is Gretchen."

Greg grinned. His eyes danced with pleasure. He knew he would love showing her just how she would thank him. He extended his gloved hand to shake. "My name is Ben, Ben Orr. It's nice to meet you. Now, let's have a look see Ma'am." He squatted in front of the tire, running his hand over the rounded surface "Looks like you may have a small puncture. Do you have a spare in the trunk?" The serious expression on his youthful face looked genuine. "If you do, I have time to change this. I can have it done faster than you could get anybody to come out."

"Are you sure you wouldn't mind?" Greg loved the pleading look on her beautiful face. "I can pay you for doing it."

"Don't worry about it. I don't want money. This will be my pleasure. If you can open the trunk, we can get started." He made a bowing motion, sweeping his arm outward for her to lead the way. As she turned toward the back of her car, Greg pulled the syringe from his pocket. "Gretchen, that's a lovely name. There is a city just across the Mississippi from my home town of New Orleans named Gretna. It will be easy to remember your name." As he ended the sentence he sunk the needle into her skin while pushing the plunger to administer a fast-acting sedative.

She felt a slight sting. Turning, her eyes grew wide with shock when she saw the gun in his hand. "What–" Before she could say anything else Greg interrupted her.

"Don't scream. I can shoot you and be gone before anyone knows what happened. Be a good girl, get in." He used the barrel of his Glock to motion for her to get into the passenger seat of his car.

By the time Greg found an inexpensive looking motel in a shabby part of the city, Gretchen was out cold. Parking the car near the end row of rooms, he looked around to make sure there wasn't anyone parked near him. After registering under yet another fictitious name, he carried her into the room he requested near the alley. He tied her to the bed, gagging her to be certain she wouldn't scream when she woke up. While he waited for her to awaken, he cut her clothing off to have a better look at her. A few minutes later she started waking up to the feel of his hands on her naked flesh.

"Gretchen, it's time to show you what you can do to pay me back for my kindness." He ran his hands over her struggling body. "You must work out a lot. Your body is perfect. I like a small waist with nice rounded hips. Your breasts could be a little larger, but they're nice anyway. I personally prefer a full busted woman. Your breasts looked larger with that padded bra you were wearing." He was enjoying himself, laughing he continued. "How tall are you? Since you can't answer I'll guess." Striking a studious pose, tapping the fingers of one hand on his chin, he seemed to be seeking an answer to the question he had asked. "About 5 foot 10, I would say. Isn't this fun?" The anger in her eyes turned to tears when he viciously pinched her nipples. "Good girl, I thought that might get a response out of you. This is your fault you know." His eyes blazed with anger while he spat out his words. "You shouldn't have acted like I was invisible when I said hello. It hurt my feelings."

Greg continued to talk while he undressed. He told her, in detail, everything he intended to do to her before he brutally raped and sodomized her. When he finished he took a long hot shower. Gretchen was still tied to the bed. She was too traumatized to attempt an escape. Greg still had her gagged. The only sound coming from her was an occasional small whimper. While he was getting dressed he continued to speak. "I worked up an appetite. When I get back we can play some more." Before leaving the room he gave her an IV injection of 6 milligrams of Versed to knock her out. He knew he wouldn't be gone more than twenty minutes; but, he didn't want to risk her getting away. There were still several things he intended to do to her before he finished.

It only took fifteen minutes for him to find a fast-food drive thru, get a burger meal and get back to the room. When Gretchen started coming out from under the sedative, Greg was sitting across the room eating what was left of his French fries. Grinning, he spoke with his mouth full of food.

"Looks like my sleeping beauty decided to wake up." He took a swig of soda before he got up, belched, then crossed the room to a bag he had sitting on the table. "Now we are going to have some real fun. You may not like it but I will." Greg prepared another injection while singing an old Beatle's tune. Coming to the chorus of It's Been a Hard Day's Night, he withdrew a bone handled fillet knife from the bag. The knife was honed razor sharp. "Look what I have here." He held up the knife, then a syringe for Gretchen to see. The terror reflected in her eyes thrilled him. He smiled a lopsided grin. "They call this the amnesia drug. It's Propofol, you can experience this game with me. When we are finished playing you won't remember a thing." The room was silent for a short time while he prepared the syringe and drew up the drug.

"Hope you like my singing." Greg held the now struggling woman down, picking up the chorus where he left off. He pinned her down more securely with a knee to her abdomen. Grasping her arm he smiled at her while he administered the injection. "It helps to know people that have access to this stuff." Resting the edge of the knife beside her breast, he started cutting long strips of flesh from her sides. "I'll turn this into something I can keep to remember you by." Laughing, he held up the first bloody strip for her to see.

***

Bud Lowe pulled the car into the driveway at Larry Joe and Brenda Lou Green's home. Before the car came to a complete stop Ben, aka Larry Joe Green, was standing in the open doorway.

Ronald Arnold was disgusted by the look of satisfied glee on Ben's face. Angered further he hissed: "That bastard has caused too much trouble for me. He's never worried about being a liability to the safety of the business. After I speak to him, I'll take a drive. How long will it take for you to wrap things up here after I leave?"

Bud couldn't believe his good fortune. He disliked Ben Orr, and had for some time. "Give me forty-five minutes, no, make it a full hour." He was whistling as he exited the car. It had been a while since he had been given the opportunity to do a job like this. Looking forward to having fun while disposing of someone that he considered a threat to the organization, he was already thinking ahead. "Boss, this will be my pleasure."

"Come on in." Ben was waving the two men into the house. "I made coffee. There is beer in the fridge; or, I can fix you something else if you want it."

The smile on Mr. Arnold's face didn't quite make it to his eyes. "Don't bother. It's getting late, this won't take that long."

Ben looked from Mr. Arnold to Bud. Bud was grinning from ear to ear. "I'll take a beer. I can get it while you talk to the boss." Bud headed toward the kitchen as the other two men sat down in the living room.

Ben was sitting on the edge of his chair with his hands clasped in front of him. The eager look on his face bespoke of anticipation at the large amount of money he expected to come his way. "What's my cut? She brought plenty, didn't she?" It was hard for him to sit still. He was almost drooling at the thought.

Mr. Arnold allowed a rather bemused smirk to cross his face as he watched Ben. "There are a couple of things we need to discuss Mr. Orr." He watched Ben deflate in front of him. "You know I told you not to draw attention to yourself. You quit your job. That would have been fine if you had gone to work somewhere else, which you haven't. Bodies have started turning up in this area, again. You knew the reason I put you into a different branch of the business was because you got sloppy with the women before. Remember a few months back? They found that fourteen-year-old with your signature all over her. It's bad enough when they are adults; but, that has put some major heat on the operation. Then these last two women, you didn't even try hard to hide them."

He gave Ben a moment for that to sink in before he continued. Ben no longer had that overly eager anticipatory look about him. He sank as far back into the cushion of the chair as he could get, concern showing on his face. "Your wife didn't bring much. Why did you try to pass your wife off as someone else? The cost to secure her was higher than normal, almost as much as what she brought. I have never seen a man so eager to sell his own child before. You should have told me she was pregnant before I met with the buyer. I don't like surprises, Mr. Orr."

Bud was standing just inside the kitchen door, leaning against the wall. He was listening, enjoying every word. Without seeing Ben, he knew that the man had to be getting the idea that his time on earth was fast approaching an end.

"Boss, the way I set it up, no one could suspect me. I will be the grieving husband. Everyone will feel sorry for me. Not only will my wife be missing, but my unborn child too. No one will think I had anything to do with it. It's perfect." Ben's voice had taken on a pleading quality. When Mr. Arnold didn't speak, Ben dropped his voice while focusing his eyes on the floor separating the two of them. When he spoke, it was barely above a whisper. "How much was my cut after expenses?"

"Considering her age, the fact she is pregnant, the cost of the two men obtaining her, all the other expenses factored in, including medical expenses, your cut is $1,500.00. You better be glad it's that much." Disgust mixed with anger oozed through the slowly spoken words. "I'll be back shortly, I have another errand to run. Bud will settle up with you." Ben started to object, but seeing the look on his boss's face thought better of it.

Ronald Arnold stood. Before turning toward the door, he leaned in close to Ben's ear. Dropping his voice, he spoke so softly Ben could hardly hear him. "The person I have to answer to is very upset about the things you have been up to." Standing, he placed a hand on each side of Ben's face causing him to look up into his own. "Do you understand now?"

"Mr. Arnold, I left the keys in the ignition." Bud had his hands behind his back as he entered the room with a smirky grin on his face. "I should be finished up here by the time you get back." Mr. Arnold was closing the door as Bud crossed the room toward Ben.

Ben was pale, eyes as large as saucers, knowing whatever Bud had on his mind wasn't a cash payment. He had seen that look before. In an attempt not to show fear, he looked Bud in the eye when he spoke. "Have a seat so we can get down to business. I need to be in Bloomfield before long. If I don't go play the grief-stricken husband, it will look suspicious." Attempting to keep his voice from cracking, he couldn't hide the stark terror in his eyes.

Bud brought his hands around in front of him. In his right hand was a small pocketknife he started using to clean his fingernails as he seated himself across from Ben. "Don't worry, you'll get what you have coming." He smiled at the thought of what he was about to do. Seeing the smile, Ben started to relax a little.

"What if the kid is a boy? Wouldn't it bother you if your son was put in a brothel, in say Turkey or someplace like that, when he reached the age of eight or nine, maybe younger even?" Bud was watching Ben for any reaction to his words. Not seeing any response, he continued. "I'm going to tell you something no living soul knows about me." He could tell he had Ben's attention from the sudden look of pure fear that crossed the man's face. "I had this uncle that I thought hung the moon. Until I got to be around ten, I never knew the things he was doing to me were wrong. He always told me that it was our secret. He claimed it was a special way to show me how much he loved me." Bud was speaking very slowly in a distinct monotone, while watching Ben's face. "I started to figure things out. I wasn't very old when he started making fun of me. There isn't any way to describe the hurt it caused. One night when he passed out, I'd had enough. I tied him up and gagged him before I woke him up. When he saw what I was about to do he sobered up real fast. That night after I showed him how it felt to have a baseball bat shoved up his ass, I castrated him, slowly. Your kid will love you that much when it gets older." The sound of Bud's laughter, along with the expression on his face, caused Ben to know exactly what to expect. "Hey man look at that, you just wet yourself." He said waving a hand toward Ben's crotch, to indicate the spreading area of darker material.

Next door to the Green's home a man appeared to be working on a vehicle in the garage. The man had the hood up on the car, but the ear buds he was wearing weren't for listening to music. Brenda had allowed her home to be bugged when she was informed of her husband's plans. Every word spoken anywhere in the house was being recorded by Special Agent Allen Burner. Agent Burner had been instructed not to act until he had enough to put Arnold away. He had to wait until his principal came back to the house to make a move.

At his farm near Bernie, Robert Moffield was getting ready for company. The cabin out back that was once used to house farm hands, was now a guest cottage. Robert's friends from St. Louis had already arrived. As soon as Robert called them to let them know what was about to happen, Eula and Henry dropped everything to make sure they were there. Eula had already unpacked and started cleaning. She wanted the main house to be ready for the arrival of the others. Robert was anxiously awaiting the call to pick up the group flying into the Malden Airbase while Eula bustled around. Eula was already planning the feast for the following day.

Liz Smith met her husband Tom, at the door. "I just spoke to Lou. They will be out at Dad's tomorrow if Larry Joe isn't there. I was careful about what

I said, just in case. I invited the whole family, so it wouldn't sound funny if anybody was listening in." She looked sheepishly at Tom. He had told her the importance of keeping things quiet. She knew that there were too many people becoming involved. "I hope you're not too upset with me."

Tom loved Liz as much as any man could hope to love a woman. He had loved her most of his life. They finally got together, after the death of her husband. "We have to be careful, you know that. It's alright though. I've been keeping Chet up to date on everything. He still isn't too happy about Brenda Lou being at Mr. Payne's, but he knows it's necessary. For some reason, he doesn't feel comfortable about Anthony Payne. I've never seen him act this way about anybody before. I guess it's because of the situation his daughter is in. God only knows how I'd act if it were me in his shoes." The strain of worry showed on Tom's face. Chet Perkins was one of the best men Tom knew. He felt fortunate to have him as a friend. The thought of something like this happening so close to home bothered Tom more than he was willing to admit.

Liz's daughter, Linda came down the stairs carrying two-year-old Casey. "Hey Tom, I think we have everything ready for company. Grandpapa Bob says we can expect a surprise. I talked to him a few minutes ago to make sure he was ready to pick up Susan and her brood." She laughed as Casey poked at her eyes, ears, and nose, naming each as she acted it out. "Wonder what he has up his sleeve."

"Knowing Robert, there is no telling." Tom said with a sigh. "I just hope he isn't doing something he shouldn't. We can't afford to lose Arnold this late into it. They have been working on the case for years. I'm glad they brought us in on it."

"I don't think you have to worry. We will all keep our mouths shut and our eyes open." She stopped talking long enough to kiss her daughter's forehead. "Mom is in the kitchen. You just missed Joe; he ran to the store for Mom. He should be back soon. Mari and Doug are bringing the kids down to the farm tomorrow. Sandy told me her and Mark will be there too. I can't wait to get my hands on their baby." Linda started dancing around with her little girl. "We're going to have a party." She sang.

While Linda chattered away, Tom watched his step-daughter with a look of pure love and adoration. "I still can't believe how blessed I am. I never dreamed I'd be lucky enough to have a family like this. If I died tomorrow, I could honestly say all my wishes on this earth had been fulfilled." He held out his arms to take the curly haired wiggling toddler when she reached her chubby little arms out for him. "I wonder who she took her eyes after; they are as blue as the sky." He mused, running a hand over the child's silky blonde curls. In turn, she reached up pulling the hat off his head so she could run both her tiny fingers through his hair. Casey loved her granddad, Tom; she made a game out of almost everything he did. He started laughing, holding the little girl out in front of him. "Phew. Young lady, I think a skunk crawled up in your diaper and died there."

"I was just on my way to change her. She loves sitting on her potty chair; but, she hasn't figured out what it's for yet. I will be so glad when she does." When Linda took the child from Tom, Casey squealed her displeasure. She wasn't ready to go back to her mother. She wanted to continue to play with Tom. "Is everything set with Chet and Lou? They have to be worried out of their minds over Brenda Lou. I have never seen Lou as closed mouth as she is now. I'm worried about her too." She hesitated at the look of concern on Tom's face. "We have things ready here."

"So far, so good. I'd better go see if Liz needs help with anything." Looking from Linda to Casey and back he chuckled. "Looks like she doesn't think she needs to take time out of what she's doing to use that potty. It's more a play thing to her. When you get her changed, I'll take her again." He reached out ruffling the curly head before heading for the kitchen.

***

Agent Trout was helping Anthony move the women from the house into the waiting limo. Brenda Lou was the first to be taken from the house. Neither man had thought it a necessity to pull the car door closed as they intended to go right back inside for the other woman. They were halfway supporting the still groggy Brenda while leading her to the limo. Going down the steps, they almost had their legs knocked out from under them as a flash of fur ran between their legs. Brenda was barely in the vehicle before the small creature jumped onto her lap, refusing to move. Looking up at the driver, Anthony noticed he was smiling at the dog's antics.

When the men came back out with the second women the old man was sitting in the seat beside Brenda, petting the little fur ball. After securing the other woman in the seat, Agent Trout was rewarded with a vicious growl when he reached for the dog. "Buddy, you want to get this little beast out so we can take off?" Trout gave a nervous laugh. "I thought it liked me until now."

"It does like you; but, it looks like it likes her more. Let it ride with her. It seems to have a soothing effect on her. I'll pick it up later." Anthony went back to lock up his house before getting into the Bentley. He noticed the old man chatting amicably with the man posing as the sheik; but, every time he looked at Anthony it was anything but friendly. The man barely spoke two words to him, then only when it was necessary.

Initially the plans had been for Anthony to follow the limo until it was out of sight where he could transfer Brenda into his vehicle for the ride to Tom and Liz's house. Before pulling away from the house, Special Agent Trout let him know that the plans had changed once again. They were going directly to Officer Smith's home. He wondered if Trout had waited to tell him due to the bugs in his house. Tony would have to wait to find out what brought about the changes. The way the limo driver acted toward him he was afraid something had gone wrong.

"You think it's safe? What if Arnold or one of his goons sees us?" Anthony asked.

"Not to worry. We have all of them accounted for." Trout replied.

When the limo slowed to a stop, Trout jumped out. Holding his garment up to avoid tripping over it, he told Anthony to pull around behind the house to park. Anthony did as he was asked, going in through the back door. Once inside he followed the Chief of Police into the living room. Unnoticed, he watched in surprise. The women were hugging the old black man, welcoming him like part of the family.

Anthony cleared his throat to let them know he was there. When little Casey saw him, she released the old man's leg to make a bee-line toward him. Stopping just short of where Anthony stood, the toddler checked out the size of his shoes before slowly looking up to his face. Casey's eyes were wide with wonder while she checked Anthony over. Satisfied with what she saw, Casey gave him a smile that warmed his heart.

James Trout stuck his head in the door. "Want to help get the lady in here. She's still a little out of it and the little pooch won't let me touch her." He stepped on into the room. When he saw Casey, he squatted down in front of her. At first he thought she was going to cry when she let out a loud squeal. Instead of crying she grabbed his beard with both hands and started laughing while she twined her tiny fingers in the fake beard. He picked her up, hugging her close while she started trying to pull the turban off of his head. When his glasses went flying, he decided it was time to turn her over to Tom, to the amusement of everyone watching. "We better get this done. We need to get gone before we draw too much attention." He patted Casey's curls again before heading toward the door with Anthony following close behind.

Agent Trout opened the car door for Anthony to take the dog so they could get Brenda into the house. Brenda was still slightly groggy. When she looked up to see Anthony bending down toward her, she reached for him with a welcome smile on her face. The little dog started to back away. It seemed to understand what was going on. It changed direction, going to Anthony. With the dog under one arm, Anthony's other arm supported Brenda Lou. Agent

Trout took her free arm in case she wasn't as alert as she appeared while they made their way into the house.

When Brenda was safely tucked into the bedroom upstairs, James Trout turned to Anthony. "We'll pick you up when we get the other lady on the plane. We should be back before midnight easy. You need to stay here until I get back. I'll be going to the farm with them tonight. We'll have a chance to talk more tomorrow." The fake chauffeur was already out the door heading for the limo when Agent Trout turned to leave. "By the way, I think the lady really likes you." The whispered remark was followed by a wink.

Chapter 13

Robert pulled the van up beside the main office at the Malden Airbase to wait for the plane to land. The location had been changed several times in the space of a couple hours due to unspecified circumstances. For a while it looked like the plane might be routed to Poplar Bluff or Cape Girardeau. The airstrip at Dexter was too short to accommodate the jet they were flying in on. Word came from Agent Allen Burner that it was finally confirmed safe to land at Malden. It was a much more convenient location for everyone involved.

When he saw the plane making the approach for a landing, Robert got out of the van to go wait in the office. It had been a few months since he had seen his daughter and her family. He had turned the operation of his insurance business over to her when he decided to retire to Southeast Missouri. Even with their busy schedule Susan and her husband managed to fly down fairly often. He was tickled they would be staying with him for a couple days. He intended to go back with them when they returned to New York.

Seeing the plane come to a complete stop, he got back into the van, driving out onto the tarmac just as the door started to open. The first one out was the nanny carrying the youngest child with the oldest set of twins closely following. Behind her was Susan with the second set of twins. Both sets of twins made a beeline to their grandpapa Bob to see what treats he had for them. Being surrounded by his family, he thought to himself that this was all anyone could ask for.

"Don't trample your grandpapa." Susan good-naturedly scolded her brood as she hugged her dad. "Your daddy will be here in a minute; we need to get all of you settled in the van. No candy, we're going to see Aunt Liz and Uncle Tom. I don't want her thinking you're a bunch of heathens. Stay clean and mind your manners." She started ushering the children into the vehicle while the nanny fastened the baby into the car-seat.

Worn out from the trip, the baby was sleeping peacefully in the car-seat. The nanny spoke to Susan. "I can help you and Dr. Fields with the luggage. Your dad wants to visit with the children." Not having seen the way Robert still worked around the farm, she was afraid for the octogenarian to try to lift the suitcases.

Susan looked into the van where Robert was already deeply engrossed in some sort of game with the four older children. Seeing the look on the nanny's face, she reassured her. "You don't have to worry about Dad, but, he does look busy. If you are alright with it, I would be happy to have your help loading things. My husband brought more equipment than I realized."

Abe was amused to find his wife in the passenger seat when he started to get into the van. The inside light came on when he opened the door to the driver's side, illuminating the inside where his father-in-law was busy playing with the children. "Your dad is an overgrown child himself." The affection he felt for Robert showed on his face as well as in his voice. "You'll never know how glad I am that they called me that day he had the heart attack. If it hadn't been for that, I may never have met you. I owe him so much."

Susan reached over gently patting her husband's arm as they pulled out onto the street. "I still can't believe how fortunate I am that things happened the way they did. To think, I never knew he was my father until I almost lost him. Now, my big brave handsome love, are you prepared for the madhouse when we get to Liz's?" Susan teased.

"You know flattery will get you anything you want, I like it." Abe teased back.

The sedative Brenda took earlier wore off completely before Robert arrived with Dr. Fields' family. As badly as Anthony wanted to speak to her, he was hesitant. He had no idea how she would react to him, or more precisely, what happened the night he met her. He was afraid if he didn't speak to her now he wouldn't get another chance before she left.

Anthony excused himself from the group downstairs, gathering his courage, he headed for the room where Brenda was resting.

The light tapping on the door brought Brenda up into a sitting position. She was apprehensive. "Come in." As the door opened, Anthony cautiously entered the room. The surprised look on Brenda's face didn't go unnoticed. Her voice showed no hint of anything being out of the ordinary. "Tony, I'm surprised to see you. Can you tell me what's going on? I'm not exactly sure what all has happened since the agent took me to your house. Things are kind of mixed up and foggy."

How could he explain the feeling of admiration he felt for the way she was handling a situation like this? His feelings for her grew stronger every time he saw her. She was in his thoughts constantly. Careful to keep his emotions hidden, he cleared his throat before speaking. "Cotton–I–sorry. Brenda Lou, I wanted to see how you're doing. May I come in? I'd like to speak to you about a few things." He stood, expectantly waiting, hoping she would hear what he came to say.

Hesitating for only a second, she looked at his face before she gave her answer. "Yes, by all means. Come in and have a seat." She gestured to the chair against the wall near the bed. "I'm glad you came. There are too many things I can't remember, I hope you'll be able to give me some answers." Brenda looked pleadingly at Anthony.

His voice soft, he sat on the edge of the chair with his hands clasped in front of him, head down because he couldn't look her in the eye. "Brenda Lou, I want to apologize. I'm ashamed of myself, for the way things turned out the night I met you. I'm not going to say I'm sorry for what happened, just for how it happened." He looked up then, hoping to gauge her reaction to his words. "I'm very glad I met you. I wish it had happened under different circumstances."

Sitting quietly for a moment, Brenda thought about what she just heard. "I'm not sure about too much that happened that night. We had sex, right?"

She hurried on, not giving him a chance to answer until she said what she wanted to say. "Tony, I need to know what happened, all of it, for my peace of mind." There was such a tormented, beseeching expression on her face that it hurt Anthony to see it.

Taking a moment to compose his thoughts, Anthony chose which questions to answer first before he started. "I'm sure you know part of what has been going on by now. I'm working with a Federal Task Force. They have been gathering evidence against a man for several years. He has managed to slip away every time they thought they had him. Ronald Arnold is a very bad man. We are about to put him away. You know now that the man you married was working for him when you two got together."

Anthony gave Brenda time to digest what he said before continuing. "There isn't time for me to be anything but blunt. For a long time your husband was the one procuring the women and children from this area for Mr. Arnold's flesh trade. By now you know your husband isn't who he claimed to be.

The FBI found out about some things in my background. There are a lot of reasons I started working with them. I worked my way into the organization to take over your husband's position for several reasons, mainly to stop the deaths and sale, of these human beings. Your husband has tortured, murdered, sold-" he paused to consider how much information to pass on to Brenda. "Suffice to say, your husband isn't your husband. His name isn't Larry Joe Green. He is a monster."

Holding up her hand, palm out to stop Anthony, she asked "You mean I'm not legally married to him?" It was hard to tell what she was feeling. He couldn't read her facial expression.

Grinning briefly, Anthony answered. "No, Larry Joe Green doesn't exist. You can't be married to someone that doesn't exist." He became serious again. "The night we were together turned out differently than it was supposed to. Ben, or Larry Joe, whatever you want to call him, tried to have you sold. The information he gave me about you was false. The only true information I had was your name and description. At first I intended to pick you up to be taken straight to the farm. The farm is a safe place where the abducted females are kept, instead of becoming victims of the human trafficking operation. There isn't time to go into detail about all of that now. After talking to you, I decided to just take you back to your house and leave. I was under the impression you were married to some dumb schmuck that would be afraid to try selling you a second time. My mistake. The thing is, if that had been the case, you would have figured out the man was a creep then divorced him." He paused briefly, shaking his head. "I had no idea they were one in the same."

Anthony studied Brenda's face for a long moment. Silently he prayed she would understand when he told her how he felt. "When I took you to your house, I honestly intended to see you safely inside then leave. That changed when you kissed me. I never sleep with the women I take. Never. Please believe me. For some reason–this is hard to explain." He paused briefly to gain control of his emotions. "I don't know what came over me. Brenda Lou, you are so different from any woman I ever met. I didn't rape you. I swear I didn't. You have to believe me. I'm not trying to justify my behavior. I knew better. I just–, I didn't have sex with you intentionally. I don't know what came over me. My desire for you was so powerful that I wasn't thinking at all. You don't know how bad I feel about myself for letting it happen. It's not something I can take back or change. The thing is, –well–, if circumstances were different, –.What I'm trying to say is that I care for you."

Brenda had looked away. She did not want him to see her cry. When she turned back, there were still tears in her eyes.

"When this is all settled I hope–" He hesitated, trying to find the right words. "I need to tell you about my background, who I really am. There isn't time for all of that now. Maybe when you come back I can see you again. Please don't hate me."

She was shaking her head in disbelief. "Right now, I don't know what to think or believe. Hate you? No, I don't hate you. I think about you often.

We'll see what happens later. At least now I'm not completely ignorant about that night. You know I'm expecting. At this point I don't know if the baby is Larry Joe's-well-the man who claimed to be Larry Joe, or if you are the father. All of this is too confusing right now."

The look on Anthony's face was priceless. For it to be put into words for the first time was a shock. He sat there dazed, his mouth open in surprise. "It might be my son, for real?" He regained his composure. "Before you consider abortion or anything-. Brenda Lou, please don't abort the baby. I know-" He looked pleadingly at her. "Girl we need more time to talk. We really need to talk. Don't make any decisions about this child until we can have a chance to talk, please." Unable to speak, Brenda nodded in agreement. She thought abortion was murder but she didn't tell him that. She was afraid to admit how much she really wanted the child. How could she explain this baby was an answer to a prayer, no matter who fathered it?

Anthony wanted to stay with her. Hearing voices coming close, he decided it would be best for him to leave the room. He looked back streaming down the face that had become so dear to him. He told himself he would leave the dog with her tonight to give him a reason to see her tomorrow. He descended the stairs.

Before Anthony had a chance to speak with Tom Smith, his phone rang.

Chapter 14

The farm was beautiful. Anthony loved the countryside in that area of Missouri. Situated between Winona and Eminence, it was so far out that you would have a hard time finding it if you didn't know exactly where you were going. He had visited Peck Ranch in the past few months just to look at the Elk they brought in to repopulate the area. It amazed him to find so much open land left anywhere. There were reports that some of the Elk had wandered off already. He couldn't help but wonder how long it would be before the Elk wandered onto the ranch he was headed to. He had heard that fences weren't made that could stop the majestic creatures.

On his visit in April, he stopped to watch the newborn calves playing in the pasture he was now nearing. It surprised him to see how curious the calves were. They came up to the fence to examine him while he watched them. If the calves didn't take off when he got too close, a cow would head toward him. He stopped again briefly to see how much they had grown since his last visit. Again, it appeared the cows took turns babysitting the calves.

He felt at peace standing there. A gentle breeze carried the earthy smell of nature with it. Closing his eyes he inhaled deeply enjoying the clean fresh air. He had never been around open pastures before moving to Missouri. Anthony loved the smell and the sounds that surrounded him here. Cows were grazing contentedly across the expanse of green while a group of calves raced and played. He was surprised to find himself thinking how good it would be for his son to experience all of this one day.

Anthony marveled at how the showers made everything look and smell so fresh and clean. If it kept raining there wouldn't be a threat of drought this year. The year before, the drought was so bad throughout the heartland that a lot of people had wells go dry losing most of their crops. People with gardens even had a hard time keeping them from drying up.

Before moving to Missouri, he had never really stopped to consider what kind of impact something like that had on the entire country.

Anthony's thoughts turned to his brother. He knew Raymond would have loved all of this. Had it not been for Raymond's death, Anthony may never have seen this part of the country. He wished once again that his brother could be with him now.

Since moving to Missouri, he learned more about animals than he ever thought possible before. When he was really young he would visit his great grandfather's farm in the Deep South; but, he couldn't remember much about it now. He remembered chasing chickens and trying to milk cows. At the time, his goal was learning to squirt milk into the kittens' mouths the way his great grandfather did. It brought a smile to his face every time he remembered watching those eager kittens at milking time.

Lost in thought, Anthony drove along the winding lane that led to the main house. Halfway to the house, he spotted one of the women using a chainsaw on a downed tree. These women constantly amazed him. There wasn't much that they couldn't handle. Some were taking classes at a nearby college outreach program while others were learning to sew or cook. They had a beautiful garden that was beginning to produce all kinds of food stuffs. Jewel was teaching a few to preserve food the old fashioned way. He remembered how hot the kitchen was while they used the pressure canners and hot water baths to can the different foods they put into the jars. Some of the women had shown talent in arranging the different flowers grown there, into strikingly beautiful floral arrangements.

It was nearing the end of April. They awoke to a heavy frost. He was glad they heard the freeze warnings in time to cover the tender plants they recently put in the ground. After being at the freezing mark that night, it had turned out to be a beautiful warm day.

These women understood what lengths Anthony went to in order to insure both their present safety and their futures. They knew he was instrumental in starting the programs for them to learn a trade while keeping them safe. A couple of the ladies at the farm made Anthony a quilt to show their gratitude. Because it had his name embroidered on it, he was allowed to accept it. At first he was afraid he would have to turn it down. Jewel informed him she had already checked to make sure he wouldn't be breaking any rules, before she allowed them to present it to him. He was glad to hear he would be able to accept the quilt. He didn't want to hurt their feelings, and he had never seen one quite so beautiful. It was hard for him to imagine how much work had gone into the intricate, hand-sewn pattern.

On a day like this, Anthony wished it had been possible to drive the convertible. With the ruts, pot-holes and other obstacles on the roadways farther into the farm, he was glad he had the Range Rover. Nearing the house, he veered off the lane toward two women fishing the pond closest to the house. Driving across the rocky expanse, he stopped a few feet from the levee. The women were fly fishing from the bank. Seeing him they motioned him closer. He drove up the incline, stopping on the flat ridge of the levee that ran around the top.

"Having any luck?" he asked as he approached.

In response one of the women held up a good size bass. "We have at least a dozen of these already." She hurriedly put the fish back into the bucket to help net another fish the other woman was reeling in. "You gonna stay for dinner? We're having fresh fish, hush puppies, fried potatoes, Cole slaw, and ice tea. It's those little potatoes we canned with the skins on. We roll them in the fish coating before they are fried in the fish grease. In my opinion they are better than hush puppies."

It was hard to believe the majority of these women could look like models, work like men and cuss like sailors. Most of them hadn't had a fair chance at life from the time they were born.

"That sounds too good to pass up. If I get finished up in time, I can help clean those." Anthony joked good naturedly. The women knew he was a city boy without a clue, when it came to cleaning fish. They had seen him attempt it before.

After checking out the catch, Anthony went on to the office in the main house. Passing the chicken coop, he noticed the Cornish Cross chicks were already big enough to go into the freezer. When he was there in April they were just tiny chicks. He was glad he wasn't going to have to help kill, gut, or pluck the birds. His stomach rolled at the thought. That the chore didn't seem to bother most of the women surprised him.

Jewel came out onto the porch when she saw Anthony pull up. "Hi Tony. Come on up. What brings you all the way out here?" She yelled out when he was close enough to hear.

Anthony waved, speaking as he approached the tall, stout built, middle aged woman wearing blue jean shorts with a denim shirt hanging open over a tee shirt. "Looks like you're canning something purple." He grinned, motioning toward her hands which were indeed covered with a purplish red-colored juice from berries she had been working up. "Do I get a sample when you're finished?" He hugged her before they went into the house.

"I think I can spare a few jars, maybe even a cobbler. Now, what brings you all the way out here on a day like this? I know it's not because you can't live without me so tell me what's going on. It's not time for your scheduled visit."

A stern worried look crossed Anthony's face. "Let's go into the office for a minute if you can." He looked at her hands.

"You've had a long drive. Grab a glass of tea on your way in. I'll be there as soon as I wash." She had been straining berries; but after seeing the serious look on Anthony's face, she would have dropped whatever she was in the middle of to find out what was wrong.

As soon as Jewel closed the office door behind her Anthony spoke. "Are you still armed?"

She raised her shirt tail to show him the gun she kept strapped to her waist. "What's going on? This can't be good."

"They found the body of a man that used to work for Ronald Arnold. They suspected it was him last night; but, it took some time to make a positive identification. He had been butchered after he was beaten and sodomized. It happened in his home. When they finished they moved his body. From the looks of it, he was alive for most if not all of the torture. He was still alive when whoever killed him started cutting him up." He didn't tell Jewel that someone had used a wooden colander bat to sodomize the man or that the man's genitals were found shoved deep in his throat. "It appeared that his fingernails and toenails were pulled off before his fingers and toes were severed. After cutting each part off, he was cauterized. By keeping him from bleeding out, the person that did this kept the victim alive longer."

Jewel appeared deep in thought before she spoke. "Do you think Arnold was afraid the man was going to talk?"

"At this point no one knows. It may have something to do with Ben's recent activities. Ben's the victim's name. He was Arnold's man from Malden. I don't think he knows anything about this place; but, we can't be too careful."

She motioned for Anthony to follow her to the other side of the room. When Jewel pulled the bookcase away from the wall, he saw a doorway he hadn't known existed. The door opened revealing a wall covered in monitors showing several different areas of the ranch. He hadn't known there were cameras spread throughout the property. "I can watch everything that goes on here." She waved at the monitors. "When no one is in here, everything is caught on film. All we have to do is push a button to lock the buildings down tight. Somebody might be able to get over the fence." She pointed to one of the frames on the monitor. "It has an electric charge running through it when we are on lockdown, but it can be shorted out. There are alarms to warn us if that happens."

"I'm impressed. I figured there was more security than I knew about; but, I had no idea this existed." Anthony paused a moment, deep in thought. "I can't help feeling responsible for all these young women."

"If there appears to be any danger, we sound a siren to alert the girls to head for the main house. There is a safe room that can't be accessed unless you know how, even if they could find it." Heading for the door she motioned for Anthony to follow. "There are enough supplies in that room to safely stay for two weeks if need be." Jewel paused in thought before adding. "I'll put somebody on the cameras full time until this is over."

"That would be a good idea for now." He agreed. "How are you set for defense?"

"Don't worry, Tony. Me and the other workers are armed to the teeth. There are a couple of the girls giving marksmanship lessons to the ones that want to learn. I think we are good." Jewell hugged him.

"Thanks for the concern."

Amy and Ruth were approaching the house with a full stringer of fish when Anthony and Jewel stepped out onto the wide front porch. "I'll get Jenkins to clean those while you two get cleaned up. Check the schedule for tomorrow, there may be changes. We will have a meeting after supper tonight." Jewel was speaking as they descended the stairs.

When the girls were out of sight Anthony brought up the main reason for coming. "We're sending a couple women FBI agents out here to help in case there is trouble. No one is to know that they aren't witnesses. Everyone agreed that, at this point, there isn't any reason to assume there is a threat. This is strictly a precaution. These women will fit right in. They are trained in just about everything; but, they will be armed anyway."

Jewel showed Anthony the safe room. "Just let me know who to watch for. I'd hate to sic some of these gals on the wrong people." She laughed. Anthony knew what she was referring to, some of them had grown up having to scratch and claw their way to stay alive.

He filled her in on the new evidence they had on the case, explaining that they were getting ready to make the arrests even though one of Ronald Arnold's main players was now confirmed dead.

"It couldn't have happened to a more deserving sadist." Jewel said. She took him by the arm, leading him down a hallway to a small bedroom. "I know something about that dead guy. He was a real sadist. There is something I want to show you."

They were able to look into the room through a small window in the upper part of the door. "This is where we keep someone if they get sick or injured. We can keep an eye on them without disturbing them. We have had this girl in here for the last ten days. The poor little thing is on suicide watch."

Anthony couldn't remember ever seeing Jewell look so sad. He looked into the room. There was a female siting on the floor with her legs crossed, clasping her hands in front of her. She looked about twelve years old. Her thick red hair was plated into a long braid hanging down her back. Anthony thought she looked like a porcelain doll, her skin was so fair. She continued to rock back and forth while looking straight ahead.

"What's wrong with her?" He asked

"The way she's sitting you can't see the other side of her face. With the long sleeves and pants you can't see anything of her body either." Jewel looked like she would cry. She shook her head before continuing. "The authorities down in Kennett found her stark-naked standing in the middle of an intersection down there. She was badly injured, dazed, half dead really. They said she didn't appear to be aware of where, or even who, she was. The officer that tried to get her out of the road said she looked catatonic. When they got her to the hospital, they put her in a cubical with nurses staying right there by her. She never made a sound until the doctor tried to examine her. When he touched her she started screaming and wouldn't stop until she was sedated."

Jewel wiped at a tear, took a deep breath, continued. "She had been brutally raped. They said the poor little thing won't ever be able to have a child of her own now. There are bruises all over her body. She must have fought like a tiger, the way her fingernails were broken down into the quick and her knuckles were bruised. She had some broken fingers too. The rope burns on her wrists and ankles are healing, but there will be permanent scaring. Her ear was half ripped off. They were able to fix the ear. Some bones in her face were shattered, but they will mend pretty well. She has a tic-tac-toe game cut into her back. There will be scaring where the strips of flesh were cut out for the game board. Lord, Tony if you saw her stomach–. Looks like he tried to gut her."

"Ben was responsible?" An expression of pure hatred crossed his face. Anthony had to make an effort to keep his voice level. "How old is she?"

"She's a tiny thing, with the baggy sweatshirt she looks even smaller. She doesn't look it but she is twenty. A straight A college student. They had a female shrink work with her for a couple weeks before she would say a word. The woman finally pieced together what happened to the poor girl. He left her laying halfway in a ditch. Left her for dead. After she saw the picture of that monster she went off the deep end again." Jewel took a deep breath, let out a sigh, then after regaining her composure again she spoke. "Yes, Ben did this to her. You need to see her for yourself. Speak quietly, move slowly, and be gentle."

Anthony opened the door to the room. Jewel turned to look at him. The anguish she felt was apparent. She entered with Anthony following quietly behind her. Once inside with the door closed, Jewel spoke to the young women. "Misty, honey there is somebody here to see you. He is one of the good guys. He won't hurt you sweetie. Don't be afraid, I'm not leaving you alone with him. I'll stay right here. He's okay, I promise."

Misty stopped rocking to look up at Anthony. When she saw him she looked scared to death. She put her head back down, shut her eyes tight, and started rocking again. Anthony walked around where he could see the other side of her face. Seeing the damage, he drew in a sharp breath.

The young woman kept her eyes tightly shut as she started quietly chanting. "Me oh my, I just want to die. He stuck the needle in my thigh. Me oh my, I cry, I cry, I cry. He slammed the lid, I could not see the sky. Me oh my, I just want to die. I told him to stop, he hit me in the eye. Me oh my, I cry, I cry, I cry. I can't get loose, no matter how I try. Me oh my, I just want to die." The chanting continued, telling the horrifying tale of unimaginable things she endured while still conscious.

"How long has she been like this?" Anthony swallowed, trying hard to maintain the contents of his stomach. Some of the things he heard caused him to come close to retching. He took a deep breath to calm his anger before he had asked.

"She is getting better. I was afraid she would start screaming again when she saw you. She started that chanting a couple days ago. The psychiatrist said it is a defense mechanism to help her work through what happened to her. It will take time. It may take a long time. She's stronger than she looks. According to the psychiatrist, this is a good thing."

Jewel took another deep breath, releasing it slowly. "They aren't sure how long she was in the muddy ditch water. There were a couple teenage boys out hunting saw her first. There was a camo print blanket thrown over her. At first they thought there was some kind of animal moving around under it in the weeds. They went to investigate. When they pulled the blanket back, they thought they found a dead person, the way she was cut open. She was laying there with her eyes wide open. I guess, from what they told, when they started yelling she jumped up and took off running with her intestines pretty much hanging out. They called it in when they got to a phone. Nobody believed the boys until she was found the next day."

They closed the door softly behind them, leaving Misty sitting the way they found her. "She was in the hospital for a long time. Nobody thought she had a chance one to live. The authorities brought her here when they figured out who was responsible for doing this. They didn't know his name but knew it was the same one killing those women. So, they were afraid if he, Ben Orr, found out she was still alive he might try to finish her off." Jewel explained. "What it boils down to is, they didn't know where else to put the poor girl."

Having seen the security cameras and the way the ranch was guarded made Anthony feel less anxious about the safety of the women he had sent there. He enjoyed his visit. There was lively conversation with the other women while they ate the freshly caught fish, filling him in on their newest accomplishments and dreams for the future. After the meal he made the long drive back to Dexter. Jewel sent jams, jellies, fresh produce, and the cobbler she had promised him. The aroma made the trip very enjoyable. Since it was dusk, he kept a close watch for deer feeding along the roadside while he thought about Brenda.

Chapter 15

Chet hadn't seen his eldest daughter for two months. He was worried about her wellbeing. Donna paid her dad a visit earlier that day to invite her parents to dinner. Donna was showing already, which made him wonder all the more about how Brenda looked and how her pregnancy was affecting her both physically and emotionally.

Donna and Mac took Chet and Lou out to dinner to celebrate finding out the sex of their unborn child. They were so happy it was hard for them to keep from blurting out the news that they were going to have a girl. Donna wanted to wait until the right moment to see her parent's reaction to the news. During the meal, they filled them in on how Brenda's shop was doing in her absence. As the evening progressed, Chet became more agitated. "Larry Joe is dead. I don't understand why they think Brenda Lou has to stay gone now. They wouldn't even let her go to his funeral."

"Daddy, she didn't want to go to the funeral. Are you forgetting what that no good sorry excuse of a man tried to do to her? The feds, or somebody, are still trying to sort that out. If it hadn't been for Anthony and his friend, Larry Joe would have sold her or worse, maybe even killed her. She stays in touch. Now, –we came here to celebrate that you and mom are going to have a granddaughter. Tonight isn't about Brenda Lou's mess, it's about my baby. The baby Mac and I are going to have. You know, your first grandchild." Donna was getting upset. Mac was patting her leg, trying to sooth her. He didn't blame his wife for feeling the way she did. He knew Chet and Lou were worried about Brenda; but, it seemed that was all they ever wanted to talk about. He couldn't understand why Chet was so obsessed about Brenda

Lou's wellbeing now that Larry Joe was dead and Brenda was tucked safely away in hiding.

Chet abruptly rose from his chair, almost knocking it over. He slammed both hands down on the table, glaring at his daughter. "How did I raise such a self-centered bitch?" He was almost shouting, causing the other patrons to look over at their table. "What if it had been you instead of your sister? You would expect us to worry about you if the tables were turned." He grabbed Lou by the arm yanking her out of her chair. "Come on Lou. We're leaving!" His face was red with anger as he practically dragged his wife toward the door. Donna was shocked. She burst into tears looking after them as they went out the door.

Mac drew his wife into an embrace as she burst into tears. He was holding her tight, brushing his hand down her hair trying to absorb some of the hurt he knew she felt at her father's harsh words. "Shush, shush, baby you know he didn't mean what he said. He is just really upset. Your daddy loves you. I don't know what's eating at him. I've never seen him like this before." He was gently rocking his wife in his arms. "You go on to the car, sweetheart. I'll settle up so we can go home. Alright?" He held her out away from him enough to see her face. "Will that be alright, or do you want me to go pay and come back to the table for you? Donna Mae, baby, I love you."

She nodded as she stood. Holding back her sobs she looked pale and shaken. It was obvious that she was hurt to the core. "Let me have the keys, I'll meet you at the car." Her answer came out in a whisper. Head down so she didn't have to look at the pity on the faces of the people sitting near them, she took the keys and made her way to the door. Once inside the car, the dam broke. Donna Mae wept as she had not wept since she was a small child.

Mac wasn't just confused, he was angry. He couldn't believe how his father-in-law acted. He had known Chet since before he and Donna met, never before had he seen this side of him. He knew Chet had been acting funny ever since he found out what Larry was up to. What he couldn't understand was that, with Larry Joe out of the way, Chet shouldn't be still worrying about Brenda's safety. He was starting to wonder if Chet was showing effects of Alzheimer or some other brain disorder.

Chet had Mac to make a new will after the incident when he passed out at Brenda's. Even thou his health checked out fine he was still acting odd. Mac was starting to wonder if Chet had something to do with Larry's death due to the way he was acting every time the subject came up. If it hadn't been for client privilege, Mac would have asked his wife about some of the accounts her dad mentioned in his will. Chet had several bank accounts, but refused to tell him the amounts in any of his accounts, just who would get which if something were to happen to him and Lou. Mac's thoughts raced on about Chet's behavior tonight. Maybe they found something wrong with him that he neglected to tell his family. Maybe he really did have Larry Joe disposed of if he knew he didn't have long to live.

***

Lou didn't say a word to Chet until they were back inside their own home. She sat on her side of the car, looking straight ahead all the way home. Once inside the house, with the door shut behind them, Chet started toward the bedroom when Lou stopped him. "What in God's name got into you tonight? How could you say something like that to your own daughter? You were loud enough for the whole town to hear. Everyone in the place was staring at you. What is the matter with you Chet Perkins?" Standing with her hands on her hips, she was almost yelling at her husband. Lou had never raised her voice to him in all the years they had been married, but he had never displayed such cruel actions toward one of their children before. She was livid with rage. "You're supposed to be a preacher, a man of God. How could you say something like that to anyone, let alone your own flesh and blood, and in public to boot? What's got into you? Tell me right now and it better be good."

"Nothing. Woman, it's nothing you need to know about. Leave me alone." He turned his back on her, going into the bedroom he closed the door behind him.

Lou was dumbfounded. Her husband hadn't treated her in this manner since they came to live in Bloomfield. There was a time early in their marriage that she had almost divorced him because he acted like he was acting now. They had made it through the rough time, moved to Missouri, and Chet had gone into the seminary. Without the stress he had in the city, he calmed down. After he became a minister, their marriage flourished.

Chet had always made a couple missionary trips a year by himself, but took the family on a cruise each year. While he was gone, Lou took the children on trips with her. After the children were older, he let Lou choose more of the destinations for his mission work. He enjoyed that the two of them could travel more without the children. She would keep busy sight-seeing, shopping, or whatever she wanted to do while he was tied up with business, it was enjoyable for them both. Over dinner, she would tell him stories about her day while they laughed, holding hands like teenagers.

Lou sat on the sofa going over the scene at the restaurant in her mind. After a while, she calmed down enough to call Donna Mae. Chet leaned against the door listening to make sure his wife wasn't following him, before he locked the door to the bedroom.

When he was certain Lou wasn't going to try to come in, Chet took his gun down from the shelf. It had been years since he had used the gun so he checked it over, cleaned it, and made sure it was loaded before returning it to its hiding place. He hadn't told a soul about what he witnessed in Brenda's bedroom. He needed to find out more about Anthony Payne before he could be sure what he was going to do about him. The whole situation had gotten out of hand. It was bad enough to find out that his son-in-law worked for Ronald Arnold. Now he wasn't sure where Payne's loyalties lay. Whatever it took to ensure the safety of his family, he was willing to do. Chet had never kept secrets from Lou until this happened. He knew he couldn't talk to his wife about his plans this time.

Chet moved his family to Bloomfield when his children were very young to keep them safe. The city was a better place to make the kind of money he wanted to make, but with that came the danger also. This kind of thing wasn't supposed to happen to his family. He made necessary changes for their safety then, now he would take the steps to insure it didn't happen again.

***

Brenda was torn between wanting to see Anthony one minute and never wanting to lay eyes on him again the next. She sat on the edge of her bed debating with herself whether she should call him about the flowers she received earlier along with a very sweet card, or not. The note said he would be happy when he could see her again, asking how she was. She cried when she read the part asking how she was getting along with the little dog. When he didn't show up to pick up the dog she took it with her to Manhattan.

Brenda found New York an amazing place to visit. She was seeing sights she never dreamed she would see in her lifetime. Her weight had gone down with the diet combined with an exercise program the doctor put her on. She found out the baby was a boy the same day she felt it move. There was just the slightest bit of a bulge to indicate there was a child growing inside her. She was aglow with good health. While the Fields' family was treating her like one of their own, she was learning a lot of useful parenting tips from them. She loved the children. They were all very well-behaved, and the dog loved the children as much as the children loved the dog. It was amazing how it stood for them dressing it up in doll clothes and painting its toenails without so much as a whimper.

Brenda was told of Larry Joe's death. She was also informed his death caused the investigation to change course drastically, lengthening the time it would take to pull the case together. Since finding out her husband wasn't who she thought he was, then that he was planning to do away with her, she wasn't grieving his death. It made her angry with herself as much as at him, because she didn't see him for what he was until recently.

Picking up the small dog, Brenda hugged it against her. She held it in her lap petting it while it looked up expectantly. "Well Rascal, he wasn't Larry Joe so I wasn't ever really married. He wasn't the man he pretended to be so I never really had him. You can't mourn the loss of someone that never existed. Isn't that a hoot? Between you and me, I don't think this baby is his anyway. I've really got myself in a mess! Is my daddy going to be happy or what? Thank goodness I still have my business. Or, at least, I think it's still mine."

When Brenda first left southeast Missouri, she thought she would be home by now. Her dad called to check on her every couple days. It didn't seem to make him very happy to learn that she didn't know any more about the progress than he did. When it all started, no one in her family thought Larry Joe was capable of the kind of things they were finding out he did. Her family was keeping it all from Brenda. They weren't sure how much she found out before she left. The authorities refused to give her any details. All she knew for sure was that someone had killed Larry Joe, or whoever he really was.

Shopping for baby clothes and maternity clothes was getting old. Brenda had started taking foreign language lessons, exercise classes for expectant mothers, and nutrition classes. Her days were filled but she missed Missouri, missed her family. She was glad she had the little dog to talk to, and took pleasure in watching it play with the children.

Susan took a couple days off from work to spend with her dad before he had to return home. Every time Robert visited he would accompany her to work, for at least part of the time he was in New York. He still enjoyed having an involvement in the company he started. His youngest daughter was doing a good job running the business for him. He couldn't be more proud of her than he already was. There were a couple of charities he backed that he wanted to continue to work with himself. His attorney had instructions for Susan as to what needed to be done after he passed on.

The women were still sitting at the breakfast table talking and listening to what was going on in the other room. Susan had been informing Brenda of bits and pieces of information about the investigation when she heard anything. Abe was at work, Robert had finished his meal, then taken the children into the living room to play. Susan and Brenda could hear the peals of laughter from the kitchen. The nanny had been given the day off because Susan knew the woman would be upset with the complete disregard for the schedule she attempted to keep the children on. There was also a rule pertaining to roughhousing that totally went out the window, because Robert was the biggest duck in the puddle when it came to that. This way they were all happy.

"How are you feeling today Brenda Lou?" Susan noticed how homesick Brenda recently started acting. "I'm glad to see there isn't any more morning sickness, bet you are too."

Brenda had been lost in thought. When Susan spoke she looked up pleadingly at her. She knew now was the perfect time to ask. "I feel great. There is one thing though, maybe you could help with."

Susan had a feeling she already knew what Brenda was going to ask. "Sure, I'll be glad to if I can. Has this got something to do with Dad returning home?" She leaned forward grinning at Brenda. "Maybe you want to ride along? Tell me if I'm wrong." She teased. Not waiting for an answer, she continued. "I put a call into Tom Smith yesterday telling him how miserable you are. It was good of them to let me warn you about what all they found out. I can't promise they will let you go for a visit yet; but, as homesick as you look–." She hesitated briefly "I should hear something by this evening. I was going to wait before saying anything until I was positive what their answer would be."

"When this all started I had no idea it would be this long. It never entered my mind that the man I thought I was married to could have been involved in so much. Organized crime, even the sound of it–. He was a monster. Pure evil. How could I have lived with him that long and not seen any of it? You and your husband, your whole family, are so kind. I don't want you to think I don't appreciate it. I just wish all this was over so I could get back home."

"I can't claim to understand what you must be going through. Pregnancy is hard enough without everything else. I was lucky enough to have a wonderful husband to support me while I carried my babies. I wish there were more we could do for you. You realize you have a home here as long as you need it."

Susan reached over clasping Brenda's hand in her own. Tears started slowly making their way down Brenda's face. "You don't know how much all this means to me."

Wanting to lighten the mood, Susan smiled, got up from her chair, and went around the table to hug Brenda. "How about we take the kids to Central Park? I think Dad will enjoy it as much as the little ones. We'll get them tired enough so you and I can have lunch out, get a massage, manicure, pedicure, the works. I will keep my phone on in case we get that call while we're out. Does that sound alright with you?" When she saw a look of hesitation on Brenda's face, she continued. "Dad will want some time with the kids without me hovering. I tend to cramp his style when I make him stop teaching them to make those weird funny faces and things like that. He thinks I'm a party pooper." She laughed causing Brenda to grin at the thought.

"Sounds great, I'm going nuts sitting around. I've already outfitted the entire nursery. The baby has more clothes than it can possibly ever wear. There isn't anything at all I can think of that is left to shop for. Count me in. Let's go, Central Park sounds interesting. It will only take a minute for me to be ready, then I'll help you with the kids."

After Central Park, while Susan dropped off her father and children at the apartment for their nap, the expected call came in. She was glad she was in her bedroom with the door closed. This way, Brenda couldn't hear any of the conversation. Chief of Police Tom Smith, her brother-in-law from Dexter, was calling her back.

He told her he was able to get permission for Brenda to come home over the weekend; but, she had to be under constant surveillance. The man they were after appeared to have slipped out of the state. They thought they knew where he was, but they weren't positive. "It may not be safe for Brenda to stay here very long. Anthony will be picking her up. He will take her where she wanted to go and be able to protect her if the need arose. That is the only way they will agree to Brenda Lou coming back even for a little while." He said.

Tom also told Susan they just found out Ronald Arnold wasn't the main person in the operation. "It looks like there is someone Arnold answers to. No one has a clue to his identity. One of the agents told me Arnold is only over part of the territory, it looks like it's divided up into four sections. This whole thing is bigger than I dreamed. Brenda Lou may know more than she realizes she does. It's really important that no one finds out where she is. She could be in a lot more danger than it looked like at first. Damn!"

Susan was shocked. "Do you think she should stay here then? This is turning out to be worse than the Mafia crap you see in the movies. It doesn't sound safe for her to go home at all."

"I hope they aren't trying to use her to draw the others out. Susan, that family is the salt of the earth. I know Chet is half mad with worry and he doesn't know hardly any of this. We aren't allowed to tell him. You can't tell Brenda Lou any of this. I doubt I should be telling you."

"I have an idea." Tom knew his sister-in-law. He could almost see the wheels turning in her mind as he listened to the brief silence. "Here's what we will do. I have people in the company that work with insurance fraud. They are great at disguises. Since I'm taking Brenda Lou to get a makeover in a few minutes anyway, it can be a real makeover. Her own family won't recognize her when we're done."

Tom cleared his throat. "How are you going to get her to go along with that without telling her why?" He sounded as skeptical.

Chuckling, Susan answered. "How long did it take for me to come up with an answer to the problem? Leave everything to me. I have to run. There is a lot to be done before we take off tomorrow. Give everybody my love."

"Whatever you say." Tom answered. He was amused. He laughed at the thought of what she might come up with. He knew how capable Susan was at accomplishing whatever she set her mind to. "Hold on. Before you hang up, are you and the kids coming?"

"I hadn't planned on it, but–yes. It will help with Brenda Lou's cover. We will see you tomorrow night. Bye" With that there was a click and the line went dead.

On the way to the salon, Susan convinced Brenda to alter her appearance. She said it would be fun to play a trick on her family while keeping everyone else unaware of her presence. Susan told her it would enable her to check up on her salon without her employees knowing who she was. Brenda knew her body looked totally different, what with the exercises, taking off the weight and her baby bump starting to show. She thought about it, deciding it would be fun.

While the women plotted they giggled like teenagers, laughing out loud at times. They picked up a couple of stylish outfits for Brenda that she would never have normally considered wearing, before getting in shape. With the new haircut and color, darker makeup, different shades of nail polish, in addition to a couple well placed scars-compliments of Susan's investigators, Brenda looked like a different person. They bought dark sunglasses to hide the color of her eyes. When she saw herself in the mirror, she couldn't believe the transformation. She was ready.

Chapter 16

Anthony was pacing the floor. He had just been informed he would be guarding Brenda while she was home for a visit. Normally, walking on the cool tile floor barefoot helped soothe him when he was distressed. Today his thoughts were in such turmoil he couldn't hold a single train of thought long enough to come to a decision about anything. The plane wasn't due in until 2:00 PM. He looked at his watch every few minutes in disbelief. It seemed like time was standing still one minute, then flying by the next. It was only 9:30 AM.

Jumper had been tilting his head first one way then the other while he sat silently watching his master pace back and forth across the room. When Anthony noticed him, he bent down eye level to the dog. "Buddy, I wish you could talk." When the dog answered with a low throaty "woof" it made Anthony laugh. "Maybe it's a good thing you can't talk. Let's take a run."

Recognizing the word run, Jumper danced around the room with his leash in his mouth while Anthony changed into a jogging suit. "I'm ready if you are." He spoke to the animal, ruffing his fur while he snapped the leash on him. On the way out the door, he made sure the house was locked up securely.

The six mile run helped clear Anthony's head and tired Jumper out. The dog was ready for a nap when they returned. "Okay you beast, I guess it wouldn't hurt for me to stretch out for a while too. By the time I get up, it should be late enough to get ready to meet the plane." He started undressing as he spoke. Within a few minutes, he was sound asleep.

The sound of laughter brought Anthony wide awake. Sitting straight up in the bed he looked at the figure sitting in the chair across the dimly lit room.

"Now what? As you see, I have the dog, and thank you for suggesting it. He turned out to be good company." Anthony yawned, rubbing his eyes.

Standing up, the ghost strode across the room to look at the dog. "Well now, I must say you chose the ugliest creature you could find." He laughed while Jumper looked up at the tall figure, cocking his head sideways, trying to figure out if he should be frightened or not. "Some fierce watch dog you have there. All a body need do is look at him. His size alone is enough to scare one to death." He chuckled. "If he started toward them they would break something trying to get away." The ghost propped his elbow in the palm of his hand as he rubbed his bewhiskered chin with his free hand, still studying the dog. "I like him. He kind of grows on you, doesn't he?"

Anthony was sitting on the side of the bed with the sheet drawn across his lap, shaking his head. "I don't think you appeared to talk about my choice of pets. Don't you think it's about time to let me know why you started showing up? I don't think you attached yourself to me because you like me. What's going on?"

"Actually young man, I do like you. You need me, you just don't know it yet. I was a lawyer you know. More than that–," the ghost paused for effect watching Anthony for a reaction, before continuing. "If it had not been for me and the beautiful young lady, my first true love, you would never have been born. I was in the hereafter until your father was murdered. You are the reason I am here."

Anthony lowered his eyes, closed them while he shook his head, before looking up at the ghost. "You have hinted at this before. Are you trying to tell me that you had an illegitimate child by a black woman, and, that the child was one of my ancestors?"

The ghost chuckled. "I believe you finally have it. For a smart young man, sometimes you can be rather slow." He grinned down at Anthony, still seated on the bed with a look of astonishment on his face.

Squinting his eyes, giving the ghost a rueful stare, he spoke. "So, I am to believe that Abraham Lincoln, President of the United States, that has no living descendants on record, is my great-great-great whatever grandfather, come to help me out with some problem that you won't even tell me about?"

A hint of a small mischievous smile appeared on the face of the ghost. "I think that about sums it up. Although, they may find more from a different woman someday, if they have not already. There is something I need to tell you and you are not going to like it. Close your mouth young man, that's unbecoming."

"Is that what you wanted to tell me, to close my mouth? No, I don't like it." he fumed.

"No, no, no, no, that's not what I need to tell you." The ghost seemed to be enjoying himself. The grin was replaced by a more somber expression as he started pacing once more, rubbing his chin in a manner that made it look as if he were lost in thought. "What I have to tell you concerns the woman you will marry; I believe her name is Brenda Lou."

"Wait just a minute, who said anything about me getting married?" Anthony jumped up, pulling on his lounge pants.

"Don't get so upset. I know so many things you are yet to understand." He watched Anthony with what appeared to be a half grin. Anthony was tripping in an attempt to get his leg into a pant leg that was half inside out. "If you sit back down you won't do damage to yourself. You need to learn to control your emotions better before you hurt yourself."

Anthony plopped back down on the bed. "What the-"

The ghost cut him off. "Consider what I have been telling you. Someone wishes your entire bloodline removed from existence through no fault of your own. There isn't time to go into everything just now. You are a bright young man; but, there are some things you are in the dark about. Some of the things you learn will be hurtful and some will bring you joy. I will be back soon. For now, watch the girl closely, her life does depend on you." The room filled with the ghost's laughter once more. "You are in for a surprise when you go to meet her." He faded away leaving Anthony and the dog looking at the spot where he had been, both with a bewildered expression on their faces.

"Hey, wait a minute. What has my bloodline got to do with any of this? Come back here!" More confused than he had ever been, he found himself yelling into thin air.

After taking a quick shower, Anthony changed clothes half a dozen times before he was satisfied that he looked good without appearing to have done so. Looking around the room, he couldn't believe the mess he had made. Clothes and shoes were strewn on the bed, not to mention all over the floor. Empty hangers lay in a tangled mess on the floor of the closet. "Jumper, the cleaning lady is going to wonder what happened. She may think I've been burglared." He laughed at himself as he fluffed the fury head of his pet. "Too bad, there isn't time to straighten things. I better hurry up."

Rushing toward the door leading to the garage, Anthony stopped in his tracks. His cat was lying on the kitchen counter. Someone had used a knife to attach a note to the animal. He rushed to where the cat lay. It was still alive, but barely. Grabbing a towel from the drawer, he wrapped it carefully around the injured cat before picking it up. Placing the poor animal in an empty box, to keep from further injuring it, he hurried out, careful to lock the door behind him. With tears in his eyes, Anthony gently placed the box containing the cat beside him on the seat of the Bentley.

At the veterinarian's he explained what happened, while the animal was being examined. The Dr. told Anthony he would take photos before removing the knife. The veterinarian also offered to write a detailed report on the incident for the authorities.

Anthony wrote his cell phone number on the notepad laying on the vet's desk. He asked to be called as soon as the animal's condition was confirmed. "Under normal circumstances I would stay to find out how she is doing. Then again, under normal circumstances, this wouldn't have happened. I need for you to keep this quiet, I'll return as soon as possible."

"I'll be here for several more hours. She's in shock. Even though she lost a lot of blood I think you got her here in time. By you getting her here so fast, I think surgery will make that leg as good as new. Even without the note, it's easy to tell someone was sending you a message." The veterinarian was already busy preparing the animal for surgery.

Anthony raced from the building to his car, thankful the clinic wasn't too far out of the way. He drove just over the posted speed limit, hoping he wouldn't get stuck behind any farm machinery or be stopped for speeding. He was making the turn into the Malden Air Base when he saw the plane start its approach to land.

The car came to a stop beside the hanger as the door of the airplane opened. The first one out of the plane was Robert followed by the children being ushered out by Susan. A woman Anthony couldn't place followed Susan. There was something vaguely familiar about her, but he wasn't sure quite what it was. The pilot was the last one out. The door closed leaving Anthony feeling bewildered. He crossed the space to where Susan stood talking to the pilot. When he stopped beside Susan to ask where Brenda was, the woman with her pushed her sunglasses up on top of her head. Without saying a word, she turned to face Anthony. His mouth dropped open when he saw her face. Even with the disguise he knew it was Brenda.

Susan turned toward Anthony and promptly burst out laughing. "I'm sorry. I didn't mean to laugh; but, you should see the look on your face. Big difference, right? If you hadn't known she was coming, you wouldn't have recognized her at all from a short distance. Am I right?"

On the ride back to Dexter, Robert sat in the front with Anthony. The children were crowded in wherever they could be. Anthony wasn't informed they would be coming or he wouldn't have driven the Bentley. He was afraid he would be stopped and ticketed for seatbelt violations. Susan and Brenda were in the backseat with three of the children. The men discussed the crops while the women spoke in whispers about Anthony. They knew with the children chattering and the radio on, they wouldn't be overheard in the front seat.

Chapter 17

After arriving at Tom and Liz's house, Anthony seemed distracted. Brenda was puzzled by his silence as well as his distant behavior. When Anthony called Tom to the side to speak to him before leaving abruptly, Brenda wondered if he was upset with her. With everything that had happened to her, she had little self-confidence. By him leaving without saying anything to her, she was afraid he didn't have the same feelings for her that she had for him. She wondered if there was someone else in his life.

Tom wore a worried expression he was attempting to hide from everyone in the room. Approaching Brenda, he made an attempt to appear casual when he spoke. "He'll be back for you soon. Susan and Robert are spending the night here." Looking closely at the outfit she was wearing his face split into a genuine grin. "What look are you going for? I see you have the dog in your purse. Girl, Paris never looked so good." His laughter filled the room. "Sorry, you look really good, I didn't mean to laugh. It just surprised me to see the dog." As if on cue, a head of fluff with a bow on top appeared from the top of the bag giving a yap of approval at being noticed. Tom blushed as he reached out to stroke the silky fur of the little dog.

Liz found Tom's embarrassing himself funny. She chuckled, wrapping an arm around his waist. "Before you put both feet in your mouth, let's get these weary travelers something to eat. Where did Anthony take off to?"

"He had to go pick his cat up at the vet's. He'll be right back." He winked at his wife. "Do we have ice cream to go along with the sandwiches?"

"There is ice cream churning as we speak. I put blue berries in it just for you." She was pushing him toward the kitchen with the rest of the group following.

Robert overheard Liz above the den of voices. "Real homemade ice cream? With real blue berries?" He called out. "That's my girl. Her momma taught her well!"

While Liz, Tom, Robert, Susan, Susan's children, Linda, Joe, baby Casey, and Brenda gathered around the table at the old Robin's house, Anthony was on his way across town.

It was 4:00 PM. Traffic was heavy due to people getting off work. Anthony had time to go over and wonder about what the ghost said to him meant. Finally giving up the attempt to sort it out, his thoughts shifted back to Brenda. He couldn't believe she looked more appealing now than she had when they had been together. Her pregnancy agreed with her. She glowed. He noticed her breasts looked about the same size, only more firm than before. She looked like she had lost weight and aside from the slight baby bump, she looked trim.

"Damn it girl, I'm in deep trouble." he mused aloud. His started thinking about the night they shared. On the way to her house, she started out calling him by her husband's name. It wasn't long before she tried kissing him. When she called him by his own name he stopped pushing her away, returning her kiss. She made love to him knowing who he was. Remembering how she had been so eager, leaning into him, and undressing him, touching him while commenting on his body. She called out his name while they made love. He knew it was him she wanted him that night, not her husband.

Remembering the feel of her hands exploring his body caused him to become physically aroused. He didn't notice the light changing from red to green until the car behind him honked. "I have got to stop this or I will go crazy." He turned the radio on for a distraction. "Damn it girl. You already got me crazy." He quickly turned it back off, the song that was playing was about making love. "Shit, I don't have any right to be thinking like this. I need to be thinking about who did that to my cat anyway. I hope the poor little thing is alright."

The receptionist was getting ready to leave when Anthony pulled into the parking lot. She met him at the door with a huge grin on her face. She was an attractive woman in her early twenties. The way she checked him over, it was obvious she liked what she saw. "Mr. Payne, your baby is going to be good as new in no time. The Dr. just finished closing the wound a bit ago. She's waking up already. Would you like for me to take her to your car?" She was looking at the Bentley with longing written all over her face. Anthony wondered if she was going to start drooling.

"Thanks. I appreciate the offer but I can manage. It looks like you're ready to leave anyway. Is it alright if I go on back? I need to speak to the Dr. about something." He started toward the door at the back. Turning toward the disappointed young woman he asked, "Do you want me to pay now or are you sending the bill?"

"We don't have the bill made up yet. You can stop by later to pay, or I can send it to you." She had such an expectant look on her face that Anthony had a hard time smothering a chuckle.

"You can send it." He couldn't help but smile when he saw the dejected look she gave him.

The veterinarian looked up when Anthony entered. "Hi Tony. She is going to make a full recovery. I think she was in shock from fright, as much as from blood loss. I think the person that did this used one of your kitchen knives. Man, it's sharp as a razor. I made sure to wear gloves when I put it and the note in a baggie for you. What surprised me is that the blade passed between the muscles, there wasn't much damage to the connective tissue either. I cleaned the wound and stitched it up. Either she was very lucky or the person that did this knew what they were doing. She's going to be sore for a couple days; but, she should be up and around later tonight."

After going over the instructions on how to care for the incision, he took the bag and the cat to the car. While he placed the still sleepy cat on the seat, he thought about Bud.

Bud was the only person he knew of that had the knowledge and experience to be able to intentionally do something like this. He understood the man enough to know he wouldn't do anything to permanently harm an animal he intended to let live; but, at the same time this was something he would do to deliver a message for the boss. He thought they had gone back to Chicago and couldn't understand what he could have done to cause them to suspect him. With Jumper in the house, it had to have been Bud or the dog would have sounded the alarm. He would pick Brenda up first, but intended to view the tape as soon as he got home.

The adults were still around the table in Tom and Liz's kitchen. Linda answered the door, showing Anthony in. When they were headed toward the kitchen he was almost bowled over by the children. He stopped briefly to watch a game of tag they were playing with the tiny dog. Linda couldn't keep from chuckling at the stunned look on his face when he turned in her direction. "Look at that. The only time it ever acknowledged I was on the place is when it wanted fed. The rest of the time I never even knew where it was."

Linda laughed out loud. "Tony, she has her bluff in on you. She was just showing you who's boss. Animals are like children when it comes to that. Looks like you have a lot to learn." She waved him on through the doorway. "We saved some food for you. I hope you're hungry."

Tom was pushed back slightly at an angle from the table far enough to cross one leg over the other, but close enough to rest the coffee cup he was holding on the table's surface.

"Have a seat." Patting his rounded stomach he grinned up at Anthony. "I'm full as a tick. Around here when these women say we are having sandwiches; they don't tell you it comes with all the fixings. I think they could all walk away with blue ribbons at any fair around." He paused to take a sip of coffee. "I'm trying to decide which pie to have for dessert. The blueberry is the best you'll find anywhere; but, the meringue on that coconut crème is piled mountain high and golden brown. That's my favorite and the best I've ever tasted. I think I just talked myself into a small piece of each. If there is room after that, I'll have a little ice cream."

"My man is a mess." Liz looked affectionately at her husband. "Don't worry Tony, there is plenty. I know to make two of each whenever I make pies." She pulled out a chair. "Have a seat. We have turkey, ham, and roast beef for sandwiches, potato salad, coleslaw, baked beans, and home fries. Would you like whole wheat or white buns?"

As soon as he was seated a cold glass of iced tea was placed in front of him. "I didn't think I was hungry. Looking at this spread, I think I changed my mind. I have my cat in the car so I'm going to have to eat and run." He looked over at Brenda. "Are you going to be ready to go soon?" It was obvious to everyone that she was apprehensive. Taking a deep breath she looked up making eye contact with Anthony before answering. "I didn't unpack anything. My luggage is still in your trunk. I let Rascal run after the flight, but she will come when I call her." Brenda had been caught off guard at first. It looked like she had regained her composure by the time she finished answering Anthony.

Anthony piled coleslaw on roast beef on top of a whole wheat bun. He was spreading mayo on the top half of the bun when he directed a question to Susan. "How long are they letting Brenda Lou visit?"

"We have three full days here. I have a list of all our phone numbers for you in case you need them. Brenda Lou has them written down too." Susan was watching the different emotions race across Anthony's face as she spoke. It didn't take long for her to see just how worried he was about Brenda and how much he cared for her. "I think we should all get together at Dad's in a day or two instead of you trying to run all over the country to take Brenda to see everyone." She turned to look at Robert. "How would that be with you Dad?"

"Day after tomorrow would be great. We will have us a picnic. I'll call the others; it will be a party." He first cut his eyes toward Anthony, hesitating just a second, before looking back at Susan. "Maybe I'll see if Henry and Eula can come too." Nodding his head, looking slightly amused, he continued. "I'll do just that."

Susan thought she saw a hint of a wry smile, causing her to wonder what her dad was up to.

It soon became apparent that Anthony would be staying longer than planned. He borrowed a pet carrier from Tom to put the cat in so that it wouldn't get overheated in the car. After dessert the men went into the living room while the women stayed in the kitchen. Their discussion of what had happened to the cat earlier that day, turned to speculation about the safety of Brenda and Anthony. Robert was entertaining the children in another room; but, was in and out enough to catch pieces of conversation. Without being informed of several details involved in the investigation, Linda's husband, Joe was included in making plans for Brenda's visit. The men decided to keep some of the information from her father, so Chet wouldn't worry any more than he already did. At first, Tom suggested telling Brenda the incident with the cat was a weird accident so she wouldn't let it slip to her family. No sooner was it out of his mouth than he knew she wouldn't believe it.

Tom agreed to contact the agent in charge of the task force, because Anthony asked for more surveillance to cover the places Brenda would be visiting while home. The time frame was already pretty well set so that was covered. The women wouldn't be told all the details, so the chance of Brenda finding out wouldn't be as great. Tom would have more officers, both city and county, drive by Anthony's house. After the details were decided on, the plans were put into action and the conversation turned to other topics.

Anthony gave Tom the baggie with the note and knife to pass on to the FBI, when they went to the car to put the cat in the pet carrier. After hearing all the steps everyone was willing to take to keep Brenda safe he felt much better. He decided to change his security codes the minute he stepped into the house, because Bud had the current codes. The cameras would have to be disabled while Brenda stayed there; but, there would be two dogs there and the little one would bark and growl if Bud came around.

Robert was sharp for his age. He heard enough of what was being said to come to the conclusion that not only was Anthony really working on the right side of the fence, but he liked the man. He noticed the concern shown for Brenda was more than a job to the tall black man. Robert could see how much she meant to him. He already knew that Brenda was pregnant; now, he wondered if the baby just might be Anthony's. He knew he had to call Henry first thing in the morning.

"Alright fellows, it's bedtime for the kids." Liz's voice carried into the living room. "Some people had to get up with the birds this morning. They may want to get around too." She appeared in the doorway grinning. "I think Dad wants to get on the way to the farm if you're done."

"Sorry, I didn't realize it was getting so late." Tom rose and went to put an arm around his wife's shoulder. "Gentleman, it's been a pleasure. I think the little lady has spoken." She gave him a playful elbow to the ribs. "I mean, my lovely wife is right. It is getting late and tomorrow will be here before we know it."

They all grinned at the antics of their hosts. Susan and Robert decided to go on to the farm instead of spending the night. While the group headed out the door, Anthony watched Brenda in silent amazement. He couldn't believe his eyes when the little dog jumped into the bag when she motioned for it to. Tom helped settle the pet carrier into the car while Brenda said her goodbyes. When Tom and Liz went back into the house, Linda and Joe were getting the kids settled into bed.

Anthony drove Brenda to his house with a strained silence hanging heavy between them. While they waited for the garage door to raise, Anthony asked Brenda to stay in the car until he was certain everything was safe. When the door came down, he got out immediately going to work changing codes and turning off the cameras in the basement. Brenda was lost in thought when he returned.

"Girl you look like you have the weight of the world on your shoulders. Would you like to talk about it?" Anthony opened the car door for Brenda before going around to the trunk. Motioning for her to follow him, he handed her a stun gun he kept hidden there.

Brenda looked surprised as she took the stun gun from him. "What am I supposed to do with this?" She was inspecting it. It looked smaller than the ones she had seen in the past; but, when she pushed the button on the side, the area around them lit up causing Anthony to jump back.

"It may not look too impressive, because it doesn't have the light on the end, but you just found out that it is more powerful than the bigger ones." He looked at her with a lop-sided grin. "Keep that in the side compartment of that suitcase you call your purse and please don't use it on me." He joked in an attempt to lighten the mood. "You just saw how that arch reached out. I thought you had me with that thing there for a minute." He started to reach into the car for the pet carrier. "I never thought to ask, do you know how to use that?" He pointed at the stun gun she was pushing down into her purse.

"Aren't you suppose to touch the little prongy things to bare skin before you push the button?" As she lifted the bag onto her shoulder, Rascal stuck her head out to look around.

"Ideally, but if that isn't possible, try to press it against the person anywhere you can. As you just saw, it is powerful enough to deliver a jolt even if it isn't in direct contact. Be careful with it. I don't want you to hurt yourself." He had an overly large suitcase by the handle in one hand and the pet carrier in the other. "Will you open the door, please?" He grinned at her, still finding it hard to believe she was at his house.

After Brenda held the door for him to pass through, Rascal started wiggling to get out of the bag. As soon as she set it on the floor the little dog jumped out, lifted its head and howled. Jumper came running into the room. When he saw them he tried to stop. He had enough momentum going that he slid on across into the wall stopping with a thud. Rascal ran over to him to say hello by licking his nose. It was easy to see who the boss was. Both Anthony and Brenda laughed at the antics of the two dogs.

Anthony reached up, retrieving the cat's bed from the top of the refrigerator, he placed it on the countertop. When he lifted the poor creature out of the pet carrier, he placed it gingerly in its bed. The cat looked around like it wanted to run before announcing displeasure at being out in the open. Anthony rubbed its soft fur, murmuring quietly to ease the cat's distress. He pushed the bed farther back into the corner created by the wall and the refrigerator before opening a can of food to put in a dish beside the cat's bed. "After she finishes eating I'll take your suitcase into the room for you. If I don't stand guard Jumper will try to help her with it."

They watched as Jumper came over to see what was going on. He stretched his long neck enough to get his head above the counter top. "I see. He doesn't even have to put his paws up there to reach things near the edge. That is one large puppy." Brenda found it amusing. They both watched as Rascal leapt onto Jumper's back then onto the counter top.

"I wondered how she was getting up there. Now I've seen everything. That's why the cat's things had to be moved to the top of the fridge." They both laughed when Rascal licked the cat in greeting. The cat hissed its disapproval before slapping at the dog's nose for the unwanted attention.

Anthony finished putting Brenda's things in the bedroom she would be using before giving her a tour of the house. Rascal stayed right at her heels while they walked, making a point to let Brenda know there was a space under the shelving in one of the guest bedrooms.

When Anthony bent down to look in the space, he found a couple of the small dog's toys hidden near the wall. "I believe this is where she's been hiding. I looked everywhere I could think to look and never could find her. She would just appear and then disappear just as fast." He straightened up with one of the toys in his hand. He looked amused as he tossed the toy across the room. The dog scampered after it, quickly grabbing her toy, took it right back to the hiding place. "If I didn't know better I'd think she was proud of herself."

"She probably is. She's a smart little thing that knows Jumper can't get under there to get to her toys."

When they started for the door, Rascal let out a howl. They stopped, turning they saw the dog run to Brenda with a toy. She took the toy to put it back; but, before she could get back to the door the small creature ran to stand between her and the door with another toy in its mouth. Brenda started to go around Rascal, but stopped when the dog dropped the toy in order to raise its little head so it could howl again. Brenda looked down at the dog while speaking to Tony. "If I were prone to bet-I would bet she wants me to sleep in here with her."

"I think you hit the nail on the head." He was standing with his hands on his hips, shaking his head, while laughter bubbled up engulfing them both. After taking a moment to catch his breath Tony made a decision. "It looks like we are moving your things and Rascal's. She will howl all night if she doesn't share a room with you and you can't stay in this part of the house. I hope you understand that you need to be close enough for me to keep you safe. We already know she won't stay in the room I started to put you in. How does that sound to you?"

Brenda had been watching his changing emotions as Tony spoke. It was plain that he wasn't sure about how she would feel staying in a room so close to his. His consideration touched her. It was obvious he felt ashamed about his part in what happened between them. Although Tony had called her a few times while she was in New York, there hadn't had much of a chance to talk about the possibility of him being the one that fathered her child. The subject had barely been touched upon.

Seeing the look in his eyes when he looked at her made Brenda's heart melt. She was pretty sure she was falling in love with the man standing in front of her. The way he looked at her caused her to wonder if he may feel the same way about her. She hoped it was true. Wanting to lighten the mood, Brenda grinned up at him as she answered his question. “Anthony Payne, I think that is a great idea. It’s been a very long day and we could both use a good night’s sleep. If she sees my things and her things put in there at the same time she should be good with it. I hope you don’t mind if she sleeps in the bed with me. She has kind of taken over as my protector.”

Rascal seemed to know she was the topic of conversation. The little dog was standing on her hind legs dancing and hopping around in circles. It looked so comical they both laughed. “If it makes you feel safer, it will be fine with me. Brenda Lou, I-. Never mind, we can talk later. Let’s get you settled in.”

Chapter 18

Lou was pacing the floor. She was too angry to stand still. She found out her daughter had flown in without getting in touch with her, and wondered why she hadn't heard from her yet. Instead of calling Tom Smith's house, she had attempted to call Donna Mae. Donna's phone rang several times without her or Mac answering it. She wondered if Donna was still upset enough she wasn't taking calls from them; or, if there was another reason they weren't answering. The last thing she wanted to do was call Anthony's home to reach her daughter.

On top of everything else, Chet was acting so funny she didn't know what to expect from him. She wondered if part of it wasn't her fault for making him go to Ben's funeral with her. She thought someone should go; and well-after all-he had been their son-in-law for a long time. The thought of what he had done still made her want to torture him worse than he had been before he died. A smile lit her face at the thought of what she had been told about the torture. Brenda wasn't her favorite daughter; but, she was her child. Lou had to see the man in his coffin to be sure he was really dead. What Ben had done was unforgivable as far as she was concerned. She wanted to kill him herself with her own bare hands.

When they moved from the city to Bloomfield, Chet became a different person. If he hadn't changed he and Lou would have ended up divorced. Thinking back to some of the things he had said and done in Chicago still bothered her. Lou liked being in charge. While living in the city, Chet wanted her and their children to do exactly as he said. She started to resent him, feeling like an underling he thought he could control. Since he had entered the ministry and they moved back to her hometown he had been a wonderful husband and father. Lou no longer felt like he wanted her to be an obedient child, with the need to let him know where she was or what she was doing at all times. With the freedom to do as she pleased, she had fallen in love with him all over again.

Chet came in through the back door looking like the weight of the world sat on his shoulders. He looked up to see his wife glaring at him.

"I found your gun. That's not the one you were using to target practice with when you and Tom went to the range. Didn't you tell me you got rid of those? What else can I expect to find out?" Her voice was low with a hard threatening quality.

"Nothing else Lou. There is nothing else to find out. With everything that has happened I wanted to have some extra protection around. That's all there is to it." He looked defeated and it came through in his voice. "Have you heard from Brenda Lou yet?"

"No! She hasn't seen fit to call yet. We're her parents. I can't believe they don't want us to know she's here. Why are you so worried about her? Why can't you treat Donna Mae half as good as you treat Brenda Lou? She bends over backwards to try to please you. She not only helps Brenda Lou; but, she has her husband helping with everything too. All you can do is bite Donna Mae's head off and criticize her. She is expecting your first grandchild and you-you could at least say you're sorry." Her sharp words cut to the quick like the hot edge of a finely tempered blade right off the forge, striking deep into his heart.

He looked at his wife with the saddened eyes of a beaten down puppy. "If you had asked where I've been, you would know why Donna Mae wasn't answering her phone. Before I left she checked the caller ID so I know you tried calling her. She understands why I was snappy and yes, it hurt her feelings. I apologized to her and Mac. She showed me the ultrasounds they sent home with her. She also admitted that she got pregnant when she did because she knew that Brenda Lou was trying to have a baby. She wanted to have one first. Why haven't you gone to see her?" His last statement caught Lou off guard. Lou had claimed to be at Donna's a couple times since the night Donna and Mac had been over.

Lou paused before answering. Chet knew she was making things up. He was too tired to ask why she was lying. "I started over there when I told you I did. I just couldn't face them after the way you acted. Don't try to turn this back on me, it's not me that hurt her." "I just asked a simple question. I love all my children equally. You know that. Brenda Lou was our first born is all. Donna Mae resents that she isn't the oldest. She admitted it to me. She knows too that things have always came easier to her than to her big sister. You know you have always babied Donna Mae more, taking her side in everything at the expense of the others for whatever the reason." He looked as exhausted as he felt. The anguish in his voice couldn't be hidden if he wanted it to be. "I've always tried to please you. I'm not trying to hurt your feelings. I just don't know what's going on with you anymore. I need to take a walk." He turned and quietly went back out the door leaving Lou standing there smoldering in rage, wondering if he knew more than what he said.

***

St. Louis, Missouri

Henry laid the receiver back into the cradle. Laughter spilled into the living room from the other side of the house. He knew what he had to do, but the thought of it was hard to come to terms with. The someday he had dreaded for so many years had arrived and he wasn't ready to face it. The sound of Eula and Dixie nearing the room caused an anxiety he hadn't felt in years because he knew this had to be done now.

Eula stopped short when she saw the tortured look in Henry's eyes. Looking at her husband, she knew there was only one thing that could upset her Henry so badly. The time had come. "Henry, was that Bobby on the phone?" She went to his side, putting her arm through his and gently squeezing it to her side.

Dixie looked from one to the other knowing something was about to happen from the way they were looking at each other and at her. She knew she hadn't done anything wrong but her scalp prickled in fear. "Grandpa, what's wrong?"

Henry attempted a smile he didn't feel. "Let's all have a seat. You're old enough now to learn about your daddy and what happened to both your momma and your daddy."

The stricken look on Dixie's face caused her grandmother to go to her and coax her to sit on the sofa. Eula sat beside her with her arm protectively holding the young girl close. Henry started pacing in an attempt to gather his thoughts before he broached the subject he had avoided for so long.

"I thought you said my parents were dead. You told me my daddy died before my mother knew she was pregnant and she died right after I was born." Dixie looked pale. The tears that were forming were threatening to spill over any moment. Watching her grandparents, she knew there was something dark and terrible connected to what she was about to hear. It hurt her deeply to realize that things about her parents had been kept from her.

Eula was patting Dixie, trying to calm her. "Now, now, we told you the truth. Nobody lied to you. We just didn't tell you everything." Eula looked up pleadingly at Henry. She had dreaded this day since Dixie had been left with them.

Henry looked at his lovely granddaughter. He wiped at the tear trying to escape from his own eye. He looked lovingly at the beautiful young lady she had grown up to be. Clearing his throat, he attempted to keep his voice level. "You know how much we love you. We always tried to do what was right and good for you. You were never lied to about your parents, Dixie. There are things we didn't tell you for your own protection. It looks like the time has come for you to know the whole story."

"Henry, are you sure she needs to know everything?" Eula sounded almost hysterical. When Dixie looked at her she saw the fear her grandmother suddenly felt. "I knew we would have to tell her more; but, do you think she needs to know it all?"

Dixie sat in stunned silence wondering what could be so awful as to cause this kind of reaction in her normally calm, plainspoken grandmother. She couldn't remember ever seeing her grandmother afraid of anything.

With downcast eyes, Henry slowly nodded his head before looking at his wife. "Yes, I'm sorry Eula. Other things have happened; she has to know for her own safety. We're making a trip down to Dexter early in the morning. Bobby is expecting us."

"What if he wants to take her away from us Henry?" Eula was almost in tears.

Watching in stunned silence, Dixie listened to the conversation bantered back and forth between Henry and Eula. She stayed quiet while she wondered why old Uncle Bobby would want to take her from the only home she had ever known.

Henry shook his head. "Nobody is going to try to take our little girl momma." He smiled lovingly at his wife. She was nearing ninety but to him she was still as beautiful as she was when they fell in love almost seventy years earlier. He had a somber look about him when he turned to Dixie. "You know your momma was really our granddaughter even though we say you are our granddaughter instead of telling people you're our great granddaughter, right?" He knew he was rambling while he tried to think of a way to make what he was about to say easier to accept. When he looked down at the floor, trying hard to compose himself, Dixie noticed that a light film of perspiration had formed across his forehead. She knew how disturbed he was as she watched him rub both his hands up his face and draw his fingers through his hair.

After what seemed a much longer time than it actually was, Henry looked back toward Dixie.

When Dixie nodded he continued. "Your momma was as beautiful as you are, and just as smart. She was in college when she met your daddy. They planned to get married. What happened to them never should 'a happened to anybody. You are going to meet your daddy's brother tomorrow."

Dixie looked up wide eyed in astonishment. "I have an uncle I didn't know about? How could you not have told me? Are you afraid he is going to try to take me? Is that what this is about?" She had never raised her voice to her grandparents until now. The shock and hurt showing on her face told them how this was hurting her.

He knew this was tearing Eula's heart out but he had to tell Dixie the whole story. The people responsible for her parent's deaths were still out there and they were too close for comfort. It would be too easy for them to find out that Anthony Payne was her uncle.

Henry swallowed hard, suddenly looking every day of his advanced age. He sat down bracing himself for the story he had to tell. "I'm not worried about your uncle trying to take you. Oh Dixie, sweet baby girl, I wish it was that simple. It is worse than that. It's much worse I'm afraid."

The story began with their son, a military officer, taking the men he trained into battle in Vietnam. Their son's wife and children were to live with Henry and Eula while he was away. He returned home in a coffin. After the military burial, their daughter-in-law and grandchildren continued to live with Henry and Eula until the children were grown.

Their youngest granddaughter was Dixie's mother. She was a 4.0 honor student, accepted into a college in Chicago, IL. on full scholarship. Peggy Elizabeth left home right after high school graduation to get a job for the summer before her classes started in the fall.

Peggy found a job working in the office of a manufacturing factory located near Elgin, IL. Not long after she went to work, there was a problem with a computer program the factory used. The young man that was sent to update the program made a point to take his lunch break the same time Peggy did. He felt dumbstruck the instant he laid eyes on her. There was only one way he knew of to get a chance to speak to her. He approached her table and was delighted when she asked him to sit with her. They started talking. When he found out which college she was attending he couldn't believe his luck, they would be attending the same college. Before the end of the day he asked for Peggy's phone number.

It didn't take long for the two to fall in love. After a while, there were times when Peggy called home she seemed evasive when asked about Raymond. She finally admitted there was something that her boyfriend was keeping from her. Eula told her that if he really loved her he would open up about what was bothering him. One evening Raymond seemed more distracted than usual. Peggy finally demanded he tell her what the problem was. Raymond saw how important it was for her to know everything. He told her about his past, his parents, then about his brother's connection with Ronald Arnold and the reasons behind it. He told her it really worried him, but nothing he said seemed to make any difference.

Halfway into the first semester, Peggy was spending several nights a month at the apartment Raymond shared with his older brother. Between studying and making wedding plans, time wise, it worked out better that way. One evening while Anthony was away from the apartment, Raymond and Peggy were there cramming for an upcoming test when Mr. Arnold showed up looking for him. Raymond flatly told Ronald Arnold to leave and not to come back.

Mr. Arnold wasn't a person that took being told what to do lightly. Less than a week passed before Ronald Arnold stopped Raymond on the street demanding that Raymond work for him. He was told something might happen to Peggy if he refused. Several people were passing by on the sidewalk as Raymond threatened to turn him in to the authorities for the threats.

Unable to do anything to Raymond right then, he walked away with a smirk on his face.

A couple days after the encounter, Ronald Arnold showed up at the apartment with two men while Peggy and Raymond were alone in the apartment. They pushed their way in when Raymond demanded they leave. Raymond was knocked to the floor and made to watch while the woman he loved was brutally raped. When they were finished with Peggy, Mr. Arnold held her, making her watch while the two men nearly beat Raymond to death before tying a tourniquet around his arm. When she saw them inject the contents of the syringe into his arm, she knew he was dead before they dragged her limp body from the apartment.

Peggy wasn't showing, but she was well into her first trimester of pregnancy when she was abducted. Ronald Arnold kept her drugged and prostituted her to wealthy clients. When he found out she was pregnant he sold her services in a common brothel for two months. Upon her release, he told her if she tried turning him in he would take her child to do with as he pleased. She knew he had connections with some of the police so she believed him.

Throughout the remainder of her pregnancy, she was addicted to drugs. Peggy stayed depressed while constantly looking over her shoulder. Ronald Arnold was finished with her but her fear of him was still strong. Her tiny daughter was born an addict. When depression finally got the best of her, she decided to end the constant misery of her existence by taking her own life. Peggy took her daughter to St. Louis, leaving the newborn baby at the home of her grandparents with a long letter. The letter contained the horrid details of the beatings, rape, and Raymond's death, along with everything else she had endured after that. She apologized for letting them down, for not being the person they had raised, and thanked them for all they had done.

It broke Eula and Henry's hearts when they read the details about her being forced to watch the murder of the man she loved and what it did to her. Part of her died with him in the apartment that day. She told them the only reason she stayed alive as long as she did was because she couldn't kill the only remaining part of Raymond Andrew Taylor that was left on this earth. Until they read the letter Henry and Eula were under the impression that Peggy was still attending college in Chicago.

Dixie's grandparents explained how they returned home from shopping one day to find a box on their front stoop. In the box they found the letter lying beside the infant. The tiny infant was in the process of having a seizure. At first sight, it was easy to tell the baby was undernourished. By the time Henry read a small portion of the letter, they knew what was causing the baby to seize. Normally calm, Eula was beside herself trying to help the child when Henry told her they had to get the infant to the hospital immediately. Weaning the tiny little baby off the drugs was rough but soon she started to flourish.

The whole time Ronald Arnold held Peggy, he had seen to it that no one suspected she was missing. He had her to call her family with carefully scripted conversations. There was not one thing left to chance. He was smart, careful, and experienced enough to know exactly what was necessary to keep from getting caught.

After reading that letter, Eula and Henry were careful to keep little Dixie's identity as quiet as possible. To the best of their knowledge Anthony had no idea she existed. Due to what they read, they were afraid Mr. Arnold would try to use her to get at her uncle if he found out she had been born before her mother's death.

By the time Henry finished talking, all three individuals were in tears. "Do you have any questions child?" Eula asked.

***

Chicago, Illinois

Ronald Arnold was pacing the floor. He knew his boss did not tolerate errors. He knew he had made more than one. His head was throbbing and even though the air conditioning unit was set below 70 he was sweating. No matter how hard he tried, he couldn't come up with a believable excuse as to how he had missed the things he should have seen. He knew his ego had a lot to do with part of the predicament he found himself faced with. His only hope was that his boss would think him too invaluable to kill.

The sound of the phone ringing almost caused his heart to skip a beat. Consumed with dread, he lifted the receiver. "Hello." He cringed when he heard his own voice crack as he spoke."

Bud found delight in the sound of fear he heard in that one simple word. "Hi Mr. Arnold. Did I catch you at a bad time?" If it weren't for the fact that he took pleasure in the things he was allowed to do, he would have done away with Ronald Arnold long ago. Bud didn't like the superior attitude, or the demeaning way that Mr. Arnold treated the people he had working under him.

Hearing the sound of Bud's voice, he regained his composure. "No, what have you got to report? You were supposed to get in touch earlier. Who the hell do you think you are? When I give an order, I expect it to happen." He no longer sounded afraid, he sounded like the self-centered, mean, overbearing, pompous, jerk Bud knew him to be.

"Well Boss, I've been busy doing what you asked me to." Out of spite, he waited for Mr. Arnold to repeat his request for the information. He knew how much his boss hated to have to ask twice for anything.

Painfully aware of what Bud was doing, Mr. Arnold was clenching his teeth to keep from shouting into the phone. "Tell me what you found out."

"I've been watching her shop and the house. No sign of her anywhere. You already know she didn't go to his funeral. I went through the house again but didn't find any kind of records. Hell, I even put a tail on her folks and that didn't do any good. I put bugs on the phones too. If she has been talking to any of them it has to be on cell phones. Looks like ole Ben must 'a burned the records."

Mr. Arnold breathed a slight sigh of relief. If Bud hadn't found them, then his boss wouldn't have them either. "From now on, bring the tapes directly to me. Don't take time to listen to them. She is smart enough to avoid calling them. Better yet, remove the bugs from her parent's house. We don't want the wrong people to find them. Understand?" Without waiting for an acknowledgement, he continued. "You can tail her sister but take the tail off her parents, it isn't productive. What about Payne?" he snapped

"Tony boy has been busy. He said he needed to take a short trip to keep his cover, so he will be gone for a few days. The money is in the account, I checked. As for the other stuff, I'm still trying to sort out the mess Ben left when he tried to rip you off. I'm making progress. I have meetings set up with our contacts in Little Rock and Memphis."

Bud wasn't about to tell his boss he had done some collecting and taken some time for himself after Mr. Arnold had gone back to Chicago. With Will out of the way he knew his boss wouldn't find out. The new man wasn't up to speed on the operations yet.

"Sounds like you have things under control. What about the police?"

"Mr. Arnold, it doesn't appear like they are too interested in Ben's death since they found out he wasn't the good guy he was trying to pretend to be. They blamed him for more things than he actually did but it doesn't look like they have a clue about the other branch of the business he was involved in. It doesn't look like they much care who did him in Boss." Bud chuckled for his bosses benefit.

"Good, good. If you find out anything else let me know immediately. I want that bitch dead, understand! There's no telling what Ben spilled to his little wifey. I doubt that she knows anything but we can't run a risk like that. I'll see you back here in a week if nothing changes." The line went dead.

Bud held the receiver out from his ear. "By the way asshole, your day is coming. Furthermore, you're nothing more than a prick of an errand boy!" He smiled as he placed the receiver back into the cradle, stating. "Two more days to do what the hell ever I want to without that jerk knowing!"

Ronald Arnold knew Anthony kept Brenda instead of selling her. Bud had been having him watched since Wilbur disappeared. He wasn't about to harm Brenda without hearing it directly from Mr. Arnold's boss. If shit hit the fan, he wouldn't be the one standing in front of it.

Chapter 19

Anthony stirred the gravy to keep it from clumping while biscuits browned in the oven. The fried bacon was sitting on the counter already. He didn't hear Brenda enter the kitchen. She leaned against the door facing watching him engrossed in fixing breakfast. Brenda was drawn to him. She realized she had been from the first time she laid eyes on him.

Brenda finally faced the fact that her marriage had been a farce for a long time before meeting Anthony. No matter how hard she had tried to make it work, it was based on lies. She smiled to herself, feeling a warm glow just being near him. The man in front of her was real. This was the same man who talked to her when she needed someone, the man she craved the night she met him. She had known he was acting that Sunday morning when he was trying to be a heartless jerk, she had seen the pain and fear in his eyes.

Brenda absent mindedly ran a hand over her abdomen as she felt her unborn child stir. She was filled with such a sense of protective love that it caught her off guard. She knew she would do whatever it took to protect her child.

Turning to place the hot skillet of gravy on the island, Anthony saw Brenda smiling at him. He had been so lost in thought with what he had discovered after she went to bed he was unaware of her watching him. "I hope you're hungry. When the eggs are done we can eat. How many would you like, and how do you like them fixed?" He noticed that his robe brushed the floor on her, it came to mid-calf on him. He thought she looked like an adorable little cuppie-doll, standing there. He smiled back at her. He wanted nothing more right then than to go to her and wrap her in his arms.

"Wow, you cook too! Real homemade gravy, I'm impressed. It looks like a feast. I had better stick to one over medium. What can I do to help?" She walked toward him with a big grin spreading across her face. "Is that real homemade jam on the counter? This is better than a restaurant."

Anthony turned, broke the eggs into the skillet and reached up to remove the hash browns from the microwave. "I cheated on these, store bought, home cooked." He turned the eggs then took the biscuits from the oven. "These are my specialty." He sat the biscuits on the counter and took the eggs from the skillet. "Grab a couple plates out of the cabinet over there while I get the juice and milk."

Brenda put plates and glasses on the table, then helped Anthony move the food before pouring herself a cup of coffee. "Tony, this looks great. You fixed enough for an army. Where did you learn to cook? These biscuits are perfect too. I never did have any luck making these." She hadn't been all that hungry until she saw the spread laid out on the table, now she was famished.

"Wait just a minute, I forgot something." He had started to sit but stood right back up. Anthony crossed to the refrigerator and brought back a bowl filled with fresh strawberries and cantaloupe wedges. He sat down, placing the bowl in front of her with a satisfied grin. "Now Madame, breakfast is served."

Brenda looked at the spread with the expression of a kid in a candy store. "This is better than a buffet. I better be careful or I'll end up looking like the Good Year Blimp." She was already filling her plate.

"This is all healthy food. The eggs are organic; the bacon isn't store bought. The only thing on the table that is questionable would be the hash browns. I didn't see anything on the label that looked bad though. You can eat all you want without worry. You're eating for two. Enjoy." He looked proud of himself while he gave her a rundown on everything he had on the table.

She laughed out loud. "Not to worry, I'm going to do justice to this wonderful meal. I just need to make sure I don't do too much justice to it. I want to try to keep my weight down to what the doctor said I should." She barely finished the sentence before taking a bite of the warm buttered biscuit. The divine pleasure she felt at the taste was unmistakable. "This is homemade butter too! I haven't had anything this good in a long time. You are going to have me spoiled."

"That Brenda Lou, is my intention." He suddenly realized how much he did want to spoil her. He knew what her marriage must have been like and he wanted to make up for the injustices she had suffered. He was gripped with a savage desire to protect her and the baby. Debating with himself whether he should tell her what he found out or not, he decided to wait until the problem was taken care of.

Brenda noticed the change in his demeanor. "Why the troubled look? Tony, is there something I should know?" The concern in her voice was genuine.

Looking up at her, he smiled. "No, just business. Nothing to worry about, it's under control. We have a full fun filled day ahead of us." He was determined to keep her from any kind of worry while she was visiting.

The security company would be out to fix the system after they left. Anthony had watched the recordings of the time period when the cat was injured. Someone had rewired the cameras and alarms to insure nothing showed up on the films. Anthony didn't think Bud had the knowledge to do something like that. Whoever was responsible, knew what they were doing. There wasn't any evidence to be found connected to the cat's injuries. Anthony made arrangements to have a couple extra things installed that Ronald Arnold wouldn't know a thing about. Brenda didn't need to be aware of what was being done. He wanted her to feel safe and enjoy her visit.

***

Lou knew she had to do something to take her mind off everything. She decided to dig out the baby furniture she had stored in the attic. It had been several months since she pulled the ladder down and climbed the stairs. She knew she shouldn't be jealous of her daughter but she couldn't help feeling the way she did. Until the birth of her eldest daughter, Lou had been the favorite. Now the people that had always made her feel special were so busy making over Brenda that they weren't that interested in Lou anymore. It hurt her feelings.

Crawling out onto the boards over the beams forming the floor, she reached up grabbing a rafter for support while she stood up. The floor of the attic was covered with mostly loose boards forming a basically solid floor to walk on. Lou wasn't afraid to walk across it or use it for storage. In reality, Lou wasn't afraid of much of anything.

After making her way to the back of the attic, Lou started moving the pieces of baby furniture around. When she scooted the changing table, a loose board turned up on its edge. Lou looked down into the space between the beams. Seeing what lay there, she removed several more boards. A well-stocked arsenal lay tucked away between the beams. "So, Chet, you know nothing about any of these weapons." She thought aloud as a demonic grin formed across her face. "Isn't that just wonderful. I wonder what all the loyal little lambs in your congregation would think if they saw these?"

Lou stayed busy in the attic for over an hour sorting through the contents hidden under the floorboards before carefully replacing the boards. Satisfied no one could tell she had moved any of them, she dragged the cradle, baby bed, changing table, and bassinet closer to the ladder. She intended to see to it that Donna got to use these instead of Brenda.

Donna reminded Lou of herself when she was younger. Brenda, on the other hand, she resented. In a way she thought of her as too weak to fight for what she wanted. Brenda was too softhearted, bringing home strays and crying when her feelings were hurt. Lou loved Brenda, she just favored Donna for the personality she saw as being like her. Donna didn't let anything get in the way of something she really wanted. Lou more or less groomed Donna to be like her, ignoring that aspect when it came to the upbringing of the rest of her children. Aside from Donna, only Walter came close to being anything like his mother.

Lou smiled to herself, remembering how upset she was when Donna told her she was getting married. When she found out Mac was a lawyer and that Donna tricked him into the marriage she couldn't stay upset at her. Donna had gone after what she wanted and won. "Well Donna Mae, grandmother will see to it this baby is raised the way I want it to be. I will be the primary role model while being the only babysitter. This child will do what I want it to. There won't be anyone around to stop me." She laughed out loud, thinking of how Chet would be too busy with the church to get in her way.

***

It was the middle of the evening when Henry and Eula arrived at the farm owned by Robert Moffield. The trip down from St. Louis had been quiet. To help keep Little Dixie's mind occupied, they had allowed her to drive most of the way. They were stressed by all the questions she had asked that they weren't able to answer.

Robert was sitting on his back porch thinking about the first time he had laid eyes on Henry. He knew he owed his life to Henry, Eula, and the woman that Dixie was named after. Over the years they had become more like family than friends. Henry was like the older brother that Robert wished he had instead of the one born before him.

Hearing the crunching of the gravel, followed by the dog barking, he was brought back to the present, knowing his old friends had arrived. He was walking around the side of the house as the car came to a halt in his driveway.

Dixie was the first one out of the car. She went running to meet Robert, throwing her arms around him. "Uncle Bobby I'm so glad to see you." She reached up to kiss him on the cheek.

"Lands sake young lady, you get more beautiful every time I see you." He hugged her tight then held her out to get a better look at her. "If I was a young man, I would try to court you myself. I bet you have a string of young men lined up hoping for a chance to get your attention." He winked at her and gave her a kiss on the cheek before releasing her to hug Eula.

"Just look at you. I know where she gets her looks. You're pretty as a picture and looking younger every day. I wish I knew your secret, I look older than dirt." He released Eula and grasped the hand of his old friend, Henry, hugging him also.

"I'm not kissing you. You aren't pretty enough." Robert laughed. His eyes were dancing with pleasure at the sight of the people that meant so much to him.

"Alright you old fool, you're too young for me and way too old for Miss Dixie. Besides that, I'm already spoke for. Now get your paws off my man afore I take a broom to your backside." Eula joked good naturedly, with a twinkle in her eye, she tried to keep a stern look on her face.

"Eula, love, you know you so pretty he can't help his self. Sides that, he already senile or he wouldn't be a gettin' fresh with me." Henry joked.

"When you two rascals get done actin stupid, you can put out stuff from the car to the house. I needs to see bout what all we gonna have to do for the big feed." Dixie watched the antics of the older people in an amused silence as Eula affectionately patted the stomach of each man while motioning them toward the luggage. Eula led the way into the house followed by the men. Dixie brought up the rear, thinking how much she loved each of them.

With the greetings out of the way, Eula headed for the kitchen. Dixie went in search of the animals, while Robert and Henry went out to the back porch to discuss what lay ahead. The two men were sitting in comfortable silence enjoying the sheer pleasure of being united again.

Dixie came running around the corner playing Frisbee with the dog. "You know Henry, Ms. Dix and old Gus would have loved this." Robert looked at his old friend with a grin splitting his face.

Henry took a deep breath. "I love the way those honeysuckles smell. I tried growing them but the neighbor keeps spraying the hedgerow. He thinks he's a helping us old folks out by keeping the vines down. They remind me of her. Ms. Dix was a special person. I wish I could 'a met your Gus." It was apparent that Henry was troubled. He was rocking with his hands clasped in his lap. When he spoke, his voice was so low he could barely be heard.

Robert reached over patting Henry on the arm. "It's all going to work out. I've been around that boy enough to see that he's alright. He's not going to let that monster get away again, I feel it in my bones. If we tell him not to say anything, he won't. I'm glad you're doing this."

"Bobby, she is what keeps me and Eula alive. If anything happened to that baby it would kill us sure as we're sitting here. I know I should 'a told you sooner, back then, but I was so afraid." There were tears forming, threatening to start making their way down his weathered face. He quickly reached up wiping at them before they escaped.

Momentarily lost in thought, Robert looked up. "I admit my feelings were hurt when I first found out that you kept it from me. After I thought on it a spell, I knew how worried you were. Hell Henry, if it hadn't been for you I wouldn't have been alive to have to think about it. I owe you my life. It didn't take a minute for me to get over it. I'm glad you let me help. Aside from Ms. Dix, you were the only family I had for most of my life." They sat quietly for a minute before Robert continued. "Look at us now. Isn't it something! Who would have thought?"

Henry watched Dixie disappear around the house. "We agreed to let her meet him before she decides if she wants him to know who she is. She has a pretty good head on her shoulders for a girl that age. Tomorrow is going to be tough, Bobby."

"We'll get through this together. Don't worry about it. She needs to know her daddy's family too. I'm glad to see you're doing right by her. You're a good man Henry, always have been."

The two men sat in companionable silence watching the martins swoop down to catch mosquitoes. It wasn't long before they heard Eula call them to the table.

Chapter 20

Brenda was excited. She had missed seeing her parents, brother, and sisters. Anthony had taken her by her shop the day before. He knew she was determined to go check on things with or without him. He agreed to take her after she promised to keep her identity hidden. He breathed a sigh of relief when Brenda came out the door without anyone recognizing her. One of the girls told her she favored the owner, but that was as far as it had gone. He had stood back where he could watch through the front window without being seen. Brenda kept her sunglasses on while she looked around avoiding a conversation with anyone. After purchasing a bottle of nail polish she wouldn't use, she was ready to leave. As promised, she didn't stay inside the shop long.

The drive from his house to the farm didn't take nearly long enough for Anthony. He was so nervous about seeing her parents that he wasn't paying attention to anything. Brenda kept a one-sided dialogue going most of the way from Dexter. Occasionally the dog would give a little bark to acknowledge it was listening to her.

An assortment of scenarios played through Anthony's mind. He knew what he would have done if he had been in Chet's place. The visions were not pretty. Another thing bothering him was that he pictured himself the only black in a sea of white faces with an old time KKK lynching. He could see himself swinging from a limb in a big Oak tree in the back yard with kids and dogs running around him in a circle, making a game of the whole thing. He shivered at the thought.

Brenda noticed Anthony's actions and distracted appearance. "What on earth was that about Tony?" He looked almost comical, making Brenda chuckle.

"What? Oh, nothing. I guess the air conditioner is turned a little too cool." He said, but he had a guilty expression.

"Something tells me that's not what has you looking like a child afraid of a spanking. Now, come on, fess up." She caught herself and laughed. "It's my daddy isn't it? You're afraid of my daddy." At the look of shock that crossed his face, Brenda laughed out loud. "Looks like I hit the nail right smack on the head. You're afraid of what my daddy's going to say." She was enjoying teasing him way too much.

Anthony made an attempt at acting peeved without success, he ended up laughing with her. Brenda was glowing with joy in anticipation of seeing those she loved. Her actions were so animated, it made him want to wrap his arms around her. He found himself wanting her with a desire that shook him to the core of his being. That he loved her hit him with a force akin to being struck by a bolt of lightning. For weeks he had been trying to deny it, but now he knew she was as important to him as breathing.

They pulled into the driveway already packed with cars. Lou came rushing out to meet them. Brenda barely got her door open before her mother grabbed her in a hug.

"Whoa Momma, let me get out before you fall in on top of me." She laughed kissing her mother on the cheek. Once she was standing she wrapped her arms around her mother, rocking back and forth in a long hug. "I missed you too, Momma."

Brenda was looking around at all the vehicles. "Who all is here, anyway?"

"Come on in. Your daddy is out back. I don't think he knows you have arrived yet or he would be out here." Grabbing her daughter by the hand, she headed off. "You too Mr. Payne, come on." She said as an afterthought. Motioning toward the house as she spoke without looking at Anthony.

Anthony was apprehensive. He hadn't expected so many people to be there. He stood for a moment looking at the vehicles. There were at least three official cars there making him feel more at ease about the crowd. "Yes Mam,

I'm right behind you. Mr. Payne sounds awfully formal. Just call me Tony." He slowly walked toward the house following the two women, scanning the area as he went. "Brenda Lou, did you get Rascal?"

He couldn't help noticing how happy she looked as she turned back to answer him. "Yes. I have her in my bag. Come on, catch up. Nobody's going to bite you." She teased.

"I hope not. I'm not as positive about that as you are." He said under his breath.

Lou turned toward him. "Did you say something Mr. Payne?"

"No Mam. You can call me Anthony or Tony. I only go by Mr. Payne when I'm working." He smiled at Brenda's mother hoping to make points in the charm department. There was no indication as to whether he was heard or not. Following the women in silence, Tony thought to himself that not only did he want Brenda to be his wife, he needed her. It wouldn't matter if the child she carried was his or not. It would be part of her and he wanted to be a father to it.

By the time the trio entered the house, Anthony was in a good mood. The smile on his face was genuine; he didn't have to pretend to be happy about being in this group of strangers. These people mattered so much to Brenda, he wanted to get to know them.

The sound of the old screen door banging shut was followed by a loud booming happy sounding voice. "There's my girl." Anthony entered the room to the sight of Brenda being lifted off her feet by her father. Chet was beside himself with joy at seeing his eldest child. Anthony stopped just inside the door momentarily to watch the scene.

Chet set his daughter back on the floor before looking up at Anthony. "Thank you for taking care of my girl. I wanted to dislike you but I can't. You seem to make her happy." He walked toward Anthony with his hand extended. A feeling of relief washed over him as he accepted Chet's hand to shake.

No one noticed Lou standing in the corner glaring at the men. Her face was a mask of pure hatred. She thought to herself that this wouldn't be allowed to happen. Her daughter couldn't become involved with this man. She wished for his death. Not only was he a black man; but, he had been in prison and she had developed a gigantic hatred for blacks. She knew too much about him. It was bad enough that Brenda was expecting a baby by the lowlife she had been married to. There was no way she would allow this shame on top of that in her household. It was easy to read the looks passing back and forth between her daughter and Anthony. This was too far south, her husband was a preacher, and it just wouldn't do. No, nothing about this whole situation would do. Lou thought about everything she knew about Anthony Payne and was already attempting to figure out a way to stop the relationship from starting.

Robert yelled through the door. "Come on out, it's time to eat. Eula fairly worked herself half to death to put on this spread. Let's get to it before the flies do."

When Anthony stepped out onto the back porch he had a hard time believing his eyes. His buddy Trout was churning ice cream in an old-fashioned hand crank ice cream maker. The agent was grinning at the antics of the small children that were learning to do cartwheels on the soft grass of the lush lawn. The long tables were made out of sawhorses and doors. Rows of folding chairs bordered the makeshift tables. Off to one side were two number 2 wash tubs filled with ice. One of the tubs had soft drinks and watermelons cooling. The other held bagged ice for the tea and lemonade.

Anthony turned his attention to the tables. He had never seen so much food at any picnic before. Fussing over the arrangement of the dishes was a wise old black woman that appeared to be in her element from the big smile she wore. When she looked up to watch something, he looked to see what it was. Robert was approaching, arm in arm with an ancient looking black man. It was the same man that stood in as the chauffeur for the phony sheik when

Brenda was first brought to his house. "If that don't beat all." He said aloud. "Looks like I'm going to find out who that is after all."

Brenda came up to him taking his arm in her own. "Surprised? I take it you haven't been introduced to Henry and Eula yet." She started pulling him down the steps toward the tables. A variety of wonderful aromas assailed his senses causing his mouth to water. "I want to introduce you to my other sister and my brother. I'm pretty sure you know Donna Mae and Mac."

Throughout the day, Anthony met more people than he could remember names for. There were several local officers that he knew, along with the FBI agents and other task force members in attendance. Almost all of them were in plain clothes. Tom was there with Liz in an unofficial capacity, along with her whole family. There was a young black girl that caught his attention. He had a feeling he should know her for some reason he couldn't pinpoint. She was hanging out with Liz's granddaughter, Issa. The two girls were showing the smaller children the hummingbirds hovering near the rose bushes at the side of the house.

While people were seating themselves in groups at the tables, Anthony found himself seated across from Dixie. He couldn't help but notice that every time he looked up he found her staring at him. After a bit, he started to feel like a bug under a microscope, until her eyes took on a mischievous look. The young lady extended her hand toward Anthony. "I don't think we have been introduced, Mr. Payne. My name is Dixie Taylor, I'm Henry's granddaughter." Before waiting for a reply, she nodded toward Brenda who was sitting directly beside him. "I've met Ms. Green before. Are you two a couple?" It was easy to tell she was hiding some secret behind a barely concealed grin.

Anthony almost choked on the pork steak he had just taken a bite of. Brenda laughed out loud at his response. Henry scowled at Dixie. "Girl, what's got into you? You don't ask strangers personal questions like that. We raised you to know better, now apologize to Mr. Payne. Don't forget to tell Ms. Green you're sorry too. Mind your manners you was raised with. You need to start acting like a young lady. You're old enough to know better than to be so impolite." It looked like Dixie started to say something else; but, she was cut off before she could.

"Do as I say, you hear?"

Casting her eyes at Henry, Dixie lowered her head. "Yes sir. I'm sorry. I just-well-I-never mind, sorry." She then turned back to face Anthony and Brenda... "I'm sorry Mr. Payne, Brenda Lou. I forgot my manners for a bit." She apologized looking rather sheepish. After recovering from her embarrassment, Dixie seemed to glow from the inside out with some hidden knowledge as she continued to sneak peeks at Anthony.

Brenda looked thoughtful for a moment before whispering to

Anthony. "Tony, who is that lady in the picture on your hall wall?"

"That's my grandmother, Opal. Why do you ask that now?"

Brenda looked thoughtfully at Dixie then back at Anthony. "I think Dixie looks a whole bunch like the picture when she smiles like that. Don't you?" She asked.

Before there was time for Brenda's question to register, or for him to wonder about Dixie's surname, Special Agent Allen Burner showed up at Anthony's shoulder with a platter piled high with barbecued chicken and ribs. Anthony did a double take before he burst out laughing at the sight of him. Agent Burner was wearing a chief's apron with the matching hat. To complete the outfit he had on oversized oven mitts in bright red with a chili pepper design on them. Bending low to whisper in Anthony's ear, he said "Tell anybody and I'll shoot you. Had to wear something to hide the gun. They made me do this." He teased, winking. The normally somber, straight-faced agent was enjoying himself. It was easy to see he was having as much fun as everyone there.

As the evening wore on there was laughter in the air mixed with the smell of meat cooking on the grill. Children, sticky with watermelon juice, ice cream, spilled soda, not to mention well-earned dirt, were hosed down with a garden hose, so they could play in the wading pool. Games of tag, horseshoes, washers, and lawn darts continued while the citronella torches were lit. The daybed on the back porch was full of sleeping children before people started saying their goodnights.

Brenda was deep in conversation with her family when Henry finally approached Anthony. Unable to read the old man's face, Anthony didn't know what to expect. The old black man, now stooped with age, had obviously been a force to reckon with in his prime. Even now, in his advanced age he could be intimidating.

Henry's eyes roamed Anthony's face as the old man slowly nodded his head with a half grin appearing on his face, before he finally broke the silence. "Young man, I had my doubts about you. Looks like I might 'a been wrong. Anything I can do to help put an end to those people you're after, let me know. Enslaving people is just wrong. No matter the for or how." Sadness suddenly filled the old man's eyes. "I have my own reasons for wanting to see justice done. It's long overdue." Extending his right hand to shake Anthony's he continued. "Glad to meet you. I'm sure we will be seeing more of you in the future." Without waiting for a reply, the elderly man turned on his heel walking away, leaving Anthony wondering what just happened.

Chapter 21

July 20th

Weather started out being in the 90's. Storms brought cold rain and high winds dropping the temperature to 72 degrees in the afternoon. Prior to the drop in temperature, humidity was so high it was equivalent to being in a sauna. With every breath it felt like you were suffocating due to the moisture in the air. Everyone felt much better after the storm's cooling effects.

At the farm in Shannon County, the sound of frogs singing filled the air with a delightful chorus, while there was an occasional honking of the geese to accompany them. Kittens were enjoying the cooler weather as they played at learning skills needed to be big cats. When they weren't scuffling in mock battle, they were rolling around batting balls of fur shed by the large dog. The largest dog was playing a game of tag with the smallest dog using a Rose of Sharon bush for a base. They ran circles around Anthony using him for the other base in their game.

Any other time Anthony would have been amused by the activity surrounding him. Lost deep in thought, he barely noticed any of it. He was afraid for Brenda's safety. There were too many unanswered questions to suit him. Somewhere there was a piece of the puzzle they were all missing, but where? Lately the majority of the time, his thoughts were in turmoil, keeping him awake at night.

The sound of weeping caught his attention. Walking around the building he saw the newest arrival of the complex sitting on a planter, her face buried in her hands. She was crying in loud racking sobs that shook her whole body.

"Are you alright?" Anthony cleared his throat before he continued. "I couldn't help but hear. Would it help to talk about what's troubling you?"

She attempted to speak between broken sobs. "You wouldn't understand. You're one of them. How could you, you're too old?" The girl wiped her nose on her sleeve before she looked up at Anthony. Her eyes seemed to grow to the size of half dollars before she sobbed once more then hiccupped.

He tried to hand her his handkerchief. "What's your name?" Smiling, he sat down beside her. "If you blow your nose you'll feel better."

Taking the handkerchief, she asked between gulping sobs "Who are you? You're not dressed like any cop I've seen."

Anthony couldn't help chuckling. "That's because I'm not a cop. You can call me Tony if you want to. How long have you been here?"

"What do you care? You don't know me." The response was almost a whisper. She was staring straight ahead, tears dripping off her chin.

Anthony couldn't help but notice this girl looked as lost and lonely as any he had ever seen. He wondered what had caused her such heartache. The only thing he knew for sure was that she was somehow mixed up in the abductions that were being investigated.

"I don't work here either. I'm visiting someone that was brought here. If you don't want to tell me what's bothering you, maybe you could talk to her. Looks to me like you need a friend to talk to." She looked over at him. The crying had finally stopped. "Tell you what, give me your name and I'll ask her to-"

She cut him off "They told me no one could have visitors." She was quiet for a couple seconds before she thrust her hand out to shake hands with him. "Promise not to laugh and I'll tell you my name."

"I promise not to laugh." Grinning he took the offered hand. From all appearances, she had something definite in mind.

Anthony felt like a bug under a microscope the way she was studying his face. When she spoke her voice was controlled. "My name is Eunice. I was named after my grandmother. It looks like you can come and go as you please and I have to get out of here. I have to trust someone that can help me."

Rubbing his chin, Anthony thought his response through, choosing his words carefully. "Eunice, I need to know the problem before I can do anything."

On the verge of tears once again she started talking. "Greg said he would come and get me. I've been here two weeks already and he hasn't shown up. Something bad must have happened or he would have come for me."

He had to break in to ask. "How could he come for you if he doesn't know you're here? I know they don't allow phones. For that matter, why are you here? You don't look very old."

The questions seemed to make her angry. "I'll have you know I'm almost eighteen. I'm not a child anymore and Greg is my boyfriend. I sent him a text when we stopped at that McDonalds in Van Buren. When I went to the bathroom a girl let me use her phone. That cop that brought me here told me we had another thirty minutes to get to where we were going. I told Greg so he should have been able to find me by now. Greg said it might take a couple days to find me but he would."

Hearing what she said shocked Anthony. His thoughts were going in circles. Nodding his head he asked the question again. "Why did they bring you here?" He wondered who Greg was and how much of a threat this would be. When Eunice started speaking again all his worries were confirmed.

Her story started with her telling him she lived in Louisiana until she was seven years old.

Eunice had been named after her grandmother Eunice so her family called her Nicky. Her only sister, Ramona was ten years older than her. Nicky had a hard time pronouncing Ramona's name so she shortened it to Ra, soon the whole family did the same.

Nicky was five when Ra started dating a man named Greg. Nicky attached herself to Greg, begging to go places with her sister and Greg. The little girl thought Greg hung the moon.

"Those were the happiest three months of my whole life." Eunice said. "Then Ra went missing."

Nicky said nothing was right after her sister disappeared. At first it was believed she and Greg eloped until Greg showed up with a story about an out of state job interview. He appeared to be devastated when they told him about Ramona. He practically lived at their home most of the week the search went on for Eunice's sister.

Eunice didn't understand why everyone was so upset. She missed her sister but was delighted to have Greg to herself that week. She cried when Greg told her he was moving away.

In the months following Ramona's disappearance, Eunice felt lost. Everyone was sad all the time and no one seemed to notice she existed. She started doing whatever she wanted without fear of punishment, it made her feel invisible and unloved.

Grandmother Eunice lived in Missouri. When she became ill, Nicky's family packed up and moved to Missouri hoping to escape the pain. Nicky was never referred to as Eunice again; she was barely noticed at all.

Summer rolled around without a word about Ra or another word from Greg. Grandmother Eunice passed away. Nicky's parents were making the final funeral arrangements which left Nicky home alone. When the phone rang she expected it to be another of her grandmother's friends. It was Greg.

He told her he read her grandmother's obituary in the paper, saying he had no idea they had moved until he saw that. When she asked how he got their number, he told her he got it from information, even though it was unlisted. They spoke for several minutes. She was too young to understand some of the questions he was asking.

At the tender age of fifteen, Nicky was a wild child. She liked to think of herself as a free spirit. Her grades were good enough that her parent's didn't notice she was skipping school. She had a fake ID she used on a regular basis.

The similarity between Nicky and Ra was too much for her parents. Every time they looked at her it reminded them of the daughter they lost.

The older crowd that Nicky ran with planned her birthday party. For her sweet sixteen birthday they took her to a night club in Cape Girardeau. The group was there for about an hour before Nicky recognized a familiar face.

Crossing the room to the man's table, Nicky stood back watching him. He was inspecting the people around him, seeming to be by himself. Nicky approached him. "I never thought I'd see you again." The cheerful sound of her voice matched the smile on her face.

Caught off guard, not recognizing her, he appraised the girl before speaking. "Aren't you a bit young for this place?"

"Oh Greg, you do know who I am. I was afraid you wouldn't know who I was."

When he heard her call him Greg, he looked more closely at the girl in front of him. "I'll be damned. You're not Ra's little sister are you?"

"In the flesh." She slurred her words just a little. "I was so afraid you would forget me."

He panicked. "Quiet, okay? I changed my name, no one calls me Greg anymore. My name is Larry Joe Green now."

Eunice giggled, plopping down in the chair beside him. "They still call me Nicky. Why the hell did you change your name to something like that? Greg is a good name."

Thinking quick, he put on a sad face for her benefit. "Before I left Louisiana they kept questioning me about your sister's disappearance. They wouldn't leave me alone and I was heartsick anyway. I needed a fresh start. It took me a long time to get over her. Where is she now? It almost killed me, her leaving without even telling me goodbye, or why she took off." He grabbed a napkin to wipe at an imaginary tear.

More sober now, Nicky pulled Greg close. She held him with his head resting on her shoulder while he pretended to cry. "It wasn't only you. No one has seen or heard from her. My parents said she is dead or something. You never got over her did you?"

He straightened up, wiping at his eyes. "I thought I had. Seeing you, well–, you look so much like her." He gave a sniff or two, a sharp intake of breath, let it out slowly before he spoke again. "That's probably why my marriage hasn't worked out."

Nicky reached over laying her hand on his leg. "Poor guy. Are you divorced?" She asked.

Looking straight into her eyes, he watched for her reaction. "I don't seem to be able to get a break. Yes, I'm divorced. It's tearing me up. Nicky, all I ever wanted was a family, children, you know. I bought this great house and she is taking it. She doesn't want children, hates animals, treated me like dirt. I worked hard and made good money, never enough for her. I caught her in our bed with another man."

They ended up in a motel room that night. For the next month they saw each other once a week. He asked her to meet him at the East City Park in Dexter.

Nicky woke up in the hospital. She had no memory of what happened. No one would tell her anything. She wasn't allowed to make any calls. The police told her she was being taken into protective custody, her parents had been informed.

She couldn't believe she hadn't received another text from, or seen her Greg, aka Larry Joe Green.

Anthony listened to her story without saying a word. When Eunice stopped talking he sat silently, taking in everything she had said before he spoke. "Tell you what, Nicky I promise to check into what happened." He knew he had to find out more. "Can you give me the number you sent the text to? Maybe it will help track the phone. If it wasn't Greg that sent the text, maybe I can find out who did and what's going on."

Tom Smith found all the answers Anthony asked for. He told Anthony he called Louisiana for a background on Ramona. He found out that Gregory Wayne Johnson had been questioned in the disappearance but there was never any positive evidence. The officer told Tom when they questioned her friends they found out Ra wasn't a goodie-two-shoes, she played Greg. They thought he overheard her making fun of him before she went missing.

Ramona's decomposed body was found in the next Parrish over three years after Eunice's family moved. Her neck appeared to have been broken. When her parents were notified, they asked for the remains to be cremated with her ashes sent to them. When the authorities told them how old Greg was they were shocked. He looked so much younger and lied to them about his age.

Anthony realized Eunice had never been told of her sister's death. He assumed they were trying to protect their remaining child from the truth.

The task force was notified about the text messages and given the number. They weren't able to locate the phone. This put a new element of danger into play. Someone knew the general location of the farm and it wasn't Eunice's Greg. Since the man calling himself Greg was definitely dead, it was the person in possession of his phone.

Chapter 22

Time was flying by. It was the middle of September and finding out who the main player in the dangerous game was proving to be as elusive as finding a needle in a haystack.

Every time it looked like they were about to latch on to a lead, they came to a dead end. The person running the show was somehow a step ahead at every turn. There had to be a way to find out how the evil creature was able to obtain information about the steps being taken to capture the elusive puppet master. It seemed like they were all just marionettes in some sort of twisted game. Time was running out to find the one pulling the strings.

Anthony paced the floor. He hadn't slept well for several nights. Not only was he getting desperate to find out what was causing the problems in their search; but, he was plagued by his dreams.

She came to him, slipping into his bed while he slept. He felt her soft warm body snuggle against him. Her hair was soft as he reached up to stroke it, running his fingers through the silky strands. He inhaled deeply, intoxicated by her. She smelled like fresh air after a rain mixed with flowers and a hint of powder. The warmth of her body as she pressed against him was arousing. When she kissed his lips it was soft at first, testing and tasting, turning to a hunger with a demanding urgency. Running his hands down the smooth skin of her back, he pulled her even closer to him. The groan of need that rose from deep in his throat startled him awake. It had all seemed so real but he was alone in his bed. Still drowsy, he closed his eyes again and groaned. Laughter filled the room. Anthony sat straight up, still in a sleepy daze, causing the bed pillow he had recently been wrapped around to fall to the floor. Running his hands down his face he noticed the sound of laughter, causing him to come wide awake with a start.

"Now what? What's so darn funny? Why are you bothering me anyway?" He glared at the space he knew the ghost would appear.

The snicker could be heard before the voice responded. "You seem to be awfully fond of your pillow." While he spoke the white mist appeared taking on the shape of the ghost.

It wasn't long before Abe Lincoln was sitting in the chair he favored. "Dreaming about her, were you?"

"That's none of your damn business. You probably know exactly what I was dreaming anyway. Why would I want to embarrass myself by giving you an answer? Couldn't you at least knock or something? You might give me some forewarning before you just pop in."

"That would not be any fun at all. A little testy aren't you?" The ghost seemed to be having a hard time keeping a straight face as he continued. "You know, in some countries it might get you executed for doing the kinds of things you were doing to an inanimate object. Then again, in one prominent myth originating out of New Guinea, the human race started when the first man made love to a stalk of cane." Looking amused and very pleased with himself, he continued. "To answer your question-I wasn't privy to your dream; but, it must have been a good one from what I saw."

Anthony didn't find the conversation amusing in the least. He almost growled when he spoke. "You seem more like a pervert than a president. Isn't it about time you gave me some straight answers? These visits aren't giving me any warm feelings filled with love for my long lost departed great-great whatever you are. I hope that's not why you decided to haunt me."

"Oh goodness, you heard about what, my drinking, or the so called off colored jokes I liked to tell?" Suddenly serious, Abe got up to pace the floor. One arm behind his back, his head was bent down, the other hand stroking his beard as he walked back and forth at the foot of the bed. Apparently lost in thought, he looked up when Anthony spoke.

"I hate it when you do that. It kind of freaks me out." Anthony's voice was raised enough to cause the dog to look up at him with its head cocked to the side as if to ask what the problem was.

He stopped pacing, standing with his feet spread shoulder width, arms behind his back, he held his hat in his clasped hands behind him, giving Anthony his full attention. "I just wanted to make sure of the wording before I spoke. There is a reason you aren't able to find the answers you seek. A tree starts from a seed. The roots grow, spreading out from there. Some put out shoots forming other trees, before you know it a forest has grown. You can't trace every root back to every tree to find the first one because the seeds are carried by birds or on the air causing trees to grow other places also. To find the original tree, you have to go to the heart of the forest. When you find the stump that's left you can count the rings. By doing that you will find the trees' age, indicating which tree first grew off the root to take its place."

Shaking his head, Anthony looked disgusted "Parables, you're giving me parables. I need help here, not more confusion. Good ole honest Abe. Sometimes I doubt that."

Abe studied Anthony before he continued. "I am giving you answers. As far as the Abe part, my name is-or-was Abraham. I never answered to Abe. You have to figure the other out for yourself. Not only that, you aren't going to like what you find. There will be people hurt that you care about. If you continue to do what's right, and you will, things will work out the way they have to. The truth will heal the wounds left behind. You will also find something you never believed possible, and you will have to work to keep it. You have grown into a fine and honorable man which I am greatly pleased with." As he faded out, his voice could still be heard. "I bet she has been dreaming about you too." The last sound to be heard was a quiet laugh.

After padding barefoot to the bathroom, Anthony tried going back to sleep. He tossed and turned, punched his pillow while cursing the ghost until finally giving up. According to the clock it was 4:30 AM. The things the ghost said kept running through his mind.

Anthony put on a pot of coffee, while it brewed he booted up his computer. Telling himself he would try changing the direction of the search to humor the ghost. "Alright. If you can hear me, I'll try this your way." He said aloud before mumbling to himself. "I feel like a fool talking to the walls. Hell, who am I kidding, I am a fool for taking directions from a ghost."

According to the reports there were two young women and seven children reported missing in the area last week. Reading the information the police had on each one, he knew some had been abducted. There was one fifteen-year-old boy that had ran away several times in the past. The twelve-year-old fair-haired Boy Scout had been selling magazine subscriptions. His bicycle was found beside the road, no other evidence of any kind was found. The child was a straight A student without any behavioral problems. His family life was reportedly above reproach. He was the delicate, quiet type that the overseas brothels paid a good amount for. Of the five girls, it appeared one left with her boyfriend to elope. One girl had a habit of being gone with friends for two to three days at a time, conveniently forgetting to ask permission first. Another one had been with her stepfather; his gun was missing. The abandoned car was left with the doors open, his body in the driver's seat. It was reported one of the girls had been telling her friends she was going to quit school to become a movie star. She told them she could do better without a diploma than they could with a college degree. The fifth girl disappeared walking home from school. She had told her parents she felt like someone was watching her for the last two weeks. They thought she had an overactive imagination until she went missing. The two missing young women were friends. They had gone out together Saturday night and had not been seen since. Their car was found abandoned in a mall parking lot three days later.

Venice Beach, California was a good hunting ground for the man who considered himself to be the king dog. He thought that was a befitting name since he had a stable of young girls he called his bitches. It wasn't too far from Sacramento which was known to be the number one city in the United States when it came to human trafficking. This was the ideal place for the man to recruit poor unfortunate young girls for his trade. K. Dog knew his business. The police that weren't on the take had their hands tied by the way he had his operation set up.

No matter how many times the police set up the raids to rescue the underaged girls K Dog was tipped off. He had more than one property and would move the girls the day before the raid. It would just be a matter of time before they would get lucky. Until then, he would continue ruining lives.

Even though Anthony had no connection to the investigation into K Dog's activities, he had heard how the man operated. The girls lucky enough to escape him told how the man would offer to help, claiming to befriend them. He would offer them a place to stay, claiming to have connections to the movie industry. Before long he had girls using drugs if they weren't already. When he had them dependent on him, he started making them earn their way by pimping them out. K Dog liked to use the ones he knew would be eighteen soon, until then they were supplied with fake IDs. For fear of their lives, they knew better than to report the beatings they took. On their eighteenth birthday, he arranged for their families to be notified that the girls would be coming into the local police station. K Dog took them to the police station to give their statement while he waited outside the back door. With the girl's family waiting, the girls gave a scripted statement to the police, telling them that they were with him voluntarily and wanted to stay where they were. After signing the statement, they went out the back door to get the fix they had been promised. The police had no choice; they informed the family members that the girls left of their own accord and didn't want to see whoever was waiting.

It was still too early to call anyone else. To give him something productive to do, Anthony started pulling up articles about mob activity in the late 50's to the late 60's. After printing out the articles with names of the major players, he started researching what happened to them. He also pulled up all the information to be found on all their close family members, living or dead.

A knock sounded on the front door along with a persistent ringing of the doorbell. Hurrying to the door, Anthony left the machine to print out the information without reading it while he went to answer the door.

Seeing the two men standing in the early morning rain, he hurried to turn off the alarm. By the time he unlocked the deadbolt, they were pushing through the door past him.

Henry was the first to speak. "My girl is gone. I'm worried sick." The old black man appeared to be on the verge of tears. Standing there, soaked to the skin with rain running off of him, he appeared to have aged twenty years overnight. "Do you know anything about this? Is she here? Do you have her?" He was almost yelling at Anthony.

Robert Moffield laid a hand on Henry's shoulder to quiet him. He could feel his friend trembling with a mixture of grief, fear, and anger. "You have to calm down. It's not going to do anybody any good if you stroke out on us. How about I talk to this young man to see if he knows anything? Would that be alright with you?" Speaking softly, he locked eyes with his old friend, the two were silent for several seconds while some deep secret message passed between them. "So, you haven't told him?"

"No Bobby, I didn't. She wanted to, the opportunity never came up." Henry looked lost. Barely whispering, he answered Robert's question. Covering his face with his hands he sobbed while trying to speak. "Bobby, maybe it would-, you go ahead." Henry's voice was so quiet it was hard to make out what he had said.

Tightening his arm around his old friend's shoulder, Robert cleared his throat to keep from crying along with Henry. When he looked up at Anthony, seeing the rather puzzled blank look, he knew it would be best to start from the beginning. "Mr. Payne, this may take a while. May we come in?"

Anthony took a step backward, unaware the door was still open until his bare feet touched water where the rain had puddled in the entry. The octogenarians had taken him by surprise, so much so, that he hadn't paid attention to the fact he hadn't ask them in. When Robert addressed him, Anthony turned closing the door while motioning them toward the kitchen. Recovering from the surprise, he regained his composure. He wondered why they thought Dixie would come looking for him. "I'm not used to company this time of the morning, sorry. Come in, I've made coffee. Have a seat while I get the both of you a cup."

Two hours and a pot and a half of coffee later, Anthony was at a loss for words. He had a hard time believing what he had just heard. He had a grown niece he never knew existed that might now be in mortal danger, if not dead. After believing he had no living family left for so many years, this was almost more than he could comprehend.

Henry excused himself after asking directions to the bathroom. In his absence Robert told Anthony that he blamed himself for having Henry bring the girl to meet him. "I should have waited until they caught the devil behind all of this. I just don't see how they made the connection to you."

Before either man could say anything else they felt rather than saw Henry standing in the doorway. He appeared to be in some sort of a trance, standing there perfectly still looking straight ahead, most of the color had drained from his face. As they watched, he seemed to crumble.

Rushing to his side before he could fall, Robert was the first to get to him. Anthony had grabbed the cordless phone on the way and was in the process of calling 911 when he thrust the phone in Robert's hand in order to catch Henry before the two of them ended up in the floor.

"Speak to me Henry. What's wrong?" Robert way frantic. He wasn't aware he was holding the phone as he dropped down beside his friend. Henry's eyes had started to roll back into his head. Gently cuffing Henry's face with his free hand, Robert saw Henry start to respond. "Stay still, I think you may have had a stroke. You just about scared the life out of me. Don't get up until we check you over. We'll get you to the hospital."

Looking directly into Anthony's eyes, Henry found his voice. "Boy, that picture, who is it? The woman, the older woman?"

Sounding as puzzled as he was by the stern pleading voice of the elderly man, it took a moment for him to answer. "That was my grandmother. What has the picture got to do with this?"

Henry ignored Anthony's question, looking first to Robert then back to Anthony, he demanded "Who all that was at Robert's that day has seen that picture, or other pictures of her?" When Anthony didn't answer right away he continued. "Somebody brighter than you made the connection."

Feeling like a child someone had just put a dunce hat on wasn't making his mood any better. He finally realized just how much Dixie looked like his grandmother and felt a fool for not questioning the resemblance along with the fact her last name was Taylor. "Okay old man." He stopped himself, took a calming breath before he continued. "My name is Tony, not Boy. I'm not sure who all has seen my grandmother's picture. Very few people that were at Robert's get together have ever been inside my home. Now–what are you talking about when you refer to a connection?"

Glaring at Anthony, Henry then turned to Robert patting his hand. "Bobby help me up off this damned floor." Seeing the reluctance in his friend, he grinned. "I'm fine, just took me by surprise is all. I'm still as tough as shoe leather. I guess the boy, I mean Tony, has to have everything spelled out for him." Once Henry was back on his feet he turned to Anthony. "I should 'a let the girl tell you who she was when we were at Robert's and maybe none of this would have happened. By the way, when you get to be as old as me any male your age is still a boy."

"You think someone abducted her because they figured out she was Raymond's daughter?" Robert asked.

Robert was attempting to be the voice of reason before tempers had another chance to flare. "There is a chance that someone who saw the picture may have made a comment about the resemblance after seeing Dixie at my place." He told Anthony. "I doubt anyone that was present that day would have had anything to do with her going missing. Now we know she didn't come here looking for you. You have to admit that it is something a girl that age might do under the circumstances."

Anthony sat quietly for a moment. It was apparent to the geriatric duo that he was considering something, something that was troubling to him. Looking from one to the other then back again, his voice had a hard edge to it when he spoke. "I know she was raised right, I'm not questioning that. There is something I have to ask and there isn't time for feeling offended. Believe it or not, I know something about how a young girl's mind can work. I wish I knew her well enough to know how she feels about herself. I need to know if she maybe thought about being a model or perhaps hoped to be discovered as an actress."

Robert already knew part of what Anthony had to explain to Henry. After filling the men in on how many missing girls were signed up with places like Model Mayhem, among the other talent sites on the internet, he explained about the modern flesh trade and how easily the young girls were being duped into believing they were headed for auditions instead of the bondage they ended up finding themselves in. Both young boys as well as girls found themselves being prostituted, sold overseas, used as slave labor, or a number of other things. Most of the missing that didn't end up in other countries were drugged until they became addicts dependent on their captors to the point they were afraid to leave them for fear they wouldn't get the fix needed. Some were used up then either killed or kicked out on their own, ashamed to go back to their families.

"Well Mr. Payne, Tony, I'll tell you straight. That girl just wants to get an education. She likes her tumbling. She likes her gymnastics. Above all she likes her learning. Her goal is to get good enough grades to get her education paid for so we don't have to pay her way. She says she is too shy to get in front of any camera. There have been real offers made for her to do just that. She didn't want any part of it. I think I can say no, she wouldn't of fell for anything like that." Henry sounded tired, with the worry punctuating every word he uttered.

It wasn't noon yet but Anthony felt like he had put in a full day. After closing the door when his surprise guests left, he leaned against it remembering the remark made by Brenda Lou. Just the thought of her brought a smile to his face. "So I have a niece by the name of Dixie. Wouldn't grandmother be proud if she knew? To think, Brenda Lou, you saw that right off." He mused aloud becoming somber. "I hope to God the wrong people didn't see her and make the connection."

Heading for the shower, he convinced himself her disappearance had nothing to do with who he was. After all these years, how could it? No one would remember his grandmother, and the people he had connections to in organized crime thought he was on their side. He convinced himself it had to be something else.

Chapter 23

Lou was so angry she was shouting out loud as she paced the floor. She was glad there wasn't anyone around to act calm in front of. The conversation she had with her eldest daughter earlier left her livid. After making an excuse to get off the phone, she threw it across the room. "That black bastard! You think you might be in love with that creature! How could someone so stupid be a daughter of mine? First you marry a man that tries to sell you and now this-this-this convict? No way will he be my son-in-law! No way will he raise my grandchild! I don't care what you think. I don't care how much money he has. I don't care, I don't care, I don't care! This is not some big city! Things like that aren't acceptable here! You aren't using the brain you were born with! You have no idea what, or, who he is. I know all about him! No, Brenda Lou, you will not marry him. I will not allow it!"

Continuing to fume for at least another hour, Lou told herself that the only reason Chet seemed to be warming up to Anthony was because of their daughter. There was no way her husband could really like that creature. She thought they were both being drawn in by someone she considered lower than dirt. If she had her way about it Anthony would pay dearly for worming his way into her family. The worst part of it was that it looked like he seemed to have Donna and Mac fooled along with everyone else. She even thought he had all those around them convinced he was almost a saint, including Tom Smith. Hatred was too mild a word for the way she felt toward Mr. Anthony Payne.

After composing herself, Lou took care of the errands she felt were essential before returning home to prepare for her ladies' church group meeting.

The smell of lemon polish and fresh baked apple pie filled the room while Lou hummed alone to the sound of gospel music. It had taken some time; but, she knew exactly what she would do to put a stop to Anthony working his way into the lives of her family. At first she had just wanted him out of their lives, but that had changed. After seeing how all those she was close to were turning toward him, now she wanted him to hurt!

***

New York

Brenda was in good spirits after her conversation with her mother. "Susan, I was afraid mom would be upset about me getting involved with someone so soon after all that mess with my late–whatever he was. I finally got up the nerve to tell her, my daddy has known for a while. She actually told me she was glad I was happy. Sometimes Mom isn't too keen when it comes to others that aren't exactly-well-white."

Susan looked up from the laundry they were folding. "Your mother loves you, of course she wants you to be happy. Have you told her yet that the baby probably belongs to Anthony?"

"Daddy knows. I just haven't built up to telling my mother. I don't want her to be disappointed in me again. I've made so many mistakes that have hurt her so bad. When I figure out how to do it without hurting her, the time will be right to tell her. Oh, Susan, I wish I knew how to get her to be proud of me." Brenda reached over to lay the towel she had folded on the stack. She quickly became lost in thought.

Susan reached over grabbing Brenda's hand. With her other hand she raised Brenda's face where she could look her in the eyes. "Don't put yourself down. You are a smart lady and as brave as anyone I've ever had the privilege to meet. You have a heart as big as all outdoors and on top of that you are a good honest person. There isn't a person alive that hasn't made some mistakes at some time in their life. So, you trusted the wrong person. That was something that could have happened to any young girl the age you were. It has happened to several, including me. You are doing something important girl. There is no way to know how many lives you are saving. Your mother is a very lucky woman to have you for a daughter."

"I certainly don't feel brave. It feels like I'm hiding from life. If that's the way it has to be to protect my baby so be it. Susan, why does life have to be so hard sometimes? I love the man I think fathered this child. I don't know what to do about it. Even though the south has changed a lot, where I came from it's still the Bible belt. Most people there just can't understand how blacks and whites could be equal, let alone fall in love with each other. What's worse is, I know he is attracted to me but I'm not sure how he feels aside from that."

Susan couldn't keep the wry smile from crossing her face. "You fret too much. All a person has to do is see how he looks at you to know how much he loves you. As for the other people, don't try to let other people live your life for you. It's not up to them to make you happy, so make your life happy for yourself. They will either accept it or not, it's up to them. The people who truly care about you will accept him if he treats you right."

"I know you're right. I guess being brought up in that part of the world makes it hard to see things differently sometimes, no matter what my heart says. With my whole life on hold it's easy to let my thoughts go in the wrong direction when I start thinking too much." She laughed at herself when she saw Susan's smug smile.

"That's more like it. You have a great smile, glad to see you using it. You go do whatever you need to do. It's about time to take my darling little monsters for a walk in the park. When you're ready let me know and we can take off."

***

Chicago

Dixie lay in a fetal position on a thin stinking mattress covering the small cot in a strange room. Blankets covered the windows to either keep the light out or so no one could see in. She wasn't sure which because she had been blindfolded when they put her there. The room smelled of cheap booze, dirty socks, stale smoke, rotting garbage, sweat and urine. She didn't have to see to know how filthy the musty room must be. It wasn't long before she heard a rustling sound not far from where she lay. Uncertain of the source, she was gripped by terror until she realized it had to be a rat instead of her captors.

After her eyes adjusted to the dim light, she started thinking of a way to get herself out of the situation she was in. Dixie started working to free herself from the ropes she was tied with. The ropes binding her ankles were tied to the legs of the cot. Her wrists were tied behind her back tethering her to the other side of the cot. Struggling to pull her feet free had only resulted in the rough fiber digging into her flesh as it tightened around her ankles. There was just enough slack for Dixie to work her hands around to reach the knotted rope binding her wrists.

Working franticly to loosen the ropes, Dixie froze when she heard a voice as the door creaked open. "I'm just gonna check on the little nigger bitch. It won't take me too long so just cool your jets out here for a minute." She heard someone enter the room before the door clicked shut. "Looks like you're still safe and sound. Glad to see you finally woke up. For a while I was afraid we might 'a give you too much of the stuff. That would a pissed the boss off big time." He smirked.

Dixie glared up at her captor as the voice of the other man came through the door. "Remember the boss don't want her deflowered, so keep your dick in your pants." This statement was followed by a sickening laugh. She heard the man again. "I reckon we can look all we want to after while. Boss didn't say nothing about that. Hurry it up and get back in here."

The man that entered the room was leering at Dixie as he spoke. "Cat got your tongue little girl? I can tell from that look you would like to tell me off, probably worse." He laughed. "Too bad I'm not allowed to do what I want. I could loosen up that little tongue of yours and a few other things too, if you know what I mean." He stepped closer, running his hands slowly over her body. In the process he lingered over her breasts and ran his hand between her legs, lingering again at her crotch. "Like that don't you?" Seeing her squirm, he laughed. "Maybe I'll spend a little extra time with you tonight when I bring your food. I know ways to make you feel really good without doing anything to piss off the boss. I'll have to take you to the bathroom before long anyway. Don't go messing yourself before I get back or I'll have to wash you." He winked down at her before turning to go out the door he had just opened. "You just might enjoy a sponge bath the way I give em. By the way, don't get any ideas about escaping. It could be more hazardous to your health than what's planned for you." He was laughing as he closed the door behind him.

Now Dixie understood what it really meant when someone made a statement about someone making their skin crawl. Having that disgusting man putting his hands all over her made her skin feel like it was crawling. She felt so violated she wanted to throw up. Until now, she had been sheltered from most of the unsavory aspects of life. This was her first taste of how horrible human beings could really be. No book she ever read prepared her for what she was now experiencing. She knew she had to escape. Until now, situations in the fictions she read all seemed so unreal they couldn't actually happen to anyone. Not anymore.

Dixie knew it wouldn't do to lie there feeling sorry for herself. No one knew where she was. She had no idea where she was or how she got here. Help wasn't on the way. Her cellphone wasn't in her pocket. All she had to work with were her wits.

The two hours it had taken to work her hands free seemed more like an eternity. While untying her ankles and rubbing them to bring back the circulation, Dixie came up with a plan for her escape. When she was free of the ropes, she looked behind the blanket covering the window. The window was raised enough to let in a little fresh air. Although she was several stories up, there was a fire escape, or what was left of one.

She wasn't worried about the bloody abrasions on her wrists as she eased out through the partially open window to flee down the fire escape in the dusky evening light. The time spent in acrobatics and tumbling were paying off. More than once on her way down, there where rungs or other sections missing. At one point there was a drop of several feet to negotiate. She used the skills she learned on the uneven bars to bridge the gap she could not have accomplished otherwise. Once on the sidewalk five floors below, she ran like the hounds of hell were on her heels. She didn't stop to catch her breath until she knew she was well away from the building.

When she finally stopped, Dixie tried to figure out where she was. It wasn't hard to tell she was in a very bad area of a city. There was broken glass and other trash littering the sidewalks. Leaning against the side of a rundown store, she took a deep breath and put on the calm demeanor of a person used to these surroundings. Taking another deep breath, Dixie steeled herself for what she might find inside before opening the door.

Chapter 24

St. Louis, Missouri

Eula sat in her husband's favorite chair. She was filled with a despair born of fear and she had never felt more alone in her life. Sitting in his chair made her feel closer to her husband. Tears streamed down her face. Henry was on his way home but had not arrived yet. The phone rang causing her to jump. Because he was overdue, she was afraid it might be more bad news. "The old fool shouldn't be driving his self around anymore. I should 'a made him take one of the kids along to do the driving. He's getting too blamed old for this, so am I." She thought out loud. On the way to answer the phone she dried her eyes, blew her nose, and steeled herself for whatever she was about to hear.

"Gram, I'm in Chicago, Illinois." Dixie whispered. "Don't worry, I'm alright. Someone stole my purse and cellphone, that's why I called collect. I need to get farther away from where I'm at, so I can't stay on here long. When I find a safer place to stay I'll call back and tell you where I'm at. I love you."

"Dixie, thank God. What happened? We have been worried half to death. Honey, have the police help you until we can come pick you up. Why are you speaking so softly? I can barely hear you." Eula's legs suddenly felt weak. She came close to falling to the floor as relief flooded her senses.

"I don't have time to explain right now Gram. I'll call as soon as I can. I'll call Aunt Ruth's phone. Tell everyone I love them."

She was afraid the phone was bugged. She knew if she didn't hang up right then she would be bawling and she didn't want her grandmother to know how frightened she was. Before her grandmother had a chance to say another word, she hung up and started running again. She was sure if she didn't get far enough away they would catch her again.

Sticking to shadows as best she could, she noticed a lawn service truck pulling a trailer coming toward her. The trailer was filled with equipment and mowers. When the vehicle slowed in front of her to make the turn, she didn't think twice before jumping into the trailer behind some equipment large enough to conceal her from sight. She laid flat on her stomach wedged comfortably between two mowers. The position allowed her to see under the board being used for a tailgate. There was a good-sized gap across the end of the trailer giving her an unobstructed view of the street behind her. The open rails on the sides made it possible to see the rest of the area. Wiping the perspiration from her eyes, Dixie breathed a sigh of relief as she watched her surroundings change from bad to decent to good. When she saw a motel about a block ahead, she started preparing herself to jump. She saw the truck's turn signal start to flash. Before the truck could turn, thankfully, the light turned red giving her enough time to safely slip out before the truck sped off again.

Dixie entered the lobby of the motel. It was just busy enough for her to place a collect call without being overheard. By the time she placed the call her grandfather, Henry had finally made it home and Eula had him go with her to their neighbor's.

She gave them the name of the motel and asked them to use the same phone to book her a room under a fictitious name. After promising to call that same number back, once she got into her room, she disconnected. They knew there had to be a reason she didn't want to take any chances of someone finding out where she was.

While waiting, Dixie acted like she was reading a magazine. She kept watch over the top of the magazine until she overheard the desk clerk make the arrangements. After hearing her room was booked she slipped off to the bathroom. Seeing a side door leading out of the building she took it. When she came back into the lobby from the front of the building, she went to the front desk to check in, acting as if she had just arrived.

After Dixie was safely tucked into her room, she called her grandparents once again. She told Henry everything she had been through. She told him she was almost positive that her captors worked for the same people that were responsible for the deaths of her parents, repeating some of the bits and pieces of conversation she could remember overhearing when she was first captured. It sent a chill throughout his body. Dixie wasn't a random victim; she was the objective.

Later, laying on her bed, Dixie was glad she hadn't told her grandfather everything she overheard coming through the wall from the room next to hers. Remembering the screams of the captives in the other room was terrifying. She knew the women had been beaten and raped.

Warm tears slid down her face while she relived listening to them beg not to be hurt anymore. It made her stomach roll when she thought about the way the men laughed while they talked about keeping the girls still, joking about it while they tied the tourniquets around their captives' arms. The women were told to hold still so the needle wouldn't hurt too badly. The men laughed about how good the stuff they were giving them would make them feel, about how friendly it would make the women.

If she hadn't heard them talking about inviting some of the police over for fun and games, she would have reported them as soon as she escaped. There was no one in the whole city she knew of to call for help for herself or the others that were being held in the building. She had escaped from them but Dixie never felt so helpless in her young life as she prayed for their safety. It was almost daylight before she drifted off to sleep wondering if the other females were still alive.

Hanging up the phone, Henry was thankful Dixie told him she was afraid the house phone might be tapped. He knew he was so distraught he wouldn't have thought of it. There was one more call to place from the borrowed phone.

Robert Moffield was shaken by the news he just received from Henry. Robert told his oldest and dearest friend he would use any recourses necessary to retrieve Dixie and do whatever needed to be done to keep her safe.

10:00 PM

"Anybody lays a hand on that girl will have to answer to me. I watched Henry go through hell and back when that little lady's mother died. I was afraid Eula would die of grief over what happened back then. There is no way I will sit on the sidelines and watch them suffer like that again. We may not share blood but we are family just the same. I know how I would feel if it were my granddaughter." Robert's voice had a steely resolve that booked no argument. It was a voice of someone who built an empire with his own sweat and sheer force of will. He was a man accustomed to being in command.

When Anthony looked up from the papers he was going over, the look in Robert's eyes backed up the words he had just spoken. If he hadn't known Mr. Moffield to be a good-natured easygoing man, he would have thought him to be a ruthless cold-blooded killer. He was glad he was on the same side as the old man. It made him wonder what the man had encountered in his life that could have been bad enough to enable him to have that kind of buried hatred and anger. There was no doubt in his mind, if it came down to it, Robert could and would kill to protect Dixie.

The private jet was approaching an airstrip near Chicago's O'Hare Airport. The flight from Malden, Missouri passed in relative quiet. Anthony thought Robert was asleep until he spoke. After hearing what he had to say, it was obvious Robert had been mentally covering all the bases. Most of the trip he sat quietly with his eyes closed.

"Mr. Moffield, I hope you don't plan on being physically involved in getting her back. It's too dangerous. You have to let the trained authorities handle it. She is a smart young woman; look how well she has done to this point. So far she has done everything exactly right. I can't believe how smart she is." Anthony let a small smile play at the corners of his mouth when he remembered what he had been told of her escape. He was still finding it a heartwarming shock to know that Dixie was his brother's daughter, his own niece.

"I can't help wonder just how many of those so called authorities are in league with Ronald Arnold. "He spat out in a hiss. "Call me Robert. I'm glad she thought about phone taps. If she hadn't told her grandmother to use her Aunt Ruth's cell phone, it might not have gone as well as it has. Tony, Dixie truly is a bright girl. I wish this whole mess was over and done with. It's gone on way too many years. How many deaths? How many ruined lives? This monster has to be stopped now." His jaws were clenched shut hard enough to cause the muscles to stand out. He turned, looking out the window at the lights fast approaching from below as they made their descent.

"Who is Aunt Ruth? I haven't heard her mentioned before. The name never came up on any background checks. Is she a close enough relation to have to worry about them checking into getting protection for?" The concern that came through when he spoke was genuine.

Merriment danced in Robert's eyes as he answered. "There is no Aunt Ruth. She was smart enough to have Eula go next door. The old woman's name is Rothalund. When Dixie was small she couldn't pronounce that or the last name of Wunderlich. She referred to her as Aunt Ruth until she was old enough to pronounce her name. Anyone listening in wouldn't have a clue who she was talking about."

"I'll be damned. She is a bright young lady." Admiration was growing by leaps and bounds for the niece he hadn't known existed until a short time ago.

Both men sat in silence until the wheels touched the tarmac. Anthony was the first to speak. "Robert, the thing I haven't been able to figure out is who could have seen the picture and put two and two together. I know Brenda Lou thought there was an uncanny resemblance; but, that was as far as that went.

How could anyone with ties to Arnold have figured it out? Grabbing Dixie? It doesn't make any sense."

Robert rose from his seat, turned to look back over his shoulder briefly, before he started off the plane. "Tony that is the puzzle we need to solve if we are going to find out who is behind all of this." He answered over his shoulder.

Anthony was shaking his head as he picked up his briefcase, following Robert off the plane. "There is no we Robert. This is too dangerous for you to be any more involved than you already have been. I know how you feel; but, you can't put yourself in harm's way. The plane is appreciated more than you can imagine; but, you're being here for her and helping get her to safety is more than enough."

"Son, let's get something straight right now, you use that word but too much. Furthermore, I'm too damned old and ornery for you to tell me what I can or cannot do." The sardonic grin didn't quite reach the eyes that looked as hard as any Anthony had ever seen. He knew if looks could kill that he would be stone cold and shriveled at that very moment. "Get used to it."

Not another word was spoken until the men were seated in the limo speeding toward the motel to find Dixie.

Robert made sure Dixie was safe before calling her grandparents. After speaking to Henry and Eula, both men agreed it would be best to spend the night in Chicago before boarding the plane to take her to safety. They assumed she would be sleeping, worn out from all she had been through. Had they known she was still awake they would have collected her right then for the flight back home.

Once inside his own room, Anthony finally had a chance to look over the pages he printed out before his early morning visitors arrived. So much happened since then he had almost forgotten about the papers. With time on his hands, he was glad he had remembered to grab them before leaving to retrieve Dixie.

Reading the articles several times over didn't change the names he found there, even though he hoped it would. He was having a hard time believing the information could be true. Anthony hurriedly started placing calls to all the agents on the task force he was working with. He told them what he had found, asking that they go back over everything to see if they could come up with a different conclusion from the one he had formed. He faxed everything he had to each of them before attempting to grab a couple hours sleep.

Chapter 25

It was a beautiful fall day. The breeze carried the soft dusty smell of approaching rain into the house through the open window. Oblivious to the surroundings, the boss's thoughts were on the upcoming meeting. Things were finally being set into motion. An old fashioned Southern hanging was about to take place. "I want the bastard to choke to death on his own balls before he's strung up." The icy sound of the boss's voice echoed in the empty room.

The cell phone buzzed as the boss started out the door. "Yeah. How did you get this number? You know better than to call unless there's an emergency." White hot anger filled the air.

"Ugh, - well, - we got sort of a problem. We couldn't get hold of Mr. Arnold. The girl, that little black girl, she got away." Came the hesitant answer. "But she don't know this place like we do and we're lookin." He hastily injected before continuing. "Not to worry, me and Russ will find her fast enough. We got people out lookin all over already. We're gonna find her real fast for you." The flunky stated.

"You idiot. How the hell did she get away? I specifically gave orders for someone to be with her at all times. Who is responsible?"

"Me and Russ was right outside the door. We had her tied up real good. When I looked back in she was goin out the window. Boss, we was five stories up with a no good fire escape she could try to get down. We looked around outside and she didn't fall or die or anything. After that we searched the whole building. We got guys going over it with a fine tooth comb. She's gotta be hiding somewhere in the building. She had to of gone back in the next floor down. There weren't no other windows except them she could of got in through. We'll find her. She's gotta be hurt bad if she jumped, so she couldn't a got too far." He paused then continued. "I don't see how she could of got them ropes undone. Russ trussed her up real good, tied them ropes tight. I double checked them ropes too."

"You better hope she is found soon. Someone is going to answer for this. You know that, don't you? What have I got, morons working for me now?" Flipping the phone shut without waiting for a response, the boss stormed to the car, slamming the door shut before speeding off to locate Ronald Arnold.

Arriving at The Plantation Inn, in Cape Girardeau, in record time, it didn't take long to locate the room in which Mr. Ronald Arnold was booked.

Ronald barely had the door opened before his visitor pushed past him. Once the door was closed he spoke. "You're early." He hesitated before continuing. "It looks like there will be a slight delay. Payne wasn't home when my man went there to pick him up."

"I'm surrounded by idiots, imbeciles, and dumb asses." His boss shouted turning toward him. Looking him straight in the eye, the voice held a calm but deadly sounding quality. "You have lost track of Payne? Your men in Chicago have lost the girl. They aren't even supposed to know who I am; but, somehow they even have my cell phone number. Should I guess how they came by their information? Do you have any idea how badly you are screwing up? I pay you to get things right."

Ronald's boss turned, looking out the window, while still speaking. "I know who's responsible for Ben's death, do you? Oh, you were there for a short time weren't you? You were supposed to stay. When I arrived you were nowhere around, were you? Didn't you wonder why dear Ben was mutilated so badly? Bud followed my orders, that's why! Why the hell wasn't I informed Benjamin Orr went by Larry Green? It's not your job to withhold information. You, Ronald, are supposed to tell me everything. It isn't your job to pick and choose what I am told."

There were several seconds of silence before his boss turned back around, looking him in the eye once more. Ronald was sweating as his boss' voice broke the silence. "Can you tell me why you aren't aware that Payne is working both sides of the fence? By the way, that is something else you didn't fill me in on. Anthony Payne is Tony Taylor."

Ronald Arnold was shocked. Not only was this news to him; but, he feared what he would hear next. He knew his life could end suddenly or slowly with great pain and suffering if he didn't think fast. He was trying to think of something.

"Come on Ronnie boy, haven't you got anything to say?" The voice was taunting. Without giving him a chance to answer, his boss continued. "We are going to see to it that our buddy Payne has a surprise waiting for him when he returns from wherever it is he went. I'm dropping my car off in the Wal-Mart parking lot. You pick me up so we don't have both cars in his driveway. Can you at least get that right, Ronnie?"

***

After Anthony finished speaking to his early morning visitors, he tried calling both Robert's room and Dixie's. There wasn't an answer in either room so he thought they were both still asleep, and left messages for them before heading to the exercise room. He was surprised to find the two already there working out. Robert was on the rowing machine, while Dixie was on the exercise bike. She had on headphones, preventing her from hearing Anthony when he came in the door. With her head down, eyes closed, and pedaling like she was trying to outrun someone chasing her, she almost jumped off the seat when she looked up to see Anthony standing in front of her.

Grinning sheepishly, Dixie watched as Anthony motioned for the two to join him. "Let's go grab breakfast. Staff says the food here is good." Eyes squinted, he looked closely at Dixie's face. "After you get some food in you, get some more rest. You look like you need it. I'll buy you a change of clothes and a toothbrush. We aren't leaving for a couple hours anyway and I know you don't have any packing to do."

She started to protest until she saw the look in his eyes. Closing her mouth, she went through the door ahead of Robert. Once Dixie passed by, Anthony put his hand on Robert's shoulder to stop him until Dixie was far enough away for him to whisper without her hearing. "After she goes to her room we have to talk."

Over a breakfast of scrambled eggs, toast, bacon, and juice Anthony and Dixie had a chance to talk. "Young lady, I can't begin to describe how thankful I am to have you as my niece. Why didn't you tell me that day we were out at Robert's?" Anthony asked.

Dixie looked embarrassed. "I started to. If I hadn't started right out asking questions that got me yelled at I would have. I just kind of felt like I made a fool out of myself so I lost my nerve." She took another bite then asked "Can I call you Uncle Tony or should I still call you Mr. Payne?" Dixie started to say something else. She hesitated casting a brief glance at Robert deciding the question would wait.

"I hope you call me Uncle Tony. Yes. I like the sound of that." He grinned. "When I met you, I wondered why you kept staring at me. I went in the bathroom to see if I had food stuck between my teeth or what." He teased her.

Dixie's expression was intense. Her voice had an amused quality to it when she spoke. "I wondered why you used the name Payne instead of your real name. I figured it out now."

While finishing breakfast, she filled Anthony in on her extracurricular activities, her likes and dislikes, her friends, and which classes she liked best. His admiration for her as a person grew by the minute.

After Dixie went up to her room the two men sat alone in the dining room talking about the flight, the weather, things that they didn't mind anyone overhearing until they knew they weren't being watched. Knowing Dixie was asleep by now, Anthony asked the desk clerk if they could send someone out for the things Dixie would need while they used one of the conference rooms for a few minutes.

When the door closed behind them, Robert turned to Anthony. "How bad?"

There was an awkward pause before Anthony spoke. He had been wondering just how much he should tell Robert. "I have to trust you to go along with what I have to do. I wish things could be different. People you love are going to hurt on a lot of different levels. You can't tell Henry, Tom, or anyone, what I'm about to tell you. I sincerely wish I could but I can't even tell you everything." He looked beseechingly at the old man he had come to think of as family in the short time he knew him.

Suddenly Robert looked every day as old as he was. He stood with his head drooped slowly shaking it back and forth. "That bad?" Looking back up, his expression showed staunch determination. "Tell me what you can and what you have in mind. We'll figure how to get this done with the least amount of damage possible. Don't worry about Henry and Eula. As long as we keep that girl safe, they can handle it."

Anthony shared as much of the information he could about what had been uncovered. He told Robert about his phone conversations during the night, along with what he found out from his visitors earlier that morning. The only thing omitted were the names. After hearing everything, it didn't come as a surprise when he learned Dixie wouldn't be going back to St. Louis. Robert was surprised that Anthony refused to let him take Dixie to his farm.

Seeing the dismay on the old man's face felt like a blow to Anthony. He knew he had to tell Robert more than he wanted to. "I trust you, I trust your whole family. I can't tell you why; but, everyone needs to think Dixie has disappeared completely. Tom has to think so too. I'm sorry. You can tell her grandparents she is alright but you have to make them see that they can't tell anyone else. They can't even tell other family members. It's for their own safety, as well as hers. Let them know it absolutely has to look like they are grieving." After briefly hesitating Anthony shook his head. "Robert, we just can't risk anyone seeing her."

Pacing back and forth, Anthony gave Robert a moment for what he heard to sink in before telling him the rest of the plan. Explaining wasn't going to be easy. He had to make Robert see why he would have to keep the information from his son-in-law without telling Robert too much. "Before you even suggest it, sending her to New York won't work either. Tom can't know anything, remember? If not one of the adults, one of the children might accidentally let it slip. That's too great a risk for Dixie, as well as themselves."

"Tom's not involved is he?" The elderly man looked sick at heart for asking the question.

"No, Tom is an honest man. He is just too close to someone with the wrong connections. You don't know how much I wish I could tell you everything. I can tell you no one in your family has anything to do with any of this. It's just too easy to say the wrong thing to the wrong person without realizing it. Bob, you have to trust that I know what I'm doing. If I could tell you–, well never mind. You will know why in due time. For now, Dixie will go someplace safe. I will personally turn her over to one of the agents you met at your place before I head home. She is my only living flesh and blood and I will protect her. Once she and I are airborne I'll fill her in on what to expect. You will be going back to St. Louis. It has to be this way. Let's head back up to my room. I have to make a couple calls before we leave."

Opening the door, the first thing they saw was a blinking on the phone. The message was from agent Trout. Listening to orders to call back immediately, Anthony knew it had to be urgent. Trout answered on the first ring. "Tony here. What's happened now?" Robert watched Anthony's face go through a whole range of emotions while he silently listened several minutes without speaking. Closing his cell phone, he sat down heavily on the bed, staring straight ahead.

To break the silence, Robert cleared his throat before speaking. "Anything you can share?"

The sound of Robert's voice brought Anthony out of the shocked stupor he appeared to be in. "Change of plans. I have to be dead for a while. At least now I can personally protect Dixie." He grinned at the shocked look on the older man's face before telling him what had happened.

Ronald Arnold's body had been discovered in Anthony's house by two of the agents Anthony was working with. It was set up to look like Anthony murdered him. Arnold's vehicle and the murder weapon were removed by the agents before the murder was reported to the local authorities. Since Tom Smith wasn't aware that the two of them had gone to rescue Dixie, it would look like Anthony had first killed Arnold then fled the scene in the murdered man's vehicle. Reports would be put out that the remains of Anthony's body were found in the wrecked vehicle along with the murder weapon.

"Well son, it sounds like a plan. I don't understand why it has to look that way but there must be a reason. It will be upsetting to a bunch of people. You've made more friends than you know. How long will you have to stay dead? Somebody has to take care of your animals. Do you want me to take them to the farm with me?"

"I really appreciate it but Trout has that covered. Thanks for caring. Guess we better get going." Anthony was glad he had removed Wilbur's gun, the tapes and other information from his house before he left.

Chapter 26

Clasping her hands together, Dixie looked out the window of the plane. "Since I can't go home, at least I will have a chance to get to know you. My new Uncle Tony, wow, I have a brand-new uncle." She turned toward her uncle studying his face, her serious expression turned to a grin. "I kept thinking you looked familiar but I knew I hadn't seen you before I met you at Uncle Bob's, you know–, Mr. Moffield's. I just figured out why."

"Oh? Are you going to tell me?"

"First, I can call you Uncle Tony, right? You said I could. Mr. Payne or Anthony sounds kind of stuffy and you are my uncle after all."

"I told you earlier that I think that would be good. It sounds great when you say it. I never had a niece before. Now here you are, almost grown up and I never knew you existed. You are my brand new niece too. I can't get over how much you look like my grandmother. Now tell me what you figured out." He teased.

"You look like a young version of Abraham Lincoln. Well, you are much better looking but there are some similarities. Have you seen that picture of him before he got skinny and old?" She tried hard not to laugh. "But, of course he wasn't black. Thomas Jefferson had black children. Abe Lincoln didn't though, but he fought so hard against slavery anyway. I've always wondered why. If you were white you could pass for him, almost, when he was young. Nah you wouldn't. His beard was yucky and he had those nasty bushy eyebrows, plus ear hair. But, put more weight on him and see the profile, you really do resemble him a little bit. I'm glad you don't have a nasty beard or the other hairy thing going on. Did you know that in his youth he was considered to be a pretty handsome man?"

Anthony almost choked, covering it with a cough. "Have you always had such an active imagination young lady?" He coughed again before changing the subject. I know this will be hard; but, you need to tell me everything you can remember from the time you were taken until the time you got away from those men. Try hard not to leave anything out. Think about what you saw or heard, how many people were there, how far you went when you got away. All of it. Can you do that? I'm sorry to have to ask you to do this. I know it won't be pleasant, but, it might help save a lot of lives."

Dixie was able to give an accurate description of the building. Since it was taller than the ones surrounding it that would help too. She told Anthony how far she ran to reach the rundown store where she stopped to catch her breath. She was even able to remember the name of the store.

She asked for a pencil and paper. It took her a few minutes to draw a fair likeness of the two men that abducted her. Hair color, height, and the color of one man's eyes were written beside their likeness.

When Dixie handed the pictures to her uncle he was speechless. "I'm sorry Uncle Tony. I didn't get a close enough look at that one's eyes to be sure of the color. I only saw him through the door when it opened." She pointed to the man she was referring to. "The one that came in to check on me got right up in my face. I got a good look at his eyes. He had bad teeth and his breath was awful. He was so creepy." She shivered at the thought of his hands on her body and what he said about what he wanted to do to her.

Anthony stared at the pictures with such evident anger, Dixie shrunk back into her seat. She noticed how intimidating he could be if that anger was directed at a person. He looked like he wanted to rip them apart with his bare hands. She noticed once again, how broad his shoulders were, the size of his arms and how the corded muscles stood out, along with hands that looked to her like he could probably bend metal.

"You told me you liked to draw. Young lady, you are an artist. These likenesses are unbelievable. I've seen one of these men before.

Using these, they won't have any problem identifying them. These drawings are as good as a photo of them would be." In awe, he glanced up from looking at the pictures to give her a warm smile.

Dixie started telling Anthony everything she remembered hearing through the wall from the next room. Tears started forming in her eyes while she recounted the women's screams. She stared crying in earnest when she was almost finished. "Oh, Uncle Tony, I hope they are alive. I could hear those men hitting them. They were doing such awful things to them."

Anthony reached over wrapping the sobbing girl in his massive arms. He kissed the top of her head while he gently rocked her. He let her cry until she was ready to continue speaking.

She was able to remember the names of the men. She only heard them call one of the women by name. What surprised Anthony was that Dixie was able to tell him the two nicknames of the police officers Dixie heard referred to. No one had been able to get a lead on them until now.

James Trout was waiting for them when they touched down at the airport in Springfield, Missouri.

***

Lou bustled around in her kitchen. The windows were open allowing a cool breeze to bring the fragrance from the climbing roses into the room. She was humming to herself. It had been several months since she had felt so content. The main story in the local newscast the night before had brightened her spirits considerately.

"I don't have to worry about my daughter marrying that black bastard now." She almost sang it aloud she was so happy. The story started out with a news crew outside of his house in Dexter. They described the grizzly scene found inside the house, panning out to show the grounds surrounding the home. There were all kinds of law enforcement vehicles parked around the house with lights flashing. When they switched back to the news anchor, he finished by stating the wrecked vehicle had been found on the river road outside of Cairo, Illinois, on the Missouri side of the bridge. The anchor stated the remains were partially burned and the gun used in the murder was found at the scene. Hearing the body referred to as that of Anthony Payne brought Lou immense joy. "It's for the best, Brenda Lou will get over it. He just wasn't right for you." She voiced her feelings out loud to the empty room.

While Lou stood looking out the window drying her hands on a dish towel, she watched Chet chasing children around the redbud tree in a game of tag. They were giggling and laughing while half grown puppies joined in the chase. She laid the dish towel down and went to stand in the door. "Who's ready for lunch?" She called out.

A chorus of voices answered in response. Some of the women came inside to help carry the food to the picnic table. Chet took the dogs back to the pen so they wouldn't be underfoot or begging for food.

Chet stood beside his wife with his arm wrapped around her waist. They watched as the women started filling plates for the children. "Thanks for suggesting we have the kids over today. At times I really miss ours being this age. Remember how much fun they were?" Chet said watching the children.

"It won't be long before we have a couple little ones under foot again. You're going to get to spoil another generation soon." Lou leaned her head against his shoulder as she answered.

Looking lovingly at his wife Chet remarked, "It's good to see you in a good mood again. I was starting to worry about you."

"Let's not go into that right now." She answered, reaching up to caress his cheek with her hand. "Our girls are going to be alright now. I admit that I was worried. It's not a concern now." She let out a contented sigh. "Now we need to find a good woman for our boy."

Chet chuckled. "Hon, I think he can find his own woman. From what I've seen, he has several to choose from." He laughed when Lou playfully slapped at his shoulder. "By the way, Walter is bringing the divine Ms. Molly down later. He says to tell you not to get attached. They are only friends. I think he's trying to sell her the motorcycle they are riding here today."

After lunch Chet started playing with the children from his church once again while the women helped Lou clean up the mess. She couldn't help the pleasure she felt at the gossip she heard connected to the death of Anthony Payne.

When everyone went home, Chet sat out on the front porch in the shade. He had a cold glass of ice tea he sipped while watching the honey bees buzzing in the lush clover that blanketed the lawn.

His thoughts were on his wife's behavior. He didn't know what had been disturbing her so badly over the last couple of months; but, he was glad to see her happy again. He thought to himself, aside from that, the only thing missing to make this day perfect was having his children here.

Chet heard the crunch of gravel. He watched Tom Smith pull into the drive. Tom got out of the car, head down, he slowly made his way to where Chet sat on the porch.

"Guess you heard the news?" Tom said. His expression was grim. "Chet, he had me fooled completely."

Puzzled, he asked his friend, "Who had you fooled? What are you talking about?" motioning for Tom to sit.

Tom stood silently for a minute, wondering how to break the news. He sat down, shook his head, and looked into the now worried face of his friend. "I know you liked Anthony Payne. Hell, we all did. I trusted the guy."

"What do you mean did?" Chet asked.

"He died yesterday. Looks like he murdered that fellow everybody was looking for and took off. He wrecked the man's car before he got out of the state. From what they found at his house he wasn't such a good guy after all. They wouldn't let me in there, so I don't know what all they did find." Tom took a deep breath before he continued. "Seems FBI, ATF, CIA, God only knows who else are all over the place. Won't let any local or state on the property. They are going over the place with a fine-toothed comb. He had me fooled." Tom Smith looked as bewildered and betrayed as he felt.

Listening to his friend, Chet paled. He wondered how Brenda Lou would take the news. First she had been taken in by Larry Joe Green, now Anthony. "I don't know how I'm going to break this to my daughter. I think she was falling for the man. Are they sure he did it?"

"From what they told me it doesn't look like there is any doubt. I overheard one of them say it looked like he, Anthony was trying to ditch the man's car after he killed the man." Tom coughed to clear his throat. "Brenda Lou may have heard by now. It went out on national news this morning. Maybe you ought to call her."

"Have you talked to Susan today?" Chet's mind was racing. He was worried about what effect the news would have on his pregnant daughter. "Maybe-I hope she was with Brenda Lou when she found out."

Tom shook his head. "Thought I better talk to you first."

The sound of the phone ringing could be heard from the inside of the house. Lou came to the door holding the receiver. "Brenda Lou wants to speak to you." She said to Chet.

Tom couldn't hide how concerned he was. "I'm glad she is with our Susan. It would be awful if she was with strangers right now."

Chet had the look of a desperate, beaten down man when he got up to take the phone.

Tom stood. "Look Chet, I hate it but I have to go so I'll say bye, I have to see to business. I'll come back by later. I'm sorry buddy. If there is anything I can do you let me know."

Lou had been eaves dropping. When Chet got off the phone he looked troubled when Lou came back in the room where he was. "It's going to be alright. Brenda Lou has her whole life ahead of her, she'll have the baby to keep her mind off those men, and she has her job." Lou tried not to appear as pleased as she was while speaking to her husband.

She started to go back into the kitchen, got half way, turned back to Chet. "She will find someone else, someone better. In the meantime she has all of us." She gave Chet's cheek a peck as they heard the motorcycle pulling into the drive. "Sounds like Walter and Miss Molly have arrived. Try to act normal. Let's go say hi."

Walter brought a young woman named Heather explaining Molly had wanted to try out his motorcycle. When Molly's boyfriend found out she was looking to buy a motorcycle, he bought her a new one. He let his parents know he was dating Heather occasionally and told them they were in the same business class.

After dinner was finished they all sat around the table talking over dessert. The subject of Anthony came up when Heather saw his picture in the newspaper laying on the counter.

"I can't believe this. There has to be more to it than what we've heard. I have always been a pretty good judge of character and if this is true, he had me fooled completely. I really liked the guy." Walter said, shaking his head in disbelief.

Heather spoke up. "I didn't know you all knew him. We studied him a little in one of my classes. He was the pick to be the next self-made mega millionaire in our time. The bio on him said he started from nothing while he was in prison for something he didn't do.

While he was in prison, he earned a couple degrees in business and finance and figured out how to do what he wanted to. When he got out, he had already started his own import export business on line. The way he set it up, it has its own survey check and balance system. A childhood friend of his dead brother helped him run it. He employs about a dozen people. The money goes directly into an account that his payables are withdrawn from. He developed the whole system himself." She took a sip of coffee. "Not only is he a genius, he was selected one of the top ten bachelors of the year. They were selected on accomplishments, looks, money, and best dressed. He was number one."

Lou had to get up, turning her back to Heather. She did not want anyone to see how it upset her to hear someone talking about how wonderful Anthony was. Attempting to keep her voice level, Lou spoke with her back to the table. "Sounds like they will have to reevaluate that list now. Brenda Lou wouldn't have been able to tolerate that kind of competition very well anyway."

Lou turned to note the surprised look on Heather's face. The young woman gasped before asking "That was her Tony? His name was Anthony Taylor. I thought Walter said Brenda Lou was seeing Anthony Payne. It wasn't Payne? Oh goodness, I'm so sorry, I didn't know. She has to be heart broken."

Chapter 27

James Trout sat explaining the situation to Anthony and Dixie. They were seated at a table near the back of a room in a restaurant near the hotel they would be spending the night at. Dixie was picking at the tablecloth, flower arrangement, menu, silver ware, and anything else she could get her hands on. The men couldn't help but notice she had something troubling her.

Agent Trout complimented Dixie on her drawings. He told her that those along with the information she provided would be their biggest break in shutting down that part of the operation in Chicago. "Hopefully we can track these people to the person over the rest of the illegal activities. You gave us enough to put a stop to this branch of the prostitution, drug, and human trafficking ring."

Dixie was sad, but along with that she seemed distracted. "Sweetie, you should be happy about this. What's the matter?" She continued to pick at her food, not bothering to look up when her uncle spoke to her. "I know you don't know me that well, is that the problem? You don't feel comfortable telling me what's on your mind?"

She looked up first at the FBI agent then cut her eyes back toward her uncle. Dixie was angry. Her voice was confrontational when she addressed the men. "What about her feelings? Don't you care anything about Brenda Lou? She loves you Anthony. Have you thought for one second what will happen when she hears you killed somebody, or that you were killed? She's too good for you, you know that? She would never stand still for doing something like this to you. It's not fair." By now her voice was raised to the point the men were afraid the other diners would hear her. Tears rolled unchecked down her cheeks.

Anthony was stunned by her words. Agent Trout was motioning for her to lower her voice. Both men were surprised by her outburst. Agent Trout reached over grabbing her by the arm when she started to jump up from the table. "Whoa! Hold on and listen. Please? Brenda Green is going to be fine. Sit back down." He hurriedly attempted to reassure her.

Dixie slapped at his hand trying to break free. "Leave me alone or I'll scream. That will get attention. You're both cruel."

"Shush now young lady. Stop it and sit back down. Let James explain." Anthony pointed to her chair speaking with an air of authority. A sullen Dixie plopped back down into her chair. Her lips were clamped together in a thin line while she had her head bent until her chin was resting on her chest. Arms crossed over her chest, she cut her eyes upward at the men. She remained silent, glaring, waiting for one of them to speak. Anthony loved her spirit. He found it hard to maintain a straight face while marveling over his new found niece.

Clearing his throat, Agent Trout looked at Dixie. "I'm glad we're on the same side. I'd hate to cross you young lady." He attempted a grin to calm Dixie. She remained silent, looking as confrontational as she had before he spoke. "Do you remember Agent Burner? You met him at Mr. Moffield's." He didn't get a response from the still silent Dixie. "He went to get Brenda Lou first thing this morning. By now she knows your uncle is alive. She also knows he didn't kill anybody. Does that make you feel better?" He tried the grin again.

Dixie sat still as a stone for a moment thinking things over. She relaxed a little before she spoke. "You aren't just saying that are you?" She still looked like she was ready to take flight any second. "How can I be sure?"

Both men chuckled. It was Anthony that spoke up. "Sweetie, he isn't telling you that to get you to cooperate. You have my word. Brenda Lou will be joining us at the place we are headed to. We will all be safe there."

"Are you going to marry her?" It was more of a demand than a question. She watched her uncle for a reaction.

Anthony almost choked. "Whoa! That's something very private between Brenda Lou and me. There are things to work out before we cross that bridge. Besides, we don't need to be talking about it at all in front of James." He looked up to see the agent trying hard to keep a smile off his face.

Dixie almost glared at her uncle. "Well if we can't talk about that then tell me how Brenda Lou's parents are going to feel about all this? Is she just going to disappear too or are they going to be told she's dead? Will somebody tell them where she is?" She took a breath. "When is the baby due? Her parents will be worried to death."

She noticed the troubled expression cross Anthony's face. Turning to Agent Trout she saw the same expression mirrored there. When Anthony spoke, his words were carefully measured. "Dixie, sometimes things don't work the way we would like for them to. People aren't perfect. Life isn't always fair. All we can do is the best we can and hope things turn out right. I really wish I could explain everything to you. There are just some things you aren't ready to hear. We don't have all the answers yet ourselves." She could tell her uncle was trying hard not to show how upset he was about some aspect of what was happening.

"Uncle Tony, I think I like you." She grinned at him. "Okay, tell me when the baby is due."

He laughed. "When it's born child. When it's born. I think I'm going to start calling you Sassy."

***

New York

Allen Burner sat on the sofa with a cup of coffee in his hand. He was watching cartoons with two sets of twins scuffling in front of the TV with the little dog, Rascal right in the middle of it all. In the background he could hear the children's nanny singing softly to the baby while giving it a bath. It reminded him of how things were in his home when he was a child. He made himself a mental note to call his parents the first chance he had.

All Brenda Lou had been told was they needed to move her to another location. Agent Burner said he couldn't give her any details until she reached her destination. At first she was skeptical. The agent had to place a call to Anthony before Brenda believed him. She was still puzzled that she wasn't allowed to let anyone else know yet. Agent Burner said Susan would be notified that the move was necessary.

Packed suitcases were waiting by the door while Brenda said tearful goodbyes to the children. Rascal seemed to understand they were leaving. The small dog ran to the bedroom to give the baby a goodbye lick before dashing back for hugs from the rest of the children. The dog jumped into its bag, looking up to let them know it was ready to travel.

Once the plane was in the air, Allen Burner told Brenda about Ronald Arnold's death. He explained the importance of people believing Anthony died in a car crash. She asked him several questions he wasn't at liberty to answer. He did tell her someone set Anthony up to take the fall for Ronald Arnold's death making it imperative that Anthony appear dead also.

Before the small jet touched down at a private airstrip in West Plains, Missouri, Brenda was given a carefully scripted scenario to read. Agent Burner told her she wasn't allowed to say anything if it wasn't on the paper. She knew she was being kept in the dark about something important.

"Ms. Green, I can't tell you more. Your wellbeing and that of your unborn baby are at stake." It was obvious he knew a lot more than what he was telling her.

Brenda kept grilling him for more details. She was becoming agitated by the lack of information given her. Rubbing her abdomen, she started feeling nauseated. Rascal jumped out of the bag onto her lap to try to comfort her. "I promise not to say too much if you just let me talk to my daddy."

Sensing her growing distress, Allen Burner handed her his cell phone. The number was blocked so no one could tell what phone she was using. "Keep it down to under two minutes. Remember. Don't say anything that isn't on that paper."

Dialing the number to her parent's house, Brenda seemed to relax a little. Her mother answered. "Hi Momma. I can't talk long my battery is low. I just wanted to hear your voice." She was silent a moment, listening to her mother's reply. "Yes, Momma I heard about Anthony." There was a catch in her voice as she tried to hold back the tears. "I'm alright. Can I speak to Daddy before my phone goes dead?" She looked over at the agent while she waited for her father to come to the phone. He pointed to his watch indicating the time. "Daddy. My phone battery is almost gone so I have to hurry. I love you. I'm doing good." She listened before speaking again. "Yes, I heard about Anthony. I haven't had a chance for it to sink in yet, but I'll be alright. I'm surrounded by good people who can help. I miss you and Momma." There was another pause. "Daddy don't worry, please. This will all be over soon. I have to go. I'll get in touch with you again as soon as I can." Brenda was crying now as she looked up to see Agent Burner making a slashing motion to let her know time was up. Pressing the button to end the call she drew in a sharp breath when she reached out to hand the phone back to him.

Seeing the look of surprise on Brenda's face, Agent Burner addressed her. "Brenda Lou are you alright?"

Her faced paled noticeably. "I think the baby knows I'm a little upset. It must have turned wrong. Ouch!" Brenda wrapped her arms around herself when she cried out. Doubling over in pain, she accidently knocked the dog into the floor. "It's too early. I can't be in labor. The pain's too sharp. No!" Tears ran down her face. "Please, I can't lose this baby." She gripped Agent Burner's arm with one hand while holding her abdomen with the other.

Fear gripped the agent. "Ms. Green, Brenda Lou. Listen to me. We are about to land. I will tell the pilot to radio ahead for an ambulance with a doctor. Sit tight I'll be right back." He took a breath to steady himself. "Take deep slow breaths. Try to calm down, please." He unbuckled his seatbelt. Looking over his shoulder at Brenda he spoke to the pilot. When he made sure the pilot knew what was happening he went back to buckle in. "We are about to land. Don't worry Brenda Lou, everything is under control. They will have the necessary people waiting when we touch down. The baby will be fine and so will you. They'll know what to do." He wasn't half as calm as he attempted to sound.

While the plane taxied to a stop, the pilot yelled back to his passengers to let them know he saw the ambulance waiting. Agent Burner breathed a sigh of relief. He had hidden it well, but he was terrified. He had never delivered a baby. Even though he had taken the training required he knew it was too early for this baby to be born.

Allen Burner didn't leave Brenda's side until she was loaded into the back of the ambulance. He rode up in the front seat beside the EMT. The car that was to have taken them on to their destination followed the ambulance to the hospital.

At the hospital, the staff tried to object to the agents being in their Emergency Room. The staff were overruled. The two agents stood guard outside of the cubicle while the doctor and nurses were examining Brenda.

When the doctor finished the exam he started toward the nurses' station. Agent Burner stepped forward leaving the other agent to guard Brenda. He followed the doctor to the desk. When asked to step back away from the doctor he refused. "You have no idea what's at stake here. I'm under strict orders to have access to any and all information concerning this patient. It's imperative no one know who she is or even that a patient fitting her description was ever seen here."

The doctor turned aside ignoring the unwanted person in his ER. He spoke quietly to the nurse. Agent Burner stepped in closer. "Excuse me doctor. Perhaps you didn't understand. I am to be included in any conversation pertaining to the patient. I need to know not only your findings but also –"

The nurse had gone to the cabinet housing the meds. Cutting Agent Burner off in mid-sentence, the doctor turned on him. "You have to take your flunky and get out of my ER. There's this thing called HIPAA. Maybe you haven't heard of it but I can't tell you anything. This young lady is not a prisoner and you don't have written authorization. Get out." He pointed toward the door.

Pulling the badge from his pocket, he thrust it in the doctor's face. "This gives me the right to be any damn place I need to be. According to my orders I need to be here. We can get on the phone to the White House now if you want to speak to my boss. I'll tell you, if it goes that far you will never work in the medical profession again. Do you understand?"

The doctor's face was contorted with rage. He stood quietly, hands on hips, glaring at the federal agent.

"Guess that means we understand each other. Did you hear what I said earlier?" The doctor remained silent. "Let's hear a patient report. I noticed you didn't have a call placed to Labor and Delivery so I don't think she is in labor. What is going on with this young woman and what are you doing for her."

"I guess I should be tickled shitless you didn't insist on gloving up and coming in the exam room with me.", was the doctor's sarcastic response.

"Cut the crap. Just fill me in on her condition and what she needs."

The doctor finally dropped his attitude and gave Agent Burner a full report on his findings. "She's having Braxton-Hicks Contractions. In layman's terms, it's false labor. From what I gather they were brought on by extreme stress. She has calmed down and the contractions are much milder. We gave her an injection. The contractions should stop completely before long."

"I need to know if the mother or the baby are in any danger. Another thing, I need to know is if she told you what has her so upset." Agent Burner's voice was filled with genuine concern.

The doctor studied the agent's face before answering. "I don't know what upset her badly enough to bring this on. She wouldn't talk about it. Mother and baby are both fine. She needs to rest. I'd like to keep her overnight for observation to be on the safe side."

"Doctor, is it possible to move her somewhere safer? What I told you earlier was an understatement. If anyone found out she was here it could put the lives of your whole staff in danger. If she can't be moved we will bring in extra guards. No one can know who she is. We would have to bring in people from outside the area to guard the whole hospital."

Drawing his hands through his hair, the doctor released a sigh of defeat. "I don't suppose you used her true name when the papers were filled out, did you?"

"No sir we didn't."

"Other than the staff, only the ambulance crew know anything about her being brought in. She resembles the women they have been showing pictures of on the news. Is she connected to that mess?"

"I'm sorry doctor. I'm not at liberty to say."

"Let her rest for another hour or so. I'll check her again to make sure the contractions have stopped completely. If you can move her lying down, I'll let you. I would suggest she be transferred by ambulance but I don't think you want anyone knowing where she's going."

"You're a very perceptive man, doctor. Her safety is my top priority. I wouldn't consider moving her if it wasn't necessary." "Under the circumstances, I'll personally handle her paperwork. The clerk hasn't seen it yet. I still have the crew's clipboard on my desk to sign for the ambulance that brought her in. Coffee can be spilled on it before they get back from the break room. I'll make up some story." The doctor shook his head, running his fingers through his hair again before continuing. "Your response to my question about who she is said more than anything about what's going on."

"I know you think I'm an ass but I care about the people here. Not only do I feel responsible for the patients but all these other people too. I'll do whatever is necessary for the safety of all of them."

"I appreciate it. You may not believe it but I do understand. By the way, if you had asked to start with she would have given you permission to speak to me." He turned, going back to stand by Brenda's side while she slept.

An hour and a half later the doctor nodded to the agent outside the cubicle on his way in to examine Brenda. He found Agent Burner still standing rigidly by her side while she slept.

"I need to have you step out. We are going to put the monitor back on and check her over to make sure she is alright to travel." The doctor whispered.

"Can we get you to put some blankets and a pillow on the bill? I want to make sure she is comfortable on the ride." He looked a little sheepish before making another request. "Is there any way we could get something for her dog too? It hasn't had anything to eat since early this morning."

With his arms loaded down with blankets and pillows, Allen Burner went out to check on Rascal and make up the seat as a bed for Brenda. He was almost done when the doctor approached with a sandwich bag, a Styrofoam bowl, and a bottle of water.

"I asked the other guy how big a watch dog she had. The way he described it I had to have a look for myself." He was wearing his scrubs, digging in the bag, with a smile on his face. "The description he gave me sounded like the mutt we bought my little girl." He pulled a half-eaten egg sandwich from the bag. "This should work. It was left in the fridge. I have a bowl here to put the water in."

Agent Burner stood up giving the doctor an appraising look. "You're not an ass after all. You just want to give people a bad first impression." He reached into the car lifting out an oversize handbag he sat on the ground. The tiny creature jumped out of the bag sniffing the air, at the smell of the sandwich, Rascal made a bee-line for the doctor.

"I'm glad I got the food down before you let it out. That beast might have taken my arm off." He laughed, reaching down to pet the small dog.

Allen Burner quickly snapped the leash in place before Rascal decided it was time to explore the area in search of a bathroom. With the task finished, he turned to the doctor. "How long before our patient is ready to travel?"

While Rascal wolfed down the food, the doctor poured water into the bowl. "The nurse is helping her dress now. She should be ready to go in a few minutes." He was stroking the silky fur while he spoke. "I just want to caution you again, she needs to rest and try to keep her away from stressful situations. When we go back in, I'll give you her paperwork. I don't figure you want any paper trail left here for anyone to find. I'll see to it she doesn't have a file here under any name. You covered the expenses with cash so we can make it look like something else. The hospital won't be out any expense, and I'll handle the payment for the unknown patient I destroyed the ambulance report on. No sweat."

"I want to thank you. I can't tell you how worried I was. After getting to know her, I would want to keep her safe even if it wasn't a job. She's a good person. I just hope she doesn't have to face too much more before that baby is ready to be born. It would destroy her if anything bad happened to that child she's carrying." Agent Burner explained.

With the car readied for the trip the doctor insisted on staying with Rascal while Allen Burner went inside. When the two agents came out pushing Brenda in the wheelchair, she laughed out loud at the sight of Rascal playing tag with the ER doctor.

The doctor brought the paper work out while the two agents tucked Brenda into the back seat. He watched them drive away thinking about all the bad things he had seen on the news lately that seemed to be connected to the women that resembled this woman. He took a minute to say a prayer for her safety. On the way back into the ER to return the wheelchair he couldn't help thinking this was one time he considered a slow shift a real blessing.

Chapter 28

All the way to the farm Anthony took great delight in watching Dixie's changing expressions at each and every new sight she took in. Nearing Cabool, she spotted a deer feeding in a field not too far from the road. Both men laughed until their sides hurt when Dixie begged, pleaded, pouted, and even mimicked a small child's voice, trying to get them to turn around so she could pet it. She finally gave up when they told her there would be deer on the farm she was going to be staying at.

By the time they reached Birch Tree, Anthony and Dixie had bonded. Anyone that didn't know better would have sworn he was her favorite uncle from the time she was born. The two were so engrossed in telling each other about their lives they paid no attention to the conversation Agent Trout was having with someone on the phone. When he turned his phone off, Anthony noticed his troubled expression.

"James, what was that about? You look like something's wrong. What's going on man?" Anthony asked as they turned onto the lane leading to the main house.

"Nothing now Tony. I'll tell you all about it as soon as we get unloaded."

Dixie looked from one man to the other. "I'm in this mess as deep as everyone else. If something is going on you should tell me too." She sounded indignant, sitting there glaring at the agent.

"Do you always take everything anybody says so personally?" He teased her. "As a matter of fact, I want you to know too. I just want to wait until I have a chance to use the bathroom and get everyone that needs to know gathered up. I don't want to have to explain things several times." He watched her relax. "Satisfied young lady?" He grinned at her, watching as she accepted his answer with a nod of her head.

After they were settled, Special Agent Trout went into detail about Brenda's part in everything that was going on and her brief visit to the ER, assuring those gathered that she was alright. When he looked at Anthony's pale face he knew how much she meant to him. He wondered just how much more there was to their relationship than he had already guessed. "Anyway, to wrap this up, she will be arriving here shortly." He watched Anthony light up like Christmas at his words.

Night was falling by the time the car carrying Brenda made its way down the twisty lane leading to the main house.

While several people were gathered around Anthony opened the car door, helped Brenda out, and started making introductions. Jewel greeted her with a hug while Anthony stood back watching, wishing it was his arms hugging her.

Eunice stood in the shadows, back away from the rest of the group, watching. She didn't miss the look of longing on Anthony's face as Brenda was helped into the house by the other women. When Anthony took the other men off to the side to talk, Eunice slipped away unnoticed to go in search of another woman she had befriended.

It was already pitch-black outside by the time everyone finished eating dinner. Anthony, Dixie, and Brenda lingered over coffee speaking with the agents that had delivered them all to the farm. Anthony found it amusing to hear Agent Burner ask so many questions about Brenda's sister, Patty. Brenda needed to rest, so they all said goodbye before Jewel and Anthony tucked Brenda in for the night with a good book to read. Dixie stayed outside with Rascal waving to the agents as they drove off down the lane.

Anthony waited until he thought everyone had retired for the night before he slipped into Brenda's bedroom. "I saw your light on. Looks like you had a pretty rough day. I know the doctor ordered bed rest. Are you sleepy or would you like to talk for a while?" He asked anxiously.

"Tony I would love to talk to you. I'm tired alright, but I feel better now that you're here. Please stay." She smiled when Rascal jumped up on the bed beside her. "She gets a little jealous sometimes if she feels left out."

"There are some things I need to tell you." He had sat down in a chair near the bed. Slowly shaking his head, he looked from her face down at the floor, clasping his hands in front of him. "Brenda Lou, I don't know where to start."

From the way he was acting, she thought he was going to tell her he was leaving for good. She took a deep breath to calm herself before she uttered a word. "Anthony I'm not a child. I can handle whatever it is you came to tell me. I've done a lot of growing up these last few months." Each breath she took was shallow in an attempt to keep the tears at bay.

Keeping his head down, his voice was so quiet she could barely hear him. "Brenda Lou, I know what your life has been like. It wouldn't surprise me at all if you don't want to see my face again after I tell you about myself." Without looking at her he rushed on. "My real name isn't Payne. My name is Anthony Lewis Taylor. I was in prison, not because I murdered someone, even though that was what I was convicted for. I did a lot of bad things when I was young. When I tried to break away from it all I was setup, convicted and went to prison for several years. While I was in there I started working for the government to put the man away who was responsible for that death and others. That's why you are in this mess now." He stopped talking, trying to collect his thoughts.

It sounded like he was trying to explain some things to her but he was rambling. She had forgotten her initial fears in her confusion. "You aren't making much sense. Why don't you start from the beginning?"

Anthony told her about his parents, brother, and grandmother. He explained how he came to be mixed up with Ronald Arnold, later ending up in prison. Skipping over his injuries, he explained how he was approached by a government official about working with the task force. Working under an assumed name had not been his idea, but he agreed to it when they explained it would help keep his name clean. Hearing him explain how he started his legitimate business in the midst of everything else fascinated her. He went into detail about the human flesh trade and his part in trying to stop it.

"I didn't do any of it for the money. In the beginning, working with the task force started out to be about avenging Raymond. They insisted I keep the house and vehicles as payment for all the years they let me stay in prison since I told them I wouldn't take a paycheck for helping them put a stop to Arnold. They were surprised I turned down the reward that was offered for his capture when I turned over what they needed to put him away for life. All that money has gone to this compound to help those victims. I have paid for the house and vehicles myself. Arnold's dead now and whoever he worked for set it up to look like I killed him. That's why we are all here now."

"Why is Dixie here, Anthony? Is she in danger too?"

He explained what happened to Dixie's mother after Raymond was killed. When he told her what Dixie had just gone through, she gasped. "Why would they want to hurt that little girl?"

"To get to me." His voice was raised almost to a shout. It took effort to calm himself down. How could he not blame himself for what happened to everyone he had ever cared for, he thought to himself. He was still shaking when he looked into Brenda's tear-filled eyes.

"God, Anthony. You have had your whole life dictated by a monster. With what you've been through yourself, how did you accomplish what you have? Most people would have given up long ago. That says a lot about your character." She reached over, running her hand down his arm.

"I am so afraid for you. It seems like everyone I get close to comes to a bad end. I don't know what to do. I tried to forget you but I can't. That night we met, I fell in love with you. No one has ever made me feel the way you do. The way you talked about Larry Joe, I could tell you thought your marriage was over, but at the same time you wanted it to work. I knew he wanted to sell you and make it look like you just vanished. It's stupid but I thought if I just dropped you off at your house and left, he would be afraid to try it again. I thought your husband was some lame brained dumbass. I didn't know it was Ben." He took a deep shaky breath before he continued.

"That wasn't a date rape drug I gave you that night, it was a simple mild sedative. You were so upset and had enough to drink on an empty stomach that, I guess it hit you hard. By the time we reached your house it had worn off some, but the alcohol you consumed was still working. You couldn't walk straight in those heels, so I helped you into your house. I swear I didn't mean for anything to happen. On the way to your house you called me Larry Joe. I thought it odd at the time that it hurt my feelings and explained away how you seemed to care so much for such a jerk. When we went inside you kissed me. I tried to make myself leave. Then when you put your arms around my neck and whispered my name and told me you wanted me before you kissed me again, I was lost."

"Tony, why did you act the way you did that Sunday morning?" Brenda was more confused than ever.

"Brenda Lou, the night I spent with you I watched you sleep. You talked in your sleep. You would call out for me one minute then beg your husband's forgiveness the next. It tore me up watching and listening, knowing what Ben said your husband told him about you. The kind of person you are, you would have done anything you had to in order to make your marriage work. I wanted to make you hate me. I wanted you to think I was the most crass, repulsive mistake you made in your whole life. After spending one evening with you, I honestly thought your husband would see how close he came to messing it all up and try to make it work." His voice had a pleading quality to it that touched Brenda's heart.

Her eyes were searching deep into his soul. "And now Tony? How do you feel now?" She was afraid to ask but she had to know for sure.

"I'm afraid. I know I love you. I tried hard not to. I lied to myself for a long time, making up every excuse I could think of for my feelings. Hell,

I even tried to tell myself I felt sorry for you and I was to blame, so what I was feeling was that I had to protect you because of that." He closed his eyes, shaking his head.

"And you, Brenda Lou? After hearing about the true me, how do you feel?" He held his breath saying a silent prayer while he watched her formulate an answer.

"It's not so easy to answer that." She watched him as his heart sank at her response.

After a moment of absolute silence, Brenda continued. "I have to think about the child I'm carrying. Your past doesn't bother me. It may have before all this happened but not anymore. The thing is, Tony I don't know who fathered this baby. Is my baby's father a dead man that did unspeakable things people will remember for years to come? If so, will his relatives show up trying to be part of the child's life? I don't even know who they are because I didn't know who he was. Could you care about a child fathered by a man like that? Would you think about him every time you looked at this baby?" She ran a hand over her abdomen. "Or." She took a breath to steady her voice. "Is this your child? I don't even know if you like children. I do know you never considered anything like this the night we were together. You have avoided any mention of the baby when we've been in the same room. At least I know your real name now, that's more than I knew about–." She stopped talking holding back a sob.

Anthony rose from his chair to sit beside Brenda. He held her close until the urge to cry passed. "Brenda Lou, I love you. This baby is a part of you. What I've been trying to do is tell you everything about me because I want you for my wife. As for the baby, just because some man plants a seed doesn't mean he is a father. If you will have me I want all of you, including the baby. I will be that child's father if you will say yes. It will be mine no matter, because I will help raise it. I will love it, cherish it, and do everything in my power to protect it. Each child is a gift and a miracle. Brenda Lou, please say yes."

He held his breath and watched as the tears rolled down her cheeks. She didn't utter a word for a full minute. When she started nodding her head he was finally able to breath. "Yes, Anthony Lewis Taylor I will marry you. I love you too. You aren't the only one who is afraid."

Anthony hadn't closed the door all the way when he went in to see Brenda. As late as it was he assumed the whole house was asleep except for the person monitoring the cameras. Neither one of them were aware anyone else was near. Eunice was standing in the dark just outside Brenda's door. She had listened to every word before she slipped quietly away down the hall and out into the night.

Chapter 29

Thanksgiving Day at the Perkins home near Bloomfield was underway. The house was filled with mouthwatering aromas and sounds of laughter. Lou was elated to have Patty Sue home from college, along with the new man in her life. The table was set with Lou's prized china, crystal, and good silverware. The women were in the kitchen busy preparing the meal while teasing Donna Mae about her size due to the advancing stage of her pregnancy. Walter's girlfriend fit into the mix, joining in with an offer to make a tent for Donna Mae to wear.

While everyone was gathered they spoke with Tom and Liz Smith. They had the phones on speaker so they could all say hello to each other. After elaborating over the menu, they briefly touched on what the members of both families were currently doing before they said their goodbyes.

Chet took the men out to his workshop to help build backdrops for the church's Christmas pageant. Donna's husband, Mac was never much use with tools so he fetched and carried while Chet and Walter did the sawing and hammering. Patty Sue's boyfriend proved useful with a sander and paintbrush.

At the sound of the dinner bell, the men headed into the house, praising their own efforts on the backdrops. With the group seated they joined hands for the blessing before Chet carved the turkey. Lou silently said her own private prayer of thanks that Anthony was no longer in Brenda Lou's life.

Patty Sue was the first to speak of her other sister's absence. "I wish Brenda Lou could be here. It just doesn't seem like a family gathering without her. I'd love to see her; bet she is bigger than a barn. I miss her. Have you heard from her lately?"

Chet looked sad at the mention of her name. Brenda was his favorite of all his children. "She called yesterday. They told her she has to stay in bed because of the baby. Travel is out of the question, but she is doing good otherwise. She sends her love."

"Why on earth can't she stay here? A bed is a bed, is a bed. It doesn't make sense to me." Patty sounded irritated.

Lou knew how Patty looked out for her oldest sister with the devotion of a puppy. "She told us the resort they have her at has a doctor there on grounds twenty-four hours a day. They pamper her half to death from the way it sounds." Lou patted Patty's hand. "Brenda Lou misses her family as much as we miss her. Don't be upset with her, they won't let her travel. We have to be patient for her sake and the baby's."

"Sounds like real torture. White sand beaches, cabana boys, massages, manicures and pedicures. What did I miss? Oh yeah, personal trainers, special menus delivered on trays where ever you're at. People waiting on you hand and foot. Poor thing. While we're here taking care of her business, running her errands, and keeping everything running smoothly for her to come back to. She's living like that Parris Hilton with that stupid little dog." Donna Mae's outburst surprised her family, amusing the others seated around the table. Donna's pregnancy made her moody. She glowed as long as she was the center of attention. Although she loved her older sister, she was envious of the pampering she thought her sister was getting in the final term of her pregnancy.

Chet slowly shook his head before he looked back at Donna. "Donna Mae you know your sister would rather be here. You also know she isn't living the life of Riley you make it sound like. How would you like it if you had to be confined to your bed? Do you really believe what you just said to be true?" He sounded like someone had just pulled the plug and drained every ounce of energy from his body.

Mac took his wife's hand as tears formed in her eyes. "No Daddy. I'm sorry. I don't know what made me say that. I'm worried about her too." She wiped away a stray tear. "I thought she would be back before now. I thought we would be going through this together, picking out baby clothes, comparing notes on the changes our bodies are going through, talking about how it feels to have a new life inside of us moving and growing, - talking about what to expect next, all of it. I miss her so bad Daddy."

"I know you do Baby, I know." He said with an understanding half smile filled with love.

Walter watched the exchange, wondering why his mother seemed to be holding back a smirk as her eyes danced watching her husband and daughter.

Caught off guard, Lou jumped when Walter addressed her, his voice stern. "Mother do you know something we don't?"

She was still weary at being caught off guard by her son. When she answered she was hesitant. "Why, no Walt. Why would you ask that?"

"You just look like the cat that ate the canary sitting there looking innocent with a feather sticking out of your mouth. That's all." He was looking intently at her face.

Lou chuckled. "Oh Son, you have such an imagination. I was just thinking about how wonderful it is to have you all here today even if Brenda Lou couldn't make it. I was remembering the bickering between your sisters when they were little girls." She was glad she had thought up a reasonable answer so fast.

When the meal was finished and everything cleaned up and put away, Lou excused herself after telling Walter and his girlfriend goodbye. She told the others she would see them when she got back from checking on the ladies from the church that had volunteered to serve Thanksgiving Dinner in the church's kitchen for those who had nowhere else to go.

***

The dining room in the main house at the compound on the farm near Birch Tree was packed to overflowing. The large table had the two extra leaves put in, folding chairs had been brought out, and sheets were used as table cloths in order to cover the entire length of the table. Place settings were a mish mash of several different sets combined to make up an attractive, colorful combination. At the center of the table sat the largest turkey Anthony had ever seen. It was golden and cooked to perfection. There was a large ham, fried chicken, chicken and dumplings, corn bread dressing, giblet gravy, mashed potatoes, candied yams, corn, green beans, coleslaw, glazed carrots, potato salad, an assortment of salads, and fresh baked yeast rolls. On the sideboard sat several cakes, pies, and puddings. Most of the bounty was either raised or made right on the farm. Some of the dishes were even fired in a kiln there and the table was hand crafted from the white oak trees that had grown there.

Everyone crowded into the large dining room. They join hands standing in a circle around the table to say a prayer of thanks for the food and safety of all those in attendance as well as asking for guidance in what lay ahead. Anthony gave his own silent special prayer of thanks while holding Dixie's hand on one side and Brenda's on the other. After the prayer some of the people left to man the camera room and stand watch until they could be relieved to come back to eat.

One of the female agents posted at the farm for extra protection of the women came back in after making her rounds. While filling her plate, she made eye contact with Anthony and Jewel, indicating with a nod of her head that they should follow her into the office. Jewel went first with the agent following her carrying a loaded plate, then Anthony followed after whispering to Brenda that he was needed in the office. He leaned over asking Dixie to help Brenda should she need anything. Dixie eagerly agreed.

Closing the door behind him, Anthony turned toward the woman. Jewel shrugged her shoulders indicating she hadn't a clue as to what the agent wanted.

The agent pointed to a chair while she finished chewing the mouthful of food. Anthony sat down, waiting impatiently for her to swallow.

Clearing her throat after taking a sip of tea, the agent started telling them why she wanted to see them. She was extracting a Ziploc bag from her pocket. "I found this buried in the bag of dry cat food in that big can in the shed. It's a good thing I decided to feed them while I looked around or I would never have found it."

Both Jewel and Anthony looked in astonishment at the cell phone in the baggie the agent was holding. "Do you have any idea who it belongs to?" Jewel asked.

"That's why I wanted you both in here. I have a pretty good idea but I want to be sure." She was removing the phone from the bag.

"Are there just phone numbers or are there text messages?" Anthony asked.

The agent was trying to eat while she spoke. "Bear with me." She swallowed again. "I went through the text messages. I already called to have a check ran on the only number on here. It comes back to that number Eunice gave you for her Greg. Whoever it is that has that phone has to be removing the battery in between uses. They haven't been able to get a fix on it. They may have given up after they tried before, thinking it wasn't still being used. Anyway, now they will have to be sure. I've seen to it that not only are they trying to track it, but–, they are going to route the messages in a manner so when Eunice gets her message, we get a copy also." A self-satisfied grin briefly crossed her face. "As the old saying goes, there is more than one way to skin a cat. Good grief, I can't believe I just said that. This place is rubbing off on me." She chuckled.

Jewel nodded her head looking thoughtful. "Well, that explains why the girl was so eager to volunteer to take care of feeding the cats. She doesn't try to make friends much. I think she has started trying to buddy up with Dixie and she talks to you, doesn't she? I thought she just really liked cats as much time as she spent out there with them." She drew her hands down her face before continuing. "How she could have gotten that on the place is beyond me. They were all searched before they were brought here."

They sat in silence for a moment before Anthony spoke. "Jewel, I was afraid Nicky was trouble. I told you about the talk I had with her. At the time it felt like she was holding something back, or lying. There was just a nagging feeling something about what she told me wasn't right."

Giving a dismissive wave of her hand, the agent addressed Anthony. "After reading those messages, I need to know what you can tell about her. Although she does talk to me sometimes it feels more like she is trying to find out if I know anything instead of her telling me anything. What did she say or do that didn't seem right to you? It doesn't matter if it didn't seem important at the time, tell me anyway."

Anthony went through the entire conversation he had with Eunice for the agent. He told her that due to circumstances, he hadn't told the girl that Greg (Ben Orr) was dead. "She sounded confrontational when she told me about using the woman's phone to send and receive the text. It certainly didn't make her happy that she wasn't allowed a phone here. From the way she acted while talking about it, I think she must have stolen the woman's phone. I just never thought about her doing something like that. It didn't cross my mind at the time."

Jewel spoke up. "What are we looking at? You read the messages. How much danger are my girls in? Do we need to worry about the ones going off the farm for classes?"

The agent stood, walking around the desk to stretch and put her dishes to the side. She thought for a minute, looking at the other two seated in the room. "They still have a few days break left before they go back to class. We'll cross that bridge when we come to it. Right now, the way things stand we have bigger fish to fry." "This doesn't sound good." Jewell said.

After sitting down facing the other two the agent took a deep breath before she spoke. "Eunice has been eaves dropping on all of your conversations that she can. She has another one of the girls helping her too. She is passing on everything she hears to the person in possession of Ben's phone. They know you're all here. As of right now, they don't know the exact location, just way too damn close to it. It sounds like they plan to lay in wait and follow someone in very soon. You're little Nicky is a mean-spirited little girl. Her friend has a crush on you. Did you know that?" The question was directed at Anthony.

His mouth gapped open in surprise for a split second. "No. I mean, I don't even know which girl you're talking about. I haven't paid any attention to who she hangs around with. I didn't know any of the girls had a crush on me. I joke around with all of them."

"Well Tony, one of them takes your joking seriously. She is nearly as mean spirited as Eunice. When you first brought Dixie here, she wanted to run her off because she thought Dixie was your girlfriend. Thanks to Eunice she knows better now and tries to suck up to Dixie to find out more about you. Thank goodness Dixie is a smart girl that doesn't gossip. Eunice's friend hasn't spoken to Brenda Lou, but she hates her with a passion." Turning to Jewel, she said, "I'll talk to you later. We need to keep that one as far from Brenda Lou as possible.

Oh, and warn Brenda Lou not to believe anything the girl tells her." "Don't worry, I can see to that easy enough." Jewel answered.

Giving a brief nod the agent continued. "We're tightening the net. There are a couple loose ends we have to tie up before we can make the arrests. It has to be air tight, we can't afford to go to trial without knowing we have all of our ducks in a row and tied down. I have to put this phone back out there before she goes out to wait on the next message. This isn't to be discussed outside this room with anybody. I mean no one at all, period. They want someone to follow in so we are going to give them someone to follow. Anthony you know all the roads around here don't you?" He nodded in response.

"I thought so. Word is going to get back to Eunice about you taking a trip to Van Buren in a few days. Like I said, they know the general vicinity of the compound; but, not the exact location. Think you can lose them on a back road bad enough they have to call for help to get back out?"

A smile crossed Anthony's face as he thought about the route he would take them on. "I know just the place, I think. As a matter of fact, there are a couple different ones to choose from depending on what they drive."

They both turned to look at Jewel who had burst out laughing. "I know where you plan to take them. I'd bet a million bucks on it!" She gasped, wiping a tear from her eye. She had laughed so hard it was hard to get her breath enough to speak. "Wonder if they have any new dogs since I went that way?" She started laughing again so hard it was hard for her to speak coherently. While Jewel laughed, doubling over with tears rolling down her cheeks, Anthony went from grinning to laughing. The agent looked on in confusion at the spectacle before her.

Chapter 30

December 4, 2013

The temperature started to fall faster than expected. The worst winter storm in three years was expected to hit the area.

It was only midmorning and the rain was already mixed with sleet. The storm was three hours ahead of the forecast.

Anthony had been waiting at the McDonalds in Van Buren for over two hours for the female agent to pull into the parking lot. She met him inside for coffee before they left together in Anthony's vehicle. They had spent thirty minutes over coffee watching to see who came and went.

Driving West on 60 Highway didn't get bad until they neared Winona. A trailer truck up ahead hit a slick spot causing it to fish tail. The driver was barely able to pull it out of the skid before it jack-knifed.

Watching the rearview mirror as much as possible, Anthony had to keep his eyes on the worsening roads ahead. "I'm glad you're along today. As bad as these roads are getting, I would never have been able to watch for our tail without you. Have you spotted which one it is yet?"

"It's a smaller medium blue car. There isn't much clearance between it and the road." She grinned knowingly. "The rough shorter route?" It was more of a statement than a question.

"You read my mind. The Low Wassie exit it is. I'm hoping he can make it far enough to lose phone service before he gets stuck."

Anthony slowed down further even though the traffic was already moving far below the posted speed limit. He put the turn signal on far enough ahead of his turn to make sure the car following them didn't miss the turn.

The agent watching their tail in her side mirror chuckled. "He's taking the bait. Don't be too obvious or he may change his mind."

After taking the turn at a crawl, Anthony sped up a little crossing the East bound lanes of slow-moving traffic. Once he put a little more distance between himself and Highway 60, he slowed again to make certain the other vehicle saw the turn signal when they turned onto the gravel road heading west. After the second turn onto another gravel road, they were both delighted to see the other vehicle had made it over the gravel washes up to that point. "Cell service should cut out pretty soon. He might make it over the next wash, I hope he does. Won't he be surprised when he reaches the curve with the wash out running across it? There is no way he will make it through there the way the water is starting to come up." She laughed picturing the welcoming picture the other vehicle would be met with.

"I drove through here a few days ago to make sure the dogs were still loose. Just wait until you see this." He laughed.

Less than half a mile down the road the agent started to worry. "Tony are you sure we didn't make a wrong turn. This looks more like a dead-end driveway than a road. It's getting awful slick too. We are starting to lose traction sometimes and the windshield is starting to ice up."

"Don't worry we don't have too far to go now. See the curve past that house?" He didn't wait for an answer. "You're not going to believe this place. After we get through there it's not too far to the paved road heading into Winona."

She sat rigidly in the seat until they started to round the curve Anthony pointed out. When she saw the sight up ahead she burst out laughing. It almost looked like a dirt path between two houses. On one side of the road there was a very large hog in a pen with a lean-to occupying a corner inside the wire. An enormous pit bulldog strained against a log chain at the very edge of the road. The other end of the chain was wrapped around a tree in the yard. The house on the other side of the curve had an assortment of large dogs running free. When they were in-line between the two houses the dogs ran out barking and growling to surround their vehicle, chasing them several yards down the road before turning back.

"Tony, you are a wicked man. Now I know why Jewell laughed so hard when she figured you would take this route. He will get stuck back there and try to walk out this way for help." They both laughed. "I wish there was a way to hide so we could watch the show when he gets here."

They didn't drive much farther before coming to the paved road heading into Winona. Cinders had been put down on the road so it wasn't as slick as Anthony had feared.

Back on Highway 60, they followed the snow plows watching carefully to make sure there wasn't another tail until reaching the turnoff leading to the farm. They were happy to see a tractor had been down the road ahead of them causing the rock to be roughed up enough to break the ice already on the road. Once they turned onto the lane, it wasn't difficult to get to the main house where they were met by a worried welcoming committee bearing cups of hot cocoa.

Dixie ran to Anthony, throwing her arms around him. She was crying tears of relief. "Uncle Tony, we were so afraid. It took a lot longer for you to get back here than we thought. Brenda Lou wanted them to send out a search team to find you and we would have but nobody knew where to start looking. I'm so glad you're back safe. Do you have any idea how much you worried us all?"

Eunice, drawn to the window by the sound of crackling ice and gravel, watched the two people get out the vehicle. Feelings of disgust and burning rage built as she watched the female agent jump up wrapping her legs around Anthony while she hugged him. Throwing her head back, it was clear the agent was laughing when she kissed his cheek before jumping down to race into the house. Anthony looked overjoyed, jammed his hands into his pockets, smiling he shuffled on to the house through the sleet.

"Just wait till I get Dixie alone. I'll tell her how wonderful that uncle of hers is. He is screwing that one too while he has that other woman knocked up. I wonder how many others he is messing with." She wiped her eyes to clear the forming tears. "He can go to hell. Greg will find me and get me out of here. I won't be stuck here much longer." Eunice was speaking to herself, her voice barely above a whisper.

While freezing rain mixed with sleet continued to fall, half a dozen people in the compound gathered round the fireplace circling Anthony and the agent. They listened intently to the story being told of how the two outwitted those trying to find the farm.

Eunice stayed upstairs until she had her emotions under control. Sounds of laughter greeted her as she descended the stairs. The agent was telling how they were trying to creep down the road, slipping and sliding barely able to see where they were going when a dog's face appeared in front of them.

She was gesturing with her hands and body while she spoke. "Here we were creeping along, trying to stay on the road. Tony had a death grip on the steering wheel, while we were snugged up as close as we could get to the windshield to see out. Our breath caused the darn thing to ice up on the inside too. I had a Kleenex trying to keep the frost off while we tried to see out through this small hole in the ice on the outside. All of a sudden there was this enormous ferocious dog's face inches from us. It was barking madly with slobber flying while it was scratching at the ice and glass trying to get at us. I thought Tony was going to lose it."

She was laughing so hard she had to stop to get her breath. Anthony glared at her before a bemused smile crossed his face when she pointed at him. "You should have heard him holler." She started laughing again.

Anthony cut in. "I wasn't the only one. That scream of yours sent that thing back up on the porch." He was laughing right along with everyone else.

"As big as some of those rocks are, I can just picture that car stuck up on one of them in that wash. Wonder how long it will take for someone to come to his rescue? Knowing he took off walking only to be chased back to the car by that pack of dogs."

They had a small hole in the ice to look through. All of a sudden a large dog's face appeared directly in front of them. It was large enough and they were moving slowly enough that the dog was half way up on the hood with its back legs still on the ground. "We were both leaning forward trying to see the darn road so we didn't see the thing until it was right in our faces. Tony let out a scream, almost jumped out of his skin. That thing wanted to get in and eat him up. It was frightening right then. Now that it's over, it's funny."

The freezing rain and sleet continued throughout the night. Snow started falling the next morning, continuing throughout the night into the next afternoon. Tensions eased since the roads were impassable taking away the worry of having their safety compromised. The only vehicles moving anywhere were the large farm tractors hauling hay to the cattle in the area. It was impossible for any kind of creature to move without leaving some kind of track.

Aside from tending to the animals, no one strayed far from the main house. Anthony, their physician, and the resident handyman went out to brave the elements, bringing back a fresh cut cedar tree. Several women volunteered to help decorate the tree after the men secured it in a five gallon can they nailed to boards for a base to keep it from tipping. It was impossible to get through the snow-covered ice to dig dirt so they used chat from a pile beside the driveway to hold the tree up straight in the can.

Dinner was over and the cleanup finished. A dozen people were seated in the large living room commenting on how beautiful the brightly lit tree looked. One of the women quilted a skirt with Christmas scenes to go around the bottom of the tree. The star on the top almost reached the high ceiling, while the twinkling lights cast a magical glow over the entire room.

Racing up the stairs, Anthony tapped lightly on Brenda's door. He didn't wait for a response before entering the room. "Guess what Aunt Brenda! Mac wants to speak to you."

Special Agent Burner called Anthony to let him know he heard from Chief of Police Tom Smith. Brenda's dad told him they needed to get in touch with her to let her know her sister had gone into labor. As soon as Anthony got the call he wanted to make sure Brenda could check on her sister. He sat quietly on the side of her bed listening, while she placed the call to her brother-in-law.

Disconnecting, Brenda hugged Anthony. "Oh, Tony, Donna Mae had a little girl. Mac says she is the most perfect baby ever born. Momma and Daddy are there and the others are on the way. Donna Mae is sleeping right now so I told him to give her a hug for me. He said she wasn't in labor very long but the baby weighed seven pounds. They haven't named her yet. I'm going to call her in the morning. Mac said Donna Mae wants to ask me if I like the name before they make it official." She started crying.

"Brenda Lou, Baby what's wrong?" He stroked his hand down her face and held her.

She sniffled, blew her nose, and answered him. "I miss them Tony. I wanted to be there with her when she had the baby. I don't know how long it will be before I get to see my first-born niece."

"Cheer up Sweetheart. I have an idea. In the morning, we will bring Jewell's laptop in here. I will have Burner take his to the hospital so you can have a live chat with live video. That way you can speak to them and see your new niece. I will have to stay out of view but can see the baby too. They still can't know I'm alive but I will be able to see them. How does that sound?"

Brenda brightened up while listening to him. "Do you mean it? That would be so wonderful. I haven't laid eyes on any of them in so long, it seems like a lifetime. I'll get to see the baby! Tony, I love you so much."

"Brenda Lou, you have to remember to keep it real short. I know it will be a secure connection, but, we can't afford to take any chances. They have to think Special Agent Trout is responsible for setting this up for you. I'm sorry. It's the best we can do."

"I know that Tony. I'm thankful for a chance just to get to see them at all." She was about ready to cry again.

Winking, Anthony started laughing. "Allen Burner, big government agent, is afraid for your little sister to know he is interested in her. He is the one that wants everybody to think Trout is doing this but it is him. Why? He hopes he will get a glimpse of Patty Sue. You know he will be watching the connection too." He laughed even harder when he saw the surprise on Brenda's face.

He looked at her thinking how lucky he was to have found such a strong, good hearted, wonderful woman.

Chapter 31

Saturday, December 7th

Anthony woke from a sound sleep to find the ghost standing beside his bed. "Now what? I'm doing all I can. Under the circumstances my hands are tied, they won't let me leave here."

"You don't want to leave anyway. Don't try to tell me different, I know better." A tone of annoyance mixed with amusement came through.

"What? No parables, straight talk for a change?"

Keeping his back turned toward Anthony, the ghost remained silent for a bit before speaking. "You may not believe this, most people don't. The first slaves to be brought to these shores arrived in 1619. It is a matter of record. They were White children. You can look this up if you don't believe me. In the 17th century there were a great number more Irish slaves sold than African. If ships ran low on supplies, they just threw the White slaves overboard. The Black slaves were worth more so they were treated better. While you are looking all this up, read about a court case involving Anthony Johnson in 1654 or 1655." He studied Anthony's face before continuing. "You have to understand about all of this. It is up to you to teach your children. Before long you will see how important it will be."

The ghost fell silent again before chuckling. "You're going to miss me when this is over young man. It looks like this will be my last visit. At least I hope I can finally rest. Looking after you all these years has been a pleasure but a chore at the same time. My work is done as of today.

I'm afraid slavery will continue to manifest itself in one way or another forever. You have accomplished more than you will ever know in the fight against that terrible plight. Because of the part you played there will be countless women and children freed from their bondage. I had to keep you safe so you could play your part in all of this."

"Excuse me. I really don't get it." Anthony was hoping for more of an explanation.

"I saved your hide several times over the years for one thing. I wanted to save your father but that was not to be. The person behind all this wanted your father. Your father refused her. She decided that his wife and any offspring should be wiped from the face of the earth. So you see, that was the reason I was called to watch over you. You may not believe it but spirits can cry too. You haven't just been avenging the death of Raymond. If I hadn't told you where to look you would never have discovered who was behind it all. You see, my dear young man, you had to live so that Raymond's daughter could live, your son could live, as well as the future generations of your children."

Anthony sat stock still listening in amazement at what the ghost had to say. Considering the implications of what he just heard, he was more confused than ever. "You were a great orator in your time. Now I can see why. Old man, you sure can talk in circles without saying what you mean. You have cleared up a few things I've questioned over the years while at the same time made me wonder about a lot of other things, including the future purpose of your blood line. There is a reason other than your wishes, that a future descendant is to be born, isn't there?"

The ghost's somber demeanor quickly changed to a quick-witted teasing mood. "Let's just say the future will be full of surprises you will live long enough to see."

Changing to a more serious note once more, the ghost cautioned Anthony to be watchful of both Brenda and Dixie. He gave Anthony a summary of what to expect in order to keep the women safe, assuring him everything would work out the way it had to.

"So old man, this is it? I won't be seeing you again, right?" Anthony joked.

"That's right boy. Take good care of that delightfully alluring delectable female of yours. I'll be there at your wedding and to see your son born even though you won't see me. I'll have a very special guest with me to watch it all. Without her none of you would be here. We will be there whenever there is a special occasion but we won't be seen or heard. Well, Anthony my boy, stay true to yourself. I don't want to have to be sent back here. Goodbye."

Anthony watched in awe as the ghost of Abraham Lincoln faded slowly away. "Goodbye Sir, it has been an annoying pleasure to know you. Thank you for everything." He heard a distant chuckle as he finished speaking.

Looking at the clock, Anthony rushed to dress warmly. There wasn't much time to spare in finding Eunice. He knew she had overheard a conversation the night before and he had to prevent her from sending a text to the person she still thought was Greg. An increased sense of urgency, bordering on panic, spurred him on. He went in search of the female agent that befriended Eunice while posing as another one of the abducted women. The agent kept up with almost every move Eunice made.

Before Anthony had the door closed behind him the person he was looking for came running around the corner. Seeing Anthony she stopped, leaning over placing her hands on her knees, she had to catch her breath before she could talk. After a couple of seconds she stood, looking at him with a stricken expression on her face. "Tony, I'm glad I found you. Where is Dixie? We have to find her right now. You won't believe what Eunice is up to."

"Whoa. Take another deep breath. I can barely understand you. Dixie is in her room. I know Nicky overheard us talking about Ben Orr last night. I know she doesn't believe he's dead. What's going on?"

"She thinks you made up the things she overheard just for her benefit. She told me she slipped in and confronted that poor woman they have on suicide watch. She said Greg or Ben or whatever you want to call him is picking her up at the cattle guard soon and she is taking Dixie down to the end of lane to wait for him with her. She wanted me to cover for her here so no one would miss her. She said when he picks her up Dixie will come back to let everyone know she is alright so no one needs to go looking for her. I don't know who she has been in touch with but I don't like the sound of any of this." The female agent was talking so fast it was hard for Anthony to keep up with everything she was saying.

"Calm down. I don't like the sound of it either. First things first. I am going to have Jewel keep Dixie with her until we get to the bottom of things. Make sure you're armed before I get back. We are going to find Eunice and bring her back even if we have to hog tie her and carry her. I'll meet you in by the fireplace as soon as I see to Dixie." Anthony hurried into the house with the agent right behind him.

Highway 60 was still packed solid with snow covered ice. Only a few brave souls attempted to risk the dangerous roads. There was some light traffic on Highway 25, mostly law enforcement or emergency vehicles tending to the health or well-being of the people in the area.

Chet had been gone most of the morning after receiving a call from one of his church's congregation. An elderly man had taken a fall while attempting to get down his steps to feed his dog. The man refused to allow his wife to call for an ambulance. When Chet arrived, the man was still laying on the steps outside his house. He wasn't about to leave his wife by herself or leave until he knew his dog was tended to. Chet covered the man with a warm blanket, fed the dog, and then loaded both the man and woman into the jeep to take them to the hospital.

X-rays revealed the man had a broken hip to go along with the frost bite he suffered to his ears while lying out in the elements. Chet convinced him to stay in the hospital for treatment, promising to look after his wife and dog until he could return home.

By the time Chet got home, Lou was walking the floor waiting on him to return so she could use the jeep. She had things she wanted to get done. There were bags of food lined up on the kitchen counter to deliver to some of their church members that couldn't get out themselves. Chet tried to talk her into letting him drive her but she refused, giving him a list of things she wanted him to do in her absence. She sent him into the house to put on dry clothes while she started loading the jeep.

Now warm and in dry clothing, Chet Perkins helped his wife finish loading the jeep. He gave her a hug and kiss, telling her to be careful. He couldn't understand the sinking feeling in the pit of his stomach as he watched Lou drive away.

Lou made it to the gravel pull-off at the intersection for highway 25 and 60, having made all her deliveries, the back seat was empty.

There was a man standing there by a car waiting on her. She stopped just long enough for him to get into the jeep. "Hello Clarence."

"Hi Boss. Please just call me Bud, everyone does. It sure smells good in here." A lop-sided grin crossed Bud Lowe's face for just a split second. "Did you bring everything we need?"

"The guns are wrapped in the blankets in the back; the rest is in the cooler. We can stop at the truck stop on the way to change and get everything ready." She was deadly calm; her voice carried a harsh commanding quality that came through each word she uttered. "You know who we're taking out, correct? Brenda Lou isn't to be harmed. The others are waiting for us in Winona. They won't make a move until we get there. We need to get in and out, no playing with any of them. Do you understand?"

"Yes Boss." She could tell from the sound of his voice that Bud was disappointed. He enjoyed torturing those he considered his enemies.

"Don't worry, we're taking Anthony with us too. You get to have him to do with as you please while I watch. I will drop you off at the entrance while I go to get Brenda Lou. I'll tell her there's an emergency with her father and you know that Payne will come along. Kill Eunice first. We can't have her talking. She will be waiting by the first cattle guard where you get out. The little fool still thinks her knight in shining armor is going to come riding in to take her away. That little black bitch will be with her. Take them both out and hide the bodies in the sink hole across the road back up in the pasture. There is enough brush no one will see you down that hill. Eunice gave us all the information we needed to do this. Too bad we can't thank her." She laughed at her own sick joke.

Bud sat quietly watching the road ahead. There were very few places that had been cleared. Even the cleared areas were slushy due to the sun melting some of the snow that was piled on the shoulder of the highway. He was glad Lou was at the wheel. She had so much more experience driving in the Chicago area where they were accustomed to conditions like this.

Under normal conditions, the trip from Bloomfield to Birch Tree would have taken two hours. Today it was taking much longer giving Lou a chance to think about the past. She had been madly in love with a married man, that no matter how hard she tried, would not have anything to do with her. Andrew Taylor was the most handsome man she had ever seen.

Lou was in the process of learning everything about the various operations of her father's organization when she first saw Andrew Taylor. She asked that he be recruited to go to work for her father, using Ronald Arnold to offer him whatever it took to win him over. In the following weeks, Andrew was in and out of the office several times, giving Lou a chance to speak to him while he waited for Arnold. She flirted outrageously with him while he paid her no attention. Lou thought his wife had to be beautiful enough to be a model, or rich at the very least, the way he side stepped all her attempts at seduction.

Thinking that if she could get him alone he wouldn't be able to resist her, Lou set up a phony meeting at the office. She was alone in the offices long enough to have dinner brought in and change into the most seductive outfit she could find. The bottle of champagne was on ice, soft music was coming through the speakers of the office, with her posed provocatively on the sofa when the knock sounded on the door. She beckoned Andrew come in.

Lou watched as the door opened. To her horror, the first persons to enter were two young boys followed by a woman before she saw Andrew. The smallest child was fair skinned like Andrew while the older child was dark skinned like the woman. The woman's hand flew to her mouth covering a gasp. Andrew coughed in an attempt to keep from laughing. Lou drew herself up into a sitting position, attempting to cover herself with the throw pillows. It was the most humiliating moment of her life.

In an attempt to salvage her pride, Lou made up a story about how the meeting was cancelled stating Ronald Arnold was supposed to have told Mr. Taylor of the change. The look of pity for Lou, Beulah had on her face was unmistakable. Lou quickly told her that she was waiting on her boyfriend. Andrew stood there with his arm wrapped around his wife's waist and his other arm protectively around his sons while Lou stammered her excuses.

Now, a smile crossed Lou's face as she relived how much pleasure there was for her in watching Andrew Taylor being tortured to death. Over the following years she kept up with the rest of Andrew's family. She delighted in the knowledge she had a hand in ruining his wife's life, and in seeing his mother humbled. By having Ronald Arnold hire Anthony to run errands, she knew exactly where he was. Later, she ordered the death of Raymond and had it arranged for Anthony to be sent to prison. Lou never expected Anthony to live long enough to get out. When it became evident Anthony would live, Lou came up with a plan to use him for a while before having him killed. She was determined to put an end to Andrew Taylor's blood-line. No one in the organization knew Dixie existed.

Things started falling apart before Lou found out that Arnold hadn't informed her of the name Ben Orr was using. She learned Ronald Arnold had neglected passing on of information to her about several aspects of her organization. Not only was Ben out of control, he was married to her own daughter. She was shocked when her children were the ones to give her that information she should have found out long ago from Arnold.

Dixie Taylor's existence had gone unnoticed by Arnold. If Brenda hadn't mentioned the resemblance of the girl at the picnic to that of Anthony's grandmother, Lou would never have known to find out who she was. She fumed to herself, thinking how Anthony Payne was really Anthony Taylor and how she had found out they were one in the same person. On top of everything else, her daughter was lying to her about where she was and with whom. She still couldn't believe Brenda, her own Brenda Lou, thought she was in love with Anthony.

Determined to get things back on track, after ordering the deaths of Ben Orr and Ronald Arnold, it was now time to see Anthony Taylor meet the fate she had planned for him.

The silence was broken when Lou spoke. "I'm giving you a bonus for this job. I think you are going to find the amount satisfactory, plus a well-deserved promotion. You will take over in Ronald Arnold's position when we get back. It's been open long enough and you've proven yourself more than once. The job you did on Ben Orr was just what I wanted."

Right ahead of them Lou noticed a semi starting to pass a tanker. She was thinking they were too close for comfort when the semi crossed the center line. As it started sliding, the driver of the semi panicked, yanking the wheel. There wasn't time to slow down on the icy pavement as Lou and Bud watched in horror. Lou slammed the breaks when the semi slammed into the tanker loaded with fuel. Their vehicle started spinning out of control when Lou slammed on the breaks. In what felt like slow motion, they plunged into the inferno caused by the exploding tanker.

***

Winona looked like a winter wonderland with everything covered in unblemished snow while the ice-covered trees glistened, casting a kaleidoscope of colors from the setting sun over the area creating a surreal landscape. Streets were nearly deserted until a group of Federal Agents pulled into the parking lot of the local grocery store just off Highway 60. They came up the hill from the North side surrounding the vehicles of armed men already parked there, surprising them as they awaited word from Lou Perkins. There was no noticeable back way out of the lot. Seeing how outnumbered they were, the men in the vehicles quietly surrendered without a shot being fired. As the last man was handcuffed for transport, Agent Trout received word that highway 60 was closed on the west bound side due to an explosion resulting from a multi vehicle accident on Freemont hill. One of the vehicles involved was a Jeep with a license plate identified as belonging to Chet Perkins. He used his cell phone to call the dispatcher in order to get information that would not be available over the radio.

"Why would they be coming this way? Has something happened to Brenda Lou?" James Trout asked in alarm.

The dispatcher seemed hesitant when she answered. "This didn't have–, ah–well, Brenda is fine as far as I know."

Agent Trout wondered why the dispatcher seemed to be avoiding answering his question. "Okay, let's start over. Does anyone know why they were over here? Who was driving and were they hurt?"

There was silence for what seemed to drag on forever before the dispatcher started to speak. "I don't have much information." "What do you know?", he snapped.

"As of right now all we know is that the road is closed because the tanker exploded and the fire burned the two people in the Jeep beyond recognition. It was difficult to even make out the license plate. The driver of the semi was thrown clear but it doesn't look like he will make it. The driver of the tanker burned up too." James Trout was stunned.

"Right now, we are trying to call around to find out who was in the Jeep for sure. I know you're close to the family. As soon as we get any information I'll personally call you back. By the time you get that bunch off your hands we should know something." She knew how much time Agent Trout had spent with Anthony and Brenda Lou.

The worry in her voice was genuine.

Chapter 32

Birch Tree, Missouri

A bright moonlit night created a frozen picture of shimmering magic. Brenda snuggled under Anthony's arm. They sat on the front porch swing, watching the stars twinkle in the clear night sky. Both were bundled up in heavy parkas against the cold damp bite caused by a gentle breeze stirring the frigid air. They had been discussing Eunice, along with everything she did to cause trouble and what would have happened if she hadn't been stopped.

"Am I interrupting?" Dixie asked as she stepped out onto the porch to join them.

Anthony lifted one side of the blanket, patting the empty spot on the seat beside him. "Are you wrapped up enough to be out here?" He asked his niece when he noticed she was wearing a coat too lightweight for the weather. She nodded, plopping down on the swing. As soon as she settled, he pulled the blanket around the three of them and settled his other arm around her. "Now I know how a mother hen feels with her chicks tucked safely under her protective wings. I have the two chicks I love both here with me."

Brenda gave him a good-natured poke in the ribs while Dixie tried hard to appear to glare. "Oh, Uncle Tony, that sounds silly." She snuggled in closer, remaining silent for no more than a moment.

"Can you believe Nicky? I mean, they had to show her pictures of that dead guy before she would believe he was dead. Did she really think I would go out there to wait on him to show up? Why would she think I would do something that stupid?" Dixie caught herself, realizing she was speaking about the same man that Brenda had been married to. Gasping as she covered her mouth with her hands, she hurriedly started to apologize. "Brenda Lou, I'm so sorry. I didn't stop to think -"

Brenda put up her hand to stop Dixie in midsentence. "Don't fret, it's alright. He has been out of my life for a long time, a lot longer than he's been dead. When I found out he was dead it was a relief."

Anthony was glad for the interruption created by Dixie's appearance. He had been trying to figure out how to go about telling Brenda about her mother. There wasn't much time left for him to break the news to her before things came to a head. According to the last text message, before the phone was taken from Nicky, someone would be attempting access into the compound within minutes. While the females talked, he continued to think of a way to tell Brenda her own mother was head of the organization behind all of the horrific things that had happened.

***

Several hours after the accident on Highway 60 occurred, Tom Smith was informed of what had happened. Apprehensive about his friend's safety, he volunteered to go by the Perkins' house instead of having the local sheriff's office send someone else. Identification of the bodies in the Jeep had not been confirmed yet.

Tom was in uniform. He tried to prepare himself for the worst while he knocked on the door. It wasn't long before Chet answered the door to find his friend standing there holding his hat with a stricken look on his face. Unable to speak, Chet motioned for Tom to enter.

Breaking the silence, Tom finally asked, "Where is Lou?" guiding his friend to the sofa. He couldn't help but notice the look of dread that came over Chet.

Suddenly looking dazed and detached from reality, Chet sank down into the cushions. He leaned forward, burying his face in his hands, understanding the reason for Tom's visit. He raised his head, staring across the room at nothing in particular. When he spoke his voice had a dreadful flat quality to it. "She went to deliver food to some of the families around here. That was several hours ago. When she didn't come back, at first I thought she may have got tied up talking or maybe she went to finish her Christmas shopping. That's what I tried to tell myself. Somehow, when she left today I knew something bad–." His voice trailed off into broken sobs.

Gathering his composure, Tom took a minute to consider the wording of what needed to be said. "Did Walter happen to go with Lou?" As an afterthought he added, "Or, anyone else you know?"

Not only was Chet worried but he was also confused as he studied Tom. He had known him long enough to know his friend was withholding bad news while trying to get information. "Tom, I know something has to be wrong. Just tell me what happened."

Consumed with dread, Tom wished now he didn't have to be the one to tell Chet what he feared to be true. "There was an accident."

Not giving Tom time to finish what he had started to say, Chet asked. "How bad is it?"

Tom suddenly felt like he had the weight of the world sitting squarely on his shoulders. A ton of grief, draining him as he dropped down in a chair across from his dearest friend. Grasping for the right words, he was clutching the brim of his hat so hard his knuckles turned white. "We don't actually know if Lou was one of the people at this point. We know it was your Jeep because of the license plate." He took a deep breath, slowly exhaling before continuing. "This is the hardest thing I've ever had to do. There was an accident involving a tanker. I wish I could say that I thought someone else was in it instead of Lou. Chet, they found two burned bodies in your Jeep. We don't know if one of them was Lou or not. I pray it wasn't. It may take a while to make a positive identification. Do you have any idea who else it might have been?"

They sat talking for well over an hour. Although Highway 60 was still patchy, 25 Highway was a mess of packed ice in most areas. The interstate had been cleared so Tom asked Walter to make the trip down from Cape to be with his father, without going into any details. All he told him was that they thought Lou had been in an accident and he didn't want to leave Chet by himself until they knew more. Brenda was far enough along in her pregnancy that Tom didn't think it was wise to tell her anything for fear she would drop everything to rush out on streets that weren't safe, to be at her father's side.

Crumbling in front of Tom's eyes, Chet sat staring off into space.

His voice was flat when he spoke. At first Tom wondered if he was just speaking his thoughts aloud or if he was speaking to him. Before long, he had his answer.

While waiting for Lou to return, Chet had cleaned the attic to keep occupied. He needed something physical to do to keep from worrying about her absence. The nagging feeling of impending doom stayed with him no matter how hard he tried to shake it. When he started moving things around he uncovered things he had no idea existed.

Some boards covering the rafters were displaced. Chet started to put them back in place when a stack of papers caught his eye. Moving more boards, he uncovered guns, phones, passports, tapes, cash, and several other things. Bewildered, not knowing what to do, he put things back the way they were except for the papers and passports. Reading some of the letters, Chet was shocked to find out his wife stayed in touch with a mob boss she had known in Chicago until the man's death. Seeing his wife had passports under more than one name, he bundled all the papers up, putting them in a drawer. He wasn't able to deal with the implications of what little he had actually read.

After he finished speaking Chet stood up, as if in a trance he went to retrieve the papers from the drawer. He came back handing everything over to Tom.

Tom was dumbstruck. "Are you sure you want to do this?"

"I can't explain it but I know she's dead. I feel it." He looked sad, lost, and older than his years. "I don't want to know everything she was into. Her own daughter, Tom, what she was doing, it hurt her own child. How could anyone do a thing like that?" He broke down sobbing. "I'm sure. Take them all. II don't want to know what else is in those papers. Take the things in the attic too. I don't want to look at any of it again."

Bloomfield was territory covered by other entities; Tom Smith was Dexter's Chief of Police. He called the Stoddard County Sheriff to come to the Perkins' home to help remove the things from the house before Walter's arrival. He knew it needed to be kept as quiet as possible until the task force could get everything straight. There would be several arrests connected to the information found in the papers Chet found. After speaking to the sheriff, Tom placed a call to the federal agents on the case.

Later that night at the farm in Birch Tree, Anthony received word about the events that took place earlier in the day. Upon hearing of Lou's death, he was glad he hadn't been able to bring himself to tell Brenda what her mother really was.

The two female agents would be taking Eunice and the woman on suicide watch with them to a rehab facility in Columbia, Missouri, the next day for intensive psychological therapy.

Anthony dreaded telling Brenda about the death of her mother, but was thankful he wouldn't have to disclose the circumstances leading up to it. Once Anthony informed Brenda of her mother's demise she would be examined to make sure she was physically able to travel. The roads would be cleared by the next afternoon and he would be taking her straight to her father's house to be with her family.

Chapter 33

Close friends and family gathered at the small church in Bloomfield for the Funeral Services for Lou Perkins. It had been several days since her death. Due to the weather, aside from those closest to her, the only people in attendance were the hardiest of the congregation and a few curious acquaintances. Chet sat with his children while another preacher officiated. He was having a hard time coming to terms with the facts involved in his wife's double life. His thoughts were troubled as he sat solemnly throughout the service thinking about the woman he had been married to.

The night after Lou's death, Chet sent all his children away stating he needed time to himself. Walter took his youngest sister, Patty home with him, while Anthony took Brenda to his home in Dexter and Donna's husband took her home after seeing their father meant what he said. Earlier that morning while Walter was in the shower, Chet found Lou's equivalent to a diary. The things she had written shocked him even more than what he already learned about her. Until that moment, he hadn't realized how much of a twisted monster she really was.

Chet learned that Lou wanted their daughter Donna to take over her operation when she retired. Things didn't work the way she planned, causing her to give up on her plans for Donna Mae. What he read next chilled his very soul. Recently Lou had made a decision to leave him when Brenda's baby was born. She planned to kidnap her own grandchild and take the baby to the Chicago area. She wanted to raise it to head up the organized crime operation once she retired.

Lou already had faked identification for herself and for the as yet unborn baby boy. She planned to start a whole new life apart from him and her children after kidnapping the baby.

That night, after he came to grips with the new found knowledge, he vowed his children would never find out who and what their mother was. He started placing calls. The first call was to his close friend Tom Smith. Chet asked him to stay with him until he could finish doing what needed to be done.

After reading what Lou had written, Tom was speechless for several minutes. The sympathy in his voice was unmistakable when he finally spoke. "Chet, she was two different people. We all loved the Lou we knew, the one you were married to. I know things like this happen more often than people want to believe, but no one expects it to be someone they know."

"I hate to even think it Tom, but I know she would have murdered her own grandchild if it turned out to be Anthony's. I never told her about Brenda Lou and Anthony. There's no telling what she would have done to Brenda Lou."

Tom looked questionably at his friend. "Are you telling me that Larry Joe–, that Mr. Payne-"

Chet cut him off. "I'm pretty sure Anthony is the father of Brenda Lou's baby. I never told you before, and didn't really mean to now, but I walked in on them Easter Sunday. Brenda Lou isn't positive either, but the way things were going with Larry Joe at the time, she thinks the baby is probably Anthony's."

The two friends talked well into the wee hours of the morning. Chet gave Tom the last of Lou's documentation to turn over to the proper authorities as evidence.

After the funeral services they lowered Lou's body into the cold ground. Chet wasn't able to shed a tear as he threw the first handful of dirt onto the top of her coffin. He had no tears left. In private he'd spent his tears and dissected his grief over the loss of his wife, the good wife, the mother of his children the person he knew and loved. There were no tears left for the remains of the creature they placed into the ground. Only Lou's ashes were in the beautiful rubbed bronze coffin they buried. Her remains had been so badly burned that cremation was the best way to handle what was left of her.

It had taken so long to sort everything out, it was already the last day of the year.

He would always love the good Lou, understanding that she had a troubled soul and split personality. The memory of the other would be buried without their children ever knowing of its existence.

Under the canopy covering the gravesite, Donna sat in the chair between her father and Mac. Brenda sat on the other side with Anthony standing behind her. Patty sat beside her with Walter sitting in the seat on the end of the row. As Chet let the dirt sift through his fingers onto the lid of the coffin, Brenda was gripped by a strong contraction. Mac reached out, grabbing her to keep her from falling as she doubled over with the force of the pain.

"Brenda, what's wrong?" The fear in Mac's voice was unmistakable. He dropped to his knees in front of his wife's sister, as Anthony pushed between the seats to grab her. She was bent forward with her arms clutching her protruding abdomen. The agents standing just outside of the canopy covering the gravesite tensed, unsure of what was happening, ready in case of any danger. Due to the individual seen running away from the parking lot in Winona, there were Federal Agents assigned to protect the family at Anthony's request. The family assumed the agents were there because they were friends of Anthony. Special Agent Allen Burner volunteered for the duty so he could personally make sure Patty was safe.

When the contraction eased, she was able to speak. "I'm in labor. It's alright, I'll be fine. My lower back has been hurting on and off all day but I didn't pay any attention to it because of everything that's been going on." She sat up straight again once the contraction ended. "That got my attention."

Jumping to his feet, Mac started patting his pockets looking for his phone. "Chet, I can't find my phone. We have to call for an ambulance for Brenda Lou. She's about to have the baby." He didn't wait for his father-in-law to answer. "Anthony, help me get her to the car so she can lay down." Mac looked up to see Anthony already carrying Brenda to the vehicle.

"Whoa, Anthony. I don't need an ambulance and I'm not going to lay down in the car. Please, put me down. Just help me stand up so I can walk to the car. We need to go by the house and pick up my bag. It's going to be a while yet before our son is born. There is plenty of time to safely drive to the hospital. Calm down."

No one returned to the Perkins' house as planned, the entire family escorted Brenda and Anthony to the hospital instead. Tom and Liz went back to their house to put away the food brought in by family, friends, and church members for the meal following the funeral. They would meet the others at the hospital later.

Anthony was glad he was the one driving Mac's car. Mac was too excitable to be driving. Donna and Mac were in the backseat and Brenda rode up front with him. When Brenda's water broke, Mac came close to hysterics. Anthony grimaced at the thought of how he heard Mac acted when Donna had their baby. He turned toward the backseat to see what Mac was yelling. "If you don't shut up we will have to put you out and leave you. You are upsetting Brenda Lou and she doesn't need that. She needs to concentrate on her breathing and you're about to scare her to death." She gave him a stern look that shut him up. "Now, calmly tell me what you said. I can see she isn't pushing the baby out, so what is going on?"

Mac was pale and his eyes were as large as saucers. "Are you sure she will make it to the hospital? I'm afraid she will have the baby before we get there." From the look his sister-in-law had given him, he was afraid she would indeed have Anthony pull over and throw him out so he carefully enunciated his words.

Brenda gave an exasperated sigh before rolling her eyes and answering Mac. "This is my first baby. I am not in any danger of having it right now. If anyone should be yelling it should be me, not you. Please, Mac, just calm down. If you have a second hand on your watch start timing my contractions.

The nurses will want to know how far apart they are. Please try to be quiet so Donna Mae can call them to let them know to meet us with a wheelchair."

Donna was patting her husband, trying to calm him. Seeing how he was acting now made her glad she had taken an ambulance when she delivered their daughter.

Dexter's hospital had stopped delivering babies years ago, so they made the trip to Poplar Bluff. Upon arrival at the ER, the staff helped Brenda into the wheelchair while Mac danced from foot to foot gripping Donna's hand. Anthony was glad they were across the room while he was trying to answer questions. To Donna's relief, she saw her dad's car turn in. Her brother, Walter and her sister, Patty Sue were in the car with Chet.

Donna and Mac waited on the rest of the family so they could all go in together. Anthony finished filling out paper work while the doctor and nurses did the work-up on Brenda, before joining the others in the Labor & Delivery Waiting Room. To Anthony it seemed like an eternity before the nurse came out to take the family to the birthing room to see Brenda.

Two hours passed slowly by before the nurse had everyone except Anthony, Brenda, and Patty leave the room. Chet, Mac, and Walter paced the halls in silence for ten minutes before they heard the high-pitched cries of the newborn baby boy.

"He sounds wonderful." Mac and Walter turned at the sound of Chet's broken voice. They saw tears of joy streaming, unchecked down his smiling face, that just a minute before had been lined with creases from worry. "Thank the Lord for sending him to us today."

The men waiting in the hall saw the door leading into the birthing room open. The nurse waving them in stepped aside to allow the Dr. to rush out on the way to the next delivery. They were greeted by the sight of Anthony standing beside the bed holding Brenda Lou's hand. He was bawling like a baby himself, wearing the biggest smile they had ever seen on his face. Brenda looked tired but triumphant, laying there, reaching up to wipe at the tears of joy coursing down Anthony's cheeks. Donna and Patty were standing beside the warming bed watching intently while the nurse tended to the new baby.

When the nurse tried to lay the swaddled newborn in its mother's arms she shook her head, pointing to her father. Chet took the child in his arms, peering into the tiny face with a look of serene wonderment. To all present, it appeared the tiny pink faced infant was checking his grandfather over as well. "He isn't just wonderful, he's perfect." He raised his head, grinning at Brenda while making his pronouncement. "I think he likes me already."

On the way to the cars, they were surprised to see the agents waiting outside. Agent Burner asked Patty about the condition of both mother and child. Patty ended up riding back to Bloomfield with him.

***

Cape Girardeau, Missouri

A meeting of the task force took place at the Federal Court House in Cape Girardeau, Missouri. The week before Christmas, all agencies involved in cracking the organized crime ring wanted to finish tying up loose ends, so they could be home before the end of the year.

After reviewing the information in the papers handed over by the Perkins family, a sweep was conducted across the entire country. The names and multiple identities for all those working under Lou Perkins' control were confirmed, leading to most of her people being found and arrested. Due to the detailed records Lou kept, there was enough evidence for solid convictions. The authorities were still searching for the few not yet in custody.

The individual spotted fleeing across a field behind the store during the roundup at Winona disappeared before anyone could find out who it was. No one knew if the man was involved with the planned raid on the compound, or if it was a local citizen. There weren't any distinct footprints in the snow leading from where those vehicles were parked. After identification of the charred remains of Bud Lowe was confirmed, it was assumed the unknown individual was a local person watching the arrests of those at the parking lot.

One letter found among Lou's papers explained her initial involvement and rise to head the organization. The letter was addressed to Lou from the sister of her mother's first husband.

Lou's mother had been married briefly to a young gangster. The marriage was short lived with her mother taking another husband within two months of a quickie Mexican divorce from the gangster. Lou's mother was four months pregnant when she married her second husband. Lou was adopted by her step-father when she was a tiny infant and raised in a good family. She knew nothing of the man who fathered her until she was a teenager. Her biological father contacted her without her mother's knowledge.

Promised a job with a huge salary, smothered in presents, lavished with spending money, Lou quickly bonded with the man who fathered her before his rise to one of the most feared organized crime heads in history. He carefully groomed her to take over in his place when he retired, cautioning her all the while of the importance of secrecy. Lou's mother went to her grave unaware Lou knew the man existed. It was a closely held secret between Lou and her biological father.

Under the circumstances, consideration for Lou's family was taken into account. It was apparent Lou hid her true identity, along with her criminal activities from all of them. Without their assistance it would have taken much longer to put a stop to the organization. Due to her death, there would be no need for her identity to be released to the press. The trials would be held at a Federal Courthouse, in the Chicago area, since Chicago was the hub of the organization. Information released to the press would only refer to Lou, using her birth name, as the daughter of the late crime boss, without referencing her adopted or married name.

All the money in Lou's bank accounts was confiscated to be used for her victims and their families. The compound at Birch Tree would continue to operate after the conclusion of the trials. Even though Lou Perkins' organized crime operation came to an end, there would always be a need for a safe haven for victims.

Anthony was delighted to finally be free to use his given name. He would no longer work inside the task force but would still be active in helping put a stop to human trafficking by donating a percentage of the profits from his business. Both Anthony and Brenda wanted to spend time helping out at the compound whenever feasible. During the ordeal, they had bonded closely with the individuals working there as well as the federal agents.

Unfortunately, human trafficking, drug trafficking, and other forms of illegal activity connected to human slavery will continue in one form or another as it has since the beginning of time. Plans were already being made for facilities to be added to the compound in order to accommodate caring for abandoned infants and children suffering from drug addiction and other forms of abuse.

Chapter 34

Dexter, Missouri

Even with the coldest temperatures in 20 years on the end of this first week of January, it was hard to find anywhere to park. Some people parked as much as six blocks away, braving the cold in order to attend the biggest event Dexter had seen in many years.

"Would you just look out there! I can't believe this many people showed up as cold as it is. The church is filled up and they are bringing in more folding chairs. I can't believe it." Donna Mae was dragging Patty Sue by the arm toward the small window in the door leading to the church's auditorium. "Where on earth did all these people come from anyway?"

Jewell helped Brenda into the dress the women at the compound made for her. Several of them insisted on personally seeing that she would have the most beautiful wedding dress ever. Anthony wasn't allowed to see the dress until the wedding. The finished creation was equal to a royal wedding gown. Creamy soft, light champagne colored, satin was accented with matching pearl covered lace. The high waist A-line cut of the front accentuated her form, with a scooped neckline trimmed in tear-drop pearls. A long detachable train extended several feet in length behind the gown. The train fastened to the dress with delicate frog fasteners looping over tiny roses made of satin and pearls, circling the raised waistline. The entire satin train was shot through with a pattern of delicate, deep golden, thread, overlaid with the lace covered in an intricate design consisting tiny pearls in the same soft champagne color. When attached, it flowed open to expose the flat satin front panel. The dress itself flared enough in the back to allow for dancing, when the train was removed. Sleeves were three-quarter length made of pearl beaded lace. A form fitting cropped jacket of matching pearled-lace covered satin, with puffed sleeves, could be worn with or without the train attached. It was made of pearled-lace covering deep gold colored satin, fastened by a single delicate frog fastener at the waist-line of the dress. Although the puffed sleeved jacket hung just long enough to appear to flow into the train, it wouldn't be worn until the bride and groom were in the receiving line after the ceremony.

Matching dresses of pastel colors were made to order for the other women in the wedding party. The satin and lace, three quarter length, A-line dresses each had matching, puffed sleeve, cropped jackets.

The men in the wedding party all wore tuxedos. The groom's tux was the only one with tails. All the tuxedos were ordered with shirts to match the color dress worn by the female they were escorting.

Brenda Lou's friend, Judy had kept her business running smoothly during her absence. Judy was ecstatic when asked if her daughter could be one of the Flower Girls. She volunteered to find the matching dresses for all the girls. The little girls looked like they stepped right out of a fairy tale, wearing three quarter length velvet peasant style dresses with big bows and long sashes. Their tights matched the crown of flowers, entwined with ribbon and pearls, atop the curls of their hair.

Brenda was sitting in a room just off the hall, where Judy was putting the final touches to her hair. She looked up at the racket made by Donna while she dragged Patty from one place to another. Brenda and Dixie burst out laughing.

"Come on Brenda Lou, sit still so I can finish this. I want to make sure the veil doesn't fall off on the way down the aisle." She sounded exasperated. "Am I going to have to run everybody out and lock the door? We don't want the bride late for her own wedding." Judy was the most efficient person Brenda knew. Now she appeared slightly overwhelmed by all the commotion.

"I promise to be good." Brenda giggled while Dixie, easing toward the door, made a zipping motion at her lips. "You know I wouldn't know what to do without you."

"I saw that young lady. Careful with the makeup, we don't have time to redo it so keep the lips straight." Judy scolded Dixie as she wagged a finger in her direction before pushing the final clip into Brenda's hair.

Judy insisted on doing Brenda Lou's hair herself even though she was part of the wedding party. Having been Brenda's best friend for several years, she was asked to be maid-of-honor. Brenda's sisters, Donna, Patty, along with Anthony's niece, Dixie were the bride's maids.

Walter stuck his head in the door, grinning at his sister. "How's it going? You sure are beautiful Sis." The warm look of admiration was unmistakable as he looked lovingly at his older sister. "Tony's about to wear a hole in the carpet. I can't believe the big guy looks so nervous. He acts like he's afraid the bride might back out." He ducked when Judy, good-naturedly threw the hair brush at his head. He laughed as he went through the door.

"Tell him I love him and we are all about ready." Brenda yelled over her shoulder before turning to look at the infant sleeping peacefully in his car seat in the corner of the room.

Susan came in to help with the baby while Judy finished arranging Brenda's veil. "Stand up so I can have a look at you." Her eyes started misting at the sight before her. "Oh Brenda Lou, I am so happy for you. You look like a fairy princess. Anthony is one lucky man. God only knows how happy I am that things are finally working out for you young lady. You deserve to be happy." She was speaking while she lifted little Raymond from the car seat. "Between my Daddy, Tom, and Liz, they have all of the children under control. The twins have taken over Donna's little girl, they act like she's one of their toy dolls. That baby girl is loving the attention."

Brenda stood up preparing to meet her father for the walk down the aisle. Susan would sit in the front pew with the baby. She would hand him to his father when it was time to join the couple as man and wife. Brenda and Anthony both wanted their son to be part of the wedding so the preacher could join them all as a family.

Susan peeked out before coming to stand beside Brenda. "There are a lot more people out there than you would believe. I guess it's because you snagged one of the riches bachelors in the state. Then again, you gave birth to the first baby born this year. The newspapers all have reporters and photographers here. This wedding is big news in a lot of ways. It's not every day a small-town girl helps bring down an entire organized crime ring." She laughed, before adding, "From the looks of it every relative you have has shown up and brought their friends too. I think your daddy's whole congregation is here too."

Afraid she would upset the bride, Susan quickly changed the subject. "I wonder what Dad and Henry are up to. They have their heads together like they are plotting something. Those two can get into more stuff than a couple teenaged boys." Susan already knew what they were discussing. Henry had the stretched limo out in front of the church. Susan's dad, Robert was telling Henry the jet was fueled and waiting to go right after the reception. The two elderly men took it upon themselves to cancel the airline tickets, and parked the limo in place of Anthony's vehicle. Henry would play chauffeur once again. This time he would be driving the newlyweds to the waiting private jet for their honeymoon.

"Well, I hope we have enough food at the reception." The worried look on the bride's face caused Susan to laugh.

"Everything is under control. Don't worry about feeding the press, they weren't invited anyway", Susan stated while attempting to maintain a straight face. "Eula says that, without an invite, they won't get in unless they are family. I'm pretty sure she has already worked all that out."

Judy turned around glaring. "You two please keep it down." The words were barely out of her mouth when the other two burst out laughing.

When the sound of the organ playing reached their ears everyone took their places.

Anthony stood beside the preacher as Brenda's brother, Walter, the best man, entered with Judy, Brenda's maid of honor on his arm. Special Agent Burner escorted Patty, while Special Agent Trout escorted Dixie. Donna and Mac were last to take their places. Following the groom's men and bride's maids down the aisle, Susan carried the baby, Raymond. She was dressed similar to the bride's maids with the exception of the burp rag over her shoulder. Attached to the baby blanket the infant was wrapped in were the wedding rings. Little Raymond was their ring bearer. When they reached the front where the bridal party stood, Susan sat there with the baby, easily accessible for his part in the ceremony. Next came the four little flower girls spreading rose petals.

As the chords of Here Comes the Bride sounded, all eyes turned to watch as Brenda entered on the arm of her father. Anthony stared in wonder at the sight of the only woman he had ever loved walking toward him. He said a silent prayer of thanks for the blessing of the family that would be his.

The End

Author pictured with the late Dr. James E. Thompson.

Jean Schick has worked in the public eye, in one capacity or another, most of her adult life. Although she is widely traveled, she is most comfortable at home near her children and grandchildren. Jean writes under a variety of pseudonyms and is currently working on her next book. Jean was born and raised in rural Missouri. She currently resides somewhere in the state.

www.ingramcontent.com/pod-product-compliance
Lightning Source LLC
LaVergne TN
LVHW020535100826
845148LV00010B/1471
* 9 7 9 8 9 5 0 0 7 2 2 4 6 *

About the Author

Dr. Geis is from Massillon Ohio and writes adult fiction. *The Rocket Scientist* is his debut novel.

He holds a bachelor's degree in psychology from the University of Notre Dame, a master's degree in counseling from Kent State University, and a doctorate in organizations and political sociology from Boston University.

Before his writing career, he was an international change management expert working with companies across four continents. His clients include Presidents and CEOs of large multinationals and Silicon Valley start-ups. He's also consulted with flag officers from several branches of the United States Military, high technology, and environmental organizations. In the process, he's conducted over 1500 presentations, public appearances, and executive workshops.

Preceding his consulting work, he spent years working in human service organizations and served as the Deputy Assistant Commissioner for Mental Health for the Commonwealth of Massachusetts. He was also a ten-year Board Chair and member of Child Haven, a non-profit serving traumatized children in Northern California.

He has lived in Boston, San Francisco, Atlanta, Singapore, Napa, Houston, and currently resides in Reno, NV.

If you enjoyed this read, please leave a review. It makes a difference and helps others discover this story. Thanks

Read more at arthurgeisphd.com.

www.ingramcontent.com/pod-product-compliance
Lightning Source LLC
La Vergne TN
LVHW010644110826
845149LV00014B/2949
* 9 7 9 8 9 9 4 5 5 9 3 0 7 *